Coming of Age ... Again

a novel

Ramune Luminaire

AOS Publishing, 2025
Copyright © 2025 Ramune Luminaire

ISBN: 978-1-990496-96-7

Cover Design: Chanelle Poupart

Visit AOS Publishing's website:
www.aospublishing.com

In youth, it was a way I had,

To do my best to please.

And change, with every passing lad

To suit his theories.

But now I know the things I know

And do the things I do,

And if you do not like me so,

To hell, my love, with you.

Dorothy Parker

One

It feels backwards to notice a person's eye colour *after* having sex with them. His were hazel. She didn't remember that from last night. He slipped a generous five-dollar bill into her donation box. "I'll take a hug. In fact, I'll take two."

Reluctantly, Lisa stood up, but as Dan's arms folded around her, she remembered the woody smell of his hair, the strength in his back, and how much she'd enjoyed kissing. She looked over his shoulder, wanting—and not wanting—someone to interrupt. This time yesterday, she'd have said she had lost all interest in sex, even with herself. Today, her body seemed to have its own will.

"Sorry I had to leave early." His lips almost brushed her ear. "Especially after we had so much fun. You were amazing. So totally British and together, and when we got into bed ..."

Lisa tried not to cringe. Through the haze, she remembered doing that special thing that men liked, but when Dan was inside her, it had hurt. *Why? Is it possible to lose your virginity twice? The first time wasn't painful. Christ, that was forty-six years ago, in the back of Tim Baker's Mini.* After going so long without, the alcohol had transported her back to when she thought sex was all about pleasing her man. No wonder Dan had such a good time. She took a step back.

He was still smiling. "Call you later? I'm meant to be in Redstock to price a job in an hour."

She nodded so he'd go. She needed to regroup, but right now she was meant to be raising money for a new CT scanner. As Dan disappeared down the street, Lisa jiggled her money box and tried to look approachable. Hugging strangers wasn't her natural inclination, but at her retirement party her boss had been overflowing with praise and too many of the appreciations sounded architectural: strong, solid, upstanding, pillar of the community. That's why she'd signed up to spend the morning on

Queen Street, under a banner that read, *Hugs for Healthcare.* She wanted to erode her image as a pillar.

Lisa had worn a fleece, hoping its texture might make her more cuddleable. The problem was that she felt sick. And shaky. She wasn't used to drinking the way she had last night, hadn't wanted to leave the house, let alone spend the morning wrapping her arms around people she didn't know. But she'd promised to be there, and she always kept her promises.

Susan had noticed straight away. "You don't look so good."

Lisa garbled something about not getting enough sleep. Susan was her closest friend, but Lisa wasn't ready to discuss Dan. That would make it real, something demanding definition, and lead to an unnecessary conversation about relationships. Instead, she joined the singsong chorus, "Donate a dollar, have a hug." But as she stood with the other women rattling their donation boxes, Lisa felt lost. Susan knew everyone. Their kids had grown up together, they'd survived empty nests together, and their days were filled with grandchildren. Lisa longed to be back in her principal's office, with staff to do all the necessary but boring tasks that now occupied her days, like keeping track of details, making coffee, and running errands. She was good at dealing with students' crises, budgeting money that rarely existed, and schmoozing potential funders—not knowing where to buy the best ice cream cake.

"So do you think you've got the flu or something?" Susan asked on the drive home.

"Actually, a friend turned up last night and we drank far too much."

"A friend with curly red hair?"

"Excuse me?"

Susan stopped for the lights. "That landscape guy who put in the trees at the back of the art school extension—Dan Mason. I saw the two of you looking cozy together in town."

Lisa felt herself flush, a child caught in a lie. "I don't know why I didn't tell you. Dan was at my place yesterday, mending my fence, and ended up staying for supper."

"Is 'mending my fence' some kind of British euphemism I don't know about?"

Lisa knew her cheeks were crimson now.

"Holy smokes, you like him. After all the hours I've spent listening to you blather on about independence and self-sufficiency." Susan leaned forward. "Honey, I hate to pee on your Pop-Tart, but if you do decide to let down the drawbridge, make sure he's not the one you invite in. My ..."

The car behind honked and Susan turned her attention back to the road. Lisa was relieved, she couldn't handle this conversation now. "You know, I don't feel well enough for lunch. Could we do this another time?" She took a bunch of keys out of her purse. "Just drop me here, by my truck. Maybe we can have coffee after yoga?"

"Sure, but I'm thinking of ditching yoga. I can't stand looking at my butterball thighs in leggings."

"Don't talk like that, your body's totally loveable. Thanks for the ride. Phone you tomorrow?"

Susan nodded. "Rest well."

As Lisa pushed open the back door, Fido rushed to greet her, squeaking his plastic duck. The noise was head-splitting. She plopped down in front of a bowl of soup-soaked breadcrumbs and looked around the kitchen: two empty wine bottles, dirty dishes, oven mitts on the floor, tea towel in the sink. How had she let last night happen, after so many years of safe solitude?

She owned fifty acres of Ontario granite and forest, but there was a wooden picket fence around the house that hadn't been repaired in the twenty years she'd lived there. Dan had spent the day working, and by the time he'd arrived at Lisa's kitchen door to talk about a new gate, it was almost dark. She had just made minestrone soup—her favourite one-bowl meal.

He leant against the door frame. "Smells good."

Cold air was cooling the kitchen. "Come in."

It was a while since she'd had a man who wasn't her eighty-year-old neighbour in the house. Dan looked out of place.

"I've done what I can with the fence, but you're going to need a new gate."

"Could you build me one that lets in friends and keeps out strangers?"

He grinned. "But what about strangers that turn into friends?"

"It's been a long while since I've had one of those." *Where did that come from?* Lisa looked down to hide her blush, but when she raised her eyes, Dan was still smiling. Fido nuzzled her hand. "He's telling me it's supper time. Would you, have you eaten?"

As well as making new friends, one of her retirement goals was to be more spontaneous, but Lisa surprised herself with the invitation.

"I am pretty hungry. I was in such a rush this morning, I forgot to pack a lunch."

While Dan went to wash, she put a loaf of French bread in the oven and opened a bottle of red wine, glad she had been spontaneous, relieved he hadn't run in the other direction, and fluttering at the thought of a man in the house for dinner. She mustn't—

"These old farmhouses are great." He was back in the room, filling it with enthusiasm.

"Aren't they?" Lisa nodded, trying not to think this was a mistake while enjoying having someone share her pride in her home.

As Dan walked around appreciatively, she wondered how old he might be. Mid-fifties? Younger than her anyway. She was happy to hear him notice the details she loved: original pine baseboards, the storm windows she'd fought to preserve, the funny little door to the cold cellar.

"And this red floor is inspired." He crouched to touch the painted wood. "Did you do the work yourself?"

"That's flattering." Lisa chuckled. "But no. I'd only just moved here from England when I bought the house. It needed renovating and I was busy taking over the art school, but luckily, I found Matt Thompson. Know him? Such a good contractor."

"I don't think so. Can I help with anything?"

Lisa set a couple of bowls on the table. "No thanks. Just have a seat while I grab the bread."

They began to eat, and she noticed how small the soup spoon seemed in Dan's huge hands. He took a sip, looked up, and as he started to talk about his landscape business, Lisa wondered how he managed such wonderfully curly hair.

"But it's been over twenty years now, and I'm ready for a change." he said, bringing her mind back to the conversation. "Spending the next twenty in the same place, doing the same thing, isn't in the plan."

She broke off a piece of bread. "I've just taken early retirement. Well, sort of. I've got a six-month contract to mentor the new principal and a position on the board, but after all those years of running an art school eight days a week, it's quite a change."

Dan nodded. "I dream of waking up in the morning with no agenda, but if I'm honest, I think I'd find it a bit scary."

This was closer to her truth than Lisa wanted to admit. After a moment's silence, he must have sensed her mood shift and changed the subject. "I know it's a kids' movie, but I watched *Dumbo* last night. It was my favourite when I was growing up, and I wanted to know if the recent one was as good as I remember. That little mouse, Timothy, still gets to me."

She relaxed as they both raved about Tim Burton and got embarrassed when they talked about music. Dan liked his artists home grown—Neil Young, Arcade Fire, Tragically Hip. She tried not to tell him she still listened to Fleetwood Mac and Elton John, but somehow Dan managed to make her show him her favourite playlist. After that, they had an almost-fight about Justin Trudeau, and when the conversation turned to Trump, she opened another bottle.

That's when they'd really started to laugh—about the ancient picture of Queen Elizabeth in the post office and the way Owl FM still played "Bat Out of Hell" every morning. Real belly laughing. How long was it since she'd done that? Suddenly self-conscious, Lisa thought she may have food stuck in her teeth, and it wasn't until she went to the bathroom that she realized how drunk she was. Holding the sink for security, she looked in the mirror and fluffed her hair—still more chestnut than grey—then wondered if she owned any makeup and where it might be. Like a character in a Jane Austin novel, she rubbed and pinched her cheeks before going back, concentrating hard on walking upright—sensible, sophisticated steps--because the wine made her woozy and liable to tilt.

"There's a bottle of Jameson in the van. I got it for my buddy's birthday. We could crack it open ... if you .... Do you drink whisky?"

Not for years, she thought, but sounded enthusiastic because she didn't want the evening to end, she was having too much fun. When Dan went out to get the bottle, Lisa tried to concentrate, to think about what she was doing, but nothing came. Only a warm feeling and a silly grin, which she tried to hide as he came back into the house. They moved into the living room and she turned on the little lamp by the bookcase and pulled the curtains. Fido was already stretched in front of the wood stove. Dan sank into the couch, opened the whisky, and handed her a glass. Lisa took a sip, enjoying its heat, but knew she'd had enough, so curled into the armchair and listened as he talked about his daughter. "She's in Manitoba now doing her masters.

Erin—my ex—left when Anna was ten. Since then, it's just been the two of us."

"You raised her on your own?"

"Everybody says that, like it's such a big deal. I guess it was a big deal, but I loved every second of it. I know it's a cliché, but Anna is the best thing that's happened to me." His face softened. "She was so funny when she was little, and clever. Once she was in high school, we used to go out for supper every time she got an "A." We ended up with our own booth at the Burger Bar. I still miss her."

"Where did she do her undergrad?"

"In Kingston. It's funny, she started there over four years ago but still came home for the holidays and worked with me every summer. It didn't feel like she was gone. Now that she's in Manitoba, it's different. She's making a life there, got a boyfriend I've never met. I guess I'm what they call an empty nester. Anyway, enough about me."

Lisa tried not to feel inadequate as she described how work-focused she'd been since arriving from England. After that, things got hazy. Dan went to the bathroom and tripped over the rug on his way back. She vaguely remembered him saying something about not being able to drive home, and her suggesting he stay.

The kissing had dissolved her. Gentle at first—tasting, nibbling, exploring—it had grown into unrestrained desire. She was a teenager again. By the time they got to the bedroom, she wanted him in every way possible. It had been twenty years. But when he slipped into her, she felt a stab of pain, and the more he moved the more it hurt. Why hadn't she said anything? Because she'd had so much to drink? Or she didn't want to ruin the moment? Maybe she just didn't want to talk about it with someone she hardly knew.

The sound of synthesized Canada geese jolted Lisa back to the present. She looked at her cell—Dan Mason, Down To Earth Designs—and swiped *decline*. Last night shouldn't have happened.

After all, she'd made a promise, all those years ago. Lisa filled the kettle, and while it was boiling, gazed at the framed photo hanging by the fridge of an old couple sitting in a bus shelter on a beach. *What will I be like when I'm their age? Jeans replaced by velour pants, hair the same but silver, a smaller dog?*

She picked up her phone and listened to Dan's voicemail. "I was thinking, I'm going to this dinner on Saturday. Maybe you'd like to come? They call it a ball but it's not that fancy, just a meal in a church hall. The Beekeepers' Association of Southern Ontario. Give me a call."

Two

Norm rang while Lisa was having breakfast. He was her nearest neighbour and didn't often phone. It was more his style to stop by. He sounded anxious. "Can you come over? I've had a letter."

Lisa had known Norm since she first came to Colville. Back then, she worked long and late at the art school, but Sundays were for home. She was outside, weeding the overgrown patch that had once been a vegetable garden, when he had first turned up in his rusty pickup, a fork, spade, and cooler of Molson in the back.

"Looks like you could do with a hand," was all he said, and they had spent the rest of the afternoon digging. Not much of a talker, Norm kept to himself, but since that day he'd always helped her—chopping firewood, plowing snow, trapping the skunk that moved in under her deck, and taking care of the place when she was away. Lisa enjoyed his quiet company. He had never asked her for anything before. This must be serious.

She decided to walk through the fields at the back of the house. The last of the snow had disappeared and it was officially mud season: trees still leafless, grass was barely green, boggy trenches between the rocks. Everything that would soon be green was brown, but Lisa still loved it. She marvelled at the expansiveness of Canada—the scale of the sky and the trees that went on forever, the sense of space and possibility, compared to the over-crowded, overworked English countryside around Oxford where she had grown up. She walked past Norm's old century farmhouse, and when his bungalow came into sight, Fido ran ahead. Norm was in the driveway, leaning under the hood of his truck, as the dog cannoned into him.

"Calm down there, boy." He reached into his overalls pocket for a treat, then turned to Lisa. "Come on in. I kept a bit of last night's liver for him."

In the twenty years they'd been friends, Lisa had hardly ever been into the bungalow, never past the front hall. Norm led her into the kitchen. He was eighty and his wife had died years ago, but it felt like she could have just popped into the laundry room to get a fresh apron.

Lisa looked around. "What a lovely, cozy room."

"This is Rose's place. She chose everything, started collecting years before we even began building. She hated the old farmhouse, always wanted somewhere new. You sit down and I'll go wash my hands. Rose never let me clean them in her sink and I still can't."

Being there made Lisa sad. She imagined Norm living alone, without his beloved, sitting at the oak-veneered table she'd picked out with the matching cushioned chairs, drinking his morning coffee out of floral mugs, cooking his meals in the antique microwave. Rose's cornflower Pyrex bowls were neatly stacked under the window and her recipe index box was on a shelf by the fridge. A china plaque hung on the wall, *Best Mom*. Lisa didn't know Norm had any children.

He put a plate of leftovers down for Fido and a cup of instant coffee on the table for Lisa and started pouring in cream before she could stop him. She usually drank espresso—black. He went to the drawer and took out an envelope. "This here's what I got. It's an order to demolish."

She scanned the letter.

The Superior Court of Ontario has found Norman O'Brien guilty of non-compliance with The Court of Colville County. The Township of Northern Colville has applied for removal. We hereby issue an order that the building at 611 Fire Route 49, Part Lot 10, Concession 3, Township of Colville, Ontario K9L 2H9 is to be demolished by November 1, 2019.

"My great-great-grandfather built that old farmhouse. He got the grant to this land in 1860." Norm's eyes were fiery. "All his six kids was born in that house and four of 'em died in it. My dad was born back there, in the same room that Mum passed." He sat for a few moments, staring at his hands. "They'll rip it down over my dead body."

"Surely this can't be the first you've heard of it. Didn't they write before, give you warning?"

"They might have sent something, I dunno, I'm no good with paperwork. I was hoping you could go to the Township and talk to 'em about the historical importance an' that. They'll listen to you, you being such a pillar of the community an' all."

Lisa suppressed a smile. "Have you tried speaking to them yourself?"

"I don't like telling people my business an' it's all city folk in the Planning Office these days. They just think I'm an old hoser, don't want to hear anything I've gotta say. All they care about is zoning and permits and crap I don't understand, and they ask too many damned questions."

She felt for Norm, they were both used to operating alone. "Why don't we go together? I doubt if they'll talk to me about your situation without you there. It'll be confidential."

His face lifted. "I thought of that. Maybe we could write up a letter giving you permission."

Fifteen minutes later, Fido and Lisa walked back through the woods. She stopped to look at the old farmhouse, tin roof rusted, windows black with soot and grime, ugly pink insulation stuffed in the crawl space—a more modern attempt to keep in the heat. But then she imagined all the life that had taken place behind those fading wood-stained walls: big family meals, laughing children, crying babies ... The kind of life that was snatched from her as a child and she'd never allowed herself as an adult. She wrapped her fingers around the note in her pocket, scrawled in Norm's shaky writing.

I, Norman O'Brien, hereby appoint Lisa West to be my agent in respect of trying to resolve the matter of demolishing the original homestead that was built on the property granted to my great-great-grandfather, Samuel O'Brien, in 1860.

Home and desperate for something to take away the taste of instant coffee, Lisa spooned fresh grounds into her little espresso pot and put it on the stove. Waiting for it to percolate, she wondered if her place was as much a shrine to Leonard as Norm's was to Rose. Lisa had used Leonard's money to buy the house, his collection of photographic prints hung on almost every wall, his LPs filled two long shelves under the TV, half of the books had once been his. She still had his expensive cameras locked away. She loved this house. Was that because, despite moving across the Atlantic, it was where she still felt close to him? Was that a bad thing? In the end, they had been perfect together. Absolutely perfect.

Dan's invitation to the Bee Ball was gnawing. Could she?

She took her coffee to the table and listened to his message again, but just as she felt a little buzz of excitement, the voice in her head amplified: *there is no such thing as a relationship without painful side effects, and God knows you've had enough hurt.* Lisa crossed her legs, then uncrossed them. Nothing felt right without work, the comfort of doing what she was good at, companionship without emotional demands. She imagined Caitlin Jeffrey, the new principal, sitting at *her* desk. How Lisa had loved the feel of that silky maple beneath her fingers. How she had loved that job—making things run smoothly, sorting it out when others didn't, and finding just the right person to teach each course.

She wondered how Caitlin was getting on with June and Brooke. Lisa missed them. She thought of everyone in the little staff room, filled with the smell of fresh coffee and donuts, remembered how they always had cake for birthdays and gingerbread at Christmas. Lisa hoped Caitlin hadn't drowned her weeping fig. Susan had given it to Lisa on her first day and, over the years, it had grown so large it wouldn't have fit through the door if she'd tried to take it with her. When Caitlin had first arrived, Lisa had phoned to welcome her, but the mentoring wasn't due to begin for another week. Lisa was to introduce her to the visiting instructors, explain the budgets, show her how to put together next year's diploma courses, maybe even be there for the start of summer school.

She took her cup over to the sink and decided to stop in at lunchtime, see how Caitlin was getting on, pick up some flowers on the way. Suddenly Lisa felt more settled.

Driving through the sculpture forest, toward the imposing post and beam building, she was proud. This was the world that she had created. She had been part of the new vision, expanded the curriculum, created the summer programme, grown Colville School of the Arts from a small offshoot of a community college in Southern Ontario to a nationally recognized institution.

The big glass doors swished open for her. Such a lovely, familiar sound. Walking along the corridor, Lisa looked for the welcome desk where Brook should be sitting, so that every visitor was greeted with a smile. It wasn't there. In its place was a young woman perched on a tall stool, staring at her phone. Her badge said *Sav, they/them.*

"Hi. Where's Brooke?"

Sav looked up. "Who?"

"She used to sit here, at the welcome desk."

"Oh, Brooke, yeah, she's in the room behind reception, so's the desk. How can I help you?"

"I'm Lisa West."

Sav gazed out from under dense eyeliner, their expression blank.

"I used to be—I used to work here. I'm just popping in to see Caitlin Jeffrey, the principal."

"Cait, okay. I'll check if she's free." Sav swiped their phone.

"No need to call. I just want to give her these." Lisa held up a bunch of white roses and winter cabbages. In the florist, she had thought the combination inspired.

"Are those—cabbages?"

"They are. Ornamental. No good for dinner."

Not even a smile. Lisa decided to keep walking. Neither Sid, the security guard, nor June the receptionist, who doubled as Lisa's secretary, were behind reception. Instead, there was a young man with a tattoo of a butterfly on his neck. His badge read *Carlos, he/him, they/them.*

"Hello." Lisa tried to sound upbeat. "Where's June? And Sid?"

"She's back there." He tipped his head toward a closed door that used to lead to the photocopy room. "With Brooke."

"And Sid?"

"He works nights now. How can I help you?"

Sav must have phoned because Caitlin came out of her office smiling. "Lisa, what a lovely surprise. Come on in." Her badge said *Principal.*

The room looked bigger. The desk was pushed against the wall, and Lisa's lovely maple chair had been replaced by something made of steel and mesh on wheels. It was swivelled around to face two very designer chairs.

"Please, sit." Caitlin sank into black mesh. She looked younger than Lisa remembered from the interview. Maybe it was just the way she was dressed, more like a student than the principal.

"I brought you these." Lisa offered the bouquet and chose the chair with an orange cover. It was surprisingly comfortable.

"Are those—cabbages?"

"Ornamental." *Don't make the dinner joke.* "With roses." *Obviously. Now it sounds like I don't think she knows what a rose looks like.*

"How unusual, thank you. I'll give them to Carlos to put in water."

Caitlin went back to reception and Lisa looked around. No weeping fig. She kept noticing what wasn't there: the paintings she'd been given by graduating students, the little rug by the window, framed awards from the Ontario Business Association. A while after Caitlin came back, Lisa mentioned the mentoring.

Something in the younger woman's eyes flinched. "Didn't Robert call you?"

Lisa looked puzzled. "Robert?"

"Director? Chairman of the Board."

Lisa remembered to smile. "Yes, I know who he is, and no, I haven't heard from him."

"That's a shame, it would have been better coming from Robert. We've been working on a plan to shift the demographic and start moving the diploma year toward a degree course and we agreed that the mentoring didn't seem necessary."

Lisa paused. *They had done all that in two weeks? And after twenty years of living and breathing this place, having practically no life outside it, I'm not necessary?* She left it a bit too long before replying. "Well, of course, if you don't think I can be useful."

"Robert said you were going to introduce me to the summer school staff, and some other stuff to do with budgets and scheduling. It's very generous of you, but I've already been in touch with most of the teachers, and I'm bringing in some of my own people, offering a few last-minute additions. As to the budgets—"

Lisa held up her hand. "No explanation needed." She took a deep breath. "Actually, it's a relief. I'm so busy that I was wondering how I was going to find the time."

"Oh good. I'd hate to hurt your feelings. You have done a wonderful job bringing this place to where it is now, and I know what a great resource you are. It's just that—"

"You're eager to do things your way. I understand."

Caitlin smiled a look of apology and relief, and with that, it was done. Lisa was redundant. She could feel panic rising, she needed to get out. No longer eager to see June or face what Caitlin had done to her lovely staffroom, Lisa headed for the exit, past Sav, who didn't even notice her leave. Lisa wished she hadn't changed out of her jeans into this officious skirt. She wished she hadn't bought the bloody cabbages. She called Robert as soon as she got home.

"Ah, yes. I didn't think you'd be going in this soon. I'm sorry that happened. The board has agreed to pay you for the mentoring package as planned."

Robert had been more than her boss, he'd been her champion, advisor, confidante—one of the most important people in her life. Now he sounded so uncaring, she could hardly believe it. "You're going to pay me to stay away?"

"I wouldn't put it that way. We made a commitment, and we don't want you to feel undervalued. It's just that, as you know, we had already identified a problem with the aging demographic of the summer school. Caitlin arrived with a strategy for attracting younger students, and she has already been in touch with U of T to talk about an affiliated degree course. As to the other areas you were going to help with, she seems quite capable."

Lisa was determined not to let Robert hear the tears gathering in the back of her throat. *Am I wrong to feel so betrayed? It's not as if he's my brother, or lover, or even best friend ...*

"Please don't take this personally, Lisa, we honestly do value your expertise. We're all looking forward to seeing you at the next board meeting."

As the call ended, she burst into tears. The life that already felt empty was looking like an abyss. Lisa had loved her independence, but now she felt alone. A familiar feeling that took her back to university, school, and even home. She thought of England, coming back from school with a Mother's Day card.

Nicky was in the kitchen reading the *TV Times*, a towel turbaned around her head.

"I made you something." Lisa stood by her sister's side, wearing her uniform skirt and cardigan, little white socks bunched around her ankles.

"That's nice." Nicky didn't look up. "Pass us a bikkie."

Lisa obediently fetched the tin on top of the fridge, then slid the card in front of it. Daisies drawn in crayon, *TO MY BEST MUM* written in glue and sprinkled with glitter.

"What the fuck?" Each of Nicky's words was louder than the one before. "I am not your fucking mother."

Lisa took a step back, eyes filling.

"Mum's dead." Nicky was shouting now. "You don't have a best mum, and I don't either. If we did, I wouldn't have to be here cooking your bloody tea every night."

"I wanted to make a card like everyone else was. I just wanted to have someone to give it to."

"Well, I'm sick of what you want. 'Lisa this' and 'Lisa that.'" Dad's footsteps were heavy on the stairs. Nicky lowered her voice. "Now look what you've done."

His frame filled the doorway, rubbing his eye with a fist. "Keep it down. My shift starts at nine. If I don't sleep now, I'll be useless later."

Nicky slid the card under her magazine and turned around. "Sorry, Dad, Lisa's winding me up as usual."

Tears prickled, but Lisa didn't let them out. She wanted to run over and put her arms around Dad's big tummy, let him hold her while she wept, but she didn't move. In the year since Mum died, he was always upstairs asleep or at work, except when he went to the football. There didn't seem time for the hugs and little talks they used to have, and Lisa missed him as much as Mum. Sometimes she had to dig her nails into her arm to stop herself from crying.

"Leave your sister alone," he scolded. "She's got enough on her plate without you making things worse. And get up those stairs and take off your uniform. I'm not buying another skirt if you rip it like the last one."

Lisa wondered what happened to that card. Knowing Nicky, she probably threw it straight in the garbage on top of the previous night's fish and chips. Years later, when Lisa was in grade ten, she saw a book in the school library called *Cold Comfort Farm*. She stood staring at the cover until those two words, cold and comfort, blurred. Keeping her hair over her face, she ran to the bathroom and kept crying until the bell went at the end of the day, stuffing her fist in her mouth when anyone used the stall next to hers. They were Lisa's first real tears since Mum died, and she honestly thought they'd never stop. After school, she went to the park and kept crying until it was dark, then crept into the house so Nicky wouldn't see her hurt.

But that little girl was gone. Now Lisa was a strong, capable woman. Except, looking around her Ontario kitchen, she felt like the unloved child again, unsure what to do next. Her night with Dan had opened a door she thought was closed forever, and should stay closed, but Lisa kept remembering how it felt to be touched—to be wanted. She also needed to do some research into painful sex. She'd read about women "drying out" after menopause but as she wasn't planning to have sex (ever again), she hadn't paid much attention. She hadn't experienced any discomfort until Dan.

She still hadn't phoned him, and the ball was tomorrow. Lisa started emptying the dishwasher. Should she? Spending the night with Dan was a drunken slip-up. Accepting his invitation to the ball would be a conscious intentional decision. It would be going on a date.

She went into the little sunroom that doubled as her home office and pulled open a drawer, trying to convince herself how great it was to have time to get her life in order. Why was it easier to throw away pencil stubs than think about having a relationship? Finally, when she'd discarded the dried-out ballpoint pens, found the perfect little box for her USB sticks, and made a pile of old envelopes to use as spare paper, she took out her phone. *Dan Mason, Down to Earth Designs.* Her finger hovered over the call button. She couldn't do it. She'd made that promise, twenty years ago. So instead, she put on her coat and boots and whistled for Fido. They would drive into town together and walk by the river. Lisa loved her new little white truck—a retirement present to herself. As she opened the door, Fido leapt past her onto the rug on the back seat. She started the engine, looked at herself in the rearview mirror, and picked up her phone.

Dan answered straight away. "Synchronicity. I was just wondering whether to ring you but I didn't want to seem pushy."

Lisa switched off the ignition. "Sorry, I should have called sooner. If I've left it too late, if you've asked someone else—"

"Course not. I asked you because I want to go with you."

She didn't know what to say.

"Still there?"

"Yes, sorry. The thing is—it's been a long time since ..."

"You went to a ball?"

They both laughed.

"Since I went anywhere with .... I don't want to presume. I mean on a—"

"Date? Don't worry, I'm kinda the same. There hasn't really been anyone since Anna's mother."

Lisa did the math and laughed again, resting back in her seat. "That's the last thing I expected to hear. You're close to beating my record."

"I can't believe that. You must have been thrashing them off with a stick." An engine thundered down the phone. "Oh, there's my backhoe with the afternoon crew. I'm outside a client's house."

"Umm, okay. So I'll see you tomorrow?"

"I'll be there at six. Looking forward to it."

"So am I." A horn bellowed and Lisa didn't know if he'd heard her. Excitement tingled as she put away her phone and started the truck. She looked at herself again in the mirror and decided to buy some makeup. He sounded so nice, and keen. Then she remembered Susan's warning. *Why did she tell me to be wary? Surely it can't be anything serious. How bad can a man be who invites you to a ball in a church hall?*

Three

Bouncing along next to Dan in his Down To Earth Designs van, Lisa tried not to giggle at the scene she had landed in. He was wearing a black dinner jacket that had once belonged to his father and her green satin dress had been in storage in the basement for years. They were like kids going to a fancy-dress party. But when she stood in the almost darkness, waiting for him to park and listening to the buzz of voices in the church hall, anxiety filled her chest. She knew nothing of these people, and it was over twenty years since she'd been on a date.

Dan held open the door. "Ready to meet a bunch of beekeepers?"

Too late to change my mind now. She took a deep breath and entered another world. They were late. Most people were already eating. A chubby man with large teeth waved to Dan and pointed to two empty seats by his side, mouthing over the chatter and clatter of cutlery, "Saved them for you."

Dan raised his hand, thumb up, and turned to Lisa. "Looks like we're going straight for the food."

The hall was charming: wooden and slightly ramshackle, lit by fairy lights, walls dotted with cardboard cutouts of bees, and a hand-painted sign proudly announcing "The Ontario Association of Beekeeper's Annual Ball." Lisa's nervousness lessened as they picked their way through the tables. Most people they passed knew Dan, who introduced her as "Lisa West, who was principal of the art school," "Lisa West, who lives in Colville," and "Lisa West, who's been brave enough to come with me tonight." It felt surprisingly good to be with him.

The diners were all ages and very dressed up—men in black dinner jackets, women in assorted fanciness: long and short dresses made of silk, velvet, and satin; hair puffed, pinned and swept up; silver, gold, diamante; and—incredibly—a woman in elbow-length gloves. The atmosphere was full of laughter and affection.

As they approached the table loaded with catering trays, Lisa sighed. "I should have mentioned I'm vegetarian."

Dan handed her a plate. "Don't worry, I called ahead. You told me you didn't eat meat the other night."

Lisa was impressed. An elderly woman wearing a nylon apron and a tiara handed her a plate of quiche with roast potatoes and peas. "Here you are, dear, we kept it warm for you."

Sitting next to Dan and opposite Warren, the big-toothed friend, Lisa felt full of optimism, until she glanced along the table and saw a face she'd hoped never to see again—Skye Stewart. Her hair was longer and scraped back, and she was wearing very red lipstick, but it was undeniably her. Lisa was about to turn away when Skye looked up, her eyes sparking instant hatred, and Lisa's whole body tensed. This was the student who had threatened to end her career. The one who knew ...

"Well, if it isn't my favourite principal."

Lisa swallowed. "Hello, Skye, how are you?"

"Shouldn't you be at work, playing God over other people's lives?" There was a slight slur in her voice and Lisa noticed a shot glass next to the one half-full of wine. The rest of the table hushed.

Lisa forced a smile. "I'm retired now, nothing to do with the art school anymore."

"But what made you think you could come *here*? You must have known I run the Junior Beekeepers. It's my job."

Lisa glanced at Dan, knowing she'd have to explain this, wondering how to keep her integrity intact. "I came with a friend. I'm sure there's plenty of space for all of us to have a nice evening."

Skye glared at him. "She's with *you*? I hope you know what you're friggin' getting into."

Dan looked from her to Lisa and back again before speaking, his voice gentle but authoritative. "Drop it, Skye."

The young woman opened her mouth, closed it, and then angrily picked up a bottle from the centre of the table and refilled her wine glass. Her expression was unreadable, but Lisa could feel her resentment. Lisa remembered Skye as a student: belligerent, rude, argumentative, always making excuses for whatever she hadn't done.

Dan squeezed Lisa's hand and spoke softly. "Don't worry. She does a good job with the kids, but we've all seen her lose it in meetings."

Gentle chatter resumed as people returned to their food. Skye was ignoring Lisa, but she had always been a ticking time bomb that could explode at any moment. Warily, Lisa turned her attention back to the table. Dan and Warren were discussing rock removal when his wife, Mattie, pushed aside her plate and sat back to talk. "Those two work together almost every day. You'd think they'd run out of things to say, but they never do. It's the same when Dan comes for Sunday lunch, the rest of us hardly get a word in."

Lisa stuffed down thoughts of Skye. "Do you live near each other then?"

"Always have. We all went to the same school."

"And now they work together?"

"They used to until Dan set up on his own. That was back when Anna was ten."

"He told me he brought her up single-handedly."

"He was—is—an incredible father. I never liked his ex. She was always looking for something bigger and better, even at school. Couldn't see how lucky she was with Dan, and definitely wasn't cut out for family life. One day, she just up and went and never came back. Anna's doing her master's now, something to do with birds and beaches." Mattie motioned to Dan. "How did you two meet?"

Lisa laughed, hoping to sound casual. "Oh, he came to do some work at my place and ended up staying for supper."

"Well, he must like you to have brought you here."

Lisa couldn't resist checking Dan's story. "So he doesn't usually bring a date?"

"He's never come with anyone before. Hasn't been out with anyone since Erin left, as far as I know. He said once that he's never going to let a woman hurt him the way she did. I told him being hurt is part of being alive, but I guess he's going to have to figure that one out for himself."

A croaky voice shouted out. "Dan's getting married?"

All heads turned to an impressively old woman sitting a couple of chairs away. Lisa tried not to blush as Dan looked up. "Not yet, Margery, I'm still holding out for you." Margery giggled, Dan winked, and Lisa felt an odd sort of pride in being with him.

Eyes magnified by ancient spectacles, Margery leaned across the table and peered at Lisa. "And how long have you had hives?"

"That's a very personal question," Lisa retorted through a big smile. While everyone else roared, Skye scraped her chair back and left the table.

Before dessert, they listened to a heartfelt talk on the destructive effects of the climate crisis from a woman in a beautiful velvet gown who worked for the Ministry of Natural Resources and kept bees herself. Everyone was riveted, and Lisa was impressed by how politicized they were. After tiramisu and coffee, the man who had introduced the woman from the Ministry stood again. "And now, while the tables are cleared and the DJ sets up, I invite you to take a ten-minute break before our fundraiser."

Dan spoke into Lisa's ear above the applause. "Forgot to tell you that I'm the auctioneer. Just come and watch, don't think you have to buy anything."

"Is there no end to your talents?" The more Lisa saw of Dan, the more she liked him. He was a wonderful auctioneer, coaxing people to part with their money for a china poodle, an electric saw, a stack of novels by Tolkien, a meal in a Chinese restaurant, piles of old beekeeping journals, and other obscure bee paraphernalia. The more Dan cajoled, begged, and challenged his audience to part with their cash, the more Lisa responded, a familiar warmth creeping through her. She loved how large and square his fingernails were. When he took off his jacket, she saw how slim his waist was. As he rolled up his sleeves, she was transfixed by his forearms.

When the auction started winding down, Lisa went to the bathroom. Running her palms over her dress, she remembered all those teenage years wishing she wasn't so skinny and her boobs were bigger. Older age was the payoff—less to droop. She combed her hair, added blush and lipstick, and thought of Dan's hands.

Back in the hall, a confused crowd was collecting around the table of auction items and he looked harassed.

"Where's Glen?" Lisa heard everyone asking. She leaned toward a woman by the door and whispered, "Who's Glen?"

"The guy that always collects the money and organizes the distribution of the items. He's supposed to be here."

Dan was at the front of the crowd giving directions to random people, but nobody seemed to be responding. Lisa rushed up to his side. "Let me help. I've done this kind of stuff at the art school."

"Please!" Dan smiled. "I am now yours to order around."

Lisa smiled back. She would take him up on that but first, the auction. Noticing that the caterers had cleaned up and left, she waved her arm shouting, "Everyone who bought something please follow me into the kitchen and form a line." Moments later she was laughing and joking, sending people back into the hall to write down a description of their purchase next to the number on its sticker. She started a ledger on the back of a menu and used aluminum serving trays to separate the coins from bills.

When Lisa had given the MC her accounts and money, and all the bidders were satisfied with their prizes, she went back into the hall. Dan was dancing with a woman in a blue turban. As the song ended, he spun around and took Lisa's hands. The music blared "15 Miles to the Love Shack." He tugged her toward him and she stiffened—dancing had always been an issue. But tonight was all about being new, so she tried to mirror his moves and relax. He didn't seem to notice her discomfort, and by the end of the track, her shoulders had loosened and her head was shaking as they laughed their way around the room.

As the next song started, Skye and her friend pushed past in a fury. Lisa almost toppled and Dan splayed onto the floor. A guy in a velvet jacket rushed over to help him up. "It's time someone told that young 'un to rein it in."

"Don't bother." Dan brushed off his pants and turned to Lisa. "We were just going, weren't we?"

She nodded, relieved. As Skye and her friend stomped to the music, Dan made his goodbyes and Mattie pulled Lisa aside. "You two should come for dinner. I get the feeling you're going to be around for a while, and I've got *a lot* of good Dan stories to tell you."

She winked and Lisa glowed like a fourteen-year-old who'd done well on her first date. These were good people, and apart from the drama, she'd enjoyed being part of something so outside her own world.

Dan turned his key in the ignition. "I'm sorry about Skye."

"So am I." Lisa clicked in her seat belt, praying he wouldn't ask what had happened to make her ex-student so angry. "I hope it didn't ruin your evening."

He shook his head and smiled. "You really came to the rescue in there, organizing all those unruly folks and their donations. No wonder the art school was such a success with you at the helm." He started driving. "Back to my place?"

Lisa's plan was to tell him she needed to go home—alone. That she had to be up early. Her plan was to just spend the evening with this man, to get a sense of him and of who she was when she was with him, to think clearly about her next step. She looked at his silhouette beside her. "Sounds good." And they started along the dark country road.

Four

Both tired, they fell into an easy silence on the way back to Dan's, but Lisa's brain wouldn't stop. For more than twenty years, she had been absolutely clear she didn't need a relationship, yet here she was driving towards this man's bed. But maybe *this doesn't have to be a relationship?* It's not as though we're in our twenties, looking to set up home together. This thought made Lisa feel easier, more in control, and although her mind was still cautious, the rest of her was ready, wanting to touch and be touched. *Take it slowly,* she told herself. *Just don't do anything you'll regret tomorrow.*

As they drove up the lane, she was distracted by the contemporary glass-fronted building that came into sight. "This is incredible. How long have you lived here?"

"I built it before Anna was born. Had to call in every favour I had. That was twenty-three years ago, and I'm still working on it." Dan switched off the ignition, unplugged his seatbelt, and leaned forward. "I'm glad you like it."

His lips were gentle and exploring. Lisa felt her body ignite, but as his hand slid under the hem of her dress, she needed to slow things down. She spoke softly. "Why don't you show me the house?"

"Good plan." He trailed his fingers back down her thigh.

As they walked to the front door, Dan took Lisa's hand and she smiled, it was such a long time since she'd experienced this simple act of intimacy. Yet she was still conflicted. Warm and homey, the kitchen calmed her. One whole wall was window, overlooking an expanse of grass studded with little lights and then forest. The moon shone brightly through the trees, creating shadows in the room.

She slipped off her coat and felt a subtle heat coming from the wood stove. Dan kissed the back of her neck and then turned her for another deeper kiss. Her fingers explored his hair—coarse and curly but soft. His hands moved down her back until they were on her buttocks, warm through the satin of her dress. Her hips moved closer in response, and as Dan went to undo her zipper, a pile of letters whooshed from the table to the floor. His eyes followed the envelopes as they scattered over terracotta tiles.

"Everything okay?"

He was staring at the mail. "I'm sorry. It's just ..." His body stiffened and his brow creased. "My wife. Ex-wife. That's her writing. It's the second time ... she's trying to get in touch with Anna."

Lisa smoothed her dress while Dan bent down and picked up the letter. "I want to burn the bloody thing. I told her when she wrote before, she can't just reappear, not after all we've been through, all we had to build. She's not taking that down."

As he took a step toward the woodstove, Lisa's eyes widened. "Surely you're not going to burn it?"

"I'd like to. She shattered Anna's heart. There's no way I'm letting that happen again."

Lisa remembered the years of longing for Mum, for any crumb to fill the hollow. She spoke gently. "Maybe it's time for Anna to make her own decisions about her mother."

"You've got no idea. Being a parent isn't a thing you change your mind about, you're either in or you're out. You've never had ..." Dan stopped himself.

Why do people think that having children gives them exclusive emotional privileges? "But I have been a daughter, and I know what it's like to lose a mother."

His face saddened. "I just love that girl too much to see her hurt again."

Lisa kept her tone low. "Maybe Anna misses her mum, whatever happened all those years ago. What if that's a need that never goes away?"

Dan looked at the letter in his hand. "All this time and that woman can still get to me." He threw it onto a pile of papers by the wood stove and sat down, looking smaller, crumpled.

Do all relationships have to include heartache? Lisa knew the answer and she didn't like it.

Dan stood up again. "I need a drink of water. Can I get you one?"

She nodded. They sat on opposite sides of the table, sipping in silence, until he let out a big sigh. "You know the thing I've never said out loud, is that living here and having a baby was never Erin's dream, it was mine. We met in high school and all we talked about was buying a van and driving coast to coast, making it up as we went along. She always wanted to go places and see things and we never thought about what would happen after that. But then she got pregnant and when Anna was born, I realized I had everything I needed right here. I never stopped to ask what Erin wanted, I just assumed ..." He looked up, his eyes watery. "I'm sorry. This isn't how I hoped our evening would end."

"Don't apologize. I want to get to know you, and what's going on in your life, but I also know that for today, it's time for me to go home."

He nodded, his face only showing exhaustion. "Yeah, of course. I'll take you."

"But you've got to be up in ..."

He glanced at the clock on the stove. "Four hours. I can't believe I said I'd look at the job on a Sunday."

"Maybe I could call a cab?"

Dan looked back at the clock. "It's too late. The taxi service is way out in Brockton and Serge doesn't answer the phone after midnight. I don't know about you, but I'm too tired to do anything but sleep." He stood up. "What if we just share my bed, hands off?"

Lisa nodded. When she came out of the bathroom, Dan was already tucked in. The huge T-shirt he'd given her smelled of fresh air and laundry soap and she was grateful for the cover as she slipped under the duvet. His breath was steady. "Night night." His voice was groggy with sleep. "Watch the bed bugs don't bite."

She smiled. He looked five years old.

Lisa woke a while later to find him nestled behind her, his arm around her waist. She'd forgotten the comfort that came from having someone at your back. Snuggling closer, enjoying the full length of his body against hers, she drifted to sleep. Deep dreamless sleep.

What seemed like moments later, she was shaken awake by the rapid fire of an ancient alarm. Dan stretched back across the bed to turn it off. "Sorry about that. I've had this clock since I was a kid."

His face was creased from the folds in the pillow. Lisa moved the hair back from his forehead. Their kiss was involuntary, inevitable. They could taste each other's sleep and it didn't matter. He pulled her toward him, his pyjama bottoms fleecy against her legs. She ran her hand up his arm, over taut muscle, bony shoulder blades, and down his vertebrae, one by one. He kissed her neck, lifting her T-shirt to taste each nipple in turn. Her breathing deepened. Lisa remembered the pleasure of kissing, of exploring—top lip, bottom, edges, tongues touching tenderly, penetrating deep. A tickle at the back of her throat, something she hadn't felt since she was a teen. She gave herself over to pleasure and he responded. He was on top, his weight on his elbows, his hands in her hair. "Is this okay?"

She nodded and reached up to kiss him.

"Hold that thought." He laughed, rolling out of bed and going into the bathroom. Lisa lay back and wondered if it would hurt, hoping it wouldn't. He came back with a condom, slipped off his pyjama bottoms, and put it on. This time his kiss felt familiar. She pulled off her T-shirt and Dan slid down, covering her belly with kisses until his tongue was between her legs. She tensed slightly—it had been so long—before relaxing into the soft warmth and her hips tilted in anticipation. Losing all sense of time and place, she lifted her arms over her head, luxuriating in pure sensation, receiving all that Dan offered, and almost came. He moved back up her body and seemed to touch every inch of her as he did. She wanted him, but when he slid into her, she inhaled. There was the pain.

He held still. "All good?"

Lisa didn't want to stop, didn't want to think about what might be wrong. In reply, she kissed him and let go into a longing she'd forgotten was there. Relishing the closeness without thinking, she wrapped her legs around Dan's back. He slipped his hands under and pulled her to him, thrusting at the same time. Bigger pain. *What's going on?* Trying to relax, Lisa breathed in deeply and out again. She wanted to be here, with him. He exhaled, changed pace. She watched his shoulder move toward her and recede, shifted slightly, took another breath, felt his hand on her breast and gradually, the pain receded. Now she moved into desire, leaving everything behind except how good it felt to be together, how good it felt to have sex. Dan came, and soon after, collapsed into her, kissing the side of her neck. She hadn't come, but her body was awake, revelling in sensation, until her brain kicked in again, puzzled. She knew that women got dryer after menopause, but that wasn't her problem. *What if it's something more serious?*

Dan kissed her. "I love that you're so real."

I wasn't very real just now. I should tell him. But as his hand slid between her legs, Lisa stopped thinking. He seemed to know exactly how to touch. Her head pressed back into the pillow, she could hear her own heartbeat, and as something inside her uncoiled, she orgasmed.

They lay still, her body snuggled into his side. This felt like more than just sex. Lisa closed her eyes. Dan was already breathing the rhythm of sleep when she remembered and stroked his face, speaking gently. "Weren't you meant to leave early to go to Whitby this morning?"

He looked at the clock. "Damn it, you're right. She's a new client, so I shouldn't be late. But you don't have to hurry. I'll jump in the shower and then call Serge, get him over to drive you home—in an hour or so? That way you can get up slowly, have some coffee and relax."

Dan headed for the bathroom but turned back and gave Lisa another kiss. After his shower, he took some socks out of the drawer, put one on, came over to show her a photo of his daughter, and dropped the other one. Lisa chuckled. With the toothbrush still in his mouth, he started telling her how to lock up when she left, dripping paste all over his T-shirt. When he was finally dressed, he stopped to give her a goodbye kiss, tracing circles on her bare shoulder. "You are *sooooo* sexy. And I love that you're so independent, not looking for anyone to fix you. It's a pretty potent combo."

"Go on, get out of here." She laughed. "I'll see you soon."

With a final look back, Dan was off. He was designing a garden and would be staying away for a couple of nights. They agreed to talk when he got home. Lisa rolled over, she could smell him on the pillow. Her body was gloriously heavy, but something wasn't right. There was no pain now, but she'd call the doctor when she got home. Turning her head, she saw a big turquoise book on the table by the bed: *Repairing Small Gas Engines*. She smiled at the paperback underneath it, *The Tao of Pooh*. On the wall to her left were floor-to-ceiling shelves, crammed with books about architecture, landscape design and trees, alongside novels: John Grisham, Guy Vanderhaeghe, Annie Proulx. On her right was a chair piled with clothes.

She padded barefoot over the honey-coloured floorboards to the bathroom—definitely a man's: tiny mirror, grey towels, Head and Shoulders shampoo, one shelf with a razor, toothbrush, comb and nail clippers. Sitting on the toilet, she imagined herself in the tub, with Dan leaning in the doorway, telling her about his day. How she had loved it when Leonard came home, tired and dishevelled, always later than her. They'd snuggle in front of the TV, listen to music while they both worked, or just go to bed together and read. Lisa knew how hard it was to find the right person; she'd waited forty years for Leonard. She pulled some paper off the roll and wiped. Blood. Dabbing again, she saw more. Not a lot, but very pink and fresh.

She tried to stop her mind from making the inevitable jump. Mum had died of cancer. It had started in her breast, and by the time it was diagnosed, had spread to her lymph nodes and lungs. That was when Lisa was six. Dad had sent her away to stay with Auntie Jean and when she came home, Mum was gone. A few years later, Auntie Jean died of cancer too. Cancer was filed in Lisa's brain. She mustn't panic. She'd phone the doctor when she got home.

Five

Despite looking twelve, Dr. Lau was wearing pearls. "So, what can I do for you today?" At least she sounded like a grown-up.

Lisa cleared her throat but hesitated before speaking. She was so keen to get checked that she hadn't considered the embarrassment of discussing her vagina. Suddenly glad that the doctor was a woman, she took a deep breath and blurted, "It's a while since I've had sex and I've done it—had it—twice recently and it was painful both times. And after the second time, there was some bleeding."

The doctor swivelled her stool to face the Health Centre's screen and pulled up Lisa's notes, then she turned back. "Quite common. Estimates are that 50-60% of post-menopausal women suffer from sexual dysfunction—dyspareunia—pain during intercourse. Any other symptoms? Dryness, itching, burning, discharge?"

Lisa's shoulders eased. There was something about Dr. Lau's matter-of-factness that made the conversation easier. "No, none at all."

More questions: Do you have a history of pain with sex? Do you have trouble becoming aroused? Did the pain continue afterwards?

Lisa shook her head to them all. "Of course, I know about women becoming dry after menopause, but I don't think that's my problem."

"You managed without lubricant?"

She nodded.

"You said it had been a while. How long has it been since you had intercourse before these two occasions?"

This was more embarrassing than discussing her vagina. Dr. Lau looked like she had been wearing diapers the last time Lisa had sex before Dan. "Approximately ... more than twenty years."

"That is a long time." The doctor turned back to her computer and Lisa's very private life appeared, letter by letter, on the screen. "Probably nothing to worry about, just some atrophy—a thinning and shrinking of the vaginal tissues. It can also cause a shortening and tightening of the vaginal canal, hence the pain. The bleeding was probably produced by friction, tearing the tissue because it has become more fragile."

The more the doctor talked, the worse Lisa felt. "So my vagina has atrophied because I haven't used it for so long?"

"I am sorry, the language around this is terrible. Even the classification 'sexual dysfunction' is punitive. No, your condition is hormonal, to do with lack of estrogen, and so easily fixable. But before I prescribe, I'd like to do an internal exam, just to rule out a few things."

"Like what?" Lisa's cancer antenna twitched. "If you're talking about ..."

But Dr. Lau was already opening the door. "Just slip off your underwear and make yourself comfortable on the examination bed. I'll be back in a minute."

Lisa had come prepared, worn a skirt to make the probing easier. She laid down and waited for the doctor, imagining her pulling on latex gloves as she came back in. The new health centre was like a cross between a kindergarten and a senior's residence. With a frieze of teddies and grab rails by the bed and chair, Dr. Lau's sliver of a room was the worst of both.

As the speculum was inserted, Lisa sucked in air audibly. It hurt the same way sex had. The doctor nodded knowingly. The examination seemed to go on forever and Lisa focused on two bears bouncing across the wallpaper. Finally, swab taken, examination complete, latex gloves in the bin, underwear in place, she was back on her chair.

"Looking at your records, I see that you have breast cancer in the family."

"My mother and her sister both died of it."

"Which is why I'm not going to suggest HRT—hormone replacement therapy. Vaginal estrogens work by increasing moisture to the tissue, via rings or creams, and I recommend you start with some pessaries—waxy tablets that go directly into the vagina. They're relatively safe."

Relative to what? Lisa asked silently. "But surely, if it's putting estrogen into my body, it's still going to increase my chances of getting cancer."

"There is always a degree of risk. The difference is that the estrogen level is much lower than if you were using HRT, but your exposure is not zero."

Lisa wondered how to weigh up the odds.

"The downside is that the dose is smaller. Topical applications might not be as effective. In an extreme case, they might not help at all. You have to use them for several weeks to find out. Most women experience some relief after about three weeks, maximum benefits usually occur after a few months, but it may take up to a year." Dr. Lau looked at Lisa enquiringly. "It's your decision."

Lisa's brain whirred. *Is it really worth it? I thought I was done turning myself inside out to please a man, and until a few days ago, I was fine without one.* Then yesterday's image flashed—Lisa, alone, grey-haired, in velour pants. Only now she was atrophied as well.

"Why don't you take some time to think about it?" the doctor suggested. "The pessaries are a very low dose. If you decide to try them, just phone reception and I'll call in a prescription to your pharmacy. In the meanwhile, all I can suggest is plenty of lubricant. You said you weren't dry, but the added viscosity may be helpful."

* * *

There was a big bunch of purple tulips waiting on the porch when Lisa got home, a card nestled in the cellophane wrapping:

Dinner on Friday? I'll make veggie spaghetti.
Dan. xxxx

Four kisses. Had he told the florist to put four? This was a declaration, an invitation to more than dinner. Lisa was churning with thoughts and feelings. Since being told she wasn't needed at the art school, her insecurities had been seeping to the surface. She'd broken her own vow by sleeping with Dan and had, confusingly, wanted more. But now she was atrophied. The only remedy still carried a risk of cancer and might take months to be effective or not work at all. Meaning she may never be able to have penetrative sex again, just when this man she likes—who adores sex—wants a relationship?

She changed into her jeans, grabbed a jacket, and called Fido. Her boots squelched along the muddy path and over last year's leaves. Fido bounded over the soggy field at the back of the farmhouse as Lisa followed through the tangle of trees and up a steep slope into wooded hills.

She breathed out loudly, letting the wind blow through the doctor's words. Here the ground was firmer, everything in tones of grey bark and limestone. *Why do people always think trees are brown?* she wondered, inhaling the smell of peaty earth. As she walked, the silence seeped into her, interrupted only by the singsong of a phoebe bird, the first sound of spring. Lisa became absorbed in the light echoing of branches and tiny patches of ice still left in shaded pools. Her legs felt strong. She enjoyed the steeper climb to the top of the rocky scarp, and when she got there, she could see Colville Lake surrounded by cottages, the water gleaming clear in the afternoon sun.

"What kind of man wants to have sex with a shrivelled vagina?" she asked Fido as he came to stand beside her.

Lisa imagined telling Dan and sat down on a log. He was so vibrant, full of energy, and had been so definite about why he liked her—because she was independent, didn't need fixing, and was *soooo* sexy. She looked out at the town, spreading around the lake, and filled with shame—about her age, her useless vagina, her lack of dating experience. She had been out with so few men, so long ago, that starting over felt like more than she had energy for. But then Lisa remembered the loveliness of her morning in bed with Dan, his boyishness, the purple tulips. She hardly knew this person, but the future felt even bleaker without him. A familiar sadness spread through her, touching a deep pit of loss.

What was Dr. Lau's advice? Plenty of lubricant? Lisa had never used lube in her life. What was she meant to do, stop mid-foreplay and say, "I might need extra viscosity, so I'm just going to squeeze on this tube of glop, and even then it might be too painful to keep going?"

Fido looked up at her. As she scratched the dog's head, an idea started to form. Not a great one, because it meant being less than honest, but maybe she could tell Dan she wanted to *really* slow things down, suggest they be platonic while getting to know each other, and use that time to secretly try the pessaries. Okay, it was a bit manipulative, but it might mean they could be together in the end. Lisa was smiling as she started the walk home. She was going to phone the doctor's office to get the prescription for topical estrogen, and if it worked, she'd be able to have pain-free penetrative sex. Then she'd send Dan a bunch of tulips with a dinner invitation.

Six

Lisa phoned Dan that evening and he answered straight away. "Perfect timing, I'm just back."

They started chatting and she told him about Norm asking for help, and that she was trying to make an appointment to see the building inspector on his behalf.

"Good luck with that. In my experience, building inspectors are a strange breed." He went on to tell Lisa about his job in Whitby, and the problems he was having with a client who couldn't make up her mind. "She keeps changing the damned goalposts. That's one of the things I love about you, you're so upfront, not a bundle of issues like some of the people I have to deal with."

They both laughed and Lisa felt uneasy.

"By the way, did you get the tulips?"

"Oh gosh, yes. They're beautiful."

"I've been thinking about you, about us."

She rushed out the lines she'd been practicing all afternoon. "So have I, and although I've loved our time together, it has brought up some old wounds. I know this is a cliché, but I think I need space to sort my head out."

Silence.

"Maybe we could take a step back for a while, try just being friends?"

"But I don't want to be friends." He paused. "I've got enough friends." She could hear him breathing. "Anyway, I know what a woman means when she says *that,* she means she's not interested."

Lisa tensed. "That's not what I mean at all. I've loved our time together, I'm just not—ready, not yet."

"So, what do I do, I hang around until you decide you are?"

Lisa didn't know how to respond.

"Sorry. I'm just disappointed. I thought things were going so well, *we* were going so well."

"Oh Dan, it really is nothing to do with you. It's just ..."

"Can't we talk about this?"

Then I'd have to tell him I'm atrophied—and I can't do that. And maybe, when I start using the pessaries, we won't need to have that conversation at all.

"Listen, if you really want to be friends, that's fine. I mean, it's not where I hoped we were going, but if you want us to get together, I'm leaving it to you to make the first move."

Lisa glanced at the fridge door, covered in flyers for potential retirement projects: Garden Club, Colville Singers, Highland Hikers, Taste & Experience at the liquor store, and there it was—a page she'd torn out of the local paper a few days ago:

Berry Jam Blues Band.
Old school and proud of it.
Patty's Pub, downtown Colville
Friday, April 19, 8 p.m.

"There's a blues band playing at Patty's in a couple of weeks. We could go to that together?"

"Okay, it's a date. Well, not a date. You know what I mean."

"I know." Lisa's toes wriggled with relief.

"Call me the day before and we can make a plan."

"I will. And Dan—thank you."

"I still love that British accent."

* * *

Leonard and Lisa were platonic for three years before they got together. They met at the Welcome Beer festival in their first year at university and for her, it was love—and lust—at first sight. He was the most beautiful being she had ever seen: tall, slim, high cheekbones and an aquiline nose, long fingers and mesmerizingly

41

pink nails. He was witty, well-spoken, and super clever, but the thing Lisa loved most about him was his Blackness. Leonard was from Ghana. Lisa knew that he would always be more attractive, intelligent, and articulate than she was, yet deep down, they were the same. They were both outsiders. But despite her dreams, she slipped into the role of his best friend. She listened to Leonard's tales of shagging around campus, commiserated when his "girlfriend back home" found out and dumped him, acted as his "plus one'" at an extravagant wedding in London and his aunt's weird party. Lisa told Leonard about growing up with Dad and Nicky in Cowley—on the outskirts of Oxford, being practically the only non-Catholic in a school run by unforgiving nuns, and about the few fruitless dates she went on with boys she met in the student bar.

When she wasn't in seminars or the dorm, Lisa was with Leonard. He tutored her through economics and she showed him how to set up psychology experiments. When they studied together in the library, he would smuggle in her favourite snacks, transferring salted nuts and chocolate into empty yoghurt pots so the crinkly wrappers wouldn't alert the librarian. They did get thrown out of the silent study area for laughing when Leonard confessed that his imaginary childhood friend was a corgi.

Three years of wonderful friendship and silent longing—there was something safe about loving Leonard from afar. All that changed in the summer of 1978 when he invited Lisa to go on holiday. "Don't worry about the money, Princess, Father's paying for everything—a perk of having a rich parent with a guilty conscience. Remember I told you I was meant to be flying back home to Ghana to see him? Typically, he's found something more important to do, but he has offered to foot the bill for me to go anywhere with anyone I choose." He tapped the tip of her nose. "And I choose you. Want to come to a Greek island with me?"

Something in Leonard's eyes signalled that he wanted more than friendship and to Lisa's horror, she felt her cheeks grow hot. "Do you mean—"

He slipped a tantalising arm around her. "Seems a shame to waste such a romantic location."

That night, they went back to Lisa's dorm room and spent the next seventy-two hours in her single bed, only surfacing for sandwiches, chips, beer, and the occasional shower. It was a revelation, the first time she understood what sex was about. Before that she'd only had one short romance with Tim Baker, and their sex life was dictated by being in the back of an Austin Mini.

Two weeks later Lisa met Leonard at the airport. As she held his hand, the engines rumbled and Gatwick Airport and the surrounding fields grew smaller and smaller until everything familiar disappeared. She had never been on a plane before, never used the passport she'd applied for "just in case." Leonard slept for most of the flight and once she had finished marvelling at being above the clouds, Lisa gazed at his beautiful profile. She loved everything about him, even the bump at the top of his nose. His irises were raven. He was perfect and they were going to be together for three whole weeks.

She thought of the last time she'd been on a real holiday when she was five, the year before Mum died. They had stayed in a caravan park in Wales, right on the beach, and she'd built castles with Dad, helped Mum make sandwiches, and Nicky had taught her to swim. That was before, when Nicky was nice.

Leonard woke as the plane was landing. Lisa fell in love with their little Greek hotel overlooking the sea, with Eleni who served them milky coffee and honey-drenched pastries, with the Aegean, phosphorescence, a moon so bright that cars parked by the beach made shadows on the sand. But the best bit was that, after all those days in lectures and evenings in bars, being part of a crowd and crashing parties together, they were alone.

Leonard hired a beach umbrella and loungers, and they spent their days reading, swimming, and playing backgammon with a wooden set they bought in a shop run by the oldest man they'd ever seen. Laughing all the way, they went back for extra dice just to check he was still alive. After lunch in a *taverna* with tables in the sand, next to fishing nets left out to dry, they'd go to their room and make love, or sleep, or both, on their mattress on the floor. They'd moved it, worried the ancient clattering iron bedsprings would wake the whole hotel. Evenings were spent wandering winding streets, choosing a restaurant, and finding a quiet place to drink *ouzo* and watch the waves, sometimes going for a star-lit swim before bed. They avoided the crowds, preferring to talk to each other, or have stilted conversations in English-laden Greek and hand gestures. Whatever they did, it felt like the whole world existed only for them. Lisa had never been so happy.

A couple of weeks into the holiday, walking back to their room after dinner, they heard what sounded like live *bouzouki* music from behind the hotel. "Time to sample the local nightlife." Leonard's shoulders started shimmying as he walked around the corner. Lisa smiled through her disappointment. She knew everyone would be dancing. They would be free and uninhibited, and she wasn't. She never had been. She didn't know how.

The bar was packed and they ended up sharing a table with an English couple. "We're in a little hotel just up the beach," Ian-from-Liverpool shouted into Lisa's ear. His girlfriend, Naomi, had an abundant body squeezed into a tight T-shirt dress. She moved with confidence, undisturbed by the sweat patches spreading out from under her arms that compelled Lisa to check her own. Naomi laughed a lot, seemed to have a great sense of humour, but they hardly had a chance to chat before she was up on the dance floor, followed by Ian and then Leonard. He looked back, giving Lisa an encouraging nod, but they both knew she wasn't going to follow.

Watching the three of them, she thought they looked like old friends, laughing and doing funny walks to the weird Greek music. *Here I am again. How many hours have I spent while people dance, reassuring them that "I'm okay, I just don't feel like it"?* And it was true, she never "felt the music." She was always too self-conscious to move. Trying not to look awkward, Lisa squeezed over to Leonard on the dance floor and told him she was going back to the hotel. "Are you sure you don't want me to walk you?" he bellowed, hips jutting, arms in the air.

Lisa put on a happy voice. "No stay, I'm fine, I'll see you later." His head turned just as she moved forward for a kiss and she ended up pecking him on the cheek, making her feel like his aunt or middle-aged wife.

The next morning, hot sunlight oozed through the crack in the blind and Leonard wasn't in bed. Lisa checked the bathroom, then went to the balcony and looked up and down the beach. Should she call the police? The holiday rep? Maybe he ended up going back with Naomi and Ian, crashed at their hotel? She went down to breakfast, too tense to eat but grateful for the distraction of chatting couples and giggling kids. She stared at the dining room door until her coffee was cold, picked up her bag, and was struggling to find her flip flop under the table when she heard his voice.

"Sorry, Princess. Drank so much that I passed out at the other end of the beach."

His tightly cropped curls were full of sand, his clothes looked like a bus had driven over them, the skin under his eyes was tinged blue, and from the way he was holding his head, he had a stiff neck. Lisa was just happy to have him back. She leapt up and threw her arms around him.

Leonard laughed, squeezed her tight, and took her hand. "Come on. I'll get my trunks. I need to sleep it off under an umbrella."

Every evening after that, to Lisa's disappointment, they met up with Ian and Naomi. Lisa had adored having Leonard to herself, but she had known it couldn't last. She wouldn't be enough. On their last night, they all went back to the *bouzouki* bar. After half an hour of dancing, glistening with sweat, Naomi plopped down in the chair beside Lisa. "I just can't get enough of this music. Going to buy a tape to take home."

Leonard was on the far side of the patio showing the waiter some of his smooth moves. Lisa was already looking forward to tomorrow's flight. She turned to Naomi. "I wish I'd got that John Irving novel from you. I've run out of things to read."

"I can fetch it now if you like. Our hotel's only a minute away."

"How about I go? Then I can have a last walk along the beach. Is the book easy to find?"

"I think it's on the chair by the window, or in a pile on the floor. The door's never locked. Help yourself. Room three."

"Brill, thanks. Will you tell Leonard where I've gone?"

"Course." Naomi was already getting up to join him.

Lisa took off her sandals so she could feel the warm sand under feet. There was no one around as she crossed the tiny hotel lobby and went into Naomi and Ian's room—a mess of clothes, towels, straw hats, piles of English newspapers, and scattered pens. Naomi carried her journal the way other people carry cigarettes. There it was, sticking out of her basket on the table by the door.

Tempting, though there can't be anything very juicy in it if she leaves it in full view. Lisa searched around for the novel and, on her way out, reached for the blue diary. It fell open as she put it down on the table:

I did read the signals right. He was all over me as soon as Ian went back to the hotel. Such a great kisser. He called me Princess and said he couldn't get enough of my curves, that I was his Aphrodite. Then we walked to the end of the beach, snogging all the way, and we did it right there in the sand. To be honest, the sex wasn't great (size does matter), but he is seriously gorgeous and exciting to be with. And it was extra horny coz Ian and the skinny girlfriend don't know. They leave in a few days. Hope we get to do it again before they go. Such a buzz. Ian's going to buy that big ceramic bowl he keeps talking about tomorrow. Don't know how he thinks we're going to get it home on the plane.

In a state of shock, Lisa went straight to the hotel and pretended to be asleep when Leonard came to bed. Her feelings were so huge, she didn't know what to do with them. What Naomi had written in her journal was definitely true. It hurt like a knife between the ribs to think of Leonard calling her Princess, but the thing that confirmed it was—"size does matter." Lisa may have only had sex with one other boy, but she knew that Leonard was small.

Her head churned. If she kept silent, what would that say about her? But she didn't want to lose him. She had waited three years for this, and until Naomi, the holiday had been like a honeymoon. They hadn't really talked about what would happen when they got back to England, but Lisa couldn't risk losing Leonard. University was over. She had nothing to look forward to except going home to her sister's resentment and Dad's depression. Lisa wanted a life of her own, with Leonard. She needed him to want her the way she loved him. She had to be enough for him, to make him so happy that he wouldn't wander. She was going to try harder.

Their flight left Athens at 5 a.m. and they were both quiet as dawn broke through the thick glass of the plane window. Lisa thought back over the past three weeks, the fun they'd had, how easy they were together, how she loved waking up next to Leonard every morning and prayed it wouldn't all end when they got back.

He took her hand. "I've only been to my aunt's flat in Ealing once, when she asked me to take round a lease for the then-tenants. From what I remember, it was quite underwhelming, and she says it's gone downhill since. I suppose that's why she's letting me have it at such a low rent." He paused, stroked Lisa's thumb with his forefinger. "I did notice that the bed looked large, a queen size, maybe even a king. I was wondering if you might like to share it with me?"

Lisa could hardly believe what she'd heard. *Thank God I didn't say anything about last night.* Harnessing the rising joy, she kept her tone level, light. "I'd love to sleep with you in something that wasn't made in Ancient Greece, but I'm not quite sure what you're asking."

He turned awkwardly, hampered by the lack of legroom, and tipped his head toward hers. "I'm suggesting you move in with me and look for a job in London."

A champagne cork popped somewhere inside and Lisa was all fizz. The dream was coming true. She unbuckled her seatbelt and kissed him, but had to be sure, she needed to hear him say the words. "So exactly what are you suggesting? Secret lovers? Friends who fuck?"

"Princess ..."

Lisa flinched, remembering reading the word in Naomi's handwriting.

"I'm talking about the real deal—Romeo and Juliet, Bogey and Bacall, Richard and Liz."

She surreptitiously wiped her eyes. "On one condition. That you stop calling me Princess."

Leonard looked surprised but then, with genuine excitement, he put out his hand. "Deal."

Taking it, Lisa could see he really wanted this too.

* * *

Moving up to London was all Lisa talked about when she got home, but Dad seemed disinterested and Nicky didn't want to hear about "the posh bloke you hooked to get out of Cowley." For the first time in her life, Lisa wasn't upset. Dad and Nicky could stick together and live in their house that never changes. She had a whole new future with the man she loved and she wasn't going to let her snidey sister bring her down.

A week later Leonard met Lisa at Paddington Station and helped heave her case to 89 Green Road, top flat, where she worked hard to become a woman that he wouldn't want to leave. He achieved his ambition of a junior job in advertising, she did a typing course and joined a temp agency. She got highlights and layers *à la* Farah Fawcett-Majors, a part-time job at *La Mode* that gave her a hefty staff discount, and she even signed up for contemporary dance. She felt like a penguin trying to fly in the classes, but if she wasn't going to leave Leonard on the dance floor, she had to persevere. And she got very good at sex. She bought *The Joy of Sex*, *Sensual Massage*, *The Kama Sutra*, and a couple of copies of *Penthouse*. Leonard responded best to the tricks she picked up from the men's magazines. She memorised the way the women arched their backs and stuck their bums toward the camera. She hadn't realized how much men liked bums. She copied the way the models squeezed their arms together to make their boobs look bigger when they were on top. She read erotic fiction, too. That was very educational.

Eighteen months after they moved in together, Leonard was promoted to assistant in the creative department of the ad agency and went to Paris for a photo shoot. He was only away for four days, but he sent roses. Lisa's eyes kept flitting back to the card:

See you on Friday. x

When Friday came, she wanted everything to be perfect. She took the afternoon off work—she was temping in a language school—and made *boeuf bourguignon* for him, a veggie version for her. *Salade Niçoise* as a starter, hers without the tuna. She even splashed out on a bottle of Burgundy for a French theme. The flat looked fantastic. Painting had been their Sunday project when Leonard didn't have to work, and she'd managed to put up the bamboo wallpaper they'd chosen. Doing it alone was a struggle, but she wanted to surprise him.

She opened the wine, ran a bath and turned up the heating. They usually kept the thermostat low to save money, but tonight was special. Strains of Miles Davis—Leonard's current favourite—mixed with steam, and as Lisa lay in the bath watching water glide off her nipples, the front door slammed and she heard him taking the stairs two at a time. He wasn't meant to be home for another two hours. His case thudded onto the hall floor and there he was, making the bathroom tiny. First, his shirt, then his Levis, hit the floor. "We got an earlier flight. The client was so keen to get back that he bumped us all."

Leonard climbed into the tub and sat facing Lisa. As water gushed onto the floor, he took her face in his hands and gave her a long lustful kiss. She still melted when he did that. Leaving him to soak, she went into the kitchen to get dinner ready. They ate in the towelling robes he'd "liberated" from the hotel. Then he moved his chair close, and turning her head with his hand, he kissed the tip of her nose and pulled a small pink bag out of his dressing gown pocket. "I got you a present, *une camisole Parisienne.*"

He undid the belt of her robe, eased it off her shoulders, and lifted her arms. Soft fabric draped down her back as he slipped the sleek silk over her head, before gently smoothing it over her breasts. As she leant back against the table, he lifted the cami and stroked her nipples. She felt so wanted, so loved. His hands were around her waist, moving her onto his lap. Lisa kissed his neck and teased her nails across his chest. She traced the muscles in his arms and slid onto him, leaning back so he could see himself in her, touching herself the way he liked. Leonard responded with his hips, moving them slowly until, almost ready, he pulled her close, his movements becoming less controlled. Lisa loved him like this, no longer cool and collected, but consumed by her.

Ignoring the dishes, they went straight to bed. Leonard lay on his side and Lisa moulded herself around him, pressed into his back. His neck smelt like almonds with a hint of Armagnac. She was home.

Seven

The Copper Bean was Colville's upmarket café, where the coffee was freshly ground and the pastries didn't have a hole in the middle. Susan handed Lisa an espresso and put a plate of mini croissants on the table between them. Black and white photos of the town as it used to be hung above tables covered with gingham checked cloths and little vases of dried flowers—in a few weeks they'd be fresh.

Nodding to someone behind Lisa, Susan forced a smile. "Diana Mosh. She's the one that bought the hardware store and turned it into a TV warehouse. I'm sure it's a front, money laundering. How many sixty-five-inch screens can a town this size support? Anyway, she's after Deb McPhee's husband. Can you believe she gave him a flyer for the new salsa nights at Patty's and asked him to be her partner?"

"Maybe she just doesn't know he's married?" Lisa picked up a tiny almond croissant.

"Like there's a hell's chance of that. Anyway, he wears a wedding ring."

"Are you going?"

"Well obviously. I'm not missing Diana on the dance floor, with or without Mr. McPhee. What about you? We could be partners. The only thing Grant's interested in moving these days is his Molson muscle, especially now that March Madness is on. You know what he's like about basketball."

Lisa was with Grant on this one. Salsa lessons in the local bar was her idea of a nightmare. "Not sure it's my thing. Can I let you know nearer the time?"

"Diplomacy in action. Now tell me all about your date with Dan."

Lisa hadn't mentioned the ball to Susan.

"A little bee buzzed that you went out together Saturday night. And?"

Recognizing her friend's insatiable need to know, Lisa shrugged. "We had a good time, but we're not dating—Christ, there needs to be a better vocabulary for this when you're over sixty."

"So if you're not dating, what *are* you doing?"

"Honestly Susan, I don't even know if I want a boyfriend—manfriend."

"My report ended when you left the church hall—together."

Lisa still couldn't tell Susan, and for the time being, there wasn't anything specific to tell. "We're being friends."

"Really? That's a relief because he's not the kind of guy you want to get involved with."

Lisa raised her eyebrows.

"This is what I was trying to tell you the other day. My niece works in a hotel in Toronto. Nothing fancy, but quite central. I stayed there when Grant had his sinuses drained at Mount Sinai. Anyway, she was with us for the weekend when we ran into Dan outside the Trading Post, here in town."

"And?"

"She recognized him, told me he stayed at her hotel regularly, once a month."

"That's what you wanted me to know? Why I'm meant to watch out?"

"No, it's the *women*. He stays there with *women*, different *women*, and it's still going on. She said so at Christmas. Sometimes it's the same one for a few months, but then he'll turn up with a new one."

None of this sounded like the Dan Lisa knew, who seemed so straightforward and honest. "Do you think they're prostitutes?"

"That's what I asked, but my niece says they don't look like *that* kind of woman, or act like them, and she should know. The reception staff is on strict orders to tell management if they suspect any of that going on. All I can tell you is Dan's been showing up with women for as long as she's worked there and that's nearly three years now."

"So, he has a string of girlfriends—women friends—that he sees in a hotel in Toronto, once every month."

"A string of somethings. They usually turn up quite late, like they've been out somewhere first, and sometimes they spend all the next day in his room. They must be having sex. What else would they be doing?"

Lisa felt drained. "I don't get it. He told me there hadn't been anyone since his wife died."

"Well, I haven't heard about him dating anyone from around here."

"And that's all you know?"

"It's enough, isn't it? Is that the kind of person you want to get involved with?"

Baffled, Lisa looked into her friend's eyes and thought of Leonard. There was no way she was going to fall for another man who was unfaithful. "I'm not sure what I want. I do know that being with Dan makes me feel hopeful in a way that I haven't for a long time—or it did, until hearing what you've just said."

As Susan looked into Lisa's eyes, her tone changed. "This guy's really gotten to you, hasn't he?"

* * *

Dan texted that evening: Hey, got a gate. Could I bring it round early tomorrow, on my way to Whitby? Lisa walked over to the sink, picked up the sponge, and threw it back into the pot she was cleaning. Dirty water splashed up onto her T-shirt. "I broke my own promise," she muttered to herself, swiping at the wet blotches with a tea towel. "There's no such thing as a relationship without heartache and this one's heading that way already. A different woman every month. He told me there hadn't been anyone since his wife died. I'll invent a reason not to go to the blues band with him and that'll be the end of it."

She looked out of the window at the newly mended fence; she did want the gate. "Okay, once the job's finished, I'll be done with him."

Lisa picked up her phone and typed: **Sounds good, see you in the morning.**

Squeezing out the sponge, she decided not to wash her hair or put on the lipstick she'd bought for the bee ball. She was old and atrophied and she didn't care what Dan thought of her. He could fix the gate and go.

* * *

"Coffee smells good."

Lisa hadn't heard the Down to Earth van come up the driveway. She was surprised Fido hadn't barked. "Is the gate in your van? I'll come out and see it. That way, if it's not what I'm looking for, you won't be held up."

"Too late, I've got it leaning against the fence. I think you'll be happy. My buddy made it for a customer and they never came back."

The sun was bright but the morning air was still cool. Dan threw Fido a stick as they walked to the other side of the house. Of course, the gate was perfect.

"Solid oak. Unbelievable, isn't it?" Dan threw the stick again. "I stopped by to pay for some tubs he's working on and there it was—waiting just for you."

"Good. Thanks. I don't have much cash, but I can e-transfer you the money."

"It gets better. The gate was already paid for, so he gave it to me. Said I could buy him a beer next time we're both in town."

None of this was altering Lisa's mood. She left Dan to install the gate and went back into the kitchen. To drown the sound of his drilling, she turned up the volume on a news report about an Eastern European comedian who was running for president, but found herself listening more to the intermittent whirr than his election strategy. She knew Dan would come back into the house when he was done. Wanting to look busy, Lisa pulled out the "everything drawer" by the sink and tipped its contents onto the table.

"Love it." He was still smiling that annoying smile. "Creating order out of chaos. You can come round to my place and do that any time you want." He took a step toward the table. "That coffee still smells great."

Lisa looked up, an out-of-date Indian takeout menu in her hand. "If you've got a travel cup, I could make you one to go."

Dan came nearer. "Have we downsized to something less than platonic?"

Answering questions wasn't part of the plan.

"Maybe I've done something to upset you?"

She didn't want to talk, she wanted him to leave, but as she imagined him going, she wanted him to stay. "You lied to me," she spluttered. "You said you hadn't seen anyone since your wife left."

"Pardon?"

"I suppose if the women are in Toronto, it doesn't count?"

His eyes widened.

"My friend Susan's niece works in the hotel."

"So much for client confidentiality."

"I don't know why I'm talking to you about this, it's really none of my business."

"You're right, it isn't, but I get why you're upset. I don't know what Susan's niece has said, but it's probably not as bad as you think."

"She said you'd been staying there, with a different woman in your room every month."

"Christ, I hate small-town gossip." He glared out of the window, then back at Lisa and lowered his tone. "But I'll explain if you want to listen."

Curiosity overtaking upset, Lisa pointed to the espresso pot on the stove. Dan nodded, pulled out a chair, and sat down in front of everything that had been in the drawer: a pile of batteries, elastic bands, pizza coupons, dog treats, fridge magnets, screwdrivers, the part from an electric whisk, and a small stuffed penguin. "When Anna was at home, I had my hands full, and in a funny kind of way, it felt like I'd be cheating on her to bring another woman into our lives. But then Anna went away to school and I got lonely. I thought it was time to try and meet someone. Mattie—Warren's wife, you met her at the ball—set me up with a friend from work and there was so much tension and expectation, it was terrible. I tried going to a singles night at a bar in Redstock and that was worse, so I gave up. Then I got this gig in Toronto that meant staying there for a week every month, and that's when I had the idea of online dating."

Lisa pushed aside the batteries and put a mug next to Dan's elbow.

"When I went online, I discovered a world of women who aren't looking for happily-ever-after, they just want to have a good time. I liked that idea, realized it was more what I was looking for too. I'd been so involved with work and Anna and building the business, I'd hardly even missed sex and suddenly there it was, no strings attached. It's not as sleazy as you'd think. I was always careful about protection and it was fun. Consensual, contained, and no one got hurt because they weren't under any illusions."

"Was?"

"I haven't had a hook-up since before Christmas. That's when I started to feel different. It was making me tired, emotionally and physically. I knew I was done the day I blew off my date and went to see a movie instead."

Lisa couldn't help but smile.

"When I told you there hadn't really been anyone since Anna's mum, I didn't think I was lying. Nothing I did in Toronto felt like it was heading for a relationship, not the way it did with you."

Lisa talked to her cup. "It's a lot to take in, but I'll admit I jumped to conclusions."

Dan let out a sigh. "I'm glad you know, if we're still going to be friends?"

She still wanted to be more than friends, but thinking of Dan having all that sex with all those women made Lisa even more embarrassed about her own condition. "I'm sorry I sounded so accusing."

She loved their long hug on the doorstep, and as Dan's van drove away, she drew a deep breath. Whatever happened with him, she wanted to feel like a fully-functioning woman.

* * *

Lisa waited until she'd had a bath to try the pessaries. Perched on the edge of the tub, she opened the cardboard packet and unfolded a sheet of paper covered in a lot of text in a very small font, most of which was dedicated to possible side effects: nausea, bloating, diarrhea, breast swelling or tenderness, swelling of the ankles or feet, headache including migraines, weight changes, dizziness, cold symptoms, acne, skin colour changes, increased facial hair, thinning scalp hair, depression, mental/mood changes, vaginal bleeding, vaginal irritation/itching/odor/discharge, severe stomach or abdominal pain, persistent nausea or vomiting, increased urination. There was a paragraph on each one. *This was what the doctor calls low risk?*

Balancing the packet on the edge of the sink, Lisa tightened the towel around her. She hadn't used much medication. Other than colds and flu, she had never really been sick. *I suppose they have to write this stuff for insurance. At least it doesn't mention cancer, and if I get any of these symptoms, I can just stop using the stuff.*

She pulled a strip of vacuum-packed pink plastic sticks out of the box, tore one off and opened it. After a few uncomfortable attempts, she finally got the pesky little thing where it was supposed to be. *Phew. I need a glass of wine.*

Opening the fridge, she saw the Berry Jam Blues Band flyer taped to the door. "Only two weeks. I'll be lucky if the pessaries have worked by then." She looked at Fido, whose eyes were glinting in the cold blue light. They flitted from Lisa to the fridge and back to Lisa. "Okay, let's see if there's a piece of cheese in here with your name on it." Closing the door, she noticed another flyer: Highland Hikers, New Spring Meet-Up, April 8. "That's on Monday," she said, but Fido was totally focused on the chunk of cheddar in her hand.

Lisa was looking forward to going on the hike. Glancing at the other bits of paper taped up, she realized it was the only part of her retirement plan she was enthusiastic about as it ticked most of her boxes: exercise, spending time outdoors, meeting new people. And she was looking forward to time away from thinking about Dan, or Leonard, or what may or may not be happening between her legs.

Eight

The car park was at the foot of a tree-covered slope with flat fields of untamed brush on either side. It was a glorious end-of-March day: the sun already high, birds chattering, and a gentle breeze blowing in the freshness of spring. Lisa sat in her truck watching the hikers arrive and gather around a couple of picnic tables near a porta-potty. She wondered if she'd know anyone. She had purposely chosen a hiking club outside Colville because she was trying to find new friends, not the workmates, parents, students, business folk, and book club members she had been mixing with for the past twenty years. But now she was apprehensive. She wanted to escape her role as principal, but missed the comfort that came with it. Happily, Fido was with her. The club organizer had said it was okay to bring him as long as he stayed on a leash.

By the time Lisa joined them, the hikers were already heading along the path toward the hill. She walked fast to catch up, smiling at a small group who smiled back but were caught up in their own conversation.

"I don't want to live to be two hundred," said the one with the walking poles.

"But you've got to admit, the phrase 'biologically younger' has some appeal," said the woman on her right, laughing.

"I couldn't get past the beard, he looked like a caveman," said the third, and Lisa worked out they were discussing a TED talk on aging. These seemed to be the kind of women she'd like to spend time with.

She looked up at the expanse of sky and breathed it in. Water oozed out from under her boots, the last of the spring run-off, but fresh shoots were already peeping from the dogwood and blackberry stems. It wasn't long before a woman in a plaid shirt came looking for her. "Welcome. We talked on the phone. I'm Sonya, the sucker who organizes all this."

"It looks like you do a great job and thank you for saying I could bring Fido. I'd have felt too guilty spending a whole day walking without him."

"No problem, we've got a couple of pups in the group." Fido sniffed Sonya's pocket. "How did you know I still carry treats?" She pulled out a little bag of bone-shaped biscuits. "My Bailey died two years ago but I still carry them." They walked side by side for a while before Sonya spoke again. "How long has it been?"

Lisa didn't understand.

"Since you retired? Most people start coming because it's part of their plan: join a hiking group to spend time outside, keep fit, and meet new people."

"Not long, and now I feel horribly predictable."

Laughing, one of the women walking in front looked around. "It's worked for me. I've been coming for ten years. Our hikes are quite the highlight of my month and I've made some wonderful friends."

Her companion agreed. "Sometimes we walk together between meetings. I'm Ellee, by the way."

Sonya nodded. "Ellee is our oldest member. We celebrated her seventy-eighth on the Kennisis trail last fall."

Of the few retirement things Lisa had tried so far, this was the most promising. The rock choir had highlighted how unmusical she was, stained glass was too much time cutting, and she hadn't gone to the second meeting of the gardening club. But she also wondered if she was looking at her future. *Do I want to be here hiking with the same group on the same trails on my seventy-eighth birthday?*

Falling into step with the others, they chatted about how dry the weather had been, Ellee's new elliptical exerciser, and the impending provincial budget. Lisa watched the walkers spread out as they went up the hill and noticed a lot of matchy-matchy, hair-done-nicely, stylish looking women. And they were mainly women. There were two men a little way ahead, one tall, the other could only be described as rectangular. His flat cap and too-long jacket didn't help. Way up ahead was the only other person with a dog, a large-framed guy with a Dalmatian. Lisa had put on some already-muddy jeans and her favourite fleece, zipped over a sweater. The rain jacket in her backpack was over twenty years old. She hadn't thought about what she was wearing, but there were a lot of Lycra leggings and form-fitting jackets up ahead. In fact, some of the women looked to be straight off the Lululemon fitness site.

They climbed the hill into evergreen woods dotted with tall maples and ash, ready to explode in the coming days. Lisa loved this time of year, so full of hope. Deeper into the woods the earth smelled peaty, still damp from melted snow, but the sky was brilliant blue and the sun blazed in the clearing ahead. The sound of panting signalled someone coming up behind, a woman in fuchsia pink. She paused for breath. "Hi."

Sonya introduced them. "This is Lisa. She's just joined."

"I didn't know we had any newcomers." The woman looked at Lisa intently before adding, "Pleased to meet you."

She was wearing shimmery powder—not a good look in bright daylight. The shimmer had caked into tiny iridescent lines around her eyes.

"Anyhoo, gotta keep moving," she said. " I need to get ahead."

"And we know why," Sonya muttered and gave a little laugh.

Lisa didn't get the joke but smiled anyway. A few minutes later another woman steamed past, a waft of heavy perfume piercing the air. Lisa cleared her throat while Sonya went on to explain where the group would stop for lunch and they settled into a quiet rhythm, each focusing on getting to the top of the ridge, talking only when they saw something interesting. A couple of hours later they stopped on a rocky crest with a stunning view: farmland and forest all the way to the horizon, newly green fields and spring-tipped trees. Everyone took out their sandwiches and Lisa let Fido off the leash. He was in heaven, touring the group, being petted and given everyone's crusts. When he saw the Dalmatian, he rushed over, tail wagging. Its owner had just appeared from the other side of the crest. Lisa ran after, but the two dogs were already playing.

"I'm sorry," she called out.

"Don't be, they're doing fine." The man's voice was so baritone it was almost a rumble. "Bring your food over, if you want, and we can keep an eye on them."

As Lisa picked up her lunch things, she thought she noticed looks from the women she'd been sitting with.

"I was going to get a chocolate Lab like yours." The Dalmatian's owner said, as Lisa settled on a nearby rock. "But then Nanny came up for adoption, and well—love at first sight."

"Great name. Guess you weren't going to call her Cruella! I'm amazed a dog as classy as that was up for adoption."

"Her owner died." He held out an angular hand. "I'm Rudy."

His skin was warm and surprisingly soft. "Lisa. And that's Fido."

As she finished her sandwich, they chatted about dogs and Lisa found herself comparing Rudy to Dan. Dan had the energy of a person who spent his time outdoors, while Rudy looked like he might have done a desk job. Now he volunteered in an animal rescue shelter. He seemed nice. Everyone Lisa had spoken to seemed nice. She opened a bag of chocolate-covered almonds, put it on the little boulder between them, and she and Rudy sat nibbling as Nanny and Fido launched a joint assault on a chipmunk's den.

Lisa was enjoying herself. Closing her eyes, she relished the sun on her face, pleased with herself for having made the effort to do something new, but as she relaxed back and took a deep breath, the scent was unmistakable. Opening her eyes again, she saw that the perfumed woman who had been climbing uphill with such impressive speed had squeezed herself onto Rudy's rock.

"Now don't be greedy." She looked over to Lisa, almost flirtatiously.

Lisa held up the bag of almonds, which the newcomer ignored.

"Hey, Nanny, come," Rudy called, and went to where the dogs were digging.

Lisa put the nuts back on the rock between them. "We couldn't have asked for nicer weather. Does the group hike in the winter?"

"Don't ask me, I'm a snowbird. Haven't spent a winter in Ontario since I stopped working. A gang of us go down to Florida and spend Christmas there together every year."

Lisa considered what it would be like to celebrate Christmas somewhere warm, and who she could go with if she wanted to try. She had never taken more than two consecutive weeks off work when she was principal of the art school.

"I'm Danuta." The woman leant forward conspiratorially. "And remember, we believe in sharing."

Lisa was bewildered. "I'd better get my dog too."

Rudy had dragged Nanny to another area, so Lisa threw some sticks for Fido until everyone had finished lunch.

Full of food and rested, the pace was slower as they hiked back along the ridge until the car park came into sight. Lisa was the last on the trail heading down to the picnic tables where they'd first gathered, and the other hikers looked like ants as they trickled down to their cars. That's when she got it. There was a definite pattern to their formation: a cluster around Rudy and his Dalmatian, another around the rectangle in the flat cap and his tall companion, and the rest lagging behind chatting. Lisa laughed out loud—it wasn't the chocolate-covered nuts that she was meant to be sharing.

When she got back to the car park, some hikers were still milling around chatting. She wanted to thank Sonya and found her talking to two women, both with remarkably black hair. Not wanting to interrupt, Lisa listened as they described their newly built house. They sounded like sisters, both widows, who had decided to live together. Between them, they had five children and seven grandchildren. Lisa wondered what it would feel like to be surrounded by the certainty of a loving family, to have a sister you wanted to spend the rest of your life with.

"The garden's a disaster," said the older looking one. "We want to give it a complete overhaul. Anyone got a good landscape gardener?"

"I know someone who'd be perfect," Lisa chimed in, thinking of Dan. "He's ..." Two blue-eyed, pretty faces turned to her. "Actually, I know he's busy, and probably based too far away."

"Shame," said the younger one. "Should I take his name, just in case?"

Lisa shook her head. "I don't think so."

Driving home, Fido stretched on his rug on the seat behind her, Lisa pulled over. She wriggled and rubbed, but the burning was growing stronger. In the end, she poured water from her drinking bottle onto some Kleenexes and slipped them into her underpants. Relief, instant and welcome. *It must be the pessaries.*

* * *

Sitting on the sofa, nursing a cup of tea, Lisa phoned Dr. Lau.

"It does sound like the pessaries are causing the irritation. I presume you've stopped them?"

"I've only been using them for four days."

"Leave it a couple more and if things haven't changed, make an appointment and come in. It might just be one ingredient that you're reacting to. When the area has calmed down, would you like to try a different brand?"

Looking out of the window at her new gate, Lisa filled with determination to get through this.

Dr. Lau continued. "I'd recommend waiting at least a week after the irritation has gone before trying anything new." Tones of the Health Centre's computer coming to life tumbled down the phone. "I'm just scrolling the ingredients of—here's one that uses a different base cream."

"Well, I suppose if I'm just reacting to the cream. Do you think it'll make a difference?"

"I'm afraid there's only one way to find out. If it's the active ingredient, estradiol, that you're reacting to, we're in trouble. That's a constant, whether we're looking at pessaries, rings, or creams."

Lisa had felt good when she was using the pessaries. Having managed to move away from her initial concerns, she liked the sense of doing something positive, going in a new direction. She didn't want to give up yet. "Yes please, I would like to try another brand."

"Good. I'm sending the prescription now. It'll be at your pharmacy when you're ready and remember, if those symptoms haven't cleared up in a couple of days, come and see me."

Lisa curled her feet under, picked up her phone, and searched "atrophied," the awful word that had hardly been in her vocabulary until so recently:

Arrested development, to become weaker, to waste away, progressive decline, any degeneration or diminution, especially through lack of use, to have lost effectiveness or vigor due to underuse or neglect.

Was this a description of the last twenty years of her life? It hadn't felt like it at the time. She had been busy and useful, helped people, helped the town to grow in wealth as well as in population. But if she thought of herself as a woman, there had definitely been some neglect. She picked up her phone again and searched Lululemon.

Nine

Lisa arrived at the Township offices and sat on an uncomfortable chair in the hallway, staring at the sign on a closed door: Chief Building Official & Bylaw Enforcement Officer. She was holding Norm's note appointing her his agent.

When the door finally opened, Garnet Holtz looked like his job description—officious, grey, and bureaucratic. "Sorry to keep you waiting."

Lisa extended her hand. "Lisa West."

Holtz's grip was firm. "No introduction necessary."

"I'm sorry, have we met?"

"Not in person, but I've seen you in the paper and I was at the dinner when you got the Township Merit Award. You've done great things for Colville."

Smiling, Lisa sat down and noticed a big fish mounted on the wall behind Holtz's desk. She felt the gaze of its glass eye as she handed over the letter from Norm, and the order to demolish. "I've come to try and sort this out on behalf of Norman O'Brien. He's my friend, an elderly widower living alone. He is, understandably, terribly upset at the prospect of losing the original homestead where his family has lived since 1860."

Holtz burst out laughing. "Are we talking about the same Norm O'Brien? The one who, over the past three years, has been in here and called every person in this building all the names under the sun? The same Norm O'Brien who was found guilty and fined for Provincial Offences for bylaw infractions and building code infractions and still not complied with what was required?"

Lisa sat down. "Go on."

"That's why the Township went to the Superior Court and applied for an order to demolish."

Trying to contain her annoyance with Norm, she struggled with what to say.

"The Superior Court has issued an order based on Norm's non-compliance."

"Oh dear, I am sorry, I had no idea. It doesn't sound like Norm has done himself any favours, but even though he's been unpleasant, maybe we can find a way to sort this out? Pulling down the homestead, destroying his family's history, does seem extreme. Maybe if I understood more, I could be helpful—to you as well as Norm."

Holtz handed her back the order to demolish. "Unfortunately, it is out of the Township's hands. The judicial system has made a determination and the building has to come down. But it's not the old farmhouse that we're talking about, it's the single-story family dwelling."

"His bungalow? But that's where he lives. If you tear it down, he'll be homeless."

"The situation is this: that bungalow was built illegally; a permit was never applied for or issued. Norm could have easily rectified the situation. We first approached him—" Holtz turned to his cabinet and extracted a bulging file, "three years ago, when his misdemeanors first came to light at a municipal level. When it became clear he wasn't going to take any action, we charged him with building without a permit and violation of the building bylaws. That bungalow doesn't have a permit, which makes it in violation of the Building Regulation Act. He cannot have two dwellings on one property, it's a violation of Bylaw-66/1966. The bungalow has to go."

Holtz leaned back in his chair. "We stated his options clearly. We told him he could tear down the newer building, demolish the original building and then apply for the permits for the newer building, he could relocate the new building, or he could get an amendment to the zoning bylaws to allow two dwellings on one property and then get all the permits for the new building. But I have to say, even if he tried that now—and it *is* too late—it's unlikely that the Council would be sympathetic. Norm has alienated the entire municipality by walking out of every meeting with one finger in the air."

Lisa pulled a lined pad out of her purse.

"There's no point taking notes. I'm afraid the judicial system has made a determination and the building has to come down."

"So there really is nothing that can be done? Maybe I could look at some of the paperwork?"

"Norm has copies of everything in this file. If he's thrown them away, come back and you can go through mine, but I'm afraid this is the end of the line, not the beginning. Frankly, O'Brien has only himself to blame. We really did try to get him to work with us, to let us help. If he'd been cooperative, none of this would have happened. We could have helped him apply for the permits retrospectively and pay for them. He's got himself into this mess."

* * *

Lisa didn't often feel angry, but now she was broiling. She loved Norm like family and he'd used her. It may have been by omission, but he'd lied and made her a fool. What did he think Holtz would do? Take one look at Lisa, a fellow pillar of society, and reverse the court orders? She wanted to drive straight from the Township offices to Norm's, but that would have to wait. She had arranged to have lunch with Susan and was already running late.

As she opened her friend's front door, she found Susan carrying a stack of laundry and apologizing, as usual, for the way she looked. "You go on into the kitchen while I put these in the machine. I've got a surprise."

Sliding off her boots, Lisa gazed around the hall. She loved the combination of sturdy log walls, white paint, and exposed beams. Grant's family had owned the house for generations. The building was perched on solid rock, the Canadian Shield, overlooking a deep trout-filled lake where they'd soon be swimming.

Three globe artichokes sat on a cutting board on the kitchen table. The last time Lisa had seen one was in London. "This really is a surprise." She picked up the biggest as Susan came back in. "Where on earth did you find them?"

"They were in that fancy new deli in Redstock. I remembered you talking about liking them. We used to have them with my Granny in Quebec when I was a kid, with melted butter and lemon juice."

"And look at these lovely flowers." Lisa went over to the vase of tulips and freesias, sniffing for scent.

"Megan sent them."

"She's probably missing her mum as much as you miss her. Aren't you going to visit soon?"

"Not till the end of August. We haven't even booked the tickets yet. Grant says the cheapest flights go via Montreal, but I want to fly direct. What airline would you use?"

"You're asking the wrong person. I haven't been back to England since I left, but I am jealous of the flowers, they're beautiful."

"I'm just going to get changed."

"You look fine."

But Susan was already on her way upstairs. She came back in a red pinafore over a green T-shirt, very elf-like. Lisa stifled a smile. After filling a big pan with water and setting it to boil, Susan took three plates and cutlery into the sunroom and laid the table. Lisa thought Grant must be joining them.

"Anybody home?" A man's voice came from the front hall.

"Shoot, it's the surprise, he's early. I was going to tell you," Susan whispered. Then, raising her voice, "Come on through, we're in here." Back to Lisa, "Now that you're finally in the market for a man, I thought I'd introduce you to someone suitable."

Susan had invited a man to meet her, now, here, for lunch? "I'm not in the market for a man," Lisa hissed.

Susan hissed back, "Well you've been out with Dan twice." Turning to the door, she smiled. "Meet my friend Mitch Edwards. Mitch was the chief engineer in Grant's company."

He was wearing a quilted jacket and cords and looked like the fit favourite grandfather in a vitamin commercial. Lisa was furious. Surely she'd put a stop to Susan's quest to find her a man years ago, after the barbeque with the guy who ran the turtle rescue centre. Lisa tried to keep the irritation off her face.

Mitch extended his hand. He had large knuckles. "Pleased to meet you. Susan's told me so much about you."

Lisa managed a smile but couldn't think of a thing to say. Instead, she nodded, smile still in place, as Mitch asked after Grant.

"He wanted to be here, but there was a break-in at the golf club and he had to run. They think it was just kids, but it's still a big cleanup. How's the new car?" Susan turned back to the stove, leaving Lisa to listen to the glories of Mitch's new Honda crossover SUV: V6 engine, fancy navigation system, top-rated for safety by dozens of magazines ...

She was so annoyed she could hardly keep still. This wasn't a surprise, it was an ambush. Mitch looked as uncomfortable as she was frustrated, especially when they sat down to eat. Susan presented them each with a head of artichoke and a side dish of liquid butter with lemon juice.

"I believe it's a member of the thistle family." Mitch obviously wished he didn't have to eat it.

"I'll just pop the quiche in the oven to warm." Susan went back to the stove.

Mitch picked up his fork, put it down again, and fiddled with his napkin until Lisa took pity on him. "Artichokes are a bit tricky, but worth it in the end. Think of it as a big flower bud and start by pulling off the petals and dipping them in the dressing. Then you sort of scrape the little fleshy bit off the bottom with your teeth."

She demonstrated but Mitch scooped up too much dressing and a stream of warm butter dribbled down his chin onto his shirt. She pretended not to notice.

"Lisa's a vegetarian." Susan took her seat at the table. Mitch didn't look like he found this comforting as he ignored the butter running into his cuff. From his stiff spine and general awkwardness, Lisa guessed it wasn't only the artichokes that were making him uneasy. She wondered what Susan had told him.

When they'd chewed at all the thick green petals, Lisa helped him out again. "Now, this is the tasty bit that we've been working towards, but first you have to pull off all these tufty little spikes—they're the choke, a bit like fish bones."

"Goodness," Mitch muttered.

Susan, determined to fill the increasingly awkward silence, was trying to convince him to buy a season ticket for the soon-to-be-starting film festival. She was head of the organizing committee. Movies didn't seem to be Mitch's thing.

Anxious to divert her from suggesting they go together, Lisa changed the subject. "Susan said you *used to be* chief engineer in Grant's company, what do you do now?"

Mitch looked relieved to stop pulling at the hot sticky stamens. "Too much mostly. I'll be in the library basement tonight, teaching life skills to men looking for work."

Teaching life skills sounded interesting, more Lisa's thing than hugging people for healthcare or going to a gardening club.

"We meet on Tuesday evenings. I mainly help the guys apply for jobs, sometimes look for accommodation, or we just chew the fat. They're a motley bunch but I've grown attached to them."

Mitch noticed Lisa looking at the ring on his little finger and explained he'd got it when he graduated, a symbol of his commitment to engineering. Her questions got them past the artichokes and through the quiche, and by the time Susan got up to clear the plates, Mitch looked like a different man. There was something welcoming about his face: kind eyes and a genuine smile, and Lisa liked his stature. He was well over six feet.

Susan came in carrying dessert. "Lisa's looking for ways to volunteer. Maybe she could come with you to the library sometime?"

Mitch's face refilled with anxiety. "Oh, yes, well, not really. It's just that she's, umm, female and it's a men's group."

Lisa sighed silently—at least she hoped she hadn't done it out loud. "I'm sorry. Lunch was delicious but I need to go."

"Really, are you sure?" Susan gave her a look. "I made chocolate muffins with almond flour, a new recipe, and I've got your favourite ice cream."

"Sounds lovely but I have an appointment and I can't be late."

Susan's voice was on the verge of sarcasm. "Nothing serious, I hope." She didn't offer Lisa a muffin to take home.

Mitch stood up. "Good to meet you."

"Absolutely, a pleasure." Lisa turned to Susan. "I'll be phoning you." She wished, for Mitch's sake, that she hadn't sounded quite so accusing.

* * *

Norm's truck wasn't in his driveway, so Lisa didn't stop to talk to him about her visit with the building inspector—probably a good thing as she was still annoyed with Susan. Instead, she went home and took Fido for a walk, complaining most of the way. Lisa wasn't sure why she was so cross. Her day out with the hiking club had made it clear there weren't many available men around, and if she did want a relationship, shouldn't she be grateful for the introduction? Mitch seemed nice, and who knew what would happen with Dan? From his point of view, she'd rejected his suggestion of romance and he might already be back in his hotel in Toronto.

In a way, Lisa could see Susan's point. Mitch was suitable. The original "nice guy", he exuded good, radiated reliable, and Lisa could tell he was unlikely to hurt her. She thought of Leonard, all the chaos he'd inflicted, but in the end, they had known a love unlike any other. Could anything ever match that?

As she walked up the hill behind the house, Lisa remembered the day Leonard turned up on her doorstep in London, holding a bunch of bleeding hearts. It had been eight years since she'd last seen him. She just stared and he looked back steadily until, smiling almost shyly, "Can I come in?"

Her initial reaction was fury. She had spent too much time vowing never to talk to him again, he had hurt her more than she wanted to remember, and because of him, she had lost her whole family. At the time, it felt like she had lost her life. But she didn't close the door.

Leonard's eyes were pleading. "Just give me five minutes and then, if you want, I'll go."

They sat at opposite ends of the sofa, her arms folded, but as he talked, Lisa could feel her resistance waning. She had never heard him so humble. "I've done a lot of work on myself. I'm different now."

Lisa knew every gesture but noticed tiny new grey curls in his tight crop, little lines on his forehead and around his eyes, and wondered how she looked to him.

"I behaved like an absolute arsehole and I'm sorry. I'm ashamed of what I put you through."

He had never talked about himself like this before. In all their time together, Lisa couldn't remember hearing Leonard apologize.

"Now I see what a self-centred bastard I was. A narcissist, according to my therapist."

"You're in therapy?" This was unbelievable.

"For two years. That's why I'm here."

"Because your therapist told you to come?"

"No, because she's helped me understand so much, regret all the diabolical things I did to hurt you and realize ..."

Is this really happening?

He slid along the sofa toward her. "That it's you. It's always been you."

Lisa had imagined this moment so many times, longed to hear Leonard say these words, but that was years ago, when she still hoped. Now she'd given up and moved on, so what was she meant to do? Rush into his arms? Leonard leaned forward and picked up a strand of her hair. "I miss you. I want to be with you, and honestly this time. No more lies. No more fucking around."

Lisa's heart was pounding. This was too much. She stood up. "It sounds like you've been thinking about all of this for a long time, but I was just going to put my dinner in the oven."

Leonard laughed. "God, I've missed you."

Here, sitting on her sofa, was the original dream: a Leonard who wanted her as much as she wanted him. A Leonard who'd had therapy, who she could trust.

He stood up. "Tell me what you need, what you want me to do."

After eight years of silence, Lisa had been sure he'd forgotten her and moved on, as she had tried to do. Instead, he'd been thinking and talking about her, still feeling love for her—without telling her? This was hurtful too. She took a breath and looked around the room, at the Matisse print and kilim-covered sofa, then back to him, the brightest thing in it, and as she saw herself reflected in his almost-black eyes, her heart creaked open. "I don't know what I want, but I guess you could stay for a drink."

Ten

Dan's van was already parked outside Patty's Pub when Lisa arrived, twenty minutes late, for their night at the blues band together. She had spent an unbelievable amount of time working out what to wear. After putting it on and taking it off twice, she had decided that the beautiful but "casual" new dress she'd bought wasn't casual enough for Patty's. She had also come home with a T-shirt with a lower-than-usual back that showed off her neck and shoulders, made her breasts look good, and accentuated her slimness. She tried it with the not-for-work-skirt she'd bought to celebrate her retirement, but decided it looked like she was trying too hard. In the end, she just wore the new T-shirt with her usual jeans and a loose shirt over the top. *Okay, at least I'll be comfortable.*

Standing just in the pub door, her eyes scanned for Dan. The place was a bit of a dive and the lights had blown on one side of the bar. Last time she was here was to see one of her students play in a band. As she gazed over the already-crowded room, she saw Dan at a table near the stage and stopped to watch. He seemed so easy with himself, taking little swigs from a bottle of beer, smiling at people who passed by. Lisa liked that he wasn't looking at his phone. He saw her and waved. The floor was sticky as she walked towards him. The band wasn't on yet, but music was still blaring. She had to pull her chair near to hear what he was saying.

"I've been doing a job application. Remember I told you how much I wanted a change? Well, I might be going to Manitoba." His eyes were bright, full of excitement. She felt hers drain away. "It's more of a summer placement really, but I still had to find all my high school certificates and send them off."

At least it's only for the summer.

"An out of the blue opportunity." Dan was shouting to be heard over the music. "Field assistant, working with Anna. She's got a grant for someone to help her collect data for her masters."

Lisa leaned in, forcing herself to sound enthusiastic. "You'd be working with your daughter?"

"It's an excuse to hang out together and travel around, camping and collecting sample bugs."

This wasn't the plan, especially when Lisa was hoping to move them out of the platonic zone.

"My buddy Warren—you met him at the Bee Ball—says he could take over my jobs for the summer."

Limbs heavy, she didn't want to hear any more about Dan's possible adventure, over two thousand kilometres away. Thankfully, a huge man climbed on stage and squeezed behind the drum kit. "Here comes the band," she shouted back.

A predictably long thin guy carrying a bass guitar came on next, followed by a much older sax player and finally the singer, wearing a leather fedora. "Y'all ready to loosen up and let go?" he yelled as the mike screeched.

Lisa wasn't sure how ready she was, but she was looking forward to sitting close to Dan, wordlessly enjoying an evening together. Her beer arrived and she savoured the semi-sweet fizziness as it slipped down the back of her throat.

"Let's try that again," roared the fedora, and when they'd shouted loudly enough, he launched into "Lay Down Sally." Dan's foot started tapping. Soon his shoulders were swaying and his head bobbing. By the second stanza, he was on his feet, his hand extended to Lisa. *Shit!* Her confidence plummeted. She was going to have to dance. She glanced at the almost-empty patch of floor between the tables and the stage—one other couple, looking like they'd won jive championships. She looked back at Dan. *As soon as I get comfortable with this man, he ups the ante.*

Lisa sort of skipped, occasionally turning, while Dan's limbs developed a life of their own. He was so free, seemed able to just let any part of himself move in any way it wanted. As more people got up to join them, Lisa felt less conspicuous. The next numbers were faster, rockier, and soon there were so many people packed in front of the stage, she could hardly move. She struggled out of her shirt and tied it around her waist, feeling a wet patch in the small of her back. Dan was working his way around the crowd, having a little dance with anyone open to it.

Fedora man yelled into his mic, "Y'all having a good time?" The crowd cheered. A woman at the bar held up her glass and whooped as beer slopped down her arm. "Here's a tune Jesse Fuller wrote in the fifties that's been recorded by everyone from Paul McCartney to Janice Joplin and Peter, Paul, and Mary, but I know you're going to love our version best—'San Francisco Bay Blues'."

A bigger cheer. The dancers started moving before the drums kicked in, then a harmonica. The beat was fast, Lisa was flagging. A woman nearby started jumping up and down and Lisa copied her, and after a few bounces something strange happened— she stopped caring. There was sweat pouring down her face and pooling between her breasts as her legs sprang her higher and higher and she could feel herself grin. Soon Dan was in front, taking her hands. They were leaping up and down in sync, laughing, and as the music subsided, Lisa didn't want it to end.

The interval was short. Dan went to the bathroom, Lisa went to the bar, and by the time she'd bought their drinks, the band was starting its second set with "Next Time You See Her." She couldn't wait to get back on the dance floor. She was soaked in sweat, her hair was stuck to the back of her neck, and she just wanted more. She jumped, skipped, shook her head, and raised her arms, loving every beat. The second set slipped by and now the singer was saying it was time to slow things down with a favourite tune by Otis Rush, "I Can't Quit You Baby." Dan slipped his hand around Lisa's waist and pulled her close. She rested her head on his shoulder. The sax oozed sex and the lyrics throbbed between them, about a love you couldn't hide.

Dan's hand moved up Lisa's back until it touched skin, heat radiating from every fingertip. Lisa knew that if she looked up, they'd be kissing. The only thing stopping her was the explanation that would have to follow. She didn't want that conversation, not now, she'd only just started the new pessaries. Closing her eyes, she breathed in his smell and imagined how salty his neck would taste. Their bodies were glued. As the last track of the evening began, she forced herself to pull away. "Let's leave before the rush."

"Really?" Dan's eyes were half-closed.

"I think so." Lisa was using every ounce of self-control. "I've got an early start in the morning."

He gave her a long look. "Okay."

Dan walked Lisa to her truck and, once inside, she lowered the window to say goodnight. "I can't believe I danced like that all evening. I had such a good time."

"Yeah, I guess being platonic isn't all bad." He broke into a smile. "My Son the Hurricane is playing in Redstock sometime in the next few weeks. Maybe we could go together?"

Relief. She'd be seeing him again soon. "I'd love that."

And by then—she didn't dare hope. Maybe she'd be in working order. Manitoba meant things needed to speed up. If Dan was going, she wanted them to be a couple before he left.

He leaned in to kiss her and she felt a stab of regret as his lips touched her cheek. "It's a date." He grinned. "Well, not a date. You know what I mean."

They both laughed.

She put her hand over his. "Call me when you find out when they're on."

"Will do. Drive safe."

Lisa left the window open wide. She wanted to feel the night air on her face.

Eleven

It was a week since Lisa had been to see the building inspector and since then, Norm hadn't returned her phone messages. She strode toward his bungalow. *Maybe he's worried I'll be angry. And he'd be right.*

Unusually, he was nowhere to be seen. She looked at the yard and everything seemed normal. His truck was in the driveshed, along with assorted tools for gardening, sweeping, and cleaning snow—all the same vintage. There was enough wood stacked by the splitter to burn for at least three winters and his two make-shift greenhouses were stuffed with plants, ready to go in the ground next month. Among the buckets, gas cans, and tires, was an old farm plough that she guessed must have been his grandfather's.

The door was locked, so Lisa knocked and waited, rehearsing the piece of her mind she was about to deliver. She knocked again, growing concerned. Something felt wrong. When Norm finally appeared, hunched, unshaven and red-eyed, her anger evaporated.

"Not been feeling too good." He led her into the kitchen. The sink was full of dirty bowls and cups; there were empty soup cans on the stove. Rose would not have been happy.

"Sit down and I'll make you something to drink." Lisa picked up the kettle. "How long have you been feeling poorly?"

"Few days. I hate being sick."

While the water boiled, she discreetly did some washing up. It felt strange looking after Norm; he'd always been the caretaker in their friendship. She stirred cream into his Maxwell House, poured herself a glass of water, and sat down.

He blew his nose into a grubby cotton hanky.

"Have you called the health centre?"

"I'd have to be a lot worse than this to talk to them. Don't want nosey Parkers knowing my business."

"I found that out on Thursday." Her irritation returned.

He scowled and opened his mouth to speak but started coughing instead.

"What were you thinking? That after years of trying to help you get the right permits, ending in two court cases, I'd walk into the Township office and they'd tear up the demolition order?"

Norm winced and put his hand to his ear.

"Maybe I should come back when you're feeling better."

He shook his head. "What did Holtz tell you?"

"The truth, which is more than you did. You made me look ridiculous."

"Bureaucratic prick." Norm sniffed. "They're trying to turn Colville into a police state. What I do on my own property is none of their damned business. I don't care what any of them says."

"I'm not talking about the Township, I'm talking about the fact that you lied to me. You used me. I thought we were friends."

Norm straightened. "It's easy for you, you're one of 'em. You don't understand. No one does."

"And no one will if you don't tell them what's going on."

He spat into his hanky.

"Norm, you asked me to help. I assumed you were talking to me honestly. Instead, you played me."

"That homestead is all I got. If they was going to tear down all you had of your past, you'd do anything to save it too."

Oh Christ, he doesn't know they're coming for the bungalow. She leaned forward, lowering her voice. "Norm, it's not the old house they're going to pull down, it's this place. As far as I understand, you never took out a permit for it, and then, when they tried to talk to you—well, you know the rest."

She watched him crumple. "Rose's? They can't take that away from me."

"What happened when you went to court?"

His voice was tiny. "I only went to the Provincial Court."

"And?"

"The judge said he had no choice but to find me guilty. He said the Township had the evidence, that I'd built the place, and I didn't deny building it, so he had to find me guilty. He only fined me a couple of hundred, told me to go home and get my ducks in a row."

"So why didn't you apply for the permits?"

Norm didn't answer. He just stared into his coffee cup and Lisa waited. After a while he sat up straight, jaw jutting. "Screw 'em, they got my fine. They started hounding me about the old farmhouse and I'd had enough. I never went to the second hearing."

It was tragic to think of Norm losing his home, and all he had of Rose, in such a brutal way. Lisa knew what it meant to have no family, to walk away from everything familiar, and in spite of all his noise, she didn't think Norm would survive it. "Holtz said you should have copies of all the paperwork?"

Norm stood up slowly and pulled open the drawer under the microwave, packed with letters and court papers, some crumpled, some still unopened in registered envelopes. Lisa put them in a heap on the kitchen table and started sifting out the ones that were still sealed while Norm sat watching. She picked up a knife from the countertop by the sink and handed it to him. "Maybe you could open these so we can see what they say?" Norm didn't move, so she put it near his elbow and started sorting some of the other papers into piles. Eventually she sighed and sat down again. "This is a big job. You're going to have to talk me through some of these ..." She pointed to a thick wad of minutes from council meetings. "It looks like—"

"Just go."

Lisa surveyed the sea of documents in front of her. "But I'm going to need your help with the order of events. If you can—"

"I told you to go." He was looking beyond her now, out of the window at the old farmstead.

Of course, he's overwhelmed. And upset. He's only just learned it's the bungalow they're going to tear down, his shrine to Rose. "You're right," she added the council minutes to one of her careful piles, put two surveys on another. "I'll come back later, or tomorrow, and we can—"

Norm pushed back his chair so suddenly that it fell over and crashed against the wall behind him. "Get out! I don't want you here. And I ain't going through these damn papers."

He slapped the table. Papers flew and Lisa's mug smashed onto the floor, followed by the knife. She sat still, scared. Norm may be old and unwell, but he was radiating anger, his face crimson, his hands in fists by his sides. He walked over to the sink and stood with his back to Lisa as she picked up her purse and left.

* * *

As she walked home through the fields at the back of Norm's, Lisa's heartbeat steadied and she decided to give it a few days before going to see him again. Clumps of mud were sticking to her boots and she kept thinking of Dad and the fight she'd had with him. That was the ultimate betrayal. It may have been nearly thirty years ago, but it still hurt. Had she made a mistake to walk away? He probably didn't know she was in Canada. She didn't know if he was alive.

She'd never told him or her sister how much they'd hurt her. No one ever talked about feelings when she was growing up. When Mum died, Lisa had learned to swallow hers down so deep that, over the years, it had become a habit. Now she needed to take stock, to process Norm and all that had happened over the past few weeks. It was time to go into the basement.

She made a cup of tea and tried not to spill it as she picked her way down the worn wooden stairs. The air was cool. Lisa loved the smell of old walls and laundry soap. She walked past the shelves filled with suitcases and storage containers, opposite the washer, dryer, and a deep sink, behind a hanging rail of clothes and coats in protective bags, to a big table scattered with magazines. Here the walls were covered, floor-to-ceiling, in cut-out pictures: people, beaches, donkeys, vintage cars, sunsets, furniture, dogs—all bouncing, overlapping, repeating and mirroring. Lisa turned on the old Anglepoise lamp and picked up her scissors.

It had started a few Christmases ago when Susan had given her an afternoon workshop called "Visioning the Future." Nothing about the write-up appealed, especially the idea of sharing her vision with a group of strangers, but Lisa had gone because it was a gift from Susan. Skeptical about the "power of visioning," Lisa found the facilitator annoyingly new age, but she did enjoy making the collage of her wishes, hopes, and dreams. She had loved going through the magazines, cutting out pictures, and sticking them down together. Although she'd been principal of an art school, Lisa considered her own creative abilities to be inferior, and she certainly wouldn't call her basement wall art. In fact, that was the best part, it didn't have to *be* anything. She adored the freedom of randomly picking an image and sticking it down anywhere she wanted, the absolute joy of switching off her brain and doing something meaningless.

Opening an old *National Geographic,* she saw a snake, native to the Sahara, and started snipping around its weird little viper ears. Once freed from its two-dimensional desert, she curled its sandy scales around a woman in her 1960s kitchen, pointing to her new Hotpoint appliances. Lisa had never wanted to be a homemaker; she was more interested in work. How different would her life be now if she'd had kids? Leonard didn't want children and the truth was, she'd always been too scared. In very different ways, they'd both had a miserable time growing up. Too miserable to risk inflicting anything similar on a child of their own. And children make you vulnerable.

Lisa turned the pages of a vintage *Good Housekeeping* magazine and paused at a photo of a woman rubbing cream into her hands. Lisa did that every night. She wondered if her mum had too. For years after she died, Lisa would repeat the things she remembered about Mum on the way to school, so she'd never forget: soft hands, loved cherries, put a hot water bottle in my bed at night, stroked the back of my neck, buried the dead squirrel we found in the garden, phoned Auntie Jean after lunch on Sunday. Fifty-five years later, Lisa still ached for love she could trust. Something she hadn't dared hope for in a very long time. She sniffed back a tear. Susan, Fido, Norm—they were her family now. She had to find a way to help him, even if he was an irascible old porcupine.

Dipping her finger in the pot, she smoothed glue onto the back of the cut-out snake and then found just the right spot on the wall. As she kept cutting out and sticking, the magic started to work, and she grew too absorbed to think.

Twelve

Lisa had taken a ton of outdoor rubbish to the dump, half of her wardrobe to the thrift store, and she'd dealt ruthlessly with the cupboard under the stairs. But the biggest victory was that she'd been using the new pessaries for two weeks with no adverse reaction. Just out of bed, she was standing in front of the full-length mirror in her pyjamas, wondering how long it would be before she could test—and enjoy—the results. Maybe it was time to invite Dan for dinner?

A van door clunked shut outside and Fido bounced into action, leaping down the stairs, as Lisa tugged up the sash window. Dan stood grinning up at her. "Hope it's not too early. I was so hyped I couldn't stay home so I went to the diner for breakfast but when I got there, I realized that what I really wanted was to come and tell you. I got the job. I'm going to Manitoba and they need me right away." Dan was hopping from one foot to the other like a ten-year-old.

Lisa's mood tanked. *Of course you got the bloody job. You're an experienced, fifty-five-year-old man willing to work for a student's salary, and you're being employed by your daughter.* "That's tremendous." She called back, leaning out of the window. "I'll put on some clothes and come down."

"Or just come down." He laughed. "Oops, I forgot. No flirting, only very platonic friendship."

"They need him right away, for the whole summer," she muttered, pulling on jeans and shuffling through her drawer for a sweater. This definitely wasn't part of her plan. As she stepped onto the porch, Dan rushed over and gave her a huge hug. "It's like a dream come true. Six months with Anna, somewhere new. No clients, or deadlines, or orders that don't arrive in time."

"Six months? I thought it was just for the summer," Lisa blurted before remembering to sound supportive.

"I got it wrong. It's more of a research position with funding for half a year. They want me there quickly because the money runs out in September. I'm on my way to see Warren and hand over the Down to Earth jobs that are already booked."

"Wow. That is soon." Lisa gazed at the fresh tufts of spring grass and new leaves exploding onto the trees, and thought her summer looked derelict. She hadn't admitted, even to herself, how much she wanted this man in her life.

"Things haven't really ramped up at work yet. Warren thinks he'll be able to step in. He's such a great guy, he knows how much I want to go."

She rallied. "Fantastic. Why don't I make us a celebration breakfast?"

"Yes please." Now the ten-year-old was shining out of Dan's eyes.

"Coffee, eggs, beans, toast?" Lisa started back into the house.

He nodded, beaming. "Would you mind if I stay out here to make a few calls? It's a two-day drive, with an overnight stop, and I've got to get the van serviced and sort out someone to look after the bees. Anna and I will be collecting data together, camping and sleeping out in Provincial Parks, it'll be just like old times."

Lisa broke five eggs into a bowl and whisked them with grated cheese, imagining all the things she wasn't going to do with Dan—see My Son the Hurricane, spend time swimming, sharing meals, and ... How were they going to make the transition from friends to lovers if he was so far away? His voice drifted in from the porch as he talked to his mechanic, full of excitement. Excitement that didn't involve her.

She grabbed a fleece and carried a tray loaded with toast, butter, ketchup, coffee, cream, sugar, and cutlery out to the picnic table on the front lawn. The sky was bright but the day hadn't yet warmed. She paused on her way back to the kitchen. Dan looked so at home, leaning in his chair, feet up on the wooden rail. She wanted to go over and kiss him. She wanted to be in bed with him, to feel his long lean body next to hers. "Breakfast'll be ready in a few minutes," she called, consoling herself with shared domesticity.

Between mouthfuls of mushrooms, omelette, and fried potato—Lisa always had hash browns in the freezer—Dan told her what he knew about the job. "We start with two days of training at the lab in the university, theoretical stuff about the species, then I'll go out with Anna and we'll sample some sites together. She has to assess my performance before the job is definitely mine."

"I'm sure it's a done deal. When we talked before, it was all about spending time with Anna. Now it sounds like you're interested in the work?"

"I'm keen to do something different. Anna's twenty-two and I started Down to Earth Designs when she was ten. I've never lived, or even worked, outside Colville, let alone Ontario."

Lisa probed with more questions, and Dan answered them with so much excitement that she couldn't let him see her disappointment.

"I'll be collecting spiders, lady bugs, grasshoppers, mayflies, ants, wasps, bumble bees—that'll be tough, killing bees." He finally stopped to breathe when his phone pinged. "I'd better check that. It might be Anna."

"Go ahead." Lisa loaded dirty dishes onto the tray. In a way, Dan had already left. While he spent the next half hour taking care of things on his phone, Lisa tried to appear busy, until she stood in front of the house waving. "Let's make sure we get together before you go."

He gave a thumbs up out of the van window.

"This is a disaster," Lisa groaned, going back into the house. "Six months till I get to kiss him again," she wailed into the empty kitchen. "And what if he doesn't like me when he comes back?" The next thought made her stomach plummet—*or he meets someone else while he's away?* She started piling their plates into the dishwasher and chipped the cup Dan had been drinking from.

This was intolerable, exactly what she'd been avoiding for so long. Lisa stomped into the mudroom and spoke to her rubber boots. "I refuse to surrender control of my happiness to a man."

She spent the rest of the day in the garden, ruminating on Dan, trying to figure out what to do about Norm, and was about to start making supper when the doorbell rang. *That's weird. Everyone I know comes in through the kitchen.*

Fido was already in the front hall, dancing on the spot. Lisa made him sit, opened the door, and gasped. The same beautiful black skin, long straight nose, raven eyes, and leather coat with the collar turned up. "Leonard?" Her hand went to her mouth, but this wasn't Leonard, he was gone. This was a replica of the Leonard she knew at university over forty years ago. And this one was female.

"He's my father."

Lisa stared, speechless. The young woman had a London accent. Her skin was a shade paler, but the features were his, only finer. She had Leonard's eyebrows, her hair was cropped exactly the way he used to wear it, and she had the same way of standing—legs apart. This person was definitely made from his DNA. Lisa went liquid. "He is ... isn't here," she stammered. "He ... died."

"Yeah, I know."

Lisa's eyes weren't working properly. Everything looked distorted.

"I want to know about him."

"You want me to tell you about Leonard?"

The young woman's face said, "Obviously."

Lisa realized she had stopped breathing.

"I've got no one else to ask."

"How did you find me?"

"Mum was always going on about you when she was off her head. She knew your name and where you used to work. There was an old bloke there who remembered you, said you'd gone to Canada. It wasn't that hard really."

"And you just came?" Lisa was trying to do the math. "Why didn't you write or phone first?"

"So you couldn't say no."

The young woman kept looking at her with frighteningly familiar eyes as Lisa's brain was exploding and her feet felt like lead. What should she do? There was no how-to book for this. Nothing in her past to guide her into an appropriate response. "You'd better come in."

Sitting at the kitchen table, her khaki backpack by her side, the young woman looked smaller. Younger.

Lisa stood on the other side of the room. "How old are you?"

"Twenty."

"When's your birthday?"

"November 17th, 1998."

Lisa and Leonard married on March 15th of the same year, and that meant she was planning the wedding while he was having sex with this person's mother. That date turned their whole marriage into a lie. "I need you to leave."

A moment of anxiety flashed, then the young woman resumed her stance. "I'm not leaving, I've just come three thousand miles to see you."

Not my fucking problem! Lisa screamed to herself. "I'm going to call a cab to take you to the hotel in town."

"I can't afford that."

"How did you get here?"

"Flew to Toronto, spent bloody hours on a bus to Minden, waited three hours for the bus to Colville that only leaves once a fucking day, then a man called Norm gave me a ride to the end of your drive. Had to keep the window open the whole way cuz I didn't want to catch whatever he's got."

Norm's face full of rage flashed through Lisa's mind. "Did you tell him why you were coming here?"

"No." Her features finished the sentence.

"Good. Norm's not a big talker, but the fewer people who know about this the better."

"Why? Don't want your husband's Black daughter turning up to ruin your good standing in the community?"

Lisa didn't want anyone to know because she could hardly face it herself. She picked up her cell and started scrolling for the local cab company.

"I told you already, I'm broke." The young woman reached into her jeans pocket and pulled out a handful of scrunched Canadian notes. "See."

"I'll ring the hotel and tell them I'll cover your bill." Lisa didn't want this person to exist, let alone have a name, but she couldn't stop herself from asking.

"Ashley Aitkin. My mum was an intern in your husband's office."

"Okay. I don't want to know any more. I'll stand you one night at the hotel, and then you're on your own."

"But I've come all this way."

"Well, I'm sorry to say it, but that's not my problem."

As the taxi drove off, Lisa buckled, sliding down the wall of the front porch and let out an awful sound. She put her cheek on top of Fido's smooth, warm head, hugging him close. "Are you the only one in the world I can trust? Leonard may be dead, but he can still shatter me into tiny pieces. And each time he does, it's worse than the one before." The tears were pouring. "What the hell am I meant to do with this?"

The thrumming in Lisa's head was so loud she couldn't think. She went into the living room, but the air was too thick. She went back onto the porch but started shivering. In the end, she opened a bottle of wine, went back into the living room, put on the TV, and focused on slowing her heart. At first, she couldn't work out what Julia Roberts was doing, then she realized she was pressing down divots on a racing track. It was strangely comforting.

She'd never watched *Pretty Woman* before. When the credits rolled, Lisa went upstairs and fell straight asleep, fully clothed.

She woke at 2 a.m., her brain tossing. *He fucked the intern just before our wedding. Christ, I hope it wasn't just after, somehow that would be worse.* The word intern implied youth. Lisa didn't want to know how young. Or what she looked like. Or how they'd come together. Or where. After an hour of gazing at the ceiling, Lisa went downstairs and put some milk in a pan to heat. Stirring cocoa powder into the warming white liquid, she noticed the taste of blood and realized she'd chewed her cheek. She poured her drink into a mug and took it into the living room.

The first thing she saw was Leonard's record collection taking up half of one wall. Lisa wanted to go around the house and get everything of his out of every room, put it in a big pile outside, pee on it, and burn it. Instead, she went to the hall closet and dragged the Hoover into the living room, moved all the furniture out of the corners, and started vacuuming. A few hours later, sunlight sliced through the windows, bouncing off polished furniture and seeping into dust-free rugs and upholstery. Lisa went upstairs to shower. She had too many questions. She was going into town to talk to Ashley.

Thirteen

Walking into the Village Inn, Lisa was tense, nervous, angry, scared, and determined to keep it together. She stopped to say hi to Janet on reception, who used to work at the art school, and after a chat, told her she'd come to see a young friend from England.

Janet winked. "She's in the dining room."

Standing in the doorway, Lisa watched Ashley get up from a seat by the window and walk over to the buffet. Her table was spread with empty dishes. It looked like she'd already had a helping of everything, but she went back to her place with pancakes, rolls, two hard-boiled eggs, and a glass of orange juice. Lisa remembered how she used to love watching Leonard. This young woman was part of him, made from his blood. She was wearing a long leather vest over a T-shirt and looked thin. Lisa could see the child Ashley was, not so long ago.

Ashley looked up, nodded, and went back to chewing.

This creature was both alien and familiar. She even held her fork the way Leonard used to, tilting her hand slightly sideways before lifting it to her mouth. Lisa hated the pleasure it gave her to see.

"Great spread," Ashley said as Lisa sat down. "Last time I ate anything was at the cafe in Kentish Town. Felt too queasy on the plane. Never been on one before and didn't want to end up with my head in a sickbag."

Lisa's first time in the air was going to Greece with Leonard. Now she was sitting in Canada with his child. She kept her tone level, business-like. "I understand you want to know about your father, and I am prepared to answer your questions, but you must realize this is very difficult emotionally for me."

"Oh yeah, like it's easy for me?"

Lisa took a breath before she spoke. "You have to admit that you've had longer to get used to the idea than I have. I only found out you existed sixteen hours ago."

"Knowing about it for twenty years hasn't made it easier."

"Listen, my life hasn't been—" Lisa stopped, reminding herself that she was the adult here, and took another breath. "Point taken."

The server asked if she wanted breakfast. Lisa ordered black coffee, probably not a good idea on top of the two she'd already had, but the 2 a.m. start was catching up with her. Ashley took a plastic bag with ice written on it out of her backpack and slipped the hard-boiled eggs and rolls into it. "So, are you going to tell me about him?" Her eyes had the same intensity as her father's.

"Yes, I am. And I'd like to know more about you, too."

"Really?" Ashley took a swig of juice. "Okay. I've got nothing to hide."

"Let's go outside onto the patio."

Grabbing her coat and bag, Ashley followed Lisa through a door at the back of the hotel. They settled at a table in the sun, sheltered from the wind by a stone wall. Ashley slid down and put her hands in her pockets. "Go on then, what was he like?"

"That's way too big." Lisa cradled her cup in her hands. "You're going to have to ask me more specific questions than that."

"Okay. Was he a player, or was Mum the only one?"

Lisa skipped a beat. "I honestly don't know how he felt about your mother. I didn't even know she existed until yesterday. I can tell you that, before we eventually married, Leonard and I lived together for eleven years in our twenties and early thirties, and he wasn't always faithful then."

The young woman in front of her looked pensive. "Did you two have any kids?"

"No, we decided not to."

"How come?"

"I'm going to pass on that one."

Ashley rolled her eyes. "Where did you meet?"

"At uni. We both went to Sussex in the late seventies."

"So he was a hippy? Huge Afro, droopy shades, big flares?"

Lisa almost smiled. "Anything but. Actually, he used to wear a long leather coat exactly like yours."

"That's weird." As Ashley fingered her collar, Lisa saw the first glimmer of genuine emotion. "So we have the same sense of style."

"He was very clever, studied politics and economics."

"Is that why you went for him?"

"To be honest, I liked everything about Leonard from the moment I set eyes on him. That was in the student bar, the first week we arrived."

Ashley looked interested, as though she'd like to hear more, but instead she asked if he had any brothers or sisters.

"No, he was an only child. Born in Ghana and when he was eight his parents sent him to England to go to boarding school. They're both dead now."

"He came from money then?"

"Once he left uni, he never took a penny from his family. His father was furious he didn't go back to Ghana. He wanted Leonard to go to Oxford or Cambridge and study law, then take over the family business, but Leonard loved advertising."

"Feeding people lies."

"That's what I used to say to start with, but it was more than that to him."

"It must have made him a few quid. Mum took me to the ad agency once. She went in to see someone she used to work with and left me in reception. I remember how flashy it was, how everyone seemed to glide instead of walk. It's gone now, bought by a big German firm a few years back."

She's sharp. Done her homework.

"So, no grandma or grandad? Uncles, aunts, cousins? Just you?"

"Sorry." Lisa meant it. She remembered how she used to long for more family than just Dad and Nicky—all her grandparents were killed in the second World War and Aunty Jean had never had any children.

Ashley picked an old ivy stem off the wall behind her and started pulling it apart, then turned to the skin around her fingernails, or what was left of them. "What other stuff did he like, apart from making money?"

"He did make a lot, but that wasn't his driving force. Leonard really did love his job. He liked the challenge of coming up with ideas, working with photographers."

Ashely didn't look impressed.

"He adored good food and wine."

"Don't tell me, he liked cooking and used fresh herbs that you grew in pots on the windowsill."

Lisa didn't want to admit that Ashley was right. "He was a great dancer, really into music."

"What kind of music?"

"Soul. Early stuff like Stax, Otis Redding, Isaac Hays."

Ashley scrunched her face. "We might have the same taste in coats, but I like music that was made this century."

"Leonard liked films, too. We joined the NFT when we moved to London. The National Film Theatre, on the South Bank?"

"All that black and white shit, like *Metropolis?*"

"Fraid so. His favourite film-maker was Sergei Eisenstein."

"Leonard sounds like a right pseudo fucking socialist. Sold lies for money and I s'pose he read *The Guardian,* too."

There must be disappointment under all this anger. The poor girl must have hoped to hear about someone like her. Isn't that what we all want from family? "Tell me about your mum. Were you two similar?"

"I hope not. I don't drink or do drugs. Mum OD'ed when I was sixteen."

No wonder she's so bitter. "I'm sorry. Who did you live with after that?"

Ashley tilted her head. "I'm going to pass on that one, for now anyway."

Lisa smiled, almost enjoying herself. "Well, whatever happened, it must have been tough. How old was your mum when she died?"

"Thirty-four."

The answer was like a kick in the kidneys. It meant that Ashley's mother was eighteen when she slept with Leonard, and Lisa was forty.

"After Mum got pregnant, she left the ad agency and went back home to Scotland. Her parents made her lie and say she was married, that her husband was overseas, but when I came out Black they disowned her."

Lisa had stopped listening. Her head was too full of Leonard having sex with someone twenty-two years younger, in the office, while Lisa was organizing their wedding.

"Me and Mum ended up in a flat above a pub in Glasgow till I was three. That's when we moved to London. Her friend had opened a modelling agency and gave her a job on reception." Ashley looked up, and seeing the change in Lisa's expression, her voice hardened again. "But you don't give a shit about my story, do you? You just want to know stuff that relates to you and your precious husband, like how long him and Mum were shagging, and if he was in love with her."

That was exactly what Lisa wanted to know, but not now. She'd had enough. Her chair snagged on a patio stone as she pushed away from the table. "It's getting cold and I'm exhausted. I need to try and get some sleep."

"Pardon? So that's it?"

They were both victims in this situation, that's what Lisa had to remember. She mustn't blame this young woman for her own hurt. "How about I extend your hotel stay till the end of the week? That way we can take it slowly and I'll try and tell you everything you want to know."

Leonard's daughter looked up and Lisa had to turn her head to hide the tears. It was the first time she had seen Ashley smile.

* * *

Lisa decided to stop by and visit Susan on her way home, but her Jeep wasn't in the driveway, the place was empty. Longing for air, Lisa walked around to the back of the house anyway. The lake was sparkling. Following the steep path, she made her way down to the jetty. Two ducks dived, flapping onto the water, rings of reflection spreading out from their bobbing bodies. Closer by, one of last year's leaves blew onto the glossy surface and started to spin.

Lisa was almost too exhausted to think, but the questions kept coming. Had she made a massive mistake taking Leonard back? She remembered the day he had turned up at her flat, holding a bunch of bleeding hearts. Was the whole "I've had therapy, I'm different now" just a ruse? But what for, if he was still sleeping around? Lisa sat on a rock overlooking the water, replaying her decision. That first night he'd appeared on her doorstep, she'd invited him to stay for a drink but had been non-committal, still reluctant to trust. It had taken two weeks for him to convince her to have a meal together. His voice on the phone was full of gratitude when she finally agreed to go. "You choose the place and I'll pay. Anywhere you like."

She picked Mildreds, a little-known vegetarian restaurant above a bookstore in Soho. In the early days, Lisa would have chosen a restaurant to please him.

"Mr. Annan," the waiter called out when they walked in. "For you, I have a special table by the window."

Leonard looked round at Lisa. "It's one of my lunch hang-outs when I'm not with clients," he explained as they settled into their seats, and from the way he knew the menu, Lisa believed him. She kept noticing ways in which he'd changed—there was something more genuine about him, even a hint of humility. His whole face beamed when she told him she'd made deputy principal. "Alexander College. That's adult education, isn't it?" he asked, before talking about his pro bono work for a charity that helped the children of immigrants get into university.

After the first half hour—and glass of wine—Lisa had relaxed. She told him about the terrible mess she'd made of a TV interview with the local morning news show, and her escapades on the staff badminton team, and when he confessed to going to bingo to win a gaming account, they laughed so hard they couldn't finish their food.

"Let me give you a lift home." They were standing outside the restaurant.

Lisa was firm. "I've enjoyed tonight, it's been good to see you, but I'll take the tube, thanks." She turned and walked away quickly.

Leonard respected her reluctance. It was eight more dates before she slid between the sheets of his king size bed in the penthouse overlooking London's glittering lights, and when she did, she was sure. She wasn't going back to anyone or anything, she was moving forward with a person she had loved before, who felt completely new. Although Leonard looked, talked, and joked the same, there was something more caring, self-aware, and respectful about him now, and that was the person she wanted to make love to.

And it honestly did feel like making love, in a way it never had before. His body was in her muscle-memory, but his kisses were more sensitive, and she could sense his need. The way he touched was responsive and full of curiosity—

A duck splashed onto the water, pulling the lake back into Lisa's focus. Sex used to be so straightforward, without worries about pain. She tugged off her boots and socks, then stood to unzip her jeans, peeling off her underwear with them. Looking down at the winter-white legs sticking out of her woolen jacket, she laughed. When she'd shed the rest of her clothes, she opened her arms wide, letting the cool April breeze touch every inch of her. The dock was cold and damp under her feet and grit stuck to her toes as she moved to the end of the jetty.

Lisa jumped as high and far as she could and for a moment, she felt suspended, before slicing through the freezing cold. Its mass consumed her, stinging her flesh, pulling up her hair as her feet sank into muddy silt. Time stopped, her body throbbed, her nipples clenched. Needles pierced her all over. Her face hurt. She bent her knees and pushed up, raising her arms to break the surface, spreading open the water so her head could follow. After gasping a lungful of air, she made a noise. A noise she'd never heard before. It wasn't a scream or a groan, or a cry or a laugh, but it ripped her throat and came from a place that had never spoken.

New energy propelled her to shore. By the time Lisa was back on the jetty, heat was pulsing through her. Skin tingling, she sat on her jacket and hugged her knees, watching the water as it stilled, listening to the rhythm of nearby frogs. A hawk soared and spread its wings, riding the air current as Lisa looked across the expanse in front of her. It was time to stop living in Leonard's shadow. The trouble was, she didn't even know what that meant.

Fourteen

Nightmares were a new experience for Lisa. In sweat-soaked sheets, she relived her wedding, standing proud at the altar in her ivory lace dress, hand in hand with Leonard in his Boateng suit. After so many years of loving, waiting, hoping, and finally forgiving, she completely trusted that he loved her too. His eyes were on hers, and he was about to slip the ring on her finger, when the vicar turned into Ashley's mother. In reality, Lisa had no idea what Ashley's mother looked liked, but now she was young, gorgeous, curvaceous, blonde, and naked.

The next nightmare took place at the reception, as Leonard was delivering his speech. "It's taken me twenty years to realize that you are the only woman who could ever make me happy. I want to give every part of myself to you, to spend the rest of my life looking after you and loving you."

But now Ashley's mother was in the front pew, cackling so loud it drowned his words, and everyone else started laughing with her.

Lisa woke with a shudder but couldn't stop remembering. They had married in a chapel in East London. Nicky and Dad weren't there, but Lisa's university roommate had come with her husband and kids, as well as some friends from work and a couple of women Lisa had grown close to at the gym. The other pews were filled with Leonard's partners and their families, the rest of his office, even a few clients. Did they all know he was screwing the intern? Was there pity, or even ridicule, behind their congratulations?

Lisa thought back to the night he proposed. She could still see the love in his eyes as he spoke. "I want to create something together, build a life with you."

Words turned to dust by a woman Lisa hadn't even known existed. The ad agency had thrown an engagement party and now

Lisa's memory scanned the faces toasting her future. Was Ashley's mother there? Did they have sex on Leonard's desk? In a hotel? Did he bring her into their home?

Lisa sat up, switched on the lamp, and decided not to go to the hotel to see Ashley. She'd been there for the past three days and needed a break, so as the dawn light glowed white, she put on her gardening gear and went outside. She worked hard, peeling off her layers as the late April sun rose. Turning over clumps of earth, she threw branches and roots onto a pile. Fido pulled out the biggest bits to chew, making a heap of his own. A woodpecker drummed on a nearby tree and Lisa enjoyed ripping out strands of tangled brush, yanking the roots, leaning her whole weight into the spade and heaving up clumps of earth. There was a sense of power that came with the work.

Exhausted, she dropped onto the grass, Fido's tail thudding as he lay down by her side, but her brain wouldn't stop churning. All that time spent hoping and trying, believing that if she could just be good enough, sweeter, curvier, sexier, her prize would be love. And then, when Leonard finally came back, she thought he was true, that the infidelity was over. She had believed in him. His love made her believe in herself. How would she ever trust again?

Barking, Fido careened down the driveway. "Surely not." She sighed, seeing the small figure staring out over Norm's fenced field and open meadow beyond. As Fido leapt up to greet her, Ashley brightened. "I love dogs. I always wanted one when I was little." She bent down and let him lick her face. "I guess he must have been here when I came on that first night, but I was in such a state. What's his name?"

"Fido." Lisa didn't care if she sounded annoyed. "I left a message at the hotel, saying I wouldn't be there today. Didn't you get it?"

"Yeah, but then I saw Norm in town and hitched a ride."

Oh Christ. I've been so busy with Ashley that I've forgotten Norm. I need to go back and make peace with him.

Ashley carried on. "I thought it'd be more relaxing to talk somewhere private, there's too many flapping ears in the hotel."

"You're used to getting what you want, aren't you?"

"You say that like it's a bad thing." Ashley walked towards the house. "This place is a fucking film set. You've even got one of those swinging sofas on the porch. I think I'm over jet lag now. That was a weird one. Never felt like it before, but then I've never been on a plane before."

As Ashley seemed oblivious to Lisa's mood, she didn't try to hide it. "I was hoping for a day off."

But the young woman was already on the porch, burying her face into Fido's neck. "No tea or anything for me, thanks. I'm still pumped from all that coffee at breakfast." Ashley nodded toward Lisa's mud-covered boots. "What are you up to?"

"I've been digging out weeds, making a new bed out back."

"Let's do that then. I'll help."

"I'm fine on my own, thanks. Anyway, it'll ruin your clean clothes."

"Come on." Ashley tipped her head and looked up, eyes wide—probably a well-practiced expression. Then she pointed to her own oversized feet. "Doc Martens. They're work boots, you know."

Exhausted, Lisa capitulated.

The sky clouded over, so the day wasn't too hot, and once she had shown Ashley how to use the fork to weed out roots, she worked hard and fast, pausing only to throw the ball for Fido. Lisa accidentally smiled a few times, and when Ashley occasionally stopped to ask a question, Lisa found herself forgetting to feel annoyed by the intrusion. The work went much more quickly than she had expected and she was at the other end of the vegetable patch when she heard the scream.

"WHAT THE FUCK?" Ashley threw down her fork and sprinted onto the porch.

"Are you okay?" Lisa ran over. "What happened?"

"You might have told me to look out for fucking snakes. I could have been killed, or was that the plan?"

Lisa put her arm around Ashley's shoulders. "Don't worry, the snakes around here are harmless."

"This wasn't harmless. It looked right at me. Huge green fucker with yellow stripes. Kept sticking out its tongue. If I hadn't legged it, I'd be a gonner."

"That's a garter snake. They usually eat frogs, not people." Lisa tried not to laugh as Ashley rearranged her T-shirt, fighting to regain her cool.

"Let's have some tea. I bought a bag of new doggie snacks yesterday, maybe you'd like to give Fido some of those?"

As Lisa washed her hands, Ashley went straight to the framed photo of a couple on a beach. "That's Margate, isn't it? I went there once on a school trip, to an art gallery right by the sea."

"That's right. It's taken by a famous photographer called Martin Parr. He specialises in pictures of ordinary people doing ordinary things."

"Cool." Ashley sat down at the table. "Have you got any more? I used to go to work with Mum at the model agency in my holidays and she'd let me look through the photographers' portfolios."

"Well, that is something you have in common with your dad. He loved photography."

Ashley frowned. "Can we just stick to Leonard? I think it's a bit late to start calling him Dad."

"Sure." Lisa hadn't realized she'd said the word. "Leonard loved everything to do with photography—taking pictures, buying cameras, collecting photos. He had quite a big collection. My favourite is of a man running through Paris in the rain. He's caught mid-air. It's in the hall. Bring your tea and I'll show you."

Ashley loved the photo and stopped to inspect the others hanging nearby. Lisa enjoyed her interest. The comments she made and questions she asked were impressive—this young woman was as bright as her father.

"Some of the best in the collection are in the living room." Lisa led the way.

As she opened the door, Ashley gasped. "Look at all that vinyl. It must be crazy expensive."

Lisa laughed. Ashley had no idea the Avedon portrait she'd just been looking at was worth $10,000, or that the Cartier-Bresson could sell for $5,000. "Leonard collected LPs too. He started at school in the seventies."

Ashley pulled a still-glossy black disc out of its cover and then, still holding it, started scanning around the room, as though she was looking for something.

"What is it?" Lisa asked gently.

"I thought there might be ... I wondered ..." Ashley's eyes moved from the walls to the mantlepiece. "A photo ..."

"Of course. You want to see Leonard." She walked over to the bookshelves by the window. "I've got albums full of pictures of him when we were at uni, and then living in London together, and our—" Lisa stopped herself before saying the words "wedding album." She pulled out a well-worn plastic ring binder. The handwriting on the front was almost childlike: *1977*. "He would have been about the same age as you are now in this one."

Ashley looked nervous as she took the book. Cradling it in the crook of her arm, she opened it carefully, as though handling something that could crumble. Lisa turned away. Seeing your father for the first time seemed like a thing you'd want to do in private, but just as she was heading for the kitchen, Fido barked and ran to the window. "Shit," Lisa said under her breath as she saw Dan's van was rumbling up the driveway. She turned back to Ashley. "You carry on browsing. I'm going to have a word with this person."

Feeling self-conscious, Lisa went outside and hoped Ashley wasn't watching. Dan hopped down and gave her a hug. "Everything okay? You didn't return my calls or answer my texts."

"I'm sorry. I've been preoccupied."

"Everything's going so fast. I'm leaving tomorrow. Heading into Toronto for a couple of days to tie up loose ends and then straight on to Manitoba."

This was too soon. "So you've been approved by the university?"

"Yup, yesterday. It's all organized. Warren's going to run my jobs and use my place as his office, but he won't be using the kitchen." Dan turned back into the van and pulled out a cardboard box of food. "I emptied the fridge, thought I could knock together a meal for us here, a kind of goodbye lunch. The honey is to keep you going till I get back."

Lisa glanced back at the house. "That sounds lovely, but I'm afraid I've got someone here."

"Someone you don't want me to meet?" Then Dan muttered, as though to himself, "I thought you said you weren't seeing anyone."

"I'm not." Lisa put her hand on his arm. "It's a young woman who turned up unexpectedly. A long story, too long to tell now, to do with my past. Let's talk on the phone when you get to Manitoba."

Looking deflated, Dan put down the box. "I guess this is it then. I'll see you in October."

Lisa wanted to grab him, kiss him, slip her hands under his jacket and pull him to her, tell him she'd never really wanted to be platonic, but it felt too late. What was the point when he was disappearing for so long, and hadn't shown any regret at leaving her?

"Oh, I nearly forgot. I'm giving Warren my cell to make it easier for work. I'll be getting one from the university once I start on the field research, so don't try using my old number."

She needed more time, to hear about his job, find out what happened with his ex, what was in the letter, to tell him about Ashley. "I'll miss you." She took a step forward. "Have a wonderful summer." Lisa almost put her lips on his before diverting to his cheek.

Dan bounced back into action. "You enjoy your summer too. Gotta go. Still a million things to do. I'll ring when I get my new number."

Watching his van disappear down the driveway, she felt empty. As she wiped her eyes, the screen door squeaked and Ashley arrived by her side. "That looked intense."

"It's tricky."

"I hate that, when people say it's complicated. It just means they don't want to talk about it but try to make out like it's some mysterious matter of national importance. Why don't they just say it how it is?"

"Okay. I don't want to talk about it."

Ashley laughed.

Lisa turned to face her. "But let's sit down for a minute. There is something we need to work out."

She glanced back at the empty driveway before going up the porch steps. Ashley launched into the swing seat, using her feet to push herself like a kid in the playground, and Lisa gave her a moment to settle. "Have you thought about what's going to happen when you leave the hotel?"

Ashley peered out across the grass before answering. "I think I'll stick around. I haven't got much to go home for, and I like it here. No one seems posh, and I'm instantly interesting cuz of my accent."

Lisa was stunned.

"Don't worry, I'm not going to turn up begging for a bed. I've done some scouting, met some people—made a bit of a friend actually. Her name's Skye."

"Skye Stewart?"

"I dunno her second name, but she knows you from the art school. I think she might have been there when you were principal."

After Skye's performance at the bee ball, this could only be bad news, but Lisa was too busy thinking about Ashley staying in Colville to worry about it now. Looking at this replica of Leonard sitting on her porch, Lisa felt her life slide into someone else's hands. Again.

Fifteen

The summer of 1988 was unusually hot for England. Security locks prevented the window from opening more than an inch and Lisa's office was stifling. Rushing through the last assessment form, she was desperate to slip off early.

"Don't worry, I'll finish the rest," her assistant offered.

"I'm done, but thanks." Lisa groped under the desk for her bag. "Leonard always makes the plan on my birthday. Tonight it's cocktails in Soho and then Vincenzo's. "

"You're like a schoolgirl going on her first date. I can't believe you've been together for—how long?"

"Eleven years." Lisa laughed over her shoulder. On the bus home, she prayed the evening would go well. Leonard had been so distant lately. His body was with her but his mind was elsewhere, and when she asked what was wrong, he just said his head was full of work.

She opened the windows and the flat flooded with warm air. Everything was perfect. Lisa had worked hard: scrubbed, changed the sheets, put roses in the vase on the dresser, and a pot of sweet-smelling freesias by the bed. After her shower, she smoothed on jasmine-scented body lotion, Leonard's favourite. Still tanned from their week in Madeira, she wriggled into her sleeveless black dress, and although the weather was hot, pulled on a pair of stockings before slipping into high heels. Leonard liked to think he was the essence of cool, but he still went crazy for anything involving a garter belt.

Sitting on the stool at the breakfast bar, Lisa tried to make sense of another set of student feedback forms. The principal had asked her to analyze them, to present an overview at Monday's meeting, and she wanted to do a good job but was too anxious to focus. Leonard was late. She phoned his office. No reply. Half an hour later she rang again, heard his secretary's voice again, slightly distorted by the recording: "You have called Leonard Annan ..."

Where is he? Maybe he's doing something extra special for tonight, as a surprise, or he stopped to pick something up.

Resisting the urge for coffee because she'd brushed her teeth and wanted to keep her breath fresh, Lisa got herself another glass of water, turned on the TV and watched the news with the sound off. One and half hours later she was staring at a silent football match. Could he have forgotten and gone out with the boys from the office? Or a client? Surely not on her birthday. Beyond disappointment and trying not to worry, she dialed.

"Casa Vincenzo, good evening."

"Hello? I need to cancel my booking in the name of Annan, Leonard Annan. I'm sorry it's such short notice."

"Is that Lisa?" The voice on the phone grew warm. It was Vince, the owner. "What a shame, we were looking forward to seeing you. Nothing serious, I hope?"

"No, nothing serious." She hoped.

Staring blankly at a late-night book programme, Lisa kicked off her shoes and curled up on the sofa. Alternating between worry and confusion, she longed for the oblivion of sleep. It was after midnight when she heard Leonard's key and rushed to the door. "Are you okay?"

He handed her a bunch of carnations, still in their cellophane shroud. Lisa recognized the label from the all-night supermarket. She followed him into the living room and watched him sit on the edge of the sofa, sink his head in his hands, and sob. "If I tell you where I've been, you'll hate me."

Lisa came close and put her arm around him. "I couldn't hate you. I love you."

He said nothing for the longest time, then, "It began three months ago, after that party to celebrate landing the whisky account. I slept with her. It was a mistake. I don't know why I did it."

Lisa couldn't keep up. She was too full of upset for Leonard's tears, relieved that he was home safe.

"Celeste. I slept with Celeste."

Acid hit the back of Lisa's throat. She had met Celeste at the Christmas party—long neck and a designer dress.

"That was it, just that one time. Never happened again. No further dealings apart from the necessary at work, until a few weeks later, when she threatened to tell everyone in the office if I didn't go for a drink with her."

Lisa pulled away, worried she was going to throw up.

"I went but nothing happened. I swear. In a sense, that was the problem."

"How could that be a problem?"

"Because she didn't get what she wanted. After that she kept leaving me notes and messages and turning up in client meetings."

As Lisa's world collapsed, her voice stiffened. "So what does this have to do with my birthday?"

Leonard had stopped crying but was hiding his face in his hands. "She got our home number, and yours at work, and threatened to tell you if I didn't meet her for a drink tonight at the Conbury. Just one, she said, then she'd leave me alone forever."

Lisa didn't want to hear the rest. She wanted to get into bed on her birthday with her beautiful man, snuggle into his back and fall asleep, but part of her already knew that was never going to happen again.

"When I got there the concierge gave me a message to go up to her room." Leonard let out a sound that could have been a sob. "It was horrendous. Blood everywhere."

Lisa's inner organs buckled. "Go on."

"I called an ambulance and went with her to the hospital. She's going to be alright, thank Christ."

He finished the water in Lisa's glass, then leant back into the sofa. "It was awful. I thought she was dead."

Leonard may have said more but there was a noise in Lisa's ears like a plane taking off and when she stood up, she felt drunk. In the bathroom she tried to vomit but nothing came. She splashed cold water on her face and looked in the mirror. A white mask with smudged eyes stared back.

In the living room, she chose the armchair opposite his. "Where is she now?"

"Still at St. Thomas's. When she came round, I told her I couldn't stay any longer."

"Who else have you slept with?"

Leonard rearranged himself on the sofa; he seemed to be rearranging his thoughts. "I told you, it was only the once and it was meaningless. If she hadn't—done what she did—we wouldn't be having this conversation."

"Your old secretary, Sita, when you went on that Levi's launch in Venice?"

His silence said more than words.

"What about Audrey, when you kept staying at work almost all night to sort out her pitch for the yoga studio?"

His head moved, an almost imperceptible nod.

"The travel rep in Formentera?"

This time the nod was real.

"That bridesmaid when you were best man at Clive's wedding? Any of my friends?"

"No, not your friends."

The next name was so terrifying, Lisa couldn't bring herself to say it. As though he'd already heard, Leonard hung his head.

* * *

They agreed he would pick up the rest of his stuff at the weekend and carrying one small bag, Leonard left. Lisa dialed her old home number in Cowley. It took seventeen rings for Dad to pick up, even though the phone was in the hall right outside his room.

"It's Lisa. I need to talk to Nicky. Can you get her?"

His voice was full of sleep. "It's four in the morning. What's going on?"

"I just need to talk to her."

"Slow down. I asked you a question."

"Just get her, will you? You *have* to wake her up."

"Mind your language, young lady. I don't *have* to do anything, and it doesn't sound like you should be talking to anyone until you calm down."

"Dad please, trust me, this is important."

"If it's that important, you can tell me. Nicky's got to be up for work in a few hours."

Still the same—always on her side. Upset and fury that she'd felt from childhood rose in Lisa's throat. "If you have to know, she slept with Leonard."

Silence, apart from Dad's breathing, dense on the phone.

"I said, she slept with Leonard. I need to talk to her."

"I can't see what you have to say now that won't wait 'til morning."

"Nicky had sex with the man I live with. The man she knows I love."

Dad cleared his throat. "It takes two, and in my experience, it's usually the bloke that makes the first move. Anyway, it was a long time ago. I don't see why you have to drag it up now."

"You *knew?*"

"Like I said, it was years ago. Go to bed. You'll feel better in the morning."

"That's it? You want me to hang up?"

"I just don't see why you have to rake it up now. Nicky's got a twelve-hour shift to look forward to, she doesn't need you shouting at her in the middle of the night."

Lisa put down the receiver, expecting her brain to explode out of her ears. Leonard was gone. He'd screwed Nicky and Dad knew. Every time Lisa had been back home, every time she'd been there with Leonard, they'd all known. Every single person she loved had betrayed her. She wanted her mum.

Finally, Lisa started to weep. She wept for the life she had just lost, for the years of loving and trying and never giving up. She cried for the mother she missed, for the father who hadn't loved her, for the sister who hated her, for the family she didn't have. And she vowed never to see Leonard or Nicky or Dad again.

Sixteen

Lisa was getting dressed. *Time to visit Norm. Maybe bring those papers home and go through them here.* She had been so consumed by Ashley that she hadn't had headspace for him, and now she felt bad for leaving it so long.

The sky was overcast and his driveway was a minefield of pits and puddles, but as Lisa jumped out of her truck, she could see that he'd been busy. The yard was freshly swept and there was a stack of cardboard boxes and bits of crates next to a smouldering fire outside the drive shed. The pile of old barrels, bits of machinery, bicycle wheels, and a rusty cast iron pot looked like he was getting ready to take a load of scrap metal to the dump. As Lisa walked toward the house, Norm came around the corner carrying an old muffler. He looked up, saw her, and scowled. "I said I didn't want you here."

"Norm, I know I should have come back sooner, and I'm sorry I pressed you when you weren't well, but—"

"I meant it. Go away."

"Just let me take the documents that were in your kitchen drawer. You don't have to go through them with me. Maybe there's something we can use."

"Are you deaf? I don't want you here. You're just the same as the rest of 'em. Only interested in the effing system and what you can get out of me."

"Come on, that's not fair." Lisa lifted her hands, palms up. "Let's just go in and sit down. I promise not to make you look at any paperwork."

"And you don't need to talk to me like I was three years old." Norm walked over to the pile of scrap metal. "I told you to get going and I meant it."

As he hurled the muffler onto the pile, the jagged clang of steel hitting steel echoed around the yard. Silently, Lisa tried to talk away her fear. *This is Norm, who's been my friend, the closest thing I've had to family, for twenty years.* The problem was she didn't recognize the man in front of her now, and she didn't like him.

He was near shouting. "I'm going to deal with this my way and I don't need any busy bodies hanging around spying on what I'm doing, so for the last time, GO."

Determined not to cry, Lisa watched Norm turn around and walk into the house. Heading back to her truck, she tripped over a coil of wire and scraped her hand on a rusty pole as she steadied herself, the pain of rejection hitting hard. *I'm done. I did what he asked, went to see the building inspector, and that's enough. If Norm doesn't want me, I'm not going to keep trying.*

* * *

"Ashley's not here," Janet called out from the hotel reception desk. "Checked out an hour ago."

Lisa was nonplussed. "Did she say where she was going?"

"No, but I did overhear them talking about Enderby Manor, that old boarding house on the edge of town."

"Them?"

"You know, the gang that's been in for breakfast. I recognized one of them—an ex-student from when I worked at the art school. Never liked her."

Lisa's eyes widened. "Skye Stewart?"

Janet nodded, pulling a face. "The others seemed nice enough. They almost cleared the buffet yesterday and today." She handed Lisa an envelope. "Ashley said it was okay to put their meals on your tab."

Lisa's pulse quickened. *She's teamed up with Skye? And didn't tell me she was leaving the hotel? And assumes I'll pay for everyone's breakfast?* Lisa took a breath, had a quick look at the bill, and handed over her credit card while trying to recall what she knew about Enderby Manor. A vague memory came to her mind, of going to see it years ago, with a view to using it to put up visiting teachers for the summer school. Lisa thought it was too run-down then. "Has the manor been renovated?"

Janet laughed. "A better question would be, how's it still standing? It was boarded up last time I drove by, but there have been some kids living there for the last few weeks and I know the police are keeping an eye on the place."

Now Lisa was annoyed—what if f Ashley *was* taking her for a ride? As Lisa left the hotel, she texted Susan.

* * *

"Great timing," Lisa's friend put her waxed paper cup on the table before sitting down. "I got your text just as I ticked the last thing off my to-do list: grocery store, dry cleaner, library—even popped into City Hall and paid our property taxes before the yellow notice came. Excuse me while I polish my halo." She dug into her bag and took out a pile of flyers. "I was hoping you could distribute these."

"For the film festival?" Lisa took a sip of coffee. "Aren't you a bit late? It starts next week."

"I know, but I've got heaps of them left. Just take a few to make me feel better."

Lisa wriggled in her chair. Heat was happening between her legs. She'd been using the new pessaries for three weeks with no problem. Surely she wouldn't be reacting to them now?

Susan was eying the donuts behind the glass counter. "I'd love an apple cruller. If only God would grant me infinite eating without calories." She turned back to Lisa. "So why did we have to come to Timmies instead of the Copper Bean?"

"I didn't want to be overheard."

Susan sat up straighter.

"I need to talk to someone I trust. I could really do with your take on things."

Her friend leaned forward.

Lisa pressed her knees together, trying to manage the hot itchiness, and told Susan everything: the way Ashley had turned up at her door, how devastating it was to find out that Leonard had slept with her mother, all the things Ashley had told her at the hotel, and how they'd worked in the garden together and ended up looking around the house at his photos.

Both coffees were cold by the time Lisa had finished. Susan slumped back in her chair. "Holy petunias. But I thought Leonard was your soulmate, the only man you ever loved. How could he do that, just when you were getting married?"

"I know. I feel so stupid and ashamed. I was totally in love, and I trusted him. That's why this has been such a wallop—I was sure he felt the same way. When we were younger, when we lived together after university, he was unfaithful." Lisa had told Susan bits and pieces about her life before she came to Canada, but never this. "He slept around and it culminated in an awful incident and when I found out, it nearly killed me. We split up for eight years."

"And then you took him back?"

Lisa's eyes were filling. "When the initial numbness wore off, and I'd worked through the pain, I had some other relationships with good, trustworthy men, but I could never bring myself to commit. Even though Leonard had hurt me so much, somewhere, subconsciously, I was still comparing them to him."

"He must have been something special, to get you that hooked."

"He was—clever, witty, handsome, captivating—too captivating. And then, after all that time apart, he turned up at my door with a huge bunch of bleeding hearts and said he'd changed. I was cautious at first, but in the end I bought every single word."

"Where on earth did he get a bunch of bleeding hearts?"

"He probably just told someone in the art department to get them. By then he was a partner in a big advertising agency." Lisa blew her nose. "I fell for everything he said and then I married the man, moved into his flashy penthouse in a super-trendy part of London. He bought me a little vintage sports car as a wedding present. I thought it was a sign of his love, that I was living my dream, except that's what it was—a dream. Because while I was doing happily ever after, he was screwing the intern."

"Oh honey, I'm so sorry." Susan took Lisa's hand. "I'm amazed you can look at this Ashley person, let alone foot the hotel bill and spend time with her."

Lisa was distracted by the burning between her legs. "It's true, I couldn't stand her at first, but none of this is any more her fault than it is mine."

Susan raised her eyebrows. "You're a much nicer person than I am, and way more trusting."

Lisa moved position, trying not to squirm in her seat. "Ashley's had a really tough time. Her mother got into drugs, which killed her in the end, leaving Ashley completely alone. She was only sixteen and she's been looking out for herself ever since."

"Which is sad, but not a reason to trust her."

"I guess I admire her grit, and I remember what it was like to long for a parent. She never even knew her father and managed to get herself all the way to Canada to find out about him."

"I wonder if that's all she came for." The little crease between Susan's eyes deepened. "Is there any way you can check out her story? Someone back home who could do a little digging?"

Lisa recrossed her legs. "She's definitely Leonard's daughter. She's the image of him and her mannerisms—the way she moves and laughs—they're all him. I think she may also have his brain. She's smart, just never been given any chances."

Susan drained her cup. "All of that may be true, but if I were you, I'd still check her out."

* * *

When Lisa got home, Ashley was sitting on the porch next to a garbage bag with something big in it. There was a shiny Schwinn bike leaning against the steps.

"You don't need to keep paying for that hotel anymore. I've found a place."

Lisa's crotch was on fire. All she wanted to do was to have a shower and ring the doctor. She tried to concentrate on Ashley's flood of words—this exuberant young woman who talked without pausing was new.

"It's kind of a squat. Skye told me about it. Most of the kids there are younger but it's a cool set-up. Huge place, used to be a boarding house, and there's a bar downtown that does live gigs and Patty—she's the owner—says I can clear tables and keep the tip money when they're busy. It's not much, but it's a start. I've been to a few other places, but they told me to come back with a resume. That's a CV, right?"

Lisa nodded. "Does Skye live there as well?"

Ashley shook her head. "She's got a room in a house in town. I thought you had to work in a bank to have a CV. What's mine going to say: cleaner, sandwich-maker, dog-walker, bar work?"

Lisa was imagining cool water running between her legs. She had to get into the shower. "You've decided to stay a while then?"

"Well, that's why I came. To ask if you're okay with it."

Lisa stopped, one foot on the porch step. So, Ashley did care.

"You've got a big life here and I can tell you've worked hard for it. I don't want to screw that up cuz I want us to be—"

Lisa wondered what they were to each other. "Friends?"

Ashley nodded, smiling almost shyly.

Lisa wanted them to be friends too. Not because of Leonard, but because she liked Ashley, and there was something about her aloneness that reminded Lisa of herself. If she'd had a child, would she—

"And I thought maybe I could use your washing machine." Ashley flashed the Leonard smile that still dissolved Lisa's heart. "I bought this sleeping bag in the thrift store but it smells funny."

* * *

Lisa stood in the bath clutching the hand-held shower, spraying cool water until her crotch temperature dropped. As she stepped out of the tub she felt better, but disappointed. Dan or no Dan, it was time to start feeling whole.

When she went downstairs, Ashley was on the kitchen floor playing with Fido. Lisa remembered begging Dad for a puppy but he wouldn't budge. It could have made such a difference in the years after Mum died.

Lisa picked two apples out of the bowl on the table and threw one to Ashley. "Tell me about the bike you've got parked outside."

Ashley sat up and Fido rolled onto his back beside her. "It's kinda funny. There's fuck all in that squat except the broken shit you'd expect, but this one guy Terry—he's really tall and skinny—he's got a laptop and a tablet and this fancy bike. He said I could borrow it cuz he's got a car as well."

No wonder the police were keeping an eye on the place. Lisa hoped Ashley wasn't getting mixed up in anything seedy. "If you're looking for extra cash, I could do with some help around here. My neighbour Norm—he gave you a ride—usually does stuff like cutting grass and stacking wood, but I don't think he's going to have time this summer."

Ashley beamed. "Really? That'd be great except I've never mowed a lawn."

"I've got a ride-on mower. It's fun. And I'll introduce you to the Weedwacker."

"I've no idea what that is, but now I can put professional gardener on my resume."

Ashley was keen to get back to the boarding house and Lisa was pleased to see her and the now-fluffy sleeping bag pedal down the driveway. Lisa wasn't feeling good. Her head was thick and her limbs heavy. She was never unwell, never had headaches, never caught the cold that was going around the office. She resented the thought of wasting an afternoon, but all she wanted was to lie down. As she lowered the sun-shades in the living room, she wondered what was wrong and collapsed onto the couch. *I hope I'm not coming down with something,* she thought, turning over. She just didn't feel right, couldn't get comfortable, and ended up with a cushion between her knees and the throw over her eyes.

She slept heavily, without moving, and when she woke up, she felt part of the sofa, her limbs too weighty to move. Fido's face was inches from her own, giving her his it's-past-my-suppertime stare.

Seventeen

Early for her appointment with Dr. Lau, Lisa stopped at Tim Hortons and recognized the shiny Schwinn bike chained outside. Ashley was sitting in a booth, back to the door, her close crop slightly frayed. Lisa got a coffee and went over. "Want some company?"

Ashley looked like she'd been in a fight.

"Oh dear, what happened?"

"Fucking fuck-pig mosquitoes, that's what happened. Every night I pull the sleeping bag over my head, but it was really hot yesterday and I must have stuck my face out. The whole side of my head's throbbing like I've been punched."

The tough street-smart survivor brought down by bugs. Sympathy suppressed Lisa's smile.

Ashley tucked her backpack beside her, as though for comfort. "I bought some food and stuff with my tip money and it's all gone off cuz there's no fridge. I'm used to dealing with feds searching the place and people nicking my stuff, not flying hypodermics and weather that makes milk stink in less than a day"

"Feds?"

"Yeah, you know, police. And the kids at the boarding house never shut up or go to bed. They're so *young*."

Lisa didn't say what she was thinking. "That eye looks infected, have you put anything on it?"

"Like there's a first aid kit in the bathroom. I've been washing in the loo at Patty's but she's not going to want me working there looking like this."

"I'm on my way to the doctor. Why don't you come with me and see if someone can do something for your eye?"

Ashley slumped back on the vinyl bench. "I haven't got insurance."

"That might not be insurmountable. We're not asking for a proper appointment, just a little TLC."

* * *

The nurse practitioner was leaning in the doorway chatting to the receptionist when they walked in. She offered to have a look at Ashley's eye straight away and just waved her hand at the lack of health card. Lisa went in to see Dr. Lau, who was still wearing pearls.

"So, you're reacting to these pessaries too." Her eyes searched Lisa's face. "How's everything else? You look tired."

Why did sitting in front of a doctor make Lisa feel like a child? She shuffled uncomfortably. "I have been feeling odd, finding it hard to focus and wanting to sleep in the daytime, which I don't usually do. And I did get a bit dizzy when I bent down to feed Fido, my dog, yesterday."

"I'll get the nurse to take your blood pressure and maybe do some blood work, check for anemia, lack of vitamin B, that sort of thing, but it might be worth listening to what your body's trying to tell you. These are symptoms of exhaustion. It sounds like you could do with a good long rest."

"That's impossible. I haven't been doing anything. I mean, I've been doing so much less than before I retired."

"Aah." The doctor looked knowing. "You've recently retired. It could be accumulated exhaustion that's been allowed to surface since you stopped. Or maybe the things you're doing *are* too much for you. Remind me of your age?"

"I'm sixty-one. Old age doesn't come on all-of-a-sudden, does it?"

"No, but exhaustion can. Is it possible that the overload you're experiencing is emotional? Sometimes we don't even realize that things are accumulating, possibly triggering old issues?"

"Maybe," Lisa answered reluctantly.

"If it is emotional, it might help to talk to someone about it, or we could take a look at some anti-anxiety medication?"

Lisa prided herself on her ability to cope, of never needing any kind of therapy. "Thank you, but I'm sure a few days of rest will do the trick."

The doctor turned toward her screen and started scrolling. "As to the topical estrogen, I'm afraid we could be running out of options. The active ingredients are in a base cream and everything I see here uses one of the two creams you've already tried."

It was a week since Lisa had stopped using the second brand of pessaries and she had only just stopped itching. She wasn't sure she wanted to put herself through another round of torture. "Are these pessaries really my only option?"

The doctor spun around on her stool. "I know a couple of women who have used a vaginal dilator, but that's not something I would recommend. You could try non-hormonal moisturizers, sold over-the-counter, designed to replenish the vaginal wall, but I don't think they're going to make the difference you're hoping for. There are rings and sponges, but judging by your sensitivity, I think you may have an even bigger reaction to those." Dr. Lau tilted her head, looked apologetic. "It's hard to generalize because this condition seems to vary for everyone. Some women are all-round dry, others produce natural vaginal secretion but it lacks the viscosity to prevent discomfort, and some experience pain on penetration even with adequate lubrication."

Lisa squeezed her hands together, not wanting to hear any more.

"And then there's the psychology. Once a woman has experienced pain during intercourse, it's hard for her body to relax. She tends to tense the next time and that makes matters worse." Dr. Lau looked genuinely sorry. "I can also say, from listening to other patients, it seems the atrophy can be more severe if you've had a long interval without penetrative sex."

Lisa felt bleak and glad that Dan was away. This was going to need more sorting out than she'd anticipated. "Will my condition get worse, or will it stay the way it is now?"

"I'm afraid that's another thing that varies from woman to woman. I have a patient who refuses PAP tests because her vagina has shrunk so much that inserting the speculum is too painful. Others haven't found it progressive at all. There are many factors to take into account, but I would say that stress could be the greatest. Finding ways to relax does seem key."

Lisa rubbed her eyes. "There's nothing else I can try?"

"You could investigate alternative treatments, though I haven't heard of any very positive results. Why don't you leave it with me for a few days? Maybe there are some new types of topical estrogen I don't know about. I'll phone my colleague in Toronto, see if she knows of anything I don't."

"Thank you, I'd appreciate that." Lisa was surprised by how emotional she felt. Suddenly the room was too small.

Ashley was in reception looking much happier. The nurse had cleaned her eye and told her what to get from the pharmacy if it continued to swell.

"I'll give you a lift back to Enderby Manor." Lisa led the way to the pickup and they loaded the bike into the back.

Driving through town, Ashley recounted every detail of her time with the nurse and held up a small plastic tube. "And she slipped this into my pocket as I was leaving, said it would help if I get more bites. Then the receptionist got me some water and was asking all about England. They were both so kind, I can't believe how nice they were."

"Welcome to Canada. Haven't you heard the jokes about Canadians being so nice they're boring?"

Ashley laughed, then talked into her lap. "I reckon I could do with a bit more boring."

As they pulled up outside the boarding house Lisa gasped. The place was beyond derelict. Piles of garbage were seeping onto the front yard, even the boards over the windows were broken and falling off. Her nose filled with the smell of decay as she turned to Ashley. "Why don't you get your stuff and come and stay with me?"

* * *

Ashley was settling into the guest room and Lisa was on the couch, wishing she didn't have to go to the opening night of the Colville Film Festival, when her phone pinged a message from Susan: Emergency, please phone.

Grant answered. "She's really sick. She had a slight cold yesterday and woke up today with laryngitis. No voice at all."

"Oh dear." Lisa hoped this meant she didn't have to go to the opening. "Has she seen the doctor?"

"We picked up some medication on the way back from the Health Centre, but she has to rest her voice. That's why she messaged. Susan wants you to open the festival and introduce tonight's movie. She's typed up everything you need to say and going to email it."

Lisa didn't stop to consider. "I'm sorry but she'll have to find someone else. I'm not feeling too good myself and I've got a guest staying. Tell her it's Ashley and she'll understand."

A shuffling noise came down the phone and Lisa heard something raspy, like the air being let out of a tire, then a vicious cough followed by Grant's voice again. "Susan really can't talk. She's just scribbling what she wants me to tell you: Please, please, you HAVE to. Have is in capital letters and underlined. Here she goes, there's more. Creative Director great at finding films but can't make speech. Tech guy will be busy doing tech."

Lisa really didn't feel up to doing this, even for Susan. But over the years she had always been there for Lisa, from the moment she stepped off the plane and Susan had invited her to stay until she found her own place, through to the surprise sixtieth birthday party she'd thrown for Lisa last year. "How long is the speech?"

"Susan's holding up her laptop, it doesn't look like too much. She's emailing it, and now she's scribbling again. More capitals: THANK YOU SO MUCH. And a big row of kisses."

* * *

It felt weird leaving Ashley alone in the house, but as soon as she arrived at the library, Lisa forgot about her. Melinda, the creative director, was waiting by the front door and it was instantly obvious why she couldn't introduce the festival—she spoke very quietly and only to her shoes. Lisa had to bend down to hear what she was saying. It sounded like, "Thank you for standing on my Botox." It might have been, "stepping in at short notice." Melinda kept talking as they walked down the library stairs to the basement and Lisa just nodded, hoping that nothing needed a reply. As they made their way toward the community room, the dry smell of books was replaced by the welcome aroma of wine, and when Melinda mumbled next, Lisa prayed she was offering her a glass.

Most of the audience were already sitting on the moulded plastic chairs that were set out in lines. Lisa nodded and smiled; she knew quite a few of them. When she looked to the back of the room, the young man fiddling with his laptop pointed to his watch and held up three fingers. It was almost time to make her speech. She took a mouthful of Cabernet Sauvignon.

The lights went off, except the ones above Lisa's head, and she unfolded her print-out of Susan's speech. Looking up, she counted seven rows of ten chairs, seventy people, one hundred and forty eyes. She'd better start by explaining why she wasn't Susan. "I'm afraid I am not one of the people who have worked long and hard to put together this year's festival, and it's the director, Susan Shewan, who should be standing here now, but she's home with laryngitis and has asked me to be her voice."

After thanking the sponsors, staff, and volunteers, and giving a round-up of the movies that were going to be shown over the next ten days, Lisa introduced the film. "This year opens with a real favourite, starring Meryl Streep and Laura Dern, as well as lots of other familiar faces. *Little Women* brings Louisa May Alcott's novel to life like never before in a respectful but bracingly current version which I believe—" she looked up at the tech guy and he gave a thumbs-up, "is ready to roll."

The lights dimmed and Lisa retreated gratefully to her seat. As she leaned back and slipped off her shoes, she found that the film was exactly what she needed. She loved the characters and costumes as the perfect world of the March family unfolded. She hadn't really relaxed since that first fateful night with Dan.

By the time Amy declared "you love him" to her sister, Lisa had almost forgotten that she had to get up and address the audience again. She felt dizzy when she bent to hunt under the seat for her shoes. Applause filled the room as she searched Susan's script for her closing comments, but the words were hard to make out. "Tomorrow's movie is something completely different. An environmental documentary." All Lisa could think of was that gorgeous family chirping together like chickadees and how miserable she'd been at home. "Produced and narrated by Leonardo DiCaprio." Meg, Amy, Beth, and Jo, all full of joy and quirky energy, all loving and forgiving each other. To Lisa's horror, big fat tears started to plop onto the page, making puddly circles around the words. *"Ice on Fire* explores the possibility of an extinction-level event caused by arctic methane release." The letters were fading in and out. She tried to focus on the lines, but she faltered as the words in her brain blurred with the ones on the page. "And in the end, they all found lovely men who didn't do hook-ups or screw the intern." Lisa looked up and a hundred and forty eyes were staring back, all wider than they should be. Had she just said that out loud?

Eighteen

Lisa heard a mug land on the night table beside her. Eyes still closed, she breathed in the smell of freshly made tea and remembered how she used to love mornings at home, the quiet calm before Nicky was up and Dad got back from his night shift. Lisa would fill the brown teapot and let it brew as she nibbled her way through a slice of Marmite on toast, and just before setting off to get the bus to school, she'd take a cup upstairs and leave it by her sister's bed.

Opening her eyes, Lisa looked past the steaming mug and saw Ashley. "I dunno what happened last night, but your phone's been vibrating like a nun's knickers. I turned off the ringer so it wouldn't wake you up. People have been coming with food and there's a woman downstairs who can't talk but *has* to see you. Apparently it was her husband who brought you home."

Lisa flashed back to opening her eyes and slowly focusing on a sea of concerned faces. She must have fainted. Her next clear memory was sobbing in the front seat of Grant's Jeep. Sobbing up things that had been gripped in her belly for years. Sobbing so hard she gasped for breath and couldn't stop.

"Loads of people have been round. So far you've got two pots of stew—both veggie, a tin of dodgy looking biscuits, and a bag of muffins which, by the way, are delicious."

"Oh God, that's what they do here when someone dies. They bring casseroles. I made such an idiot of myself last night, I'll never be able to go out again."

"No one's said anything about you being an idiot. Or dead." Ashley opened the curtains. "Most of 'em said stuff about hoping you feel better soon, like they cared. I don't know anyone who'd bring me a four-course meal if I was on the verge of a nervo."

"Is that what they told you?" Lisa leaned up on one elbow.

"Not exactly, but it didn't take much to work it out." Ashley chuckled. "They looked a bit scared when they saw me." Her eye was less swollen, but she was still distorted.

"What did you tell them?"

"That I was a friend visiting from England."

"I meant about your eye."

"Two huge men jumped me and I put them both in hospital."

Lisa laughed and sat up, still wearing the white linen shirt she'd put on for the festival, now scrunched. Out of the window, the sun was high and further west of where it should be when she woke up. "What time is it?"

"Just after two. The woman in the kitchen, the one who can't talk, is desperate to see you. She's got a big blue book and a Sharpie and scrawls stuff faster than I can read. I told her I'd see if you were awake."

"Of course, Susan. It was meant to be her in front of the crowd last night. Someone must have phoned her, and she sent Grant to come and drive me home. Would you mind asking her to come up?"

Ashley opened the bedroom door and yelled, "She's awake, you can see her now," then came back and settled in the little armchair by the window. Fido's nails clattered on the wooden stairs as he ran and launched onto the bed. "He's been desperate to get up here too, but I thought we should let you sleep it off."

Bizarrely, Lisa felt great—rested, with a clearer head than she'd had for days.

Susan steamed in with a glass of water and a bottle of pills, notebook tucked under her arm, Sharpie behind her ear. She looked like a nurse in an old war movie, but when she sat on the side of the bed, Lisa noticed the grey under her eyes. She put her hand on her friend's arm. "You shouldn't have come, you're not well yourself."

Susan scribbled: I brought Diazepam. How are you? What happened? Then she turned and fixed Ashley with a steady gaze.

Ashley stood up. "I suppose this is the bit where I remember something I'm meant to be doing downstairs and leave you two alone."

As she left the room, Lisa turned back to Susan. "I'm fine and I definitely don't need sedating. I think I was just exhausted." She remembered Dr. Lau's concern. "And possibly suffering from a bit of emotional overload."

More scribble: But isn't she the reason for the overload? What's she doing here?

Instantly defensive, Lisa reminded herself that Susan was only trying to help. "I invited her to stay because she was living in that dreadful derelict boarding house on the edge of town. It's fine, really. I like her. She's going to help me with some chores around the place."

Susan's Sharpie exploded onto the page: Are you crazy? What do you know about her?

"I know she didn't ask to be in this situation any more than I did. She wants to find out about her father, that's all. And she's always lived in London. I think it might do her good to be here for a while. Good for both of us."

Susan started coughing and her whole face went red.

"You're the one who should be in bed, not me. Please don't worry. I promise I'll rest and Ashley isn't an issue. The fantasy that was Leonard is over. Nothing about him can hurt me again."

* * *

When Susan left, Lisa pushed off the duvet and stretched into the warm day, then had a shower. She washed her hair, scrubbed her skin, and felt fantastic as she walked out into the corridor. The guest room door was shut with some kind of electronic dance music coming from inside, so she went downstairs to get her phone and found it vibrating on the kitchen table: *Caitlin Jeffrey, Colville School of the Arts.*

Surely she can't be calling about last night. Lisa was about to press *decline* but something made her slide the flashing icon to *accept.*

"Hi, it's Caitlin. How are you?"

"I've had a good long sleep and I'm feeling much better, thanks." Lisa was going to have to work out what to say to people about last night.

"Oh, I'm sorry, have you been unwell?"

So she doesn't know. Lisa fabricated a reply about being over-tired.

"This doesn't sound like a good time, but I'm desperate. I'm ringing to ask for your help."

Lisa smiled.

"Our technician, Dominique, is pregnant and just been told to take bed rest and Carlos, on reception, has mono. I've made a few calls, but no one's free at such short notice. I wonder if you can think of anyone who might be able to come in and help out?"

Now Lisa grinned. "I might have just the right person. She's a friend, recently arrived in Colville."

Caitlin wanted to meet Ashley as soon as possible. "Do you think she could come in at the end of the afternoon today?"

"The problem is, she's had a fight with a mosquito recently and got a bad bite on her eyelid. She looks a little swollen."

"Don't worry about that, I'm sure I've seen worse. This afternoon would be great. I'm taking a few days vacation soon, trying to have a break before summer school starts."

Lisa knocked but the music was too loud for Ashley to hear, so she opened the guest room door and peeked in. The love seat was pushed up against the wall, the bed was under the window where the desk had been, and on the floor was a small cylindrical speaker. Ashley was dancing, her body fluid, each roll a sensual wave. Her arms flowed freely as she twirled, stopped and twirled again. When she saw Lisa, she turned down the music. "I moved stuff around. Hope that's okay."

The room felt bigger, more spacious. "Absolutely, but ..."

Ashley's eyes followed Lisa's to a blank spot on the wall. "The picture's in the wardrobe. I found it depressing."

Lisa laughed. "So did I. That's why it's tucked away in here." The painting had been part of her retirement present: a slightly gloomy still life by a student who'd gone on to show in high-end galleries. "I've just had a call from the principal of the art school where I used to work. She's got two staff members signed off sick and wondered if I knew anyone who could help out. I thought of you."

"Really? A proper job in an art school?" Ashley's face transformed.

"It's not really a job, more of a temporary thing, and we'll have to find a way around you not having a work visa. She's asked us to go in this afternoon."

Ashley caught sight of herself in the mirror. "I can't go like this. Tell her I'll come next week when I don't look like an ugly goblin."

"She's going away. I'm afraid it has to be today, but don't worry about your eye, I already explained on the phone."

Ashley scowled into the mirror.

Lisa used her confident people-managing voice. "It'll be fine. You get changed and I'll make us both a sandwich."

* * *

As they drove onto the campus, Lisa imagined seeing the art school through Ashley's eyes. The grass was lush green and newly mowed, the steel roof washed clean by recent rain, the windows gleaming.

"It's a bit barren." Ashley sounded disappointed. "I thought there'd be loads of arty stuff and students all over the place."

Of course, she wants people, not a beautiful building. "The summer students start in a couple of weeks. That's probably why the principal wants you here in a hurry, so you can settle in and be ready to help when they arrive."

Lisa watched Caitlin take in every detail of Ashley. The tiny top, calf-length leggings and leather tunic, looked like an outfit she'd put together for going to art school—in London. In this office, overlooking trees and a lake, she was someone who'd stepped into the wrong movie. The huge retro shades didn't help. Lisa wished she'd helped Ashley pick an outfit.

As she leaned forward to shake Caitlin's hand, Lisa took a chair to the side, leaving them face to face, but whispered to Ashley to take off her sunglasses. Ashley's expression grew surly, so Lisa tried to lighten the atmosphere. "This is the young friend I was telling you about, who's spending the summer with me. It's her first time in Canada."

Nodding, Caitlin asked Ashley if she had brought her resume.

Ashley looked like she might giggle so Lisa intervened. "She's never worked in this kind of environment before, but is keen to learn how the school functions, and she's used to dealing with people."

"Bar work, mainly. I'm pretty good at figuring stuff out and most folk I work for want me to come back."

Caitlin's face was unreadable. "Do you have any experience of the arts, of drawing or painting yourself? We've got a woodworking studio, pottery facilities, and a new metal space."

Lisa leaned forward. "I think it's more about transferable skills."

Ashley cut in. "My mum worked in a modelling agency so I'm used to being around photographers and models and photo shoots. And I'm assuming you'll be wanting me to clean up the paint, or order it or something, not use it myself."

Caitlin smiled. "You're right. The things we'll be asking you to do aren't rocket science and we are very short-handed." She glanced at the calendar on her desk. "How about we start with a trial week? See how you fit in?"

Ashley raised her eyebrows. "No pressure there then, but—if it doesn't kill you, an' all that."

As Caitlin started to talk about money, Lisa interrupted again. "I'm afraid we're going to have to find a way around Ashley's lack of a work permit. Maybe pay her for the first week out of petty cash? If everything works out, I'll have a word with the board about a way the money could come via me."

Caitlin looked concerned.

Lisa leaned forward and talked to her quietly. "Trust me, there really is nothing to worry about. I don't think you'll be disappointed if you take a risk on this young woman, and I know a way we can sort out the finances."

Caitlin paused and then replied to Lisa. "Actually, this is a life saver. I really need a few days off, and if you can find a way to make this work, I'd be truly grateful."

* * *

On the drive home Lisa felt triumphant but Ashley hardly spoke. When they arrived, she shot out of the truck and thundered into the house.

Lisa was confused. "That went well, don't you think?" They were both in the kitchen.

"You are NOT my fucking mother," Ashley yelled.

"I know, I just—"

"You talked about me like I wasn't there and answered for me and made me look stupid."

Lisa filled with shame. *Yes, I did. I slipped into person-in-charge-managing-the-situation, even used my principal's voice.* "You're right. I was—"

"I know how to take care of myself and I could've got that job without you. I don't know why you even came in with me. Except I do. To make sure I didn't embarrass you, say the wrong thing in front of your precious colleague."

Ashley stomped upstairs. Lisa stared out of the window, regretting every word. She considered following Ashley to apologize, but instead, she called Fido and changed into her hiking boots.

It was dusk and Lisa was tired when she got home, having walked the long trail that went behind Norm's house to the water's edge before coming back along the lane. She went straight upstairs but Ashley's door was open and she wasn't in her room. Lisa couldn't find her downstairs either. Guessing she'd gone out, Lisa noticed how muddy Fido's bed was, so scooped it up to wash.

The basement light was already on. She piled the dog's bed into the machine and walked to the far end of the room, past the hanging rail, towards her secret refuge. The place she went to be alone and process, with scissors and glue and walls covered in cut-out pictures.

Ashley looked up. "This is off the roof. It's fantastic. How long have you been doing it?"

Lisa felt invaded, exposed. No one had ever been down here and now Ashley was sitting in her chair.

"You look weird. Oh, I'm sorry about earlier, I shouldn't have lost it like that. My bad. I was a bit freaked out by the whole thing. You were only trying to help."

Lisa was the one who should be apologizing. She had the whole speech planned in her head, but right now all she could think about was how to get them both out of the basement. "Could we—"

"Yeah, that's just what I was going to say. Let's do some together, or if you don't want me to stick on any pictures, I could just cut out the ones you choose."

Lisa hovered by the side of the table. *But this is my private place. How am I going to manage a whole summer with her the house and maintain any kind of control over my life?*

"Oh, and I forgot to give you this." Ashley had changed into jeans and a T-shirt. She reached into her back pocket and pulled out a postcard. "I got it out the mailbox. Looks like Mr. Tricky's in Manitoba, wherever that is."

Nineteen

July 1ˢᵗ, Canada Day. Lisa hoped her postcard had arrived in time. She'd found it a couple of weeks ago in a funny little gift shop in Redstock—a picture of a baby goat nibbling the red maple leaf out of the middle of a flag. Looking for silly, retro, or beautiful cards was Lisa's new hobby. She had quite a collection of them in the top drawer of her dresser, next to the pile she'd received from Dan.

His first was a hand-tinted photo of a building with four Corinthian columns supporting the words University of Manitoba carved in stone. It arrived a week after he came to say goodbye.

Made it! The campus is so huge I keep getting lost but the old buildings are beautiful. So great to see Anna. Turns out she's been in touch with her mum for months. They've even met up twice. Anna didn't tell me because she didn't want _me_ to feel hurt! I guess you were right, she is old enough to look out for herself. My two-day training starts on Monday. xxxx

Four kisses. Lisa had read the card so often that its corners were creased and soft. In the two months he'd been away, Dan had sent nine and she almost knew them by heart. She'd replied to the first with a photo of old Colville, in an envelope addressed c/o the Department of Environmental Studies. She'd used an envelope for privacy—the entire university didn't need to know what she had to say. Dan had sounded satisfyingly pleased to get it and written back on a card showing an old pavilion overlooking a river.

Your card arrived yesterday. Love it. I'd forgotten how nice it is to read handwriting, how much closer it makes you feel, so can we stick to snail mail? I've copied your idea and put my card in an envelope to give me more space to write. The place in the picture is now a fancy restaurant where I had supper with Anna and Gavin (her guy). He's impressive, coaches the university rowing team and he paid for the whole meal. Thought that seeing them so in love might make me lonely, but quite the opposite. Their energy is infectious. Puts me in the mood myself. xxxx

That last sentence made Lisa flutter like a fourteen-year-old as she wrote her reply.

I know what you mean. Feeling the early summer sun on my skin, having more free time on my hands, being around my twenty-year-old house guest, all make me feel new and different, like anything's possible.

Over the course of their correspondence, which sometimes stretched onto paper as well as a postcard, Lisa had told Dan about Ashley. At first he'd replied with shock and sympathy, and like Susan, surprise that Lisa had "taken the girl under her wing so quickly." But now he would ask after her, and on one card, even told Lisa to send Ashley his love. More recently, Lisa had written about how well Ashley's job was going at the art school, how much fun they had sampling Leonard's "ancient vinyl" and taking turns to make supper.

Ashley's cooking has made meals much less predictable. So far we've had pasta with licorice sauce, carrot risotto with olives, and oven fries topped with peanut butter (weirdly good). When it comes to movie nights, our tastes have converged in *Pulp Fiction* and *Thelma and Louise*, but little else. I got Ashley to watch a couple of my black and white favs—*All About Eve* and *12 Angry Men*, and in return we are working our way through the entire series of *Shaft*. She found a boxed set in her favourite hang out, the thrift store.

Sometimes Dan's cards were short, like the one showing a beautiful sunset over a beach in St Malo Provincial Park.

A bunch of us came for a weekend camping but it rained so hard we nearly drowned. In the end we all squeezed into Julie's cottage instead (she's Anna's supervisor). Had a blast. Haven't played Clue for years. xxx

But Lisa's favourite card was the one where Dan said he was missing home.

A gruelling three weeks on the road collecting samples. Rain and more rain. Ground sheet leaks, sleeping bag still hasn't dried out. Now I know why the other field researchers are 30 years younger. Missing my bed, the bees, my friends. xx

Bicycle tires crunched up the gravel driveway and Lisa looked out of the bedroom window. Ashley's tight crop was growing into an Afro, and under her young friend's supervision, Lisa's hair was shorter with bangs. Looking forward to their evening together, she went downstairs to check on the progress of the baked potatoes. They'd planned a quick supper before heading into town for the Canada Day display.

"I know we said we'd go and see the fireworks," Ashley kicked off her sneakers by the back door. "But there's a party at one of the student summer rentals tonight."

Lisa masked her disappointment. "That sounds fun. Don't worry about me. I can always go with Susan and Grant."

"Skye's coming to pick me up, but I'm going to put my bike in the back of her car, in case I need to cut. I don't want to depend on her for a lift home."

A wise decision, Lisa thought, her stomach sinking at the idea of Skye coming to her home, but she looked up at Ashley with a smile. "You'd better run up and get dressed, so you're ready when she arrives."

As soon as the shower started, Fido barked and Lisa watched Skye get out of a beaten-up Sunfire. She heard Skye's boots on the step and then the door shoved open as her ex-student came in with a sense of purpose that Lisa didn't like. Her dirty blonde hair was pulled tight into two knots on either side of her head, and she was wearing too much makeup.

"Hello Skye."

Skye nodded. "Lisa."

Lisa had never heard Skye use her first name and it didn't land well. "Ashley's upstairs getting ready."

Skye pulled out a chair and sat down with the confidence of someone who knows she's going to get what she wants. "Good. I was hoping we could have a private chat."

Lisa recognized the calculated curl of the young woman's lip.

"I need another reference—a better one this time—and I need it quick. The closing date's on Tuesday and this job's the only way I'm ever gonna get out of this going nowhere town."

How is be happening all over again? Lisa shook her head, "I don't even work at the art school anymore."

"So? You can still do it. You were running the place when I was a student, weren't you?"

As she considered her options, the Skye dread that had been building in Lisa's gut turned to resolve. She walked over to the table and sat down, looking directly into the self-assured eyes across from hers. "You need to listen to me. You've had your reference and now it's done. No more."

"And you need to listen to me. You're not the one calling the shots here. That reference didn't work. I never got through the probation and now I'm stuck back in Colville again, telling friggin' kids about friggin' bees. This new job's perfect. It's in Toronto, it comes with accommodation, I've already chatted with them on the phone and I know I've got a good chance of getting it."

Lisa almost laughed at the audacity. The reference didn't work because Skye didn't make it through the probation period! Lisa changed tack, decided to sound helpful. "Why don't you ask someone from the Beekeepers Association for a reference, since they're your latest employer?"

Ashley's voice called down the stairs. "Sorry to make you wait, I'll be down in a minute."

"No worries." Skye sounded light and breezy. "We're having a nice visit." She turned back to Lisa. "The bee job doesn't count. It's crap and too part time and anyway, I've fallen out with ... Dan doesn't know about it yet, but—" Her eyes narrowed. "I bet you haven't told *him* about your little cover-up at the art school. I wonder what he'd say if he knew you'd lied and cheated and hid missing funds."

Lisa imagined explaining to Dan. She knew he'd understand, but she didn't want to go there, and she certainly didn't want this getting back to Caitlin or the board. Lisa needed to stay calm, try to think of a way out that didn't involve writing another reference. As she heard Ashley's footsteps on the upstairs landing, she had an idea. "Why don't you just re-use the reference I wrote you before? Change the date and no one will know any better."

Skye looked suspicious. "But how can I? It went straight from you to my employers?"

"Phone the art school and ask for a copy. Say you can't get a reference from the new principal, as she doesn't know you, but you need it to attach to a more recent application."

"And if it doesn't work?"

"Let me know and I'll see what I can do."

Ashley bounced into the kitchen, wearing a flouncy dress over leggings and her Doc Martens boots. Lisa stroked Fido, feeling both relieved and shaky, while the young women worked out whether to go to the pub for a drink or straight to the party. She had no idea what would happen when Skye phoned the art school, but at least she'd managed to buy herself breathing space.

* * *

The hall light was still on when Lisa woke up and she felt a nudge of nerves. She always left it on when Ashley was out, and Ashley would turn it off when she came in. She never forgot. Lisa checked her room. It was fuller every time she looked in, with thrift store treasures: endless clothes, kitsch china ornaments, an embroidered "Home Sweet Home" cushion, all kinds of books, and a road sign that probably didn't come from any store at all. The bed was neatly made. Ashley had never stayed out all night before, but Lisa hesitated to phone or text. Since the "you are not my mother" episode, she was scrupulous about boundaries. The weather forecast promised 28°C by noon and Lisa wanted to get some work done outside before it got too hot. Although it was meant to be Ashley's job, she hadn't had much time for cutting grass, so Lisa made a quick coffee and went into the yard.

She loved the ride-on mower, the way the chunky little wheels glued her to the ground. The small steering wheel and tight turning circle took her straight back to the bumper cars at St. Giles. The fair came to Oxford every September and Dad always took her and Nicky, even though her sister was "too old really." It was one of the precious times when they all had fun together and Lisa's joy was when Dad came on a ride too.

"Hold tight," he'd say, as the Zipper started to swing.

"Eeeeeeee Noooooooooo." Lisa's fingers clutched his jacket. His arm was on the back of the seat, his hand on her shoulder. She felt like she belonged, like they belonged to each other. That was so long ago.

It was lunchtime when Ashley arrived back. Lisa was cooling off in the shade on the front porch, next to a pitcher of iced water. "Get a glass and join me. There's a tiny bit of breeze here."

Ashley produced a can of Sprite from her rucksack and sat down. She pulled the tab slowly to stop it spraying, making it sound like a hissing snake. "This heat is unreal. I should have set off earlier."

"Good party?"

"Bit shit, didn't stay long. Ended up back at the squat with Terry, who now has a bug net over his bed."

"Is Terry a name I should know?"

"He's the one that leant me the bike. Turns out his family lives in town and they're loaded. That's why he's got so much gear. What a joke. Who'd choose to live like that if they didn't have to?"

"So, what's he like?"

"He's got a surprisingly large penis for someone so skinny."

Lisa nearly spat the water she was about to swallow, but she loved that Ashley was talking to her like a friend. A real friend. "Does this mean you're going to see him again? Could he be boyfriend material?"

"I don't really do boyfriends. Anyway, it might be big, but he's clueless about how to use it. When he was done, I asked him to finish me off and I practically had to draw him a diagram. I kept telling him, clockwise. How hard is that to remember?"

Lisa couldn't imagine being so blunt when she was Ashley's age—or now. "I'm impressed. I've never even been able to flirt, let alone explain what I need in that kind of detail."

"Oh, I don't flirt, I just tell them what I want, though with some guys it's a waste of time. Of course, women always do it better, but I just can't get into them. What about you? Don't tell me Leonard was the only one?"

"Remember, we split up for eight years, when I was in my thirties. And I did have one boyfriend before I met Leonard. He was my first, in a very guy-next-door kind of way."

"And now? What about Mr. Tricky?"

"He's away for the summer. If I'm honest, Dan's the first man I've been seriously attracted to since Leonard, and it *is* complicated."

"He's married then."

"No, nothing like that. Actually, the problems are at my end." Lisa wanted to be honest, to share the way Ashley had, but could she tell this glowing young woman that one day she might be atrophied too?

"You're probably better off on your own. I reckon sex is like everything—the best way to get it done properly is to do it yourself."

Lisa smiled, trying to remember the last time she'd done it herself. For a while, she used to masturbate to get to sleep, but that was years ago, and since then she'd hardly bothered.

Ashley stood up. "I'm going to have a wash and a nap, then I've got to get to Patty's. I'm working tonight."

A few minutes later, Lisa heard the shower spray. She envied the way Ashley was so open about her needs. Lisa tried to imagine telling Dan that she was atrophied, and how he might respond, and found herself thinking about Leonard instead. They'd been living together for two years before she had her first fully blown orgasm, and that was more down to him than to her.

He had just been promoted, again, and booked a weekend away in the Cotswolds to celebrate. It was the most luxurious place Lisa had ever stayed. The weather was amazingly hot for May and she had splashed out on a new sundress—red with white polka dots and buttons down the front.

Leonard had bought a soft-top Triumph Vitesse. The roof was down as they drove through manicured farmland and picturesque English villages, built with honey-coloured stone. "No wonder it's where all the nobs and politicos live." He reached over and rested his hand on her thigh. "Let's buy a cottage here when I make partner."

Lisa went warm. This was the first time he'd talked about them in the long-term and somewhere, deep within her, something unfurled.

The Parson's was a seventeenth-century coaching inn set in acres of beautiful gardens and woodland walks. After leaving their bags in the room, they went straight to the bar for lunch and shared a cheese platter and a bottle of wine. Afterwards, they decided to explore the hotel grounds.

The trees were heavy with blossom as they walked past clumps of exotic looking peonies, toward a blaze of azaleas and rhododendrons. The grass smelled freshly mown. Almost buried in the bushes to their right was a faded gold finger cut out of wood: To the Rose Garden. They followed the gravel path. Of course, it was too early for the roses to be in flower, but the little hedged-in space was sun-filled and secluded. Lisa leaned back on the warm stone bench, legs outstretched, and shut her eyes.

The sun's heat on her skin was soporific and just as she was starting to doze, she felt Leonard part her thighs. He was kneeling in front of her. He lifted her dress and used one hand to pull aside her panties. Holding her open with the other, he began to lick. It was wonderful. As he moved his hands to spread her farther, every bit of Lisa focused on the sensations swelling her. Languid and excited at the same time, she kept completely still until slowly, something new. Her hands tightened, her head filled with the sound of white light. *This is it.* The orgasm exploded from between her legs into her belly and then every bit of her body. Her back arched, she heard a deep groan, and collapsed back into the bench.

The voices seemed distant, as though they were a long way off, until Lisa grasped they must be on the other side of the hedge. Sitting up with a jolt, she almost did Leonard damage as she snapped her legs together and buttoned her dress. He rolled onto his back on the grass chuckling, and they were both laughing hysterically by the time the two women came through the gate.

Twenty

"I don't know why you're so obsessed with getting me in water." Ashley was always grumpy when she got up early.

"But it's summer and you're in the land of lakes, and I'm taking you to one of my favourite places in the world." Lisa had been looking forward to going to Sleeman Creek all week. She'd been there with Norm years ago and it had been her secret swimming place ever since. Norm. Had she'd taken the easy route by walking away? But then she remembered him yelling her out of the house. She'd had enough rejection in her life; she didn't need to invite more.

"An hour and a half seems like a bloody long way to drive for a swim." Ashley tugged at her seatbelt. "Especially when I probably won't go in."

"People come from all over the world to plunge into Canadian lakes, I don't get why you wouldn't want to. Anyway, didn't you tell me you won a prize at school for swimming?"

"I only swam fast so I could be first out of the fucking pool. I told you, I hate cold water and I look stupid in a swimsuit."

"Well it's August now, so it won't be cold, and I promise there won't be anyone to see you. We'll be at Timmies in ten minutes."

Ashley perked up. Since she'd discovered iced capps they could barely drive past a Tim Hortons without stopping. She saw the sign. "Mmmm, 18% cream and loads of sugar. Let's have a donut too, deep fried and plunged in syrup." Taking her phone out of her rucksack, "I made an Aretha mix. Mind if I put her on?"

"That sounds like Leonard music. Has his vinyl finally penetrated your soul?"

"Ha bloody ha."

As Aretha sang about feeling like a natural woman, Ashley slurped her iced capp and put her feet on the dashboard. They made their way north until the tarmac gave way to a dirt road that looked like it could only lead to old farms and barns. When Lisa could smell pine and hear gurgling on the other side of the woods, she pulled over.

"This is it?" Ashley frowned at the scrubby brush and trees ahead.

Lisa took her basket off the back seat. "Prepare to be amazed."

Half a kilometre down a dusty path, they came to a clearing filled with light sparkling off water. They were on a huge chunk of pink granite, next to a stream tumbling over rocks into a small, almost turquoise lake. The sun was high in a perfect cyan sky.

Ashley smiled. "Okay, this place is pretty special."

"We can jump in from here or climb down the rocks to an old jetty on the other side."

"I'll take the jetty."

Lisa was already wearing her swimsuit, so took off her skirt and T-shirt and spread her towel. Ashley, in vest and shorts, sat with her feet dangling over the side of the dock. Still slim, she'd filled out and looked stronger, healthier.

"If my mates in London could see me now. Terry keeps stalking me. Maybe I should marry him and stay forever."

They both kept clear of talking about what might happen when Ashley's job at the summer school ended. Lisa could hardly stand to think about it. "Even if you could put up with Terry, I'm not sure it's that simple."

"Only joking." Ashley made thoughtful circles under water with her feet, watching the ripples move away and gradually disappear. Lisa was just settling onto her towel when—

"I DON'T BLOODY BELIEVE IT." Arms and legs flailing, Ashley almost tumbled into the lake but managed to leap to her feet instead. "That can't be real."

Two huge black and grey legs appeared over the edge of the jetty, followed by six more and a big round body. As big as a plate, it was the largest Lisa had ever seen, but she kept her voice calm. "It's a dock spider. Don't worry, they don't often bite humans."

Ashley was hopping from one foot to another. "I'm not sticking around to find out. Where to now?"

Lisa stood up and held out her hand. "How about a running jump?"

Ashley didn't take her eyes off the spider. "Can they swim?"

"Come on. We'll be safer in the water."

Ashley ran toward her, grabbed Lisa's hand, and pulled her into the air. Feet first, they slid into the cool deepness. Letting themselves sink, they hit the bottom and bounced up again, still holding hands.

Lisa let go and lay back floating. "Isn't this the best?"

"It's fucking freezing." Ashley snorted. "I can't believe I just did that."

Lisa looked across the clear clean water. "I'm going to swim around a bit."

"Don't leave me." Ashley caught her up and as they swam, Lisa looked at the huge cedars and boulders, and saw an osprey overhead. This place was her heaven. After another lap of the tiny lake, she led the way back to shore and they climbed onto some rocks.

"I'll go and get our stuff." Lisa set off for the jetty. "So you don't have to face the monster." Once back, she took a can of Sprite from the basket and handed it to Ashley, found a Perrier for herself, and opened a Tupperware full of mini-iced donuts. They sat silently, watching the unmoving water, listening to the quiet, until the shade caught up with them.

When it was time to leave, Ashley jumped up. "Let's drive back a different way and stop somewhere you've never been."

"Deal," Lisa said, putting her key in the ignition.

* * *

The Pig's Ear would not have been Lisa's choice, but Ashley said it looked like something in a road movie, so they turned off Highway 62 and their little white truck felt very girlie as they parked beside two Big Horn Dodge Rams.

Coming in from bright sunshine, the cavernous bar was dark, but as Lisa's eyes acclimatized, she was grateful that the tables were clean and there was enough food listed on the chalkboard to satisfy the gnawing in her belly. They chose a spot not far from the only other table that was occupied, by three large men and a pitcher of beer. A sun-ravaged woman with a leathery cleavage came to take their order. She was wearing denim shorts. "No food. You want a drink?"

When Lisa looked at the server's face, she was shocked. Beneath the makeup, they were probably the same age. "Are we too late to eat, or too early?"

"You're in the wrong place today. Cook's sick, but we got beer."

Ashley did that flirty thing with her eyes. "Couldn't you make us something? We've had such a long drive."

The woman sighed. "I'll see what I can do."

A couple came in, said hi to the men at the other table, and slid onto stools by the bar.

"Sorry." Ashley fiddled with the mustard pot. "I'll leave the choosing to you next time."

"Don't worry." Lisa smiled. "Look, she's coming back. Let's hope she found a three-course meal in the freezer."

"Grilled cheese, but you gotta buy a drink to go with it."

"Absolutely." Lisa nodded. "I'll have a club soda, and a Sprite for my friend."

The heavily made-up eyes rolled as she walked away.

While they settled to wait for their food, Ashley looked at her phone. "It's a message from Skye."

Lisa didn't want to know, she was having too nice a day.

"She's leaving town soon. Apparently she's got a job in Toronto, in some kind of hostel. She's happy cuz she gets to live there, too."

Lisa hadn't heard from Skye since she'd demanded another reference. Asking for her old one from the art school must have worked. What a relief. Finally, the Skye-shaped thorn in Lisa's side would be gone.

Ashley put away her phone. "Why would anyone want to go and live in the dirty, noisy city when they could work here, with all the trees and lake and fresh air?"

"Maybe she thinks it's boring." *Or she ran out of people to blackmail.* "I never had the impression Skye was happy here. But what about you, will you miss her?"

"Nah. She was the first person I met, and she fixed me up with the kids in the squat, but we weren't super close or anything." Ashley looked past the men at the next table and her eyes lit up. "I can't believe there's a real jukebox." She pushed her chair back. "Any requests?"

"I dread to think what's on it. Surprise me."

The biggest of the three men at the other table started talking loudly, obviously for the benefit of everyone in the room. "D'ya see the news last night? About the boy who dresses like a girl and says he's "trans?" They only had his teacher talkin' about what you're meant to call him by. I know what I'd friggin' call him." The friends laughed. "Wife says there's a fuck-up like him in Bella's class at school. Can you believe it?"

Lisa looked at Ashley, who was taking too long to choose a song. There was no music as she walked back from the jukebox. The man turned to her. "And what am I meant to call you? Brown, black, half 'n half?"

His buddies loved the joke. Ashley kept moving.

"Hey, I'm talking. I asked what to call you?"

She turned around. "Ashley. The name's Ashley. And I know what you should call yourself."

"Yeah?"

"Yeah. Little prick."

His friends laughed again and then stopped. It took a moment to sink in before the big guy's eyes opened wide and he put a huge paw on Ashley's arm. "I'll show you what kind of a prick I am."

She stared straight at him. "Get your racist hand off me."

The only sound in the room was the click of the ceiling fan.

"I said, take your fucking sausage fingers off my arm."

All eyes were on the man's hand, huge and red against Ashley's smooth dark skin. Lisa approached the table. Her face felt tight, but she was calm and strangely articulate. "There seems to have been a misunderstanding. Maybe everyone should take a breath and—"

"Butt out lady. I don't need you telling me what to do." The man's eyes flashed as he tightened his grip on Ashley, his face an overheated furnace. Sweat dribbled toward one eye. Lisa needed to diffuse this situation, and fast. Or did she? Leaning between his friends, she picked up the man's glass and threw what was left of his beer straight at his face. Some splashed back, some stayed in the creases and started to run toward his chin. Snorting, brown liquid sprayed out of his nose as he pushed back his chair.

"RUN!" Ashley's voice came from the door, which she was holding open. Lisa dashed round the side of the table, grabbed her bag, and headed for the light. She was fumbling in her purse for the key as she ran and Ashley was yelling, "open the truck" when they heard the bar door open behind them. Lisa looked round—he was even bigger standing up. Something moved in her pocket and she put her hand on the key. Panting, she started the engine, hurled into reverse, and sped out of the parking lot without looking back. Ashley was choking with laughter and soon they were both hysterical with tears streaming down their cheeks.

A few kilometres later, Lisa pulled onto the side of the road because she was laughing too hard to drive. She had to hold her crotch to stop herself peeing.

They replayed the drama all the way home, and when they arrived, Ashley made them pose on the hood of the truck for a *Thelma and Louise* selfie and went upstairs to change, leaving her phone on the kitchen table. Lisa picked it up, curious to see how they looked in the photo—dishevelled and slightly crazy, but exuberant. Looking for more pictures, she swiped sideways and found a beautiful shot of Fido silhouetted against a crimson sky. There were others, taken around the farmhouse—rubber boots sinking in mud, a dead mouse by the wheel of the mower, close-up of a spider dangling from the laundry line.

The pictures taken in the art school were just as good: hot pottery glowing orange through a crack in the kiln door, crushed pastels trodden into the art room floor, half-empty coffee cups in lockers, on library shelves, on a ladder outside. Lisa wasn't an expert, but she'd seen enough to know that Ashley had what photographers called "an eye." She went to the bottom of the stairs. "Come down, I've had an idea that might save you from marrying Terry."

Lisa was still holding the phone when Ashley came into the kitchen. "I've been looking through your photos—"

"Don't you know it's rude to look at other people's phones?"

"Yes, I do and I'm sorry, but these pictures are great."

"You should still ask first, not wait till I'm out of the room."

"Ashley, you don't understand. I think these are *really* good. Good enough to get you into art school. You could study photography, here in Colville. We could show them to Hayden, the media studies teacher, and ask what he thinks."

Ashley spoke slowly, as though Lisa was hard of understanding. "Apart from not being Canadian or having any money for fees, don't you need GCSEs or A-Levels to go to art school?"

Lisa knew she'd reverted to parent but carried on anyway. "There may be ways to get around that, especially as you're older and already well-liked at the school. And once you've been accepted, we can apply for a student visa."

Ashley looked annoyed. "Forget it, I need a shower. My pictures aren't anything special, I just take them to fill in time when I'm bored."

Puzzled, Lisa knew better than to push it, or to try and second-guess what was going on in her friend's head. But she did have another idea—Leonard's cameras. Surely he would want to pass them on to his, she paused, praying it was true, his *only* daughter.

Twenty-One

Hoping to avoid the crowds, Lisa headed into town early. Thanks to the cottagers, campers, and summer school, the population of Colville doubled in the summer and August was the busiest time. Which is why, at 8:30 on a Sunday morning, Foodland's car park was full, the diner had a line-up outside, and families were already wandering aimlessly around town. Lisa's main job was to get propane for the barbeque because Ashley had discovered a new passion—grilled veggies with pickled ginger. After loading the refilled tank into the back of her truck, Lisa popped into the deli for hot pepper relish, picked up a *Sunday Star,* and decided to treat herself to an Americano and almond croissant at the Copper Bean.

Tables spread over the sidewalk into the street, which would be pedestrian-only until September. As Lisa settled at one in the shade, two women walking past looked at her, then at each other, and whispered. Lisa lifted the paper—they must have been at the film festival when she embarrassed herself so spectacularly. She still dreaded meeting anyone who'd been there and asked how she was doing, or worse, gave her advice. So far, recommendations included eating more, drinking less, sleeping more, deep tissue massage, "seeing my fantastic therapist," and a trip to Hedonism in Jamaica which, according to Elsa who worked in the post office, "is guaranteed to take your mind off *everything.*"

Lowering her head, Lisa studied an article on immigration in Alberta. When she looked up again, he was there. Standing right in front of her. Nut brown, hair longer and even curlier.

"You look great," he said.

She had missed him so much. She stared, speechless. Why hadn't he told her he was coming home?

"Didn't you get my postcard?"

She shook her head, too stunned to speak.

"I'm back for a week to sort out some legal stuff with Warren."

A whole week. I wish I'd washed my hair. "How long ago did you send it? The card, I mean." Of all the things she could have said, that was the lamest.

"Maybe ten days. I asked if you were free tonight, but as I'm here—" He glanced at the empty chair beside hers.

"Yes, of course."

As Dan sat down, a smile spread over Lisa's face. He was next to her, right now. "You look good too. Like a man who's been on the beach for three months."

They talked non-stop, conversation pouring as though they'd seen each other last week. Lisa expanded on what she'd written in her postcards about Ashley, how her arrival had forced Lisa to reframe everything about her marriage and how much freer she was starting to feel. He talked about his daughter and meeting up with his ex, saying that being in Manitoba had released him to move forward too. He looked even fitter, almost radiant, and Lisa had to hold herself back from touching the little hairs on his arm, bleached blonde in the sun. After an hour, Dan glanced at his watch. "I'm meant to be at Warren's soon. Have to be there most of the day but, are you free later?"

"Absolutely. Come round for supper." Lisa remembered Ashley. "Or, why don't I bring some food over to your place?"

Dan hesitated. "The house is a dump. It hasn't been cleaned for months. Let's eat in town, my treat. I'll book a table at Days of the Raj, say at seven?"

Lisa struggled to contain the swirl of excitement as she watched Dan walk down the street. He felt like what she should be doing with her life.

* * *

Because it was Sunday, Lavish Locks was closed, but Lisa saw a young woman taking stock of products behind the cash and opened the door. "I don't suppose you could do me a quick wash and blow-dry, as a special favour?"

The girl hesitated. "Thing is, I dunno if I'm allowed."

To Lisa's delight, the owner's car pulled up. Lisa had known her for years. "I was just trying to convince—sorry, I didn't get your name—to give me a quick blow-dry. Could that be possible?"

"Sure, if Yvette's okay with it. Just pay her what you want, call it a big tip, but promise not to tell anyone or we'll never get any time off."

As Lisa left the hairdresser, clean hair tickling her shoulders, she was giddy. Her biggest excitement was that the latest pessaries didn't seem to irritate. Dr. Lau had called her into the Health Centre a few weeks ago to tell her about a brand made with a different base cream and a lower dose of estrogen, and so far, no adverse effects. *Maybe I can have sex with Dan after all. Maybe tonight. I'll change the sheets in case.*

When she got to the Indian restaurant, he was at the table texting but put away his phone as she approached. She hadn't eaten all day and the rich smell of spices made her feel her hunger. After they ordered, she filled both their glasses with water from a silver pitcher. "You talked a lot about Anna and her mother this morning, but you haven't told me much about the job. Is it everything you hoped?"

"It's been a rollercoaster, a lot more than I expected."

"And all because of a piping plover. I don't even know what they look like."

"To be honest, I've seen more of those birds on screen than in real life. They're kind of ugly but funny, the same colour as wet sand. They stroll up and down the beach and suddenly run. It's called hyperkinetic. They only fly when in danger."

"And you've been collecting data with Anna?"

"Not so much. She spends most of her time in the lab, but I see her quite a lot in the evenings. She's got a big social life and I'm part of it. I thought it might feel weird, being so much older, but it's quite a mixed group. We go camping on weekends, hiking, take it in turns to make picnics. Then there's live music on the grass outside City Hall twice a week and outdoor movie screenings every Friday."

Lisa was wondering how she'd fit in, and if Anna would like her, as the food arrived: baby eggplant, chickpeas, potato with spinach, daal, and although they never stopped talking, they finished everything. Time passed in a flash, and when they asked for the bill, the setting sun outside glowed orange. Dan suggested going for a walk, adding, "There's something I need to tell you."

As they stepped out into the warm air, Lisa knew she was going to tell him too, how much she'd missed him, how she regretted trying to be platonic and was ready for more. The walk across the park and down to the lake was idyllic: cicadas were singing, a loon's eerie call echoed in the distance, and people eating ice cream strolled slowly. Even the rising moon was starting to shimmer as they reached the water. Dan stopped at a bench, partly hidden by a huge willow, and they sat down. Lisa turned to face him.

"The thing is," he started, and as though pulled by invisible threads, their heads moved together. The kiss lasted a long time, turning Lisa liquid and doubling the size of her heart. Eventually, Dan pulled back. "Sorry, I didn't mean to go there. I have something to tell you." He stood up. Then sat down again. "The thing is—I've met someone. That's why I'm here, to sell Warren the business. I'm moving to Manitoba."

Lisa stared. "But—all the postcards." Surely she hadn't imagined ... "Why didn't you say anything?"

Dan looked down. "I thought I kind of did. Hinted, anyway." He took her hand and she snatched it away. "She works with Anna. She's one of her profs actually, but they're good friends.

That's how we met. It wasn't part of the plan, it just happened. Shit, I don't know why I'm feeling guilty. You were the one who said we should only be friends."

A water rat scurried out from under a bush. Lisa felt sick. "So you're just going to up and move there? Isn't your job going to end soon?"

"That's what makes it so perfect. The university has offered me a post, training and co-ordinating the field researchers across all the departments."

Lisa took a slow breath. Her only goal was to get off the bench intact. "I'm pleased for you. You wanted a new life and this sounds perfect. And you're right, you don't owe me anything—even an explanation."

"Then why do I feel so shitty?"

She stood up. "I don't know, and it's not how I want you to feel, but I have to go now."

Lisa was almost running as she retraced their steps back through the park. Everything that had seemed so perfect was making her feel worse: slow-moving people blocked her path, the live band on Patty's patio was too loud, the moonlight so bright that passers-by could see her tears, and when she got to her truck, she couldn't find her keys. She went through her bag twice before deciding to text the cab company and that's when they clattered onto the sidewalk.

* * *

When she got home, Ashley's music was blaring, and Lisa went straight to the basement. Last time she'd been in her collage corner was months ago, when Ashley first moved in. After Lisa's initial resistance, they'd had a great time together, cutting, sticking, and chatting. Having Ashley around had made Lisa feel younger and more alive, but right now, as she turned on the lamp, she felt like a withered hag who'd made a complete fool of herself. If

Dan's girlfriend Julie was a prof she clearly wasn't retired, probably not old enough to retire, and she probably wasn't atrophied either.

Reaching for a *National Geographic*, Lisa noticed the flesh on the underside of her arm wobble and hated everything about herself: her age, the way she looked, her lack of experience. Determined not to cry, she turned the pages looking for the ugliest picture she could find. Halfway through the magazine, she saw it, a blob blowfish. The creature looked like it had died and then been inflated. Her next cut-out was a grotesque star-nosed mole, followed by a monkey with an obscenely huge dangling flabby proboscis. She was lining them up on the table in front of her, ready to stick, when Ashley's sneakers squeaked on the stairs.

"Looks like someone had a shit date."

"What makes you think I've been on a date?"

"Maybe the way you were dancing round the house all afternoon, gassed like a hyena? Or the extra-flowy hair, or the dress I've never seen before, which looks boss, by the way."

Lisa groaned. "I'd call it more of a completely fucking awful date."

"With Mr. Tricky?"

"The situation just got simple—he's seeing someone else."

"Bummer." Ashley pushed aside a heap of cut up paper and sat down on the floor.

Lisa propped her head on the heel of her hand. "You said you don't do boyfriends. Why not?"

"Same as you, I guess. If you open up, you get hurt."

"Did I say that?"

"No, but we don't need Freud to work it out. First your mum dies, then your aunt. Your sister sounds like a complete bitch and Leonard pops it practically the day after the wedding. Why else would you go without for twenty years?" Ashley picked up a magazine and turned the pages without really looking. "I don't want to rub it in or anything, but I am giving myself a one-off and going on a teeny bit of a date this week. Sorry."

"Don't worry, I couldn't feel worse right now. Tell me about him. What's he like?"

"He lives in Toronto, but he's staying in Colville for the summer with his stepdad, playing bass at Patty's. He's six foot four, looks cute when he laughs, and has really sensitive hands. We're going out for Indian."

Lisa didn't have the energy to laugh at the irony and started cutting out a sphinx cat.

Ashley turned another page. "What's your Dad like?"

"Where did that come from?"

"I dunno. We always talk about mine and I sometimes wonder about yours."

"The honest answer is I don't really know. We fell out and I haven't seen him for nearly thirty years. Before Mum died he was always joking around, surprising us with chocolate or broken things he'd find and fix up at work. Once he brought home a baby rabbit for my sister's birthday. But all I've got is a child's memories, who knows what he's really like."

"And after your mum died?"

"Looking back, I can see that Dad was devastated. He went into his shell and never came out. But when I was six, I believed it was my fault that Mum was gone. That if I'd been better, tried harder ... I thought Dad blamed me, and I kept thinking it till I left home."

"That's peak, and a bit like me, to be fair. Mum was the same, kind of there but not there. Sometimes, when she was really out of it, I'd curl up and lie next to her, pretending." Ashley picked up another magazine and opened it. "But I still had to work my life out without anyone to show me how. Sometimes I used to wish she was dead, cuz that was only way I could imagine being free. But after she did die, that's when I really knew what it meant to have no one. And nothing. No money, no place to live, no one to give a fuck."

"You were sixteen?"

"Yeah. She actually OD'd in hospital. I thought she was going to get better but she got one of her girls to bring her in some gear and that was it. One day I went to see her and she was okay, the next she was gone."

"Jesus Ashley, that's awful. Who looked after you?"

"Same person as always—me. As soon as I knew she was dead I went home to get my stuff and cut. Stayed with a friend, then moved into the squat. There was no way I was going into the system."

"I'm so sorry. That's too much for anyone to deal with, let alone a sixteen-year-old."

"Well, you know what they say, if it doesn't kill you." Ashley ripped a page out of the magazine she'd been flicking through and handed it to Lisa. "Here, have this one next."

It was a picture of a teddy bear.

Twenty-two

Since she'd been seeing Chase, Ashley was softer, less cynical, and seldom around. She'd stayed at his place every night since their first date, two weeks ago, but this morning the hall light had been turned off and the retro camera case she used as a purse was at the bottom of the stairs. Lisa decided to slow her morning—she'd missed the routine intimacy of their breakfast together.

Sipping coffee, she tried not to imagine Dan's life in Manitoba with his new love, a bad habit she'd fallen into. Today's image—him spread across a big comfy sofa with her tucked next to him. They were watching a movie, her hand on his thigh in a way only committed couples drape bits of themselves over one another.

The fantasy was interrupted by Ashley appearing in the kitchen, followed by a tall young man with a beard. "This is Chase."

"I guessed." Lisa smiled through her shock that he was standing in front of her, bare-chested, his low-slung jeans displaying tiny skulls woven into the elasticated top of his boxers.

He nodded. "How's it going?"

"I'll make us a tea." Ashley, wearing her usual sleeping T-shirt, picked up the kettle.

Chase's long thin torso was topped with a remarkable amount of chest hair. Lisa envied their relaxed attitude to their own bodies, and to her. "Or I could brew you a coffee?" This young man didn't look like a tea drinker.

"Yeah, please. Ashley's trying to convert me, but it's a hard shift." He looked around the room. "This place is great. Ash told me all about it, but it's even nicer than she made out."

He had a kind voice.

"You ever get to Patty's?" he asked, as Lisa spooned grounds into her little espresso pot. "She's got some kick-ass gigs coming up. As well as my Tuesday set, I'm playing with a wicked singer from B.C. next week. She's touring without her band."

Ashley trailed a finger across Chase's back as she brought her mug to the table. "That guy you played with last night was freakin' awesome."

"Bro, you sound so north of the border." Chase laughed.

Ashley giggled. "Well shoot me when I end a sentence with eh?"

"Eh? Why don't we skip the deets and go for poutine?"

They laughed the way people do when they're in love, oblivious to Lisa. It was good to finally meet Chase, but she was absurdly disappointed that he had gate-crashed her time with Ashley. Lisa turned her attention to making scrambled eggs and learned that he was staying with his stepfather, who lived just outside Colville. His mother had "moved on to husband number three." After Labour Day weekend, Chase would be going back to his shared house on the outskirts of Toronto and resuming his job in a cardboard box factory, while gigging downtown and recording in his friend's basement.

The information kept flowing as they ate. Lisa had never seen Ashley so silent and—the only word for it—stricken. As Lisa loaded the dishwasher, the conversation swung around to reading palms and Chase became absorbed in counting the little creases between Ashley's thumb and forefinger. Lisa texted Susan. What are you doing? Shall I come over for a swim?

The reply was instant. Sounds good. Can you pick up some psyllium husks at the health store? I'm trying a new bread recipe.

* * *

Leaving the happy couple at the kitchen table, Lisa grabbed her swimming things and jumped in the truck. She popped into Clean & Lean and was carrying a small bag of pale powdery wisps down Queen Street when she saw them coming out of the bank: Dan and a woman who was undoubtedly his. They weren't touching, but there was something about the way they were in the same section of the revolving door, and the familiarity with which she glanced up at him, that made it obvious. He saw Lisa before she could hide, and looking uneasy, he came over and introduced Julie.

She wasn't gorgeous, but she was definitely younger, with enticing curves, perfect teeth, and bouncy blondish hair. The worst thing was that she seemed terribly nice: articulate, bright, bubbly—the kind of person Lisa would want to be friends with. Dan explained why he hadn't flown back to Manitoba as planned. "The business stuff was more complicated than my lawyer predicted, and I decided to take a few days to say goodbye to some of my regular clients. It seemed wrong to just wrap up without any explanation, after so many years."

"So I flew out to see Dan's old life before he gives it all up," Julie chirped. She clearly didn't know who Lisa was. There was something eager, almost innocent in the way she spoke, and a faint whiff of sweetness around her, reminiscent of vanilla.

"It all sounds so exciting." Lisa kept her tone light, hoping for enthusiasm. She turned to Dan. "What's happening with your house?"

"Nothing, for now. It's too much to deal with on top of everything else. Warren's still going to use the office, and that way he can keep an eye on the place." Dan was focusing on a point just below Lisa's chin. He never once looked at her eyes.

Julie kept cheeping. "He's got such a beautiful home in an amazing setting. Now that I've seen it, maybe we'll come back for Christmas."

Lisa's stomach twisted at the thought. After a few more excruciating minutes, she went back to her truck, swallowing the tears as she walked. She had only herself to blame. She was the one who'd insisted they be platonic. And now she'd lost him.

* * *

Grant was outside in the garage doing something loud with power tools as Lisa let herself into the hallway.

"Want a coffee or bite to eat before we go down to the lake?" Susan was already wearing her swimsuit, under something short and voluminous made of lime green lace.

"I'd love some water." Lisa's throat was still dry from her conversation with Dan and Julie. The heat didn't help.

"It's packed and ready to go." Susan grabbed the cooler and they picked their way down the steep slope from the house to the lake's edge. When they arrived, she handed Lisa a jar of chilled water with mint and lemon and launched into her most recent project. "I'm celebrating the end of bug season with an outdoor dinner party, a week from Saturday. You'll love it. I'm making veggie *moussaka,* as well as one with lamb, and five different salads, and you'll know everyone who's coming from the art school—Dianne's bringing her new partner, Roy, and Janet and Sue and their husbands. Keith's bringing the woman he met online, and I've invited Melinda and Zach, you know, from the film festival. As they're both younger, I thought you might want to come with Ashley."

Lisa shrank at the thought of seeing the festival director and tech guy again, both witness to her horrible collapse. "I doubt if Ashley will be free but I can ask her. She's got a *boyfriend* now."

Susan gave a knowing nod. "How's that working out?"

"It's ..." Lisa couldn't bring herself to be honest. Not yet, anyway. "It's lovely to see her so happy." Sitting there, against the backdrop of Susan's family and friend-filled life, Lisa put a name to the feeling that had been creeping over her—loneliness. Bleak, hollow, and familiar. She'd never found it easy to connect. Looking out over the water, she remembered school holidays, hours in the house alone, and struggled to suppress her tears. "Shall we swim?"

She and Susan breast-stroked side by side to the floating dock anchored in the bay and Lisa felt better as she climbed the little metal ladder and lay on her back in the sun. Half closing her eyes, she saw tiny circles of colour dance between her lashes and remembered how, when she was little, she thought they were clouds.

"What do you think?" Susan flopped down next to her. "Should I tell everybody to *dress,* or is that going too far?"

Susan hadn't stopped talking about the party, even as they were swimming. Lisa summoned a drop of enthusiasm. "Yes, that'd be fun. Maybe I'll wear the backless number I bought for the glass artist's wedding—I can't even remember her name."

"Monique, and you looked stunning."

"Thanks." Lisa swallowed a sigh.

"And we can have candles and fairy lights."

"Good idea." Lisa imagined herself slipping back into work mode, all front and fake smiles. "I'll come in the afternoon and help get everything ready."

Susan loved planning events. "Grant can put up a long trestle on the grass at the back of the house and we'll use the good china and silver, with a damask tablecloth."

And I'll probably be the only one to arrive and—more to the point—go home alone.

"Isn't it great to have something to look forward to? After the party, it'll only be a couple of weeks before we leave for London to see Megan. Did I tell you that Jodie's flying out to join us and we're all going to Madrid? I can't remember how long it's been since we had a family holiday together."

Lisa yearned to share how lonely she was, but couldn't do it now. She managed to sound upbeat until they jumped back into the water. "I'm going to swim out a bit further. See you back at the jetty." A few minutes later she flipped over and floated, listening to the distant drum of a woodpecker. Her body relaxed as the water gently lapped against her, the tension seeping out of her neck.

* * *

When Lisa got home, she felt better. The swimming and company had diminished the reality of seeing Dan with Julie, and the sadness of knowing that Ashley was becoming a person with a life that didn't necessitate her. Lisa gazed out of the window. Everything was too familiar: the fields, the trees, Fido lying on the warm gravel of the driveway. *If Dan can find someone new, maybe I can too.* She picked up her phone—*I bet he still uses a landline*—and searched 411 Directory. Then she typed "Mitchell Edwards, Colville, Ontario."

Twenty-three

Mitch sounded puzzled when he answered the phone, even though Lisa introduced herself as Susan's friend and reminded him they'd all had lunch together a few months ago. When he finally understood that she was inviting him out for a drink, he was first nervous and then took charge. "Okay, let me think about where we can go. When and where should I pick you up?"

Being the one who drove and decided where they went seemed important to Mitch, so Lisa left him to it. The next day, checking herself in the mirror—clean jeans and a new poplin shirt, she realized how strange it was to be spending an evening with someone she hardly knew: a retired engineer, worked with Grant, did lots of volunteering. There was something slightly formal about their phone call and the way he was coming to drive her. Everything to do with Dan had just happened. This was reassuringly different.

The Honda SUV still had a faint whiff of new car. "Is it living up to expectation? You were listing its virtues last time we met."

"To be honest," Mitch kept his eyes on the road, "I was pretty nervous and probably just looking for something to say. Susan had been talking you up for ages and then phoned and told me I had to come over right away because there was someone else interested. My wife died three years ago, and I hadn't been on a date since before we married. I was terrified."

"Oh, gosh, I know what that's like. Until recently, I hadn't been on a date for over twenty years."

"So I guess it didn't work out with the other guy?"

"Sorry?"

"When we had lunch at Susan's, you left pretty pronto. I'm guessing you went for him and now that's over?"

This wasn't the easy conversation Lisa had anticipated; perhaps she'd underestimated Mitch? She glanced at his profile:

recently barbered silver hair, strong chin, the lines at the corners of his mouth looked like he smiled a lot. Not magnetic, but an attraction could definitely grow. "It never really happened with the other guy, and you're right, I did run away, but not from you, because I felt ambushed. I thought I was going for a girlie lunch with Susan and suddenly it was a date."

"That's funny. She dragged me and tricked you. Still, it got us here now, and that's not a bad thing."

Lisa liked the way he said that. There was something gentle but solid about this man. She tried not to compare him to Dan.

"I know you retired about the same time as Susan." Mitch glanced at Lisa as he drove. "Tell me what you do now instead of work."

"I wish I knew, the days pass so quickly." Lisa tried to remember her life before Ashley. "I can tell you what I don't do. Apart from being on the board of the art school, I am not on any other committees. I decided that when I stopped working I didn't want to fill my life with more of the same on a voluntary basis."

"I took the opposite approach. When Lorraine passed I needed to be out of the house, so I signed up for all kinds of stuff. I told you about my men's group in the library. Tomorrow, I'll be coaching soccer at the high school. I'm secretary of the local chapter of the IEEE—that's an engineer's association. Then there's walking with Curtis, he's a special needs boy I know and we exercise dogs together for the animal shelter, and my woodturning, and the grandkids."

It seemed like only moments before they pulled up outside a pub in a little place south of Colville. The view was stunning—fields dotted with hay bales and picturesque places that had once been farms. Mitch looked pleased when Lisa admired his choice, a converted old schoolhouse. "You can't see it from here, but we're right by the river. There's a patio out back with a great view."

Over glasses of cold beer, they chatted easily, and Mitch seemed genuinely interested in Lisa. He was also open and willing to talk about himself, and she found his left eye fascinating: the pupil grew bigger when he talked about anything that excited him.

"Do you like mysteries?" he asked, as they were finishing their second drink.

"You mean books, like Ian Rankin?"

"You read Rankin? Tremendous. The Brits do it best: PD James, Conan Doyle, and of course Agatha."

Lisa didn't want to disappoint him, but she couldn't lie. "I'm sorry, I don't read them. I just said Ian Rankin because I knew the name."

Mitch smiled. "Yeah, I know it's a bit of a retirement cliché, but I love solving mysteries. I took a Sherlock Holmes tour when I was in England a few years back and went to his museum."

Lisa remembered being on the bus to work, when she still lived in London, and looking out of the window as it slowed in the Baker Street traffic. She'd watch the queues of tourists waiting to visit 221b and think they were lame. Listening to Mitch, she started asking herself what she was doing with the kind of man who goes on a Sherlock Holmes tour, but resisted, and when he told her about his participation in the online puzzle club, she decided to consider it was charming. He was obviously a clever man looking for ways to use his brain.

Seeing the sun become a ball of glowing orange and spread the last of its heat across the fields was glorious. Lisa had to stop herself from wishing she was watching it with Dan. As the full moon became visible, Mitch explained it was a blue moon. "The second full moon in a month. Happens rarely. That's where the phrase 'once in a blue moon' comes from." As Lisa listened, she understood that this man was all heart. Whether it was knowledge, his time, or a wonderful experience, he just wanted to share.

The drive home was relaxing. As she rested back, cool air breezed in through the open window as the trees became silhouettes against the darkening sky. The silence was comfortable. She appreciated the way Mitch didn't talk until he had something to say.

"That was fun." He switched off the engine outside Lisa's house. "Shall we risk a meal together next week?"

She turned to face him. "I'd love that. Susan's having a dinner party on Saturday, we could eat together there?"

"Hold on." He laughed. "Shouldn't we slow it down a notch? Go somewhere quiet and get to know each other better before venturing out in public?"

Lisa smiled her most inviting smile. "Let's live dangerously. It'll be fun to see the look on Susan's face when we turn up together. She thinks I'm coming with my ... with a young woman who's spending the summer with me. You'll be a good surprise."

* * *

It was still early when Lisa got home and the moon was so bright she couldn't stay indoors. She changed her shoes, slipped her phone into her back pocket, and followed Fido into the chorus of crickets. The earth smelled warm, goldenrod glowed in the moon's soft light, and a bat swooped just above her head. Every step brought Lisa more into herself. Dan was a crush, a fantasy. Mitch felt real. There was a groundedness to him, a quick mind and a gentle heart. She was looking forward to seeing him on Saturday and going to a dinner party as a couple. It was over twenty years since she'd done that.

She reached the woods and stepped into the quiet of the trees. Moon shadows crisscrossed beneath her feet and the air was warm on her skin. She had been on this path often, but tonight everything was amplified. The patterns of the tree bark were brighter, the leaf mulch under her feet softer, and Fido's darting from one scent to another was almost a dance. Her usual route was to follow the trail up to the scarp, but Lisa walked to the left, between two maples, and picked her way toward a clearing. The sky was infinite. As she took a deep breath, her eyes followed the Milky Way and then found the Great Bear, Ursa Major.

Lisa sat down on the dry grass and heard Mr. Henderson, her math teacher, just as he'd been in the classroom. "Draw a straight line between the two stars at the end and then move seven times that distance up to the Pole Star."

He'd started an astronomy club and invited the members to meet outside the gym at 4 a.m. for their first outing. Lisa was the only one to arrive alone, on her bicycle. Everyone else was dropped off by a parent in a car. Feeling desperately ashamed, she'd hidden her bike behind the shed where the wheely bins were stored and waved goodbye to no one. Dad didn't even have a car, let alone the time or interest for parents' evenings or school socials—a fancy phrase for fundraisers.

"The downside of getting a free place in a private school," she said to Fido as he settled beside her. She looked up at a group of stars shaped like a "W". Scorpio, or was that Cassiopeia? The astronomy club only had two meetings and then Mr. Henderson moved to another school. Lisa shivered at the thought of her time at Oxford Academy for Girls. She'd loved the learning, and the fact it had enabled her to go to university, but she was always on the outside. Never invited to parties. Never had a best friend. Something that her sister threw in her face every weekend. "If the girls there are so bloody great, how come you never see any of them out of school?"

As a child Lisa had never understood why her sister was so mean, now she could see that she was frustrated and angry. Mum died when Nicky was thirteen, leaving her a single parent, *to me, the child she never wanted. And while Nicky was forced to become a housewife and mother, I escaped to private school and university and got the good job and rich, handsome Leonard.* But that still didn't excuse Nicky's huge final betrayal.

Lisa stood up, brushed the grass off her jeans, and followed Fido back to the dirt road that ran from Norm's place to home. She stopped to look at his old farmstead silhouetted against the bright night sky and wondered how was he feeling now. He had been there for her so unquestioningly over the years; maybe it was time?

The moon, slightly to Lisa's left, was smaller now, more settled. She walked through an alley of sumac, velvety red clumps reaching high, and then cut back through the field of goldenrod, asters, and milkweed, preparing to explode its white fluffiness over the darkened field.

When she got home, Lisa went upstairs and lay on the bed, but she wasn't ready for sleep. Moonlight slanted through the open windows, the air smelled of cedar, and wanting to feel it on her skin, she took off all her clothes and opened her arms wide, bathing in the blue-tinged rays. Surrounded by a sense of freedom that wasn't usually hers, she put a hand on the soft mound of her stomach and lay still. The crickets were quiet now. All she could hear was silence. After a while, something stirred and expanded. She ran her fingers over her belly, very lightly, skin tingling. As her hand moved to her thighs, she pulled up her knees and started to stroke the tiny hairs on the tender part at the top of her legs. Her breasts were soft, receptive. She slipped first one, then two fingers inside herself and moved them in and out. No pain. A wave of excitement—maybe the pessaries had worked. She started to circle and stroke in her own wetness and after a few moments, she came. An enormous, long, slow orgasm.

Twenty-four

Lisa took time pinning her hair into a semi-swirl, then stepped into the dark blue dress she'd released from its plastic carrier. The back was lower than she remembered and it was an effort nestling her breasts in the built-in cups, but once done, they felt secure. Slipping on a seldom-worn pair of heels, she stood back and took stock in the mirror. *Not bad for sixty-one. I wonder what Mitch will look like in a suit.*

He looked great, and she told him so, making his eyes smile. As he opened the car door for her, he confessed that his daughter had taken him out to buy a new shirt. She had good taste—it was exactly the same grey-blue as his eyes.

"How are you feeling about tonight?" Lisa asked as they drove through town.

"A bit like I'm going to the school prom—eager and nervous and not sure what's going to happen at the end of the evening."

She laughed but didn't reply. Lisa hadn't really thought beyond dinner, but after her moonlit encounter with herself, she was open to where the evening might lead.

Susan's place looked perfect. Lisa had spent the previous afternoon putting sand into brown paper lunch bags, adding a tea light, and now they were flickering around the edges of the lawn. The trestle table was damask-covered with sunflowers and candles running down the centre, beautifully laid with five chairs on each side and one at each end. Delicious food smells wafted from the house and the warm air was filled with the gentle patter of voices, until Susan saw Lisa and Mitch standing side by side. She shrieked with laughter and rushed to greet them.

"Ashley couldn't make it," Lisa whispered into her friend's ear as they hugged.

Susan's eyes glowed big and round as she stood back. "Finally, Cinderella's arrived at the right ball."

Mitch looked confused.

"Ignore her." Lisa looped her arm through his. "Let's go and get a drink." They joined a small group under the trees. She was proud to be with him. He looked handsome and his navy suit matched her dress as though they'd planned it.

"Long time no see," said someone Lisa recognized as Alison's husband. She used to be the art school librarian. He gave Mitch a slightly stiff man-hug.

Another man leaned forward and slapped Mitch between the shoulder blades. "Hey, bud, where've you been?"

Mitch turned to Lisa. "Meet Jeff Forbes, and this other reprobate is Roy Mason. We know each other from my Rotary Club days."

"And I think you know my better half." Roy stood aside to reveal Diane, the art school admissions secretary.

Lisa hated that phrase. *Why did marriage make you half a person? And why did Roy even say that, when nothing about him looked like he thought Diane's 50% was better?* He had an expression of permanent disdain, but as they all stood chatting, Lisa enjoyed herself. Mitch was good at small talk and participating in conversations that didn't hold much interest for her: the ex-pat community in Puerto Rico, whether Mexico was safe to visit, someone's son's varsity rowing achievements, plans for the new ice-rink on the outskirts of town.

Mitch nodded. "I read something about that in the Gazette. Everything in place except the cash. $2.3 million sounds like a lot of bake sales."

Jeff stood a little straighter. "We're expecting the business community to step up and I've heard hints that our grant application might be successful. I'm chair of fundraising." He obviously enjoyed talking big money and heading up committees. "We could do with an extra pair of hands if you're interested."

Roy must have overheard because he turned around. "We could definitely use an engineer."

"Sorry guys. Anyway, I'm electrical, not civil, so I know nothing about building bleachers." As everyone chuckled, Mitch looked at Lisa. "Time for a top up?"

"I'll come with you," she replied, and they went to the candle-lit table that was acting as a bar.

As Grant offered Mitch another Grolsch, Lisa spotted the creative director and tech guy from the film festival on the other side of the lawn. She hadn't seen them since her "nervo," as Ashley called it. As usual, the memory of that evening filled Lisa with shame, but she thought she'd better go and apologize, say something to make it less awkward when they all sat down to eat. She touched Mitch's sleeve. "I've just seen some people I need to talk to. Back in a minute."

Melinda was sitting on a lawn chair and Zach was bent double trying to hear what she was saying. Lisa remembered standing on the podium, the print in front of her blurred by her own tears, just before her embarrassing collapse. But as she walked across the grass toward Melinda and Zack, she thought of Ashley's familiar shrug and remembered her motto: "if it doesn't kill you ..." Lisa took a breath. *Big deal. I had a meltdown, bared my feelings, and no, it didn't kill me. At least it shows I'm human.* As she approached, Melinda looked up and waved, and Zach broke into a big grin.

"Hi, guys." Lisa's smile was genuine. "I just wanted to thank you for looking after me so well that night at the festival."

Melinda mumbled something inaudible and Zach looked happy to see her. "Glad you're doing better now. Did you manage to catch any of the other movies?"

And that was it. As they chatted, Lisa felt lighter, brighter, oddly proud of herself. Her collapse hadn't ruined their night, and maybe the experience *had* made her stronger. When she went back to the bar, Mitch wasn't in sight, so she asked Susan if there was anything she could do to help and went into the kitchen to fetch the appetizers.

Susan had outdone herself with the food: individual mozzarella-filled pastry shells followed by two *moussakas*, one with minced lamb and one without. A platter of grilled veg passed from person to person, and everyone helped themselves from big bowls of salad and rolls. Conversation stopped as the serious eating began.

Lisa was wiping her plate clean with bread when she caught a snippet of conversation from the other end of the table, something Jeff was saying. "... taking positive discrimination too far. How's he going to understand the priorities of a community like ours?"

She nudged Mitch and lowered her voice. "Who's he talking about?"

Mitch whispered back. "The new Township CEO. Don't know anything about it myself."

"Exactly," Roy agreed. "I'd like to know what was going on with the Town Council to give him that job. There's only a handful of Black people in Colville, so I don't see why we need one in the town hall."

Lisa's shoulder blades contracted.

Roy carried on. "And I heard he comes from Quebec. I wonder how good his English is."

Susan suddenly tapped the side of her glass with a spoon. "Sorry to interrupt, but I need to clear the table for dessert. Please pass down your plates and—"

"I don't understand the problem." Lisa didn't want to ruin the mood, but she couldn't sit by and listen to such racist rubbish. And these men were Mitch's buddies? "Isn't he qualified? Doesn't he have enough experience?" She turned from Jeff to Roy. "Have you even considered that he may have simply been the best candidate, or has a great vision for how to move this town forward?"

Both men stiffened. The rest of the table was silent. As Jeff picked up his glass and took a sip of water, everyone listened as the ice clinked against the side of his glass. "The problem is that he's not one of us. And who says this town needs to move forward?"

"For one thing, all the young people are leaving." When she was principal, Lisa had been to countless council meetings about how to prevent the steady stream of job-seekers moving to the city. "And—"

"And you think bringing in a Black Quebecer is going to solve that?"

"No one else seems to have managed. What about—"

"The thing you don't understand," Roy interrupted, in an unsuccessful trying-not-to-sound-patronising tone, "is that someone of his—background is bound to have a different view of life. The council should have elected Tina Munroe who's been town treasurer for sixteen years. She could do a fine job *and* she's a woman. That would've been enough. We don't need this guy to make us look like we're moving with the times."

As Lisa was formulating her reply, Mitch spoke up. "So how do you think the Leafs are going to do this year? Anyone want to bet we'll be bottom of the standings?"

Relief spread around the table as Grant said something about hockey and Susan started piling dirty plates.

"You know Roy, I think I understand more than you realize." Lisa's tone put the tension back into every expression.

Susan's shoulders slumped. Mitch looked up imploringly and spoke softly, "Can't you just let it go?"

Lisa ignored him. "My late husband was a very accomplished, successful man." She looked around the table. Melinda nodded and Zach gave her a thumbs up. "Even in a big city like London, home to a few more people of colour than Colville, he dealt with prejudice every day because he was born in Ghana." She fixed her gaze on Jeff. "He died over twenty years ago and what I find abhorrent is that the world hasn't managed to move on."

With no more to say, Lisa picked up two empty salad bowls and carried them into the kitchen. "Thank God I didn't bring Ashley. Those two are one step away from the Klan," she exploded, as soon as Susan appeared from behind a stack of dirty plates.

"Lisa, I'm sorry. I had no idea. Grant plays golf with them, and I just know Alison and Diane from the art school. I thought—"

"Another good reason I never learned to play golf." Lisa was still fuming. "You'd think Grant ..." She looked up and saw Susan's eyes brimming with tears. "Oh Christ, I've ruined your dinner party."

"You're different." Susan wiped her face. "You never used to be so—"

Lisa made sure she didn't sound defensive. "So what?"

"I don't know." Susan picked up a spoon and pushed a piece of left-over *moussaka* from one side of a plate to another. "Opinionated?"

Lisa leaned back against the kitchen counter. "I guess when I was principal I spent too much time with over-inflated men like that, but because I was representing the art school, I couldn't speak out. Not that I ever encountered such outright, narrow-minded bigotry."

As her voice grew louder, Susan cringed and Lisa felt horrible. She took a step toward her friend. "I'm the one who should be apologizing. What can I do? I could just slink off."

"Don't you dare. And leave Mitch, after all the work I've done to get you two together?"

They both smiled. Lisa didn't know what to make of Mitch. Surely he couldn't agree with those jumped-up idiots? She dreaded going back to the table but needed to support Susan, although she doubted the evening was salvageable.

Susan started loading the dishwasher and Lisa tapped her on the shoulder. "Can we have a hug?"

Her friend beamed. "Yes please."

They stood together for a long time, surrounded by dirty pots and dishes, until Susan said, "I don't think the evening is ruined. We'll just let the boys talk about baseball and hockey and by the time dessert's over, we'll all be laughing again." She took a big cut-glass bowl out of the fridge. "Here. You carry the profiteroles and I'll be right behind with the fruit salad."

* * *

To say the rest of the evening was uncomfortable was an understatement. The tension eased, but Lisa's emotions were jumbled. She hated herself for spoiling her best friend's party, could hardly look at Jeff and his buddy Roy, and kept wondering where Mitch stood in all of this. She asked him in the car on the way home.

"You're never going to change people like that," he answered. "I don't see the point in wasting my time on them, so I just keep my head down."

Was he spineless, or just pragmatic? The wine and intense emotions suddenly took their toll and Lisa grew heavy, too tired to say more. As they drove through the countryside in silence, she wondered if he would want to see her again. Or if she wanted to see him. Relating was hard.

They pulled up outside her house and he turned to face her. "That was a roller coaster of an evening."

She stared through the windscreen at the porch steps. "I want to say I'm sorry for spoiling it, but I'm not sure I am."

"I get that, and the truth is, I admire you for speaking up."

She turned. "Really?"

His eyes were bright. "I guess we both learned something about each other tonight, but nothing I heard stopped me wanting to know more."

As Lisa wondered what she had learned about Mitch, he leaned in and touched his lips to hers. She stayed motionless,

183

confused, but as his warmth spread through her, she pulled him closer, her fingers brushing the short hairs at the nape of his neck. His lips were both gentle and firm, easy to keep kissing. He raised his hand to her face and her mouth opened, eager to explore. But then she felt something holding her back.

Twenty-five

"Oh, my days. Fuck. I got in. This can't be real. Tell me it's real." Ashley was staring at her phone. "We are writing to offer you a place in Photo Arts on the Visual and Creative Arts Diploma course ... blah blah ... classes begin September 4."

Still groggy from last night's dinner party, Lisa was reading the *Guardian* online.

"I didn't tell you I was applying because I wanted to do it on my own." Ashley was talking fast. "But I went to see Hayden in media studies like you said, and he helped me put together a portfolio, and Dominique—you know, she's the technician—helped me write a late application because she went to art school in Toronto AND I GOT IN. Fuck. September 4th, that's in—three weeks? Oi, say something. Aren't you happy? It means I'm going to be a proper student and I can stay, if you still want me to."

A big grin spread across Lisa's face as the words organized themselves in her brain. They'd be laughing and playing and living together for another two years. "Of *course* I want you to stay. It's brilliant. Congratulations! It's just that I didn't even know you'd applied."

"Please don't be angry. I know you only ever want to do good things for me, but I needed to get in because of me, not because of you. I've almost saved enough for the first semester—is that the right word? Semester, not term, right? I have to learn Canadian if I'm going to be a real student here."

Lisa stood up and opened her arms. "I'm really proud of you."

"But what if I fuck up, or I'm not good enough?"

"Come here and give me a hug. You've got plenty of talent, and doing the course will grow your confidence."

"The art school says I can work with Dominique part-time, and they'll pay me proper money. You're allowed to clock a certain number of hours on a student visa; I'm not sure how many though."

"I'll make up the rest of the money for tuition." Lisa paused. "Only if you'd like me to."

Ashley hugged her so hard Lisa nearly fell over.

"Come with me." She led the way into the sunroom that doubled as her office. There was a wooden filing cabinet against the back wall, under a print of Cindy Sherman posing as Marilyn Monroe. Lisa opened a little box on the shelf, took out a tiny key, and unlocked the bottom drawer. "These were your father's cameras. I'm sure that if he was alive, he'd want you to have one. I'm afraid they're not digital."

A black Rolleiflex, still in its original box, was next to a Nikon and a collection of lenses.

"Oh my gosh, these are so cool. Wow. There's a course on film and we get to develop our own prints, you know."

Lisa did know. She'd researched and developed the course twelve years ago and fought the board like fury to have it added to the curriculum. But this was Ashley's moment to shine, so she just smiled. "Leonard's prize camera, his Leica, is upstairs. I was thinking of donating it to the media studies department, but maybe, one day, I'll donate it to you instead."

Ashley was practically dancing on the spot. She put out her hand and touched the Rollei like it was a baby bird, before tentatively picking up the Nikon. She was looking through the viewfinder when they heard a deep rumble outside, getting louder. "That sounds like a bike." She put down the camera. "A bloody big bike."

They went to the window. The rider cut the engine and took off his leather gloves and then his helmet.

"Oh my." Lisa turned to Ashley. "I won't be long."

Outside, she felt dwarfed by the black BMW. "This is a surprise."

"A welcome one, I hope."

His jeans weren't a great fit, but Lisa had to admit that Mitch looked good in a leather jacket. "You never mentioned being a biker."

"I got it a couple of years ago—made in Germany. I came by to invite you for supper at my place."

Lisa hadn't had time to process the dinner party or the kiss in the car.

"She'd love to come." Ashley stepped off the porch into the sunshine and extended her hand to Mitch.

Lisa watched her worlds collide and cleared her throat. "This is my late husband's daughter."

Mitch looked bemused.

"It's a bit complicated. The short version is that he was with Ashley's mother before he and I were married, and she's just heard that she's going to the art school in September to study photography."

"Congratulations. All digital, I suppose. I'm old fashioned, I like the click of a mechanical shutter."

"So do I." Ashley's eyes were shining. "And Lisa's giving me a film camera. She's got two and they're both beautiful. They belonged to my dad—a Rollei 35mm and an original old Nikon."

Mitch nodded. "Both built to last. In good working order they could be worth a pretty penny." He turned to Lisa. "So I'll pick you up at six? We can go for a ride before we eat."

"The thing is," Lisa eyed the big black machine, "I've never been on a motorbike."

"Well, I'm proof that it's not too late. I'll bring you a helmet."

She looked from Mitch back to the bike. "I'd love to."

"Great. Wear jeans and some sturdy boots and I'll take care of the rest. I'd better get to the store. I've got food to prepare." Mitch looked at Ashley as he pulled on his helmet and pushed up the visor. "Vegetarian, prefers red. Anything else I should know?"

"Her favourite dessert's ice cream."

He gave a gloved thumbs-up before dropping his visor and turning back towards the road.

Ashley prodded Lisa with her elbow. "Not bloody bad. Rides a cool bike and he's going to cook your dinner."

* * *

Lisa stepped onto the footrest, swung over her leg, and settled down behind Mitch, but when the bike started down the driveway, she tensed, grabbing the sides of his jacket, her heart racing. On the paved road, she settled until they turned a corner and, desperate to stay upright, she tried to lean against the curve. The bike swerved and Mitch struggled. When they came to a stop sign, he lifted his visor. "Just let go and leave it to me. Keep your head in line with mine and I'll do the rest."

The next bend was worrying, but after that Lisa managed to trust and relax, and soon she was enjoying herself. She opened her thighs wider, slid down into Mitch's back, and put her arms around his waist. As the board and batten buildings dispersed into green countryside, she closed her eyes and let out a deep breath, feeling something welcome—free, sexy, and in charge.

An hour later they turned into a wide street and pulled onto his driveway. The house was standard issue North American ranch style with old vines winding up the front pillars. One side of the double garage was open and Mitch slowed to a stop inside, next to a little red wagon and a plastic tricycle. "For the grandkids." He laughed, helping Lisa undo the helmet clasp under her chin.

She was stirred and unsteady as her feet hit firm ground. "Is this where you lived with Lorraine?"

"For nearly forty years. We bought the place when she was pregnant and raised both our girls here. At the start, I thought the mortgage would kill me, but we made it through."

Lisa handed her helmet and jacket to Mitch. "Were these hers?"

"Good heavens no, I borrowed them from my neighbour. Lorraine was a worrier. She hated the idea of me riding. I got the bike a year after she passed."

Lisa was relieved. She didn't want to be a Lorraine substitute.

As they walked through the house, her sense of Mitch grew stronger. The hall walls were lined with framed family photos. They passed a small room with a side table next to an armchair in front of a big screen TV and she guessed this was where he ate most of his meals. The kitchen was open-plan and airy. As she sat at the breakfast bar, Mitch put a silver foil tray in the oven and poured them both a glass of wine. The fridge was covered in photos of grinning babies and a cheeky-looking toddler, plus a couple of stick-men drawings tacked up with tape. There were curious lumps of wood on one counter, a coffee percolator on another, and a highchair by the basement door. Lisa could easily imagine the many years of marriage that had been lived here, but the place still felt like his.

"What's the story with these?" She picked up a small wooden bird.

"Oh, they're for the Scouts sale. Some people use them as Christmas tree ornaments. I thought I'd get ahead of the game this year."

The birds were adorable, some small and fat, others with longer necks, all with differently shaped beaks and tails.

"Take one." Mitch looked shy. "I mean, only if you'd like one."

"Of course, how lovely." Lisa chose a squat little thing that reminded her of a dumpy chicken. "Thank you."

"I've been wood-turning for years. Grab your glass and I'll show you my shop. It's in the basement."

At the bottom of the stairs, Mitch led her to a machine that looked like a cross between a tractor engine and something in a

Bond movie. "It's a Myford, cast iron from Britain. They don't make lathes like this anymore."

Lisa picked up a curled wood shaving and held it to her nose. The smell was fresh yet comforting.

"That's apple, left over from making this." Mitch handed her a bowl, pinkish with russet streaks. Perfectly round and smooth, it was exquisite.

"You're very talented." Lisa stroked the bowl, the wood silk-smooth under her fingers. "A real artisan."

"I don't know about that, but I do love turning. Utility brought to beauty, that's what I call it."

Back in the kitchen, Mitch put out dishes and a bubbling lasagna. "It's made with spelt pasta. I hope that's okay."

"Don't tell me you're good at cooking, as well as everything else."

"Afraid not. I rode straight from your place to the deli this morning and told them I had a vegetarian coming for supper and I wanted something interesting. They suggested I buy this and a chickpea salad. I did cut up the bread myself."

Lisa took a mouthful of gooey cheesy tomatoey bliss and relaxed into being looked after. She saw a huge Tupperware of toys in the corner of the room. "Tell me about your family."

"The girls have kept me going. They've each got a bedroom upstairs, kitted out with their own stuff, and they come for a sleep-over once a week. I've just finished making bunk beds for the grandkids."

He asked if Lisa had ever wanted children. The question, and being in his love-filled home, made her sad and she answered honestly—that she had only ever wanted a baby with Leonard and by the time they married and had a secure future together, it was too late. Mitch put his hand over hers and asked about Ashley. Lisa replied with a slimmer version of the truth.

"Ice cream?" he asked, lifting the mood. "I didn't know what flavour you liked, so I got strawberry, chocolate, and green tea."

Lisa watched him line up the three tubs. "And you want me to choose one?" She laughed. "It's got to be a spoon of each."

As he started scooping, she thought back to the kiss in the car after Susan's party. "Maybe we could take our bowls, and the wine, somewhere more comfortable?"

Mitch reached for a tray. "Good idea, but I have to watch the wine. Got to get you home safe."

"Or," Lisa took a breath, "I could sleep over?"

Mitch stopped, the bowls mid-air. "That's a ... you could ... what's wrong with me?" He looked up. "Yes, please."

As he put the ice cream cartons back in the freezer, Lisa texted Ashley: Could you be home for Fido tonight if I stayed out?

The reply was instant: FUCK YEAH!!!!!!!

Twenty-six

As soon as they moved into the living room, the atmosphere was awkward. It didn't look like a space Mitch used much. The curtains were open, so as they sat at opposite ends of the floral sofa the dark window reflected back their nervousness. Three faces stared from a large photo on the mantelpiece, presumably Lorraine and the girls. Lisa averted her eyes as she and Mitch finished their ice cream. He opened another bottle of pinot grigio, and as the wine's warmth seeped through her, she slid closer but didn't make a move. It was his turn to take the lead.

After a while, he put out his hand and took hers. She gently explored the patch of hair above his knuckles and the rough pads of his fingers, before pulling up her legs and turning to face him. He inched closer. The kiss was nice—warm and steady, like Mitch. Lisa stroked the back of his neck and they kept kissing for a long time. She unbuttoned his shirt, her fingers finding thick curls and baby-soft skin. At last, he kissed her neck and moved his hand to her breast. Her whole body was waiting. After what seemed like a lifetime of more kissing, he suggested they move into the bedroom.

"Of course, I wasn't expecting ..." he muttered, turning on the light. They were standing in front of a large king-size, a heap of what looked like clean laundry on one corner. It was obvious where Mitch slept, on the side next to a night table piled with books, a pair of glasses, and a bottle of pills. He'd taken the shade off the bedside lamp, presumably to provide better light for reading. A rowing machine took up most of the floor space on the other side of the bed.

Struggling to regain the mood, Lisa covered his hand with hers and turned off the light again. "Don't worry, neither was I."

Mitch moved the washing and started to take off his clothes, so Lisa did likewise and hurried under the covers. The bed was reassuringly firm. When he was next to her, she turned on her side and slid her hand over his chest, down to the softer skin below. Although Mitch was a big man, there was a fragile quality to his body, and a hesitancy in the way he explored hers. She traced his neck and shoulder before first circling, and then kissing, each nipple. He stroked her back, kissed her again, and when he tentatively touched her breast, she let out an involuntary moan. Her nipples were so hard they stung. She was all wanting. As her hand moved down the line of hairs on his stomach, he sighed in encouragement. She traced the fine skin on his hips, the thicker hair in the dip between them and then—his soft, wrinkled penis was in her hand.

She groaned inwardly. Wondering what to do, she kissed him while working it hopefully, but still nothing. She tried another kiss, but his response was half-hearted.

"I'm sorry," he stammered, rolling away and onto his side. "This hasn't happened before."

Lisa put her hand up to his back, the skin warm under her palm.

"It's been a long time. Lorraine was a wonderful mother and we were great companions, but, the romantic side of our marriage ended years before ... I don't know what to say."

Could this be true? Lisa was naked in bed with a man, and she was sure the pessaries had worked, but *he* couldn't do it? The words, "there are still things we could do" formed on her tongue, but Mitch sounded so abject that they never left her mouth. Instead, she tucked herself into his back. She could tell he was as full of shame about his lack of performance as she had been around Dan. She knew it would make Mitch feel better if she talked about her own problems, and she almost did, but instead she said softly, "Let's just cuddle and be cozy. We probably need time to get used to each other, that's all."

She sensed the tension in his body release as he turned around. "Would you still sleep here? I'd like that, and maybe in the morning?"

Lisa wished she had a T-shirt to put on. "Of course, and don't worry about the morning, there's no pressure."

* * *

Mitch fell asleep fast, making a small gurgling snore on every out-breath. Lisa lay beside him, wide awake and thinking. About Leonard. About the day after their wedding, when they got home.

"My love, I'm sorry." They were standing by the door to the penthouse. "My back's been playing up and all that wonderful honeymoon action, plus the drive, seem to have worsened the situation. I can barely make it over the threshold myself, let alone with you in my arms."

She kissed him suggestively. Since they'd been back together, she couldn't get enough of him. Of them. "Luckily that's never been one of my fantasies." She raised her hand to his cheek. "And, unbelievable though it is, we are both in our forties."

Leonard winced as he bent to unlock the door. "I think I'll see if the doc can squeeze me in tomorrow morning. Maybe I need a chiropractor or an x-ray or something."

This was surprising. For Leonard to go to the doctor instead of work meant he must be in real pain. She picked up both overnight bags, the rest of their bridal gear was still in the car. "That doesn't sound good. How long has it been bothering you?"

"Weeks, on and off. The osteo at the squash club says it's an occupational hazard of being tall and sitting at a desk so much of the day, but it's never been like this. Lying down is agony, so I haven't been sleeping either."

"You should have told me. Why didn't you say anything?"

"I didn't want to worry you, especially with our big day on the horizon. I assumed it was made worse by the rush to get through everything at work, and pre-wedding nerves, but now we've done the deed and it hasn't improved."

They were in the huge loft apartment, their together place, overlooking the river and London beyond. Lisa still thrilled every time she saw the view. Leonard eased himself onto a barstool. Standing behind him, she felt through his sweater and started to gently squeeze and lift the thick muscles around his shoulders. "Sounds like you could do with some stress relief. Why don't you soak in a hot tub and I'll give you a proper massage with the oil you like." She kissed the back of his neck. "Then, when you're good and relaxed, we can pretend we're back in the honeymoon suite."

"Darling, I can't believe I'm saying this, but I'm not sure I'm up to it. I'll try the bath and then go for a walk. That seems to loosen me up, makes it hurt less."

The next day Leonard came home with a pack of painkillers, saying he'd taken some at work and they hadn't made any difference. By the end of the week, he was wincing every time he moved. He'd been looking drawn, but Lisa had put it down to tiredness, and thought the weight loss was due to his busy-ness before the wedding. The tailor had taken in his suit twice. "Promise you'll go back to the doctor. It must be a slipped disc or sciatica or something."

On Monday afternoon, Leonard rang her at work. "Could you meet me at the doc's on your way home? He wants to talk to us both."

"Why?"

"Don't worry, I'm sure it's nothing." Leonard spoke in the ultra-calm voice Lisa had heard him use with clients when things weren't working out. "I haven't been into the agency. Dr. Turner sent me straight to the hospital for tests. They didn't keep me in, just said he'd have the results at the end of the day."

Panic rising, Lisa used the upbeat tone she'd perfected telling students they'd failed a course. "He probably just wants me to make sure you obey his prescription for bed rest."

When she got to the doctor's office, Leonard was there, sitting on the floor. He looked up at her, already broken. "It's not good news."

Dr. Turner waved Lisa into the chair opposite his. Afterwards, she just remembered the words "liver," "pancreas," "cancer," and "not long." The doctor pre-empted the only question she really wanted to ask by saying, "Leonard has made it clear he doesn't want to hear a timeline."

That was the end of the marriage. Marriage, Lisa realized, was based on belief in a shared future. That's what the wedding had given her—permission to trust in a life ahead with the man she loved. Until that moment, she thought the loneliness was gone. Now, with one visit to the doctor's office, it was back.

It was also the end of Lisa's interest in herself, or anyone, or anything, apart from Leonard. The next day she told her boss she needed a leave of absence, and from then she hardly left Leonard's side. Her only job was to help him in any way she could: to make sure he drank enough water, to find foods that might tempt him, and to try and anticipate his every need.

When he was lucid, he was the man she had waited so many years for, and that made the crying worse. Sometimes they wept together. Sometimes he just held her in his arms, called her his love, and stroked the back of her neck while she sobbed. When she wasn't with him, Lisa cried even more. She cried in the kitchen, in the bath, and on the balcony. She cried in the 7-Eleven, when he was napping, and when he was with visitors or on the phone.

It was the crying that introduced her to Eva, the angel who saw them through. Two days after the doctor's diagnosis, Lisa's eyes were so tear-filled that she literally bumped into a woman on the street and, surprisingly, poured out everything. The woman had lost her husband a year earlier. "You need Eva," she'd said. "She's a palliative care nurse who will come and stay in your house."

Lisa had gone home clutching a torn corner of the *Evening Standard* with Eva's phone number written on it.

By some miracle, Eva was available, and she gave Lisa the timeline she so craved. "If there's anyone Leonard needs to see, you should call them now."

After that, time became elastic, and memories started to feel more real than everyday life. In the early days, Leonard would get up and stare out of the window, eating less and less each meal, but he still went for little walks with Lisa. Then she pushed him in a wheelchair. When his hospital bed arrived, organized by Eva, Lisa moved into the guest room. After that, Leonard stopped trying to get up at all.

That's when Lisa felt truly alone. They had different agendas now. Leonard's focus was physical: dealing with his pain and the constipation that came with the morphine, saying goodbye, shielding his visitors from their upset, sleeping. He and Lisa hardly spoke. There seemed little to say, except repeated versions of I love you, and the words were beginning to feel barren.

Leonard's squash buddies appeared. His secretary. The art director he'd worked with for fourteen years. The thing Lisa hated most was seeing their distress as they left. She seldom said anything, just braced herself for the goodbye hug and closed the door. Simon and Clive, his partners at the ad agency, took turns coming by every day and reading to Leonard, just picking a book from the pile by his bed and opening it at random. Eliot, Dickens, Faulkner—Leonard would lie with his eyes closed listening, a slight smile on his gradually cracking lips, and eventually squeeze their hand, signalling it was time to go.

In the end, it was just Lisa and Leonard in a silent capsule, their penthouse high above the noise of life. Everything meaningless disappeared. He didn't want to be in a hospital and

Eva made that possible. He had an IV for fluids and medication, and morphine on a pump. Lisa spent her days stretched out next to him, whispering, stroking, reassuring. Sometimes they drifted into the darkness together, sometimes she just lay listening to him breathe, trying to imprint his smell in her memory. She no longer cried. Dr. Turner came by every few days and talked to them, but it was Eva who listened, Eva who understood, and eventually Leonard was just lying there, eyes open, staring at the ceiling, his mouth slightly ajar. The covers were off, he kept pulling them down.

Lisa rang the doctor, her voice trembling. "If this is what you call a comfortable death, there's something badly wrong."

"It's because he's so young." Dr. Turner was apologetic. "His heart is still beating, while most everything else has shut down."

"So that's it, we just have to wait?"

"I'm afraid so. It's probably harder for you right now than it is for him."

She put down the phone and gazed out of the window at the grey London sky, praying this would end. After a while, she went back into the bedroom, felt the thick carpet under her feet, and knew. The air was empty, the stillness deafening. He was gone. She looked at the most beautiful hands with the pinkest nails, the tiny chest hairs she stroked after they made love, and she wanted to die with him.

Twenty-seven

Lisa was in the garden feeling uneasy about Mitch. On paper, he was perfect—kind, good company, clever, full of integrity, and the motorbike was a definite plus. But the sad truth was that being with him made her wish she was with Dan.

She picked the last of the late summer peas off their thick stems and remembered her phone call with Mitch the night before. It had been awkward. Neither of them really knew where they stood, and their attempt to check in and chat felt forced. They weren't officially dating—how she wished there was an alternative to that word when you're in your sixties. Technically, they weren't lovers, and they certainly hadn't been all over each other the morning after. That had been awkward too. Lisa had been tempting and encouraging, Mitch had been too ashamed to try again or talk about it.

Lisa knew, in her heart, that it wasn't going to work and she wasn't looking forward to telling him, especially in light of his— inability. She would be absolutely clear that what she had to say was nothing to do with this. As she picked up the basket of peapods, she decided to invite him for supper and explain that she just wasn't ready for a relationship. She'd make it all about her.

Taking a deep breath, she walked more easily back to the house, freed by the relief of having made a decision. On the porch, she slid her phone out of her pocket and looked at the time; just enough for a shower before she had to pick up Ashley.

* * *

Through the glass panels in the art school corridor, Ashley looked radiant. Sitting in her truck, Lisa watched with pride as she confidently handed the technician a sheet of paper, bent to explain something, then stopped to point a student in the right direction, before swinging through the heavy glass doors. It was lunchtime and they were going to Home Hardware to buy paint for her bedroom. The room hadn't been decorated for years, and as Ashley would be in it for the next two, she was going to pick the colours.

"This is real nice, thank you." Ashley was standing in front of the paint swatches. "I've never had a room painted the way I wanted."

Lisa tried not to be trepidatious. Thinking of the way Ashley combined foods, clothes, and put together playlists, she hoped her paint choices wouldn't be too dramatic. After careful consideration, Ashley took a colour chart over to the window and came back pointing to a tiny square of lavender.

Lisa burst out laughing. "That is not the colour I was expecting."

Ashley's eyes flashed. "What, you thought I'd have purple and black like some twelve-year-old Goth?"

"I don't know what I thought, but I love the colour you've chosen. With white trim?"

Ashley's excitement returned. "Do you think that'd be better than a creamy colour?"

"It's completely up to you." The truth was that Lisa loved this young woman so much she could have painted the walls purple, orange or dark green. "Time for some lunch before I take you back?"

"I dunno, we're pretty busy. I'm helping the pottery students put up a display in the exhibition hall."

"Take-out then?"

Ashley ordered two huge sandwiches and a chocolate donut from the kiosk by the water. Like Leonard, she seemed able to eat never-ending amounts without gaining weight.

"We didn't buy any brushes or stuff for sanding," she said as they drove back to the art school, her mouth full of tuna salad.

"Don't worry, I've got all that in the basement. And if there's anything we need, I can pick it up tomorrow."

"Cool. I'll tell Patty I can't do lunchtimes this weekend, so we can have a real go at it. She won't be happy—holidays are always busy—but I'd rather have my room nice for when I start my course."

Ashley leapt out of the truck as soon as they pulled up outside the art school. Lisa was checking the rearview mirror, ready to reverse, when a knock on the window made her jump. Skye Stewart's face was inches from her own and there was something suspicious about her cheery smile. Lisa raised her eyebrows enquiringly.

"It's okay, you can open the window, I won't bite."

Lisa lowered the glass, sensing the young woman's delight in having the upper hand. "I thought you'd moved to Toronto."

"Leaving tomorrow. I'm just here to say bye to Ash, but we should get together next time I'm in Colville. Maybe have some tea."

Now Lisa knew something wasn't right.

"Anyhoo," Skye spoke with hateful brightness. "I'll let you go. I can see how much you want to get away."

As she accelerated toward the highway, Lisa remembered seeing the same supercilious smile the day she called Skye into her office for "the chat." Skye had always been a difficult student: missing classes, claiming dyslexic status *after* failing her exams, never completing projects. But this time, she had been reported for plagiarising another artist's work—almost comical, as Skye had managed an excellent reproduction of a Picasso painting, but wasn't bright enough to choose a lesser-known artist to copy.

Lisa didn't like expelling students, even when they were as irksome as this one. As a principal, she was constantly reminding herself that troublesome students had troubled pasts, but no one knew anything about Skye's history, even the school counselor. Lisa had never worked out how Skye had managed the entry requirements, or made it through the interview. She'd been floundering and failing ever since, as well as blaming and resisting support.

Skye had been given warnings, chances to resubmit work, even retake tests, but there was no way she could leave with a diploma. Lisa had had this conversation with students before, and each time her suggestion had been met with remorse and tearful gratitude for a way out, but she suspected Skye would be different. She certainly walked into the room looking unconcerned.

"I've asked to see you because I have a suggestion," Lisa started. "Something you might find more appealing than the alternative."

Skye gazed ahead, her face unreadable.

Lisa glanced at a print-out on the desk in front of her. "Since the last time you came to see me you've been given opportunities to improve your grades, as well as your attendance and studio hours, and I've been keeping a careful watch on your progress."

Skye still didn't look worried.

"Whatever happens in the next few weeks, it seems unlikely that you're going to leave here with a diploma, so I want to give you the opportunity to take your own action, to avoid ending up with a failure on your transcript."

A slow smirk crept over the otherwise unmoving face. "The thing is, my dog's sick."

Lisa stopped dead. Surely not.

The smile broadened. "Really sick. I think it's got the same thing that Tory's dog had."

How could she know? Tory graduated a year before Skye had even started at the art school.

"So sick that I might have to put it to sleep."

Now it was Lisa who kept her face expressionless, remembering the mess she'd uncovered to do with Tory's misuse of grant money, and her own solution to avoid public disclosure—a solution that was meant to stay secret. She had no idea what to say.

Skye's eyes were unwavering.

Lisa gathered herself and managed to find her principal-in-charge voice. "As I said, in this case, there are only two options, and the one I'm offering would probably be best."

"I don't think so, not for you or me. We wouldn't want the world to know you'd failed to report misuse of art school funds, would we? Or covered it up and used your own money."

"Enough." Lisa walked over to the window and looked past the building design students practicing straw bale construction, to the new media lab she'd raised the money for, and the sculpture forest beyond. Helping that student—Tory—out of her crisis was Lisa's only indiscretion, the one time she hadn't followed the rules. She turned back and looked directly at Skye. "Whatever you want, I cannot change your grades or performance record, or the fact you so blatantly plagiarised another artist's work. Whether you leave here with a diploma is not up to me."

"I know that." The smile was almost a snarl now. "I don't give a fuck about the diploma. What I want is a job."

"You want to work here, at the art school?" Lisa didn't try to hide her alarm.

Skye laughed—a high-pitched, unpleasant sound. "No friggin' way. I'd rather stick pins in my eyes than work in this place. It's a job in Toronto, in a design studio. I've sorted a portfolio with examples of my work—well, someone's work—and now I need a reference. A really good one. The interview's next week."

Lisa sat down behind her desk. She needed time to think. "Come back and see me again tomorrow."

Skye was undeterred. "Why can't you write it now? All you have to do is say what a great student I've been and then I'll be out of your hair. I won't have to graduate cuz I got a job instead."

Lisa didn't waiver, and when the unbearable young woman finally left, she slumped back into her chair. How on earth had Skye found out? Tory wouldn't have told anyone, and anyway, after graduating she'd gone to work on a cruise ship. Lisa remembered Tory sitting in the seat Skye had just vacated, weeping. Tory was talented and hard-working, that's why she'd been awarded the Special Merit Award—$2,000 to spend on the creation of a piece of sculpture to display in the great hall, but when she'd handed in her receipts to account for the grant money, Lisa had found a discrepancy.

Tory came into the office looking like she had been waiting for the axe to fall. The receipts she had submitted were spread out on Lisa's desk, and when she pointed out that some were missing and others wrongly dated, the poor young woman had collapsed into tears.

"I know I shouldn't have done it," she stammered. "I was just so desperate for the money, and I really thought I'd be able to make it up before I had to hand in my accounts."

Lisa knew Tory came from a foster home, that her mother had died and her father was seldom around. Tory had won a scholarship to cover her tuition and received a subsidy for her rent, and she worked two jobs to support herself.

"I tried to earn enough to pay the money back, did double shifts at the diner and got a babysitting job, but Cherry's been sick and the vet's so expensive."

Aaah, Cherry must be the little dog Lisa had seen with Tory, that looked like a cross between a Dachshund and a Poodle.

"I've had her since I was seven and she's never been sick, till now. It's all the blood work and tests that cost so much, and then they said she had to have three different kinds of medication, and ..."

"You used the grant money to pay for it."

Tory nodded, looking totally lost.

Lisa felt nothing but sympathy as she thought of Fido, her best friend and only real family.

"And now they say Cherry's got to be put down. She's got a tumour in her abdomen, so big it's stopping the blood from getting to her back legs, and it could burst at any time." The tears were streaming down Tory's face and onto the front of her jacket, leaving dark drips on faded cotton.

Lisa handed her a Kleenex, close to tears herself. "I'm so sorry. I know how important a dog can be when ... Do you know how much it'll cost to have her put to sleep?"

The car in front braked suddenly, reminding Lisa she was driving and had almost arrived at the Foodland car park. As she squeezed her truck into a tight space beside the delivery van, she remembered the relief on Tory's face when she offered to cover the vet's bills and pay for Cherry to be put down. The young woman was grateful, weeping, and terrified. Lisa took her for tea in the canteen to calm her.

But now it was time to think about food. Lisa was making stuffed peppers for supper with Mitch. Shaking her head, she picked up her purse. She still didn't regret what she'd done for Tory. The only thing she regretted was giving Skye the reference. That was certainly backfiring now.

* * *

Mitch arrived on time with a bunch of zinnias and a bottle of Cabernet Sauvignon. Something about him was different, almost glowing. Maybe he'd had a haircut?

"Come in." Lisa beckoned him into the kitchen. "I don't think you've been formally introduced to Fido."

Fido wagged his greeting and then rushed to fetch the squeaky duck. Mitch gave him a quick pat and came straight to Lisa, putting his arms around her. She turned her head to make sure the embrace was a hug, but he manoeuvred them into a kiss. A different kind of kiss from the ones they'd had. There was an eagerness to it that had been missing before, and as he pressed his body into hers, she felt something else that had been missing.

She disengaged. "Shall I open the wine, or do you want to start with a beer? I've got Molson and Grolsch." He was coming close again. She took a step back. "Or I could give you a tour of the house? You've never been inside before."

"The tour sounds good."

As they left the kitchen, Lisa felt the warmth of his hand in the small of her back. She mustn't divert. If they slept together, she'd end up hurting him, and he didn't deserve that.

"These photos all belonged to my late husband," she said when they got into the hall. "He collected them for years."

Mitch walked over and glanced at a portrait by Jane Bown, then started up the stairs to have a quick look at another by Richard Avedon, and soon he was on the top landing. Lisa joined him. "That shot of Princess Diana was taken by a photographer called Mario Testino."

"Uh-huh." Mitch looked around. "Is this your bedroom?"

Before she could avoid it, they were both staring at her pale blue duvet cover. Mitch turned and kissed Lisa's neck, his hands on her hips, pulling her to him.

"I should take the peppers out of the oven," she said into his collar. This was a lie. She had only put them in when she heard his car in the driveway.

"Wouldn't it be more romantic to stay here?"

He was unbuttoning her shirt. She was going to have to tell him now. She slipped her hands over his and spoke gently. "Let's go back into the kitchen."

Mitch looked down. "The thing is, it's a matter of timing. It would be better if ... I'm not sure it'll be safe to try again after we've eaten."

Lisa perched on the edge of the bed. "I don't understand."

Mitch's head dropped as he sat down next to her. "I took tablets before I left the house. Then on my way over I was thinking about you—about the other night—and I got hard. I didn't expect that, but here it is and I don't know how long it's going to last, or what'll happen if we don't .... And it doesn't say how many hours I'm meant to wait before taking any more."

"Viagra?"

"Similar product, different brand. I took one yesterday as a test run and it wasn't very effective, that's why I took two today. So maybe you could get the food out of the oven and come back upstairs?"

Lisa wondered if they should sleep together, just so they could both see if their parts were in working order, but when she saw his vulnerability, she knew she had to tell him the truth. She took his hand. "This is terrible timing, and it really does have nothing to do with your virility, but I don't think we're a very good idea."

He gazed at her. "You want us to stop seeing each other?" There was still a huge lump in his pants.

"I thought I was ready to be in a relationship, and Susan was right to introduce us because you are exactly the kind of person I should be with, but I just can't do it. Maybe I've been on my own for too long, or I'm not ready. It really isn't anything to do with you."

He looked down, spreading his hands over his knees. "I don't think I've ever felt so humiliated."

"I'm sorry. I never should have let it get this far. You are a wonderful and brave man to have gone to such lengths and to talk about it so honestly. Much more courageous than I—"

"Please don't. The more you say, the worse I feel. Maybe you could just go downstairs and leave me here a while, to sort myself out."

* * *

The table was laid, the wine open, and Lisa was holding a tray of sizzling stuffed peppers when Mitch came into the kitchen. He seemed surprised to see the food. "I don't think I can eat, I'll just head home."

"Are you sure? It's all here. We could still spend the evening together."

"Maybe we can do that sometime, but right now I'm a bit too raw. I'm sorry, after you've gone to all this effort."

It was hard to see Mitch so dejected, especially knowing she was the cause. "You shouldn't be apologizing to me, I'm the one—"

"Just give me some time." He stepped forward, his lips brushing her cheek, and as he went through the door, Lisa realized she was still wearing oven gloves.

Twenty-eight

Ashley was a surprisingly diligent painter. She had much more patience for the prep—washing, sanding, and filling—than Lisa, who thought indoor tasks like this were something to be accomplished, rather than enjoyed.

"I did it as a job, just for a few months, helping this guy that was a painter and decorator. I loved it but then we split up and things got 'tricky.'" Grinning, Ashley made air quotes around the word, before picking up her brush and handing Lisa a roller. The room smelled softly of paint. "He gave me a whole load of emulsion that was left over from the house we were doing up, but I never got around to using it. Dunno why. It would have made my room nicer, but the rest of the squat was such a shit-hole that I could never work up the mojo."

Lisa poured paint into the flat tray. "How long did you live there?"

"Just the last couple of years. Before that I was all over the place—on people's floors, sofas, even had a few weeks on the street. But when I got my NI number I started doing proper jobs and settled down a bit. That's how I saved enough money to get here, with bar work and a bit of cleaning at weekends."

There was a pile of plastic-covered furniture, clothes, DVDs, cushions, boots, bags, and books on photography between them. Lisa wanted to stop painting and listen properly, encourage Ashley to keep talking, but she thought it might have the opposite effect, so instead she kept her back turned and her roller moving. "Was that when you worked for the firm that fixed appliances?"

"Nah, that was my second job, after the sandwich shop. I loved that lunch place. It was near the Harry Potter bridge and the tourists were great. Americans used to come in and tip me a fiver for handing them a sausage roll. Brits don't even tip taxi drivers anymore."

"So you didn't go straight to the squat after your mum passed?"

"No way. I didn't stay anywhere for very long, I was too busy avoiding social services. Like I told you, I left the hospital just before she died. When I knew it was coming, I went home and grabbed the stuff I wanted, and stayed with this boy while his parents were on holiday. I never saw Mum again, but I'd been saying my goodbyes for weeks, years really. Every time I left the house, I thought she might be dead when I got home."

Lisa remembered the years of longing for her own mother and wondered how Ashley had survived. "I'm sorry you had to go through that, it sounds really tough."

"Well, you know what they say ..."

Lisa turned around. "So you didn't go to the funeral?"

Ashley kept her eyes on her brush. "Nah, not my thing. It was time to move on."

"Oh no." Lisa looked at her phone. "I need to get going. I've got a mammogram in an hour."

"Apparently they're really painful."

"Definitely not nice, especially if you've got little boobs like us."

* * *

Setting off for the hospital, Lisa put on the radio and was happy to hear Simon and Garfunkel. She'd always loved them. But as she turned into the lane, she listened to the lyrics, about being a rock and an island, and stopped by Norm's driveway. The next verse was worse, talking about having no need of friendship, and that friendship causes pain. Lisa turned off the radio. She'd spent too much of her life being an island. She looked at Norm's bungalow, surrounded by the debris of his solitary life, and missed him. She missed his acrid comments and curmudgeonly smile, and the way he went soft at the sight of Fido. She decided to go round and see him the next day, to buy an apple pie at the market and take it as a peace offering.

She had to rush to get to her mammogram on time. Perched on the plastic chair, wearing only her bra and jeans, she answered the technologist's routine questions and paused at one she'd never noticed before: "Do you use any estradiol vaginal inserts?"

"Why do you ask that?"

"Honey, it's on the list. I just tick the boxes." The technologist kept her smile steady and obviously knew better than to offer a medical opinion. "I do know that if you answer yes you have to be checked every year, instead of every two years." She glanced at her screen. "But I see on your notes that you come annually anyway because you have a first-degree relative who had breast cancer?"

Lisa's brow creased as she nodded. "But if using topical estrogen means you have to be checked more often, it must put you in a higher risk bracket."

The same smile. "I told you dear, I just ask the questions. So when you're ready, take off your bra and stand over there, on that cross on the floor."

As the plates moved together, mangling Lisa's breast, she hardly felt the pain. Her brain was whirring louder than the machinery. *If using pessaries means a woman has to be screened annually, there must be an increased risk. Why hadn't Dr. Lau made this clear?*

Lisa felt her cheeks flush as she realized her own stupidity: by chasing the dream of making her body younger, she'd put herself in danger of getting cancer. She was such a fool, shoving all those pessaries into herself, and what for—the pretense of being something she wasn't?

"Okay, if you could just move to the other side of the plate."

The technologist's hands were warm, and as they manoeuvred Lisa's breast onto the cold piece of glass, she thought of her mother. How she'd just disappeared, and Auntie Jean had gone the same way. Lisa shivered.

When she got home, she went straight up to the bathroom cabinet and took out the pessaries. Tipping the aluminium packs out of the box, she tore the applicator strips apart one by one and dropped them in the little pedal bin. Then she ripped the cardboard box into shreds. As a scrap printed with the words "vaginal insert" fell into the sink, she said, "I'm done," and went downstairs into the kitchen. Susan would be arriving soon for lunch.

* * *

They ate on the front porch while Ashley, still in her paint-splattered jeans, provided entertainment with a story about Chase buying banana-flavoured condoms. "I like my 'nanas chopped on Cheerios, not up my vag, and the smell was disgusting—so fake. The more we did it, the stronger it got, like having sex in the bloody greengrocers. I made him go out and get the right ones for the morning."

Lisa loved seeing her two friends together and smiled when Susan talked about Ashley meeting her daughters. "You'll love them," she cooed. "They'll both be back for the holidays and Lisa always comes over on Christmas day. I hope you will too."

After lunch, Ashley headed off to the art school for her goodbye party, before returning as a student.

"She's a hoot." Susan put down her fork. "Especially on the topic of sex."

Lisa gazed at her empty plate, wondering whether to take the risk. "You and I have hardly ever talked about sex. Well, I guess I wasn't having any to talk about, but I'd love to know how, I mean, do you and Grant—?"

"Oh honey." Susan flipped her hand. "We're down to anniversaries and birthdays, and even then it's hardly worth the trouble."

"I'm amazed. You always seem so loving and happy together."

"We are, it's just that when it comes to the physical, things aren't what they were—for either of us."

"Does that mean that you—?"

"Dry as the Saraha. And even with lube, it's not the same. It takes me so long to come, I think my nerve endings have withered."

When the doctor told her that an estimated 50% of all older women experienced pain during intercourse, Lisa hadn't really believed it. Somewhere, subconsciously, she had decided she was different to everyone else—or worse. She leaned forward. "It hurt when I slept with Dan and I thought it was because I hadn't done it for so long. Since then I've been torturing myself with different brands of pessaries."

Susan shook her head. "Janet didn't get on with them either. I was on HRT for a few months but it made me hungry *all* the time and I blew up into a baby elephant. Pam got a three-centimetre cyst in her breast when she was on the pessaries, and Diane and Roy haven't had sex since her sixtieth birthday. She doesn't think he minds, says he hasn't really been into it since the kids were born."

Lisa felt foolish. Why hadn't she told Susan what she was going through?

"But it must be tough with a new man. I wouldn't want to be in your position, starting a relationship when you're desiccated. What did Dan say?"

Lisa answered into her lap. "I didn't tell him. I said I just wanted to be friends, and for us to spend time getting to know each other better, while I was secretly hoping the pessaries would work."

"And he went to Manitoba and met someone else." Susan put her hand over Lisa's. "Oh sweet pea, I'm so sorry."

Lisa's phone pinged and she was surprised to see the message was from Dan, but she waited until Susan had gone before reading it. He hadn't been in touch since that dreadful time Lisa had run into him with Julie. Going to be around for a couple of weeks after Labour Day to sign final docs with Warren and sort out stuff before flying back to start new job. Would be good to see you. Don't like the way we left it. Want to meet up?

Lisa put the phone in her back pocket and went upstairs to finish painting. She had to think.

* * *

Later that night, lying on her bed, Lisa replied to Dan's text: Next week would be great. Want to walk Fido together?

She had watched Ashley say what she thinks and ask for what she wants, and now Lisa was going to do the same. She was going to tell Dan the truth, about her feelings for him, her condition, and her fear that he wouldn't want her if they couldn't have fantastic sex. She'd explain that she'd never really wanted to be platonic, and that she was in love with him.

Rehearsing the words made her peaceful. She was sixty-one years old and had seldom risked speaking her true feelings. In the early years with Leonard, she had wasted so much time secretly longing and trying to change herself to please him. She'd never told Dad how she ached for his affection, or shown Nicky her hurt. Lisa knew it was probably too late with Dan, that he was committed to Julie and moving to Manitoba, but she had to try. She finally understood the freedom that would come from talking honestly. After that, she couldn't control what happened.

Twenty-nine

The Saturday Farmer's Market on Labour Day weekend meant the start of Ontario apples as well as the last of the summer raspberries, and Lisa wanted to be there early. She was also going to get some Brinjal pickle. The Indian restaurant had just started selling it at the jam and chutney booth and she was making veggie curry for supper—Chase's favourite. When they'd eaten, she and Ashley were going to hear his farewell gig at Patty's. He'd be leaving for Toronto on Monday.

As she opened her truck door, Lisa paused to watch a hawk hover effortlessly in the crisp morning sky. After buckling her seatbelt, she ran her hand over the steering wheel, enjoying its cool smoothness, and set off for town.

The maples were already tipped red, their silhouettes like sculptures against the brilliant blue. Two deer bounded along the road ahead, leaving a trail of dust in the newly laid gravel. Lisa didn't know how Dan would react to her declaration, but the great thing was that she wasn't afraid to tell him. Whatever happened, she was looking forward to it.

Sunlight strobed through the branches on her left, she was almost level with the tops of tall trees growing up the side of the ravine running down to the river. Lisa wanted to get to the market before it filled with weekenders. She had done this drive a million times, but today, as the road curved to the right, the truck slid sideways on loose gravel. Her mind was sharp as her hands gripped the wheel more tightly. *Steer into the skid—into the skid.* She turned the wheel and nothing happened. Her knuckles tightened around it as her tires seemed to disconnect from the road. The truck was spinning and the house she had just passed on the right was now in front of her. Road, house, trees—road, house, trees. She spun out of control onto the wrong side of the road facing backwards. Now she was gliding again, to the edge.

Lisa shut her eyes as a terrible crashing and crunching filled her ears.

Then silence. She was hanging sideways, kept in place by the seatbelt. The truck had rolled and landed on its side. Still gripping the steering wheel, she was scarily calm. *What just happened? Why didn't the airbags inflate?* She turned off the ignition and did a quick body check: head, neck, shoulders, hands, and legs. Nothing hurt. Good. If I undo my seatbelt I'm going to fall hard onto the other side of the truck. She carefully looked around. One of the back windows was blown out. She knew from watching movies that she should get out quickly before the gas leaked or something exploded.

She heard a car slow down and stop on the road above. A woman's voice, shrill. "Oh my God! Oh my God!"

Lisa eased her legs around and over until her feet were almost in the passenger footwell. Undoing the belt, she allowed herself to drop and then manoeuvred until she was standing on the passenger window.

"Are you alright?"

She ignored the high-pitched question and focused on getting hold of the driver's door handle. Her fingers were under the chrome opener but it felt backwards. It took a lot of concentration to figure out which way to tug it open. At last, the familiar clunk and she pushed but it didn't move, the door was too heavy. Lisa adjusted her feet, bent her knees, took a deep breath and jumped up, shoving with all her strength. The truck made a deafening metallic groan as it started to roll and she heard the woman scream.

Thirty

Fido finally gave up looking out of the window and lay down on the landing to nap, waking at regular intervals. Driveway. Nap. Driveway. Nap. Squirrel. Nap.

Movement upstairs. She's awake. The other one. The one that talks and tickles but doesn't take me out or feed me. She'll be down soon.

Nap.

Scratch behind the ears. Roll over, tummy rub, and there she goes down the driveway on her wheels.

Driveway. Nap. Driveway.

I want to go out. It's time for my walk.

Driveway. Nap.

I'm hungry.

When is Lisa coming home?

Thirty-one

Lisa lay still, wondering what time it was as she watched Ashley move quietly around the over-bright room. She was taking close-ups: IV bag, monitor, call button, then paused to change the position of Lisa's sneaker next to the leg of the hospital bed before clicking the shutter.

It was never quite day or night in the hospital, and Lisa never felt fully awake or asleep. From the throbbing in her leg, she thought she must be due for some more pain meds, and from the squeak of wheels stopping and starting in the corridor, it sounded like food was coming. Hopefully, the message had filtered through that she was vegetarian. Over the last four days, she had left platefuls of hamburger, chicken, and fish, but it didn't really matter—she had little appetite and the medication made her woozy. It took the edge off, but there was still a constant gnawing ache in her shin. She'd never felt anything like it. She also had a big bump on her temple, but thankfully the CT scans had come back clear.

Ashley turned around and put her camera down on the windowsill. "Hiya. You've been asleep all morning. I got some great shots of your toes sticking out of that boot contraption; hope that's okay. It cringes me out to think you've got screws in your leg."

Lisa smiled, her voice quiet. "And a metal plate."

"Disgusting." Ashley wrinkled her nose. "Oh sorry, I know you're lucky to be alive an' everything." She held up a bag from the thrift store. "I went through your wardrobe for something you could wear to come home, but all the jeans and skirts looked too narrow to fit over the big boot thing, so I got you this." She pulled out a sleeveless suede dress with fringing at the bottom. "I know it's a bit Wild West, but I thought you could put it over a T-shirt or a sweater."

Lisa laughed and started coughing. As she hauled herself up, a pain shot through her shin and the gasp stuck in her throat—no sound, no air either. Her lungs barely moved. She tried to take a breath but nothing happened.

"Are you okay?"

"Just a bit hard to—" The words prompted a coughing fit. Lisa saw her own fear reflected in Ashley's eyes, but the next breath was easier. Ashley took her hand and the contact was soothing, helping Lisa's breathing become regular until she could talk again. "It's probably just because I've been lying around since Saturday."

Ashley poured some water and Lisa took little sips. Her mouth was dry.

An orderly stood in the doorway. "Mac 'n cheese?"

"Thank you." Lisa started coughing again and something stabbed at her back. Lifting the lid off her plate, she felt nauseous and couldn't bring herself to eat the cream-covered pasta or once-frozen peas. The stabbing was in her chest now, making her anxious, but she didn't want to worry Ashley. "I think I need to close my eyes again for a few minutes."

Still looking concerned, Ashley perched on the chair by the window. "Don't worry, I'll be here."

Lisa lay still, trying to relax, trying to feel normal. Suddenly a boulder rolled onto her chest and her eyes grew round as she desperately tried to suck in air.

Ashley jumped up. "What is it?"

"Suffocating." The word was tiny. Lisa tried to move and something pierced between her ribs. She couldn't grasp the air. Now a knife was driving into her chest.

"Help. We need help in here." Ashley's voice was wobbly and loud. As she ran toward the nurse's station, Lisa started to panic. She really couldn't breathe now. Ashley ran back in, followed by the new grad nurse, who looked terrified. She yelled at Ashley, "You need to leave. Get out. Get out NOW."

Fear filled the room and Ashley raised her hand to block a sob. Another nurse came in and spoke to her more gently. "It's nothing to be alarmed about. We just need to take care of your friend. You go sit in the waiting room and we'll come and get you."

All Lisa could hear now was the sound of her own gasping, and then voices—"response team," "code blue," "ICU," "doctor." Another nurse hurried in and put a mask on her, telling her to take deep breaths. Lisa felt air blow on her face but she still couldn't breathe. Someone rushed in behind a machine with wires on it, Lisa's gown was lifted, things were stuck to her arms, legs, chest. A voice came from nowhere and Lisa just managed to grasp the words. "Stay as still as you can. We're going to do a reading of your heart." As her hand was lifted, Lisa kept focusing on the voice. "This thing I'm putting on your finger, it measures your oxygen."

Tightness around her arm, something sharp. Another voice talked about blood work.

A man raced in with a bigger machine. Sitting her up, Lisa felt dizzy as he put a big board behind her. "Take a deep breath and hold it." That hurt so much she almost passed out. Now there were nurses all around, sliding her onto a stretcher. One of them said something about a scan. "So we can get a better picture of what's happening. Then you're going to the ICU."

Florescent lights flashed and the next voice Lisa heard was Ashley's, high-pitched and strained. "What's happening? Where are you taking her?" It sounded like she was running alongside. "What's going on? Is she dying?"

Thirty-two

"Hi there Lisa, my name is Marcia." The voice was gentle but authoritative. "I'm your nurse today. It's Wednesday. You've had a pulmonary embolism and you're in the Intensive Care Unit of Colville Hospital."

Dry. Cold. Thirsty.

"It was touch and go there for a while. We weren't sure you were going to make it. It's lucky you had this PE in the hospital."

Hand on my arm. Warm. Nice.

"If you'd have gone home and had it, things could have been very different. It's a good job your friend called the nurses the way she did, could have been bad if she hadn't been there."

Fuddled head. Itchy face. What's this?

"Lisa, you need to leave that on. You've got oxygen in your nose. It's probably making you feel dry, but it's really helping you right now. Just rest. I'm going to give you a little more pain medication."

Relief. Sleep. Dream. So cozy. Mum's reading a story, my favourite, The Tiger Who Came to Tea. Nicky's on the end of the bed, her feet under my blanket.

Noise. Voices. Footsteps. Face up close.

"I'm Dr. Blunstone. How are you feeling? We did a CT of your chest. Remember we put you in that machine?"

Too-bright light, round face, beard, kind eyes.

"We took pictures of your chest and found a pulmonary embolism, which is a clot in your lungs. This tells us why you're having a hard time breathing. If you can lean forward, I'm going to listen to your chest."

Why do they keep waking me up? And that thing round my arm, the big whooshing noise as soon as I drop off. I just need to sleep, to close my eyes.

"Hey Lisa, how's it going? Remember me, I'm Marcia? Just going to open the blinds. How are you feeling today?"

Daylight. Green walls, green curtains, wires fixed to my chest. Beeping above my head. Something on my finger, the thing on my arm, needle in my hand, tube. "What day is it?"

"How long have you been here?" Marcia was putting a tourniquet around Lisa's arm, preparing to take blood. "Two days. I'm just going to check your heparin IV. It's an intravenous blood thinner to get rid of your clot."

"Ashley." The word was tiny. "My, my, young friend. Been here?"

"Not on my shift and I've been your nurse since you came in. The only visitor I've seen is that fella who was here yesterday—quite the charmer. He sat by the bed for a couple of hours while you were sleeping."

The words tangled. Lisa wanted to ask, but it was such an effort. She was too busy breathing. Breathing too fast. She closed her eyes as Marcia was holding her foot, feeling for a pulse, and woke up to see a silhouette in the doorway, behind a bunch of roses. Her heart bounced. *Could it be? Is he the one who was here yesterday?*

"Hey, kiddo."

Mitch's voice was bright. Lisa wanted to be pleased to see him, but she wished—

"No need to talk." He pulled a chair up to the side of the bed. "I don't want to wear you out, just thought I'd to pop in again before I leave for Tobermory. Terrible timing, but I'm going away with the girls and grandkids. It's been booked for weeks." He sat down and leaned toward her, speaking gently. "It's good to see you awake. You had us all worried there for a while."

"How did you?" Lisa's lungs felt too small.

Mitch bent his head near. "Know you were here?"

She nodded.

"Purely by chance. I was out for a ride and thought I'd stop by your place. I'd been meaning to come by because we hadn't seen each other since ... anyway, the young woman—"

"Ashley."

"Yes. Ashley had just come back from the hospital. She was in a hell of a state. I was glad I could be there for her, she seemed quite traumatised."

Lisa longed to see Ashley.

"I made her a cup of tea and we sat on the porch together till she calmed down. In the end she phoned her boyfriend and he came to pick her up."

"She's in Toronto?" Disappointment hit Lisa in the belly. Taking a ragged breath, she whispered "Fido?"

"He's fine. He's been with a neighbour since the accident because Ashley was spending so much time in the hospital."

"Norm."

"Correct. She said he'd looked after your dog in the past. I left a voicemail for Susan last night, told her where you were, but haven't heard back yet. She's in Madrid now—sent me a pic of them all outside the Prado."

Lisa didn't want to be rude, but her eyes closed anyway. When the nurse came to check on her a while later, Mitch was gone and there was a fat little wooden bird on the table by her bed.

Lisa asked the nurse. "My friend, the one who was here?"

She leaned forward to tuck in the sheet. "He asked me to tell you he's gone on holiday and he'll see you when he gets back."

* * *

As the days went by, Lisa was more and more exhausted. The glaring greenish light was relentless and it seemed like a nurse woke her up every ten minutes to take her temperature, check her oxygen levels, look at the monitor, or ask the same tedious questions: How's the pain? Do you know where you are? Can you tell me what day it is? Lisa was hungry but food made her queasy. She hated the catheter and was sick of wearing diapers, and she kept sliding down on the air mattress and ending up in a tangle of sheets. That was another annoying thing the nurses were always doing, "Just fixing the bed." And Lisa still hadn't heard from Ashley. Susan texted from Spain every few hours but Lisa wanted Ashley.

Lisa was also starting to think. About her life. About what she wanted from it. Cliché or not, the question was inevitable. She'd never had a bucket list, was now the time to make one? Did she want to go skydiving, hot air ballooning, gliding? See the Taj Mahal or the Pyramids? Not really. She tried to reposition her leg and remembered she hadn't done her exercises.

At first, the visits from Frank, the physiotherapist, had been a comfort. He just sat calmly beside Lisa, chatting, helping her breathe. They'd breathe together, which she found strangely comforting. He'd put his hand on her tummy, encouraging her to draw her breath down. "Remember, breath flows where the attention goes," he'd say, and it seemed to work.

But Frank's demands were gradually increasing. He'd asked her to do five deep breathing repetitions every hour, as well as pump her good ankle and tighten the calf and thigh muscles, and lift her arms above her head regularly, but she didn't have the energy.

Today the catheter was finally out and Lisa just wanted to sleep. Frank appeared, smiling that interminably encouraging smile, as he positioned a chair beside her bed. "It's time to get you up. I want you to transfer from the bed to this chair, sit in it and come back to bed. And then maybe we'll go for a walk."

"I'm too tired." Lisa turned her head away. Her whole body was leaden and weak, drugged with fatigue.

"Today's the day, Lisa. It's important to get you moving. Apart from anything, we need to make sure you don't end up with stiffness in your ankle and foot that could be difficult to rectify later on. Moving early is fundamental to best recovery."

Lisa spoke into the pillow. "I don't want to. I don't feel well enough."

"Come on, we're going to do this, with lots of pacing and breaks."

Lisa remembered Dad making her go to school when she had the flu. How she'd begged him to let her stay home, but Nicky wasn't there and he said Lisa couldn't be in the house alone. Well, now she wasn't a child and Frank wasn't her father. She looked around at him. "No." The word came out a wheezy shout and an arid cough took over. "See, I'm too sick. Leave me alone." She knew she sounded like a petulant seven-year-old and she didn't care. "I've had enough of being here and I don't want to sit in a chair. Go away, I need to sleep."

Frank crouched down next to the bed, removed the pulse oximeter from Lisa's finger and cupped her hand in his. "I know this is hard, but it's necessary. I'm right here with you. If you only manage to transfer to the chair today, that's okay, and I'll be right here with you tomorrow, and the day after."

Lisa looked into his kind eyes and her own filled. She hadn't ever believed that someone would be there for her tomorrow, and the day after, and the next. That was what she wanted in her future, someone to rely on. Someone to love her who she could love back. She started to cry. Gentle rolling tears that transformed into great big choking sobs, gripping her chest like a vice, making her cry more.

Frank stayed where he was, her hand in his. "Lisa, you've been through a lot. A pulmonary embolism is a very big deal. It's true that you could have died. And, from what I understand, one minute you were driving along the road and the next you were in here with a fractured distal fibula. You've had a great deal of pain, an operation, and a bump on the head. All that is a big shock to the system, it's not surprising you're upset."

Right there in that moment, Lisa didn't think anyone had ever been this nice to her and it made her cry more. "I'm so broken and alone," she whispered, and he kept holding her hand as she wept.

When the tears subsided, her head felt clearer. Frank handed her a glass of water. This was very new, not being able to look after herself.

"Are you ready to try transferring from the bed to the chair now?"

Slowly, Lisa nodded.

Thirty-three

"Here you are." The nurse handed Lisa her phone. "All charged up."

"Thank you." Lisa was nervous. She cleared her throat and tapped in the code for England, then her old number. She didn't even know if they lived there anymore. It rang for a long time before, "Nicky, is that you?"

"It was last time I looked. Who's that?"

"Lisa."

Silence.

"Your sister."

"Yeah, I know who you are."

The disappointment was familiar. "How are you?"

"Nice of you to inquire after, now let me see, more than thirty years?"

"It's good to hear your voice." Lisa suppressed a cough.

"Was there something you wanted, or is this just a social call?"

"I had a car crash." She tried to slow her breathing. "And a few days ago I had a pulmonary embolism—a big blood clot. I almost died."

"Huh. So you almost croaked and thought you'd better make peace with the fam?"

Lisa cleared her throat. "Not exactly."

"Still the same Lisa. Still all about you."

She wheezed, the pain of the past constricting her lungs.

"So why *did* you call?"

"I told you, I was really sick and it made me think that if I had died ... I didn't want ... so is Dad ... are you living there now?"

"Now?" Nicky's laugh was bitter. "I've never stopped living here. I did have plans, I was going away, but then the old man had a stroke."

Suddenly Lisa was six years old again, struggling to work out what was happening in her own family, her only information coming through the filter of her sister's anger. "How is he? Is he going—?"

"The first was fifteen years ago. He's had two more since then."

So Nicky was still at home, looking after Dad. "That can't have been easy."

"Fucking right it hasn't been easy. My life hasn't been easy since 1963."

Lisa was starting to understand. In a way, her life *had* been all about her.

"Anyway, Dad's okay now. We're both okay, no thanks to you."

"He must be—what—nearly ninety?"

"You don't even how old he is?"

"How about you? Still working? Is there, anyone special?"

"You sound like a bloody Hallmark card. No, no one special. Feeding and cleaning up after the old fart doesn't leave much time for anything else. And yes, I still work. I've had to earn for us both single handed since the stroke. We did manage to buy the house off the council, but that's left us with a mortgage that still isn't paid off."

"Oh Nicky, I'm sorry."

Lisa's words felt inadequate and she could hear the frustration in her sister's silence.

"Is Dad bedridden? Does he go out?"

"I told you, we're doing fine."

"Can I talk to him?"

"He's asleep, and the shock'd probably give him another stroke. Try phoning at a time that's convenient for us, not when I've just got him tucked up for the night."

"Of course. I will."

More silence.

Lisa asked tentatively, "Want to know anything about me?" She heard Nicky shift position, imagined her sitting on the bottom stair the way she used to, phone wedged against her shoulder,

"I know you're in Canada and that you've had a lot more choices than you left me with. I know you're principal of some fancy college, which probably pays quite well. And now I know you only called because you nearly died and that scared the shit out of you, not coz you care about us. Anything else?"

"Can I leave my number?"

"I've done without it this long, can't think why I'd need you now."

"Please take it, if only so you can tell me if anything happens to Dad."

With an annoyed sigh, Nicky put down the receiver and Lisa heard the drawer open in the hall table. She remembered it so well—walnut veneer with the front leg broken and glued back together. She could see her sister pushing aside minicab cards and pizza flyers, rummaging for a pen before she wrote down the number.

"And I'm five hours behind U.K. time."

"Yeah, I know. I'm not completely ignorant."

"Nicky, I never thought you were."

Her sister's voice grew synthetically cheery. "Tara then. Have a nice life."

"I'll ring again soon and talk to Dad."

Another pause. Lisa willed her sister to say something else, but with a blip, the call ended. Staring at the wall, she thought about how things congeal in memory. After all those years of resentment, she wanted to wrap her arms around her sister, to say she understood. Until this moment, it had never occurred to Lisa that she had the power to wound either Nicky or Dad, but now Nicky's life seemed tragic, and thinking about it hurt more than the coughing. Eventually, Lisa sank into the pillow and slept.

Norm was standing awkwardly at the door to her room when she woke up. He seemed older and smaller. She hadn't seen him since their big bust-up. He handed her a bunch of cellophane-wrapped blue-dyed carnations and an envelope. "Thought you'd like the colours."

Lisa put the flowers on the table by her bed, her voice stronger since sleeping. "Thank you. I'll ask the nurse to find a vase later. And a card—how lovely."

"Not a card, it's photos."

She pulled out half a dozen prints of Fido—sitting by his food bowl, with his squeaky duck, offering a paw, sleeping by the woodstove—all taken at Norm's. Lisa's heart lurched when she saw those beautiful brown eyes and she passed her fingers slowly over each image, imagining the comfort of the fur.

"Knew you'd be missing him. 'Fraid I'm not very handy with a camera. Took a whole heap but them's all that came out."

"Oh Norm, that's so thoughtful." Lisa had to pause for breath. "And thank you for looking after him."

"The young'un that's been staying at your place turned up and asked if I'd have him so she could be here with you. That's how I knew you was in hospital. Then she came round and said she was going to the city, asked if I'd take him more permanent like."

Lisa nodded and motioned for Norm to sit down. She'd left another message for Ashley, sent a couple of texts, but still hadn't heard back.

Norm looked at the plastic-covered seat suspiciously before sitting on it. "S'pose the truck's totalled."

"I guess so. I haven't really thought about it. I still don't remember the accident."

"Probably best. Have you phoned your insurance? Bottom feeders, the lot of 'em, but you best get the claim going. You might get a new truck out of it." Norm folded his arms, resting them on his little pot belly. "I been calling round to water the garden. Took the last of the beets and beans, you've still got some squash and kale."

Lisa thanked him again. She'd never heard Norm so chatty and he kept going, about Fido and how dry the weather had been, which trees were turning, and then he started fiddling with a button on his overshirt. "I want to say sorry. I'm not proud of the way I threw you out. I know you was only trying to help. You and that dog, you're the closest thing to family I got now, since the boy went to Toronto."

Lisa took her hand out from under the covers. "You know, I was planning to come and see you the day I had my accident. I realized how much I missed you."

Norm was still looking at his button. "But I shouldn'a talked to you that way."

She leaned forward and touched his arm. "You're my family too. I know it was the worry talking. It must be awful to face losing your home, and all that's left of Rose. I still wish I could help."

Norm looked up, his face full of fire. "Well, I'm not going to make it easy for 'em." He leaned forward. "I've got a plan."

Lisa was too tired to ask. Her eyes flickered shut and Norm pushed back his chair.

"But I best be going."

* * *

When Lisa woke up, the blinds were closed and the lights had been dimmed. She rolled over and—*was it? Could it be?* The smile spread all the way to his eyes.

"Thank Christ you're alright." He came closer, crouched by the bed.

Hot tears ran down her cheeks.

Dan leaned forward, so close she could feel his breath, smell the fresh air on him. Two nurses walked past the open door, casting a shadow on the floor. They were laughing. Lisa noticed tiny specks of brown in the hazel of his eyes. She closed hers and their lips touched.

Thirty-four

The next morning, Lisa moved out of ICU into the orthopaedic ward where, luckily for her, the only bed available was in a private room. The freedom was wonderful. She was off the heparin drip, could go to the bathroom on her own, and creep along slowly behind her walker. In ortho, the nurses, and the atmosphere, were more relaxed. Lisa was still a bit short of breath when she moved or talked too much, but she was starting to feel herself. And Dan was back.

He arrived the moment visiting hours began and his energy filled the room. He brought chocolates, a pile of books, and jars of honey for the nurses.

"I wasn't sure what you'd like to read." He put the books down on Lisa's bedside table. "So I brought my favourites."

She looked at the spines: *East of Eden* by John Steinbeck, *The Englishman's Boy* by Guy Vanderhaeghe, and *Winnie the Pooh.*

"And, in case you couldn't cope with too many words," he handed her a picture book called *The World's Most Beautiful Gardens,* the cover overflowing with bougainvillea. Then he leant over and kissed her. Very gently.

"Oops," they heard from the doorway and Lisa's favourite nurse, Sheldon, stood there grinning through his moustache.

Dan looked around and laughed.

"I'll be back in a while." Sheldon winked and closed the door behind him.

Dan sat on the side of Lisa's bed and leaned forward, kissing her again. Her fingers slipped under his jacket and felt the length of his back. He put his hands around her waist and pulled her to him. Her leg was glowing with pain and it didn't matter. Dan pulled up a chair and they just looked at each other, both grinning, until her brain kicked in. "How did you know I was here?"

"I only got back a few days ago, and I know we'd arranged to get together on Saturday, but I had a Japanese maple that needed a home and thought I'd surprise you with it. You weren't in, so I was just leaving it on the porch when this old guy turned up."

"Norm."

"That's it. He told me what had happened and I came straight away. My whole body buckled at the thought of losing you." Dan kissed her again. "Oh Lisa, I've been so stupid."

"But what about Manitoba? Julie?"

Dan took Lisa's hand, stroking the side of her thumb with his. "All I know for sure is that I want to be with you."

"But aren't you meant to be moving there? Living with her?"

"I'm not due to fly for another week. I know it's a big ask, but could we not talk about that now? Let's just be here, with each other."

Lisa's phone vibrated and she glanced at the screen. "It's Ashley. I haven't managed to speak to her yet."

Dan nodded. "Go ahead, I'll get us a coffee."

Ashley's voice was strange. "This is awesome. Sorry, that sounds crap. I don't know what to say, I never thought I'd talk to you again. How are you feeling?"

"Much stronger every day. All I want now is to come home, see you, and snuggle Fido."

"Any idea when that'll be?"

"Maybe as early as next week. They've just got to get me moving with crutches and make sure the medication is working. Will you be there?"

"Of course. I've been in Toronto, with Chase."

"That's what I heard. How's that going with your course?"

"I've, well I haven't, they said I could defer."

"Oh Ashley, I'm sorry. It's because of me."

"Don't be stupid. I just couldn't focus, or handle staying in the house alone. Anyway, Toronto's cool. I've got some bar work, you know, under the table. Listen, gotta go. Be back on Monday so I'm home when you get there. I'll text."

Lisa felt like she'd lost something precious. She and Ashley had grown so close over the summer and now that seemed gone, but as Dan came back carrying two red paper cups, Lisa filled with gratitude. She was alive. She could drink coffee. She had her life ahead of her, and she wanted it to include him. She took a deep breath—her first since the embolism. "Okay. Let's not mention Julie for now," she said, feeling like someone else. "But I would like to hear about Manitoba."

Dan spent the day telling stories about camping and collecting bugs, getting to know his daughter's boyfriend, and making peace with his ex-wife. Lisa talked about her summer with Ashley—the almost bar fight, meeting Chase, and realizing how cloistered her life had become before she retired. She decided not to mention Mitch. Every now and then Dan leaned forward and they kissed, making her heart swell. Lisa was surprised at how easy she found it not to think about Julie. He was here with her now, and now seemed the only thing that mattered.

Dan chatted easily with the nurses, managed to charm himself a free lunch from the trolley, and even looked like he enjoyed eating it. When he left to introduce a long-standing client to Warren, Lisa slid down under the covers, exhausted but joyous.

"You look so happy, I wonder if you still need your meds." Sheldon laughed, handing her a little paper cup of pills.

* * *

Now Lisa looked forward to Frank setting her new physio goals and challenges. Yesterday his instruction was to take three trips along the corridor and back with her walker. Today she was to ride the elevator to Tim Hortons in the foyer, where he was going to meet her in his break, to celebrate her new mobility.

Wearing two mauve gowns—one in front and another in back, since they hadn't yet worked out how to make a single gown cover both sides—and a sneaker she'd had on in the accident, Lisa made her way past a man in a wheelchair, immobile and staring straight ahead, and pushed through the swinging doors, across the corridor, and into the next ward. Glancing into the rooms, she saw pale faces asleep or blank-eyed in front of a screen, and as she hobbled behind her walker, she was proud of her strengthening body. The next person she looked at was skeletal. There was someone slumped in the chair beside them, asleep. Turning her head away, Lisa almost bumped into a visitor and gasped, he reeked of cigarettes. All she had smelled since arriving at the hospital was antiseptic, bleach, and the occasional whiff of bodies.

She loved having coffee with Frank, but by the time Lisa got back to her room, she fell straight to sleep on her bed. What seemed like moments later, she was woken by the sound of a chair scraping across the floor. Mitch looked mortified. "Shoot, I'm sorry, I really didn't mean to wake you."

He also looked quite rugged and healthy.

"It's fine." Lisa pulled herself up to lean against a pile of pillows. "I hardly sleep, night or day." She saw his beaming eyes and felt guilty.

"So, you're out of intensive care. That's good."

"Isn't it? And I've still got the roses you gave me. The nurse put in the sachet of plant food that came with them."

"Food's a bit of a euphemism. It's chiefly composed of acid and bleach, with some sugar. Still, seems to have done the trick."

She felt dishonest, knowing she should mention Dan, but not sure how.

"You look wonderful. It's hard to believe you're the same person I sat with in intensive care. How are you feeling?"

"Bored of thinking about me. Tell me about you."

He settled back into his chair. "Well, I've been camping. The girls arranged everything—they called it glamping. We had comforters on blow-up airbeds, a propane fridge and solar power, which the grandkids loved because they could watch cartoons."

"I've never been camping. I know it's shameful, as I've lived so near the great outdoors for all these years."

Mitch beamed. "Well, that's easy to rectify, when you're feeling better, if you," he looked down, "I didn't mean to overstep."

Now she felt really bad. And cornered. "All I can think about now is trying to get out of here."

"Of course. Any idea when that might be?"

"Sometime after the weekend, if all goes well."

"That's fantastic. I'll tell Susan. You know, she wanted to fly back, but I said there was nothing she could do."

"Thank goodness. She's been looking forward to this vacation all year."

"She cares about you." Mitch looked serious and sincere. "She's not the only one."

Lisa turned to the box of Kleenex by her bed, pulled one out, and started twisting it between her fingers.

Mitch reddened. "Anyway, she'll be back next week. I expect she'll get straight off the plane and make tracks for wherever you are."

"I can't wait to see her and hear about the trip." These words expanded into an involuntary yawn.

"I'll be going, I don't want to wear you out. I'll come again in a couple of days. Is there anything you need? Food, clothes, reading material?" Mitch's eyes fell on the pile of books on Lisa's bedside table. "Looks like you've got plenty of that."

Lisa nodded. "I think I've got everything I need. And thank you for keeping tabs on me for Susan."

As he put the chair back to its original position by the window, Lisa turned onto her side and was asleep again before he'd left the room. The tiredness never left her. Hospital nights were long and sleepless—the hall lights were always on, Lisa's door was kept open, and there seemed to be constant movement outside. She could hear everything happening at the nurses' station and sometimes a cry or a delirious voice calling out. That was the worst.

* * *

Two days later, Frank turned up after breakfast with two shiny new crutches. "I've just had a word with the nurse, and the good news is that if you can show competency with these, you can go home as soon as you get the weight-bearing boot. Probably not till Monday, and we have to know there's going to be someone around to help you."

Lisa started to cry. She'd been told how well she was doing, and that she'd be leaving soon, but there was still a corner of her that believed she might never see her life again.

Frank came near. "What's the matter? Going home is a good thing, isn't it?"

"I know, but there are so many people here who've lost so much. I'm so grateful."

He crouched, looking into Lisa's face. "It's true. You are one of the lucky ones, and from what I've heard, you have a good life to return to."

"Sorry, I don't usually cry all the time."

Frank laughed. "I just have that effect on people. Now let's get you up. I've got to see you can handle stairs, too."

Thirty-five

Lisa was sitting in the chair by the window. The blind was between two panes of glass and she had to turn a dial to open it. Outside the sky was limitless and over the roofs of Colville, she glimpsed a stand of tall trees and imagined all the life that was there—birds, bugs, bracken, jumping squirrels, sleeping porcupines. She longed to be outside again, and for the familiarity of her own life. She was also ready to be different. She couldn't change yesterday, but she could make sure tomorrow didn't bring any new regrets.

"Hey Lisa, I've got some good news." Marcia, the first nurse Lisa had when she arrived, stood in the doorway looking pleased. "The doctors have decided that you're ready to go home. Your blood work looks good, your vital signs are good, your breathing has improved, and you're rippin' around on those crutches. I think we can get you down for an x-ray and a fiberglass boot today, and as long as you have somebody at home who can help you, you can be discharged before the weekend."

Lisa's heart rocketed.

"Is there someone who can stay with you?"

"I think so. Ashley—my friend—said she'd be there for me on Monday, but I'm sure if I call she'll get an earlier bus."

"And someone to pick you up?"

"Absolutely." Lisa couldn't wait to tell Dan.

"Make your calls and then we'll get you all ready and check you've got everything packed up in your room."

Later that afternoon Dan was holding a plastic hospital bag while Marcia took out Lisa's IV, placing an alcohol swab where it had been. "Just apply pressure till it stops bleeding and I'll put on a bandage."

"Please thank all the other nurses who've been so wonderful. I really don't have words for how much I appreciate everything you've done."

Marcia handed Lisa her crutches. "Take good care of yourself and remember, you've got an appointment with the orthopaedic surgeon, and you need to have a follow-up with your family doctor. Here's the paperwork and do take it easy, it's going to be a while before you're feeling back to your old self."

Standing next to Dan, waiting for the elevator, Lisa was heady with happiness.

"Hang on a minute." Marcia came running down the corridor toward them. "I found this at the back of the drawer in your bedside table." She was holding out the little wooden bird.

"What's that?" Dan asked.

"It's a long story." Lisa felt another stab of guilt.

She sat on a bench while Dan went to get the van. The sun had lost its heat and was lower in the sky than last time she'd been outside, and the air smelled slightly of damp earth. An ambulance arrived at the door to Emergency and Lisa shuddered as she imagined herself inside, lying unconscious after the crash. It was so strange not to remember, but she was also grateful, and turned her head away as the paramedics wheeled out the stretcher.

Dan pulled up, took the crutches, and helped her into the passenger seat. "Nervous about getting in a vehicle again?"

"I hadn't thought about it until you said that."

They both laughed.

"Good. Don't think about it now." He squeezed her hand.

The trees were turning copper, people were wearing jackets, and there were signs of Thanksgiving outside houses. Lisa had missed so much. As they passed a boy walking his puppy, she longed to see Fido and Ashley.

When they turned off the highway onto her dirt road, she saw the familiar markers that meant home: the bent birch, the broken ash, and the two twisted maples that had grown into one. A wild turkey flapped clumsily into the brush and a huge black squirrel ran up the driveway in front of them. As the house came into view, with its beautiful shutters and the red-shingled roof, Lisa realized how much she needed its peace and familiarity, and as Dan shut off the engine, she let out a long sigh.

"How does it feel?" he asked.

"Like I'm the luckiest person in the world."

"I'd say you were the loveliest and I'm the luckiest." He kissed her lightly. "Let's get you in."

All she'd done was leave the hospital and sit in the van, but Lisa was surprised by how tired she felt as she struggled with her crutches along the side of the house to the back door. "Ashley will have locked it. There's a key in a jar behind the rock by—"

They both stopped and stared. The door was ajar, the glass in the window smashed. "You wait." Dan started walking forward. "I'll see what's going on."

He went in, calling loudly, "Anyone here?" Lisa used her crutches to hobble up the step into the kitchen and looked around in horror. There were shards of glass all over the floor, this wasn't the safe place she'd dreamed of coming back to. Dan's footsteps were mapping the rooms upstairs. Still unused to the crutches, she limped into the hall. The bare walls were punctuated by hooks— Leonard's photo collection was missing. She moaned and went through to the living room. The TV was untouched, her laptop was still on the shelf by the woodstove, and feeling leaden with dread, she made her way into the sunroom. Her little office had been uprooted: drawers left open, books pulled off shelves, the filing cabinet gaping. Lisa leaned forward, looked, and—the cameras were gone. Admitting what might be the truth was unbearable.

Dan's voice echoed down the stairs. "Police. I want to report a break-in."

Do I want to report a break-in? Lisa felt sick. *I suppose I have to now.*

Clutching the banister with one hand and both crutches under her arm on the other side, Lisa tentatively started up the staircase, which seemed much steeper than the one in the hospital.

Dan was standing in the bedroom, drawers ajar, clothes strewn around, underwear scattered all over the floor. Her bureau was open but the jewellery box was untouched. The case at the back of her wardrobe was pulled out and Leonard's Leica camera was gone. The memory of sitting on the bed with Ashley as she marvelled and clicked the shutter reeled through Lisa's mind.

Dan spoke gently. "We'd better not touch anything till the police get here."

He and Lisa were outside on the porch when they arrived, Lisa wrapped in the mohair blanket she kept on the swing seat.

"I'm Constable Maclean and this is my partner, Constable Burrie. You reported a break-in?"

Lisa stayed on the porch while Dan showed them the back door. She heard him explaining that she'd been in hospital and then they started questioning: Who has keys? Was there someone checking on the house? When was the last time they would have been here? As Dan didn't know the answers, Lisa heaved herself out of her chair.

"So you're not the homeowner?" Maclean was asking as she got to the kitchen.

The room looked smaller with the three men in it. Both constables were wearing bullet-proof vests and had guns on their belts. Even after living in North America for so long, Lisa still wasn't used to seeing police with firearms. "No that's me," she interrupted.

"I beg your pardon." Maclean looked around. "So this is your partner?"

What is he? She suddenly saw herself as sad and deluded, thinking Ashley had been her best-friend-almost-daughter and Dan was some kind of soulmate. She wobbled her way to a chair. "I suppose he's my friend," she answered weakly.

There was a slight shift in Maclean's expression as he looked back at Dan. "I'll be needing your name, address, and number then."

Burrie was over by the stove calling for a forensic identification officer. "It appears the suspect used a rock to smash the glass in a south side door leading into the kitchen. The window? Approximately half a metre by one-and-a-half metres. Yup. Then the suspect opened the door to gain entry. Open drawers. Possible fingerprints."

"Miss West—or can I call you Lisa?" asked Maclean.

She nodded.

"I see you're not feeling too good, and Dan here has told me that you're just out of hospital, but I wonder if you could take us round and point out what's been touched, anything you see that's missing."

His colleague joined them, looking both serious and pleased. "We're in luck. There's a forensic available, he should be here in about half an hour. We'd like you to both come to the station—on Monday if possible, so we can get elimination prints. Shouldn't take long."

Lisa nodded again and led them into the hall. She explained about the missing framed photos and cameras, feeling heavier with every word.

"Do you know the value of the missing items?" MacLean asked.

"I've got a list. I had to provide it for insurance."

"Excellent. Does it include values?"

"The whole collection is insured for $260,000."

The constable raised his eyebrows. "I'll need a copy of that list, and do you have serial numbers for the cameras? What's their approximate value?"

"No, I'm afraid not, and I've no idea how much they're worth."

"Then if you could give me the make, tell me how old they are, if they have any distinguishing features like scratches or engraved initials." Maclean's pen hovered expectantly over his little black book.

Lisa's thoughts were distorting. "Could we do this tomorrow?"

MacLean paused. "That's possible, but it would be better to do it now, and in your best interest when it comes to insurance."

"Okay." She sighed, and hauled herself back upstairs.

"You say that the young woman who's been staying here is currently with her boyfriend in Toronto? Do you have her phone number, and what about the boyfriend's address?"

Lisa leaned back against the door frame. "I'm sorry, I don't even know his surname. His first name is Chase. He's been working at Patty's pub downtown." The pen scribbled. "My neighbour, Norm, was probably the last person here, but he's just been watering the garden. He wouldn't have come into the house."

Maclean nodded. "Surname?"

"O'Brien."

"I'll be needing his number too. We'll start with a neighbour canvas, see if anyone has noticed any unknown vehicles in your driveway, or seen people they don't recognize going in and out of the place. We'll follow that up with contacting Ashley. We'll need her prints too. I'll be in touch with the results."

Burrie was using his phone to take photos of Lisa's clothes-covered floor, and the empty space where the Leica should have been, when the forensic officer arrived.

Maclean suggested he take a statement from Lisa, while his colleague take one from Dan. Her stomach growled and she felt faint—she'd been too excited to have her hospital lunch. "I need something to eat first, and a hot drink."

Sitting on the porch again, nibbling a chocolate chip cookie out of Dan's bag of groceries, Lisa felt despair. A regular thief would have taken the laptop, TV, found the cash she kept in the kitchen cupboard for emergencies. Constable Burrie appeared with a mug in his hand. "My aunt is British, she always said, 'milk in first, don't leave the bag for too long'."

"Thank you." The tea was better than anything Lisa had tasted in the hospital.

MacLean took a seat opposite her, notebook in hand, his voice exaggeratedly formal. "The Colville Police Service is currently investigating a break-and-enter to your residence. What can you tell me about this?"

"Well, I've been in hospital ..." Lisa started.

He prompted her through the rest of the story, stopping for specifics like, "Who has keys?" and "Has there been anyone living with you?"

It didn't take too long, and in the end, she was pleased to get it done. When his own interview was finished, Dan came and sat down, putting his arm around her shoulders. "The forensic guy's almost finished, then they'll be gone. How about a sleepover at my place? I can pop back and nail a board over the broken window when you're settled."

Lisa nodded. She wasn't sure how much longer she could stay upright, or hold down the volcano of emotions that were building.

MacLean handed them each a business card. "Here's my name and phone number. If you have any new information, please contact me, and we'll try to keep you updated on our investigation."

Now Burrie was by his side, handing Lisa another business card. "At Colville Police Service we have a victim services unit ..."

She wasn't listening. She needed an explanation for the disappearance of the prints and cameras that didn't involve Ashley. Lisa couldn't live with the thought that she could have been so blatantly betrayed, again. The words *like father, like daughter* kept playing in her mind.

"Right, good," said Burrie, as the constables put away their little black notebooks in perfect unison. The forensic officer was already walking to his car.

Thirty-six

Confused, Lisa gazed at the line of trees silhouetted against an expanding sky and tried to work out where she was. And what time of day it was. Then she remembered: the burglary, the police, and flopping into Dan's bed, too tired to undress. The now-familiar ache in her leg was bad. She had done too much yesterday and forgotten her nighttime medication, and as she raised herself onto her elbow, she thought of Ashley and her chest tightened.

Lisa's bag was by the bed and Dan had left a glass of water on the nightstand, so she gulped down two painkillers and sank back into the pillow. When she next woke the sun was high and there was a note leaning against the lamp:

Found Norm's number and called him. Gone to get your brown-eyed boy. Back soon. Will bring breakfast. xxxx

Lisa had barely finished reading when she looked out and saw the Down to Earth van making its way up the driveway towards her. She heard the engine switch off, one door slam, another slide, and moments later, Dan's voice. "Are you awake?"

A blur of brown fur leapt up, tail wagging, followed by Dan who sat on the side of the bed. Fido licked his face too, and for a moment, they felt like a family. Fido finally lay down, tail still thumping, and as Dan leaned in for a kiss, Lisa's stomach growled.

He laughed. "How about some of my famous eggs Benedict— without the ham? I can bring them in on a tray."

Lisa wanted to sit at a table and wear something that wasn't a hospital gown. "I'd like to eat in the kitchen. You go ahead and I'll get dressed and give Ashley a call. I left a message yesterday telling her I'd be at home and I want to let her know I'm here with you."

Dan looked like he was about to say something but stood up instead. "I'll get the percolator on."

Back in the bedroom, Lisa looked at the phone icon but slid her finger to *text* instead: House broken into. Phone me before you come. x

The kitchen was bright and smelled of fresh coffee. Dan switched off the radio and as Lisa moved toward the table on her crutches, he pulled out a chair. "I'll get the eggs going. How do you like yours—soft or better cooked?"

Strange. Dan was so familiar, Lisa felt so comfortable, and yet he didn't know how she liked her eggs. The truth was, they hardly knew each other. But as she ate her delicious English muffin, piled with spinach and creamy sauce, she forgot everything except the flavours bringing her mouth alive. "I'm not surprised your eggs are famous, they're fantastic."

"It's all about the butter, that's the secret. I'm with Julia Child on that."

"So you're a closet gourmet?"

"'Fraid not. I just watched the movie with ... in Manitoba."

Silence filled the space between them. Dan pushed his plate to one side and swallowed before speaking. "I emailed Julie when we got here from your place yesterday and told her I wasn't coming back."

Lisa's eyes widened. She'd assumed that at some point they'd talk about what was going on between her and Dan, about his planned life in Manitoba, about Julie. And that they'd have the conversation *before* any big decisions were made. "Have you heard back yet?"

Dan nodded. "We were on the phone till late."

So that's it? Did we have a conversation I don't remember? I have been functioning on limited brain capacity. Lisa wasn't sure what to say. "How are you feeling now?"

"Like I've had enough. Anna's been sending me ugly texts."

Everything felt surreal. "You emailed Anna as well?"

"No, Julie told her." Dan ran his fingers through his hair. "I guess it was inevitable that the shit was going to hit, but I hadn't expected it to happen so fast. I haven't told the university yet."

Part of Lisa wanted to throw her arms around him, but could she trust someone who just swiveled from one life to another?

"I think I made a huge mistake, taking that job and saying I'd move in with Julie. Looking back, I realize I wanted a change and everything with Julie was so easy. You must think I'm some kind of fly-by-night."

Lisa didn't know what she thought, except that she loved him.

Dan sounded so defeated. "I hoped Anna would be more understanding."

He had let down his daughter, the university, and a woman who expected to spend the rest of her life with him. Lisa looked at the eggy smears on her plate. "Are you absolutely sure that this is what you want? I don't think I could stand it if you changed your mind again."

"Since I saw you in hospital, you're the only thing I've been able to focus on." He interlaced his fingers with hers. "And I know we've got a lot to talk about, but I can't manage much more right now."

Lisa nodded. It was too big to think about, especially with everything else. She remembered the shattered glass on her floor, and Ashley who hadn't responded to her messages, and repressed the urge to go back to bed and stick her head under the pillow.

Dan stood up. "More coffee?"

Lisa looked through the windows at the clear blue sky. *This is good news,* she told herself. *Enjoy it.* "You know what I'd really like? To take our drinks outside. It's such a glorious day and it feels like I've been indoors forever."

"Great idea." Dan went into the mudroom and came back with a padded overshirt. "Slip this on and start getting yourself to the chairs at the front of the house. I'll be along in a minute with the caffeine."

Once outside, Lisa put her hand on her belly and breathed in the cool autumn air, held it for a few seconds, and let it go. She could hear Frank's words: breath flows where attention goes. She kept going, it was good to feel her lungs swell. The air seemed to expand out of her chest and into her arms and legs. She imagined it pouring into her big boot, swirling around her broken shin, helping it mend. She had never been as conscious of her body as she was since the accident.

"This is for your leg." Dan overturned a milk crate, then tucked a padded vest over Lisa's lap. "I'll be right back with the drinks."

She was self-conscious, didn't like feeling like an invalid, but soon they were sitting side by side in the sunlight. Fido chased a chipmunk across the grass and then picked up a stick and started chewing it. She put her hand on Dan's arm. "Thank you for this, and yesterday, and getting Fido, and the lovely food. I'm not used to being looked after."

"Well, get used to it, because it makes me happy."

As she smiled, Lisa's mind flitted. "Oh shit. I left my phone in the bedroom and I'm waiting to hear from Ashley."

"I'll get it, but I think you're being naïve believing she'll turn up."

"So she's guilty without a trial? You've never even met her."

"How much do you really know about her? You have to admit, it's a bit strange the way she turned up out of nowhere and then moved in. Did you make any checks? Do anything to verify her story?"

"God, you sound like Susan. Ashley looks like Leonard, acts like him, and we've spent the whole summer together. We've grown very close. She almost feels like a daughter to me."

"I'm not denying that, but I am questioning her motive for being here."

Since seeing the state of her house yesterday, Lisa hadn't dared give these thoughts headspace. Hearing Dan express them was infuriating. "Let's hope you're never on a jury, especially if the accused doesn't fit your stereotype of a responsible citizen. Not that you'd know—" She stopped herself just in time.

Dan scowled. "Is that the thanks—"

"I didn't—" Pain ripped through Lisa's chest. The cough was well and truly back.

He stood up, alarmed. "What can I do?"

Dan looked on helplessly as, gradually, Lisa's breathing calmed and she was able to talk again. "You know, Ashley isn't the only one who could have taken those prints. I've been wondering if Skye might have had something to do with it."

He sat down. "I know you've had issues with her in the past, and she's got a temper, but I can't see Skye breaking into your house and taking those prints, or even knowing they were valuable enough to steal."

Dan had never asked Lisa what had happened between her and Skye, and she didn't want to go into it now. "All I'll say is I know a side of her that you probably haven't seen."

"She's worked for the Beekeepers Association for nearly a year, and even if her record isn't perfect, that doesn't make her a thief. I just don't see why you're so blind about Ashley. You've said yourself she'd had a rough life, even lived on the streets."

"And that makes her a thief?" She picked up her crutches. "I'm going in." She needed to calm down, before saying something rash.

Once back in the bedroom, Lisa struggled out of her clothes, lay down, and looked at her phone—again. The only message was from Mitch, a voicemail. "Where are you? I went to the hospital and they said you'd been discharged, and I've just been to the house and your back door is broken and boarded up. I'm worried, please phone me."

Lisa's sank into the mattress. She had completely forgotten Mitch, and he'd been the one who was there when she woke up in hospital, and visited, and told Susan, and been so caring. *But I'm too tired to talk to him now.* She typed instead: So sorry, should have let you know. Discharged early. House broken into. Police investigating. Staying with a friend. Will call soon.

She was about to put down her phone when Ashley's text appeared: Shit. Hope house is OK. Hope you are OK. So won't come today. Soon. x

Lisa reread the message, Dan's words echoing. She took a couple of tablets, lay back, and drifted off.

* * *

The light was fading when Lisa's eyes opened again. She couldn't believe she had slept for so long. Dan was sitting on the bed beside her. "I'm sorry."

"No, I am." She took his hand in hers and kissed the back of it. "We're both tired and stressed and I overreacted. The truth is that I just can't bear to think it was Ashley."

"I know." His lips were warm and inviting. Soon he was lying next to her, her hand on the back of his neck, his sliding down to her breast.

Lisa stiffened. "We need to talk."

"Oh—kay."

She pulled herself upright. "There's a problem. I'm the problem. It's why I said we could only be friends."

He frowned. "I thought we'd moved past all this."

Lisa wished she'd rehearsed what she was about to say. "The thing is, I should have told you from the start, but when I, when we, it's sex. It's not working for me."

"Really?" He raised his eyebrows. "The things you said and did that first night at your place, and then when we came back here after the bee ball—"

"I know. I was. I am. It's just ...." Tears seeped onto her cheeks. "I love kissing and touching, but when you're inside me, it's painful."

Dan pulled away. "Painful? Why didn't you tell me?"

"Because I, well, the first time I was puzzled and so drunk I could hardly remember. And the second, when we were here, I really wanted to feel you. I wanted us to make love."

"How can it be making love if I'm hurting you? Didn't you think I'd care?"

"I was ashamed. I didn't want you to know I was—broken." Now Lisa was crying. "Oh Christ, I've done this all wrong. It's medical, I've got—"

He touched her cheek. "You're sick? Is that why it hurts?"

"Kind of, except I'm not going to get better."

"Cancer?"

"No, no, and I'm not dying. It's just to do with being older. I'm atro... drier ... things aren't as elastic as they should be."

Dan gazed at her, as if absorbing her words. "But, you do like me?"

"That's the problem, that's why I'm such a mess. The doctor gave me something, and I thought it had helped, but then I went for a mammogram and discovered the medication is riskier than I realized, and now I've stopped using it."

He was clearly struggling to keep up. "But you would like us to be physical?"

"Of course. Except you're younger, and so into sex and I—"

Dan silenced her with a kiss. A long kiss that tasted of her tears. He spoke quietly. "Can you roll over without hurting your leg? I'd like to give you a back rub."

Lisa turned onto her tummy and felt useless as Dan supported her big boot with pillows, but as the warmth of his hands spread through her T-shirt, she relaxed. He moved his palms in soothing circles between her shoulder blades, slid them up her spine, and then squeezed each neck muscle in turn. Lisa felt herself grow heavy, her breathing slowed and she lay still, as an invisible force compelled her to focus on every minute move of his hands. It was the first time she'd really enjoyed her body since the accident. Since before it. For years. The more Dan stroked, rubbed, and caressed, the more relaxed she became, in a way that made her feel luxuriously sensual.

"Can I move down to your legs?" His hand was warm on her thigh. "I won't go near the break."

Lisa groaned her assent, too soporific to make words. He gently massaged the back of each leg, working down the unbroken one to her foot. Heat emanated as he massaged each toe in turn. He seemed to know exactly how much pressure to use on every part of her. She longed to feel his hands on her breasts, between her legs, but she wanted to preserve the innocence.

"Thank you," she muttered, as he worked his way back up her body. "It's like your hands are charmed, as though each finger is filled with—"

"Love?"

Dan kissed the back of her neck. "That's the vital ingredient." He knelt by the bed, his head level with hers. "We may not be naked, or 'having sex,' but I'm still making love to you."

She nodded, too relaxed to speak.

"And after supper, I'd like to do it some more."

Thirty-seven

The next morning, Dan slipped into bed beside Lisa as she slept. His warm presence gradually seeped into her, and carefully maneuvering her boot, she turned to face him. They lay in silence, looking. How she loved the line of his mouth.

He slid towards her, his forehead touching hers. "Let's both turn off our phones and let the world take care of itself for a day."

Lisa thought about Ashley, the police, and how worried Susan would be if she called and didn't get a reply, and then snuggled closer. "Great idea."

They had croissants and coffee in bed, watching Fido through the huge windows as he snuffled in the grass. Every now and then he rushed to look in and share his excitement, before zig-zagging back to track more chipmunks. Lisa sighed. "Wouldn't it be great to be that carefree, so full of trust and optimism? He's never resentful, never clings onto bad feelings."

Dan's eyes widened. "I didn't have you down as someone who'd hold a grudge."

"I've certainly carried one against my sister, and Dad, for far too long."

"Is that why you never talk about your family?"

Lisa told him about growing up without Mum, enduring Nicky's constant put-downs and the feeling that, however good she tried to be, her sister and Dad were the *real* family. "Nothing I did made a difference. I was always the outsider. It didn't help that I got a free place at a private school and a scholarship to university, while Nicky dropped out of the local public school when she was sixteen. I don't think she's ever forgiven me for that."

"Sounds like she was jealous." Dan brushed a crumb off Lisa's chin. "You were the one that got away."

"I know, but at the time, all I wanted was a family."

He listened, prompting with questions, as she told him about Nicky blaming her for breaking dishes, busting the TV, and losing Dad's winning lottery ticket when they were all things Nicky had done herself. Lisa cried about Dad never coming to parents' evenings at school, and not even looking up when she read him the letter offering her a place at university, ending with a description of the way Leonard had slept with Nicky and what Dad had said on the phone.

"Jesus. Just hearing about it is like a punch in the gut. How could a father do that? I'm not surprised you walked away."

It was good to feel Dan's empathy, but since her stay in the hospital, Lisa's anger had disappeared. "I'm sorry. That was a lot of talking and probably not what you had in mind when you suggested we switch off our phones for the day."

"I didn't have anything in mind except time together. If you ask me, Nicky sounds bitter with envy."

"You think that's why she slept with the man I was as good as married to?"

"Well, it was a perfect way to get back at you. Or to get some of what you had—literally."

Lisa looked at Dan. "It was a lot of years ago. What I want right now is to be in the present." Their kisses were longer and deeper than yesterday's. Every cell in her body was reaching for his, but she was also anxious. She didn't want to disappoint.

As if he knew what she was thinking, Dan offered another back rub. "Maybe without the T-shirt?"

Lisa answered by pulling it off, she didn't want anything between them. The sheet was warm as she settled back onto the bed and sank into the sensation of Dan's touch, tracing her vertebrae, one by one, soothing and mesmerizing. As he coaxed and squeezed muscles, her breathing softened, shoulders released.

He lifted aside her hair, kissed the back of her neck, and Lisa turned over. Dan stroked her face, running his fingertips over her closed eyes and around her lips, touching softly, skimming the skin on her neck, the outline of her collarbone, but as he trailed them down towards her breast, she laughed. "I'm ticklish."

He stroked each breast and kissed her belly. Her nipples were hard with longing, but when they finally felt the brush of his lips, she was distracted again by almost-laughter and she thought of Ashley, telling her lover exactly what she needed. Lisa had never dared, until now. "When you touch me so lightly," she ventured, "I get distracted and want to giggle. Maybe you could try to be a bit firmer?"

Dan's stroking became stronger. "That better?"

She groaned her assent. He sucked each nipple in turn and as her head tilted back, he slid up the bed and kissed her mouth. "Maybe we should stop for today?"

"Not an option." She guided his hand between her legs, starting the movement she knew would work, and moments later, Lisa moaned. It was the longest, deepest orgasm she had ever had.

Dan held her tight and whispered, "Want to go again?"

It took a while for his meaning to sink in, Lisa's ears were still so full of the sound of her own heart. "You mean ... but what about you? I'd like to—"

Dan interrupted with a kiss. "Sounds good, but maybe we should wait for that leg to be a little less painful. Let's make today all about you. There's plenty of time for me."

Lisa came again. And again. And again. She had never experienced anything like it. When she was done, Dan lay down next to her and they were both still, the sweat drying on her skin. "That was incredible, amazing, thank you."

"What, you think it was only for *your* benefit?"

Laughing, Lisa adjusted the pillow. "Please don't take this the wrong way, but I'm curious. Do you do this with all the women you make love to?"

"Really?" Dan looked affronted. "Absolutely not. In fact, I wouldn't use the words making love for anything I've done with anyone since my wife left. The women I met in Toronto were fun.

We got up to stuff, pushed boundaries, but none of it involved love.”

“Tell me. What it was like?”

Dan opened his eyes wide.

“I want to know. About the hook-ups.”

“That feels weird.”

“I’m intrigued, and it’s part of who you are, isn’t it?”

“Part of who I *was*.”

“Okay, but I’m still curious.”

He leaned up on his elbow. “Well, in the beginning, I was like a kid in a candy store, and in the end, my dates were empty and exhausting.”

“So how did you get into it?”

“I guess two things happened at once. Anna left home to do her bachelor’s and I got a regular gig in Toronto, completely overhauling this guy’s huge garden in Parkdale. I had a couple of local contractors working for me there full time, but I still had to make regular site visits, so I started staying in a hotel around the corner.” Dan tucked the duvet around them. “I’d been thinking of dating and Warren’s wife set me up with a one of her friends, but that felt too intense and too public. I tried going to some bars when I was in the city, but these days it’s hard—if you approach a woman the wrong way, she thinks you’re being creepy. I honestly didn’t know how to do it. So then I had the idea of going online, in Toronto, and oh boy was it a steep learning curve.”

Lisa traced Dan’s knuckles with her thumb. “Go on.”

“When I first signed up I thought it was all about dating, but most of the women I met only wanted one thing. Some of those internet sites make casual sex as easy as picking a movie, and after a while I thought, why not? I was starting to enjoy the freedom of Anna being away, and the whole business was conveniently contained. By the time the Parkdale job ended, I was well into it, so I kept going back to the hotel. I’d flirt online all month and then spend a weekend getting laid.”

"Did you sleep with everyone you emailed?"

"Christ no. Sometimes we'd meet for drinks or dinner and I'd go back to my room alone. There was one woman who spent the whole meal sobbing into her curry because her husband was unfaithful, another who just kept scrolling through her phone, showing me photos of herself in her underwear, and the anarchist—I didn't dare go back to her place. But after a while, I learned to decode the signals online, and I met some women who were fun. Sometimes we'd keep it going for several months."

"Until?"

"Usually, until one of us decided to move on, or they found someone permanent, but even when they did, they sometimes got in touch wanting a secret weekend."

Lisa was adding up the number of people she'd slept with: Tim, Leonard, then Graham, Steve, and Emmanuel after she split up with Leonard, and then Leonard again. At least, if she counted him twice, she could use two hands. "I feel like such an innocent, and so unadventurous."

"Sorry you asked?"

Lisa kissed his shoulder. "Absolutely not."

"I think part of it was trying to work out what sex meant to me, and what kind of sex I enjoyed. I'd been with Erin since high school."

"And what did you discover?"

"That meaningless sex is exhausting, and ultimately unsatisfying. And there are no rules. Everyone's different, everyone's needs are different, you just have to make it up as you go along." He squeezed her hand. "That's what I want us to do."

"But what was the sex like with them?"

Dan laughed. "There I draw the line, but I will tell you about one woman I went with, just before I decided to pack it all up. She'd had labiaplasty."

Lisa had never heard of labiaplasty and decided not to ask.

"That date was my turning point, but it had been building for a while. In spite of the fun of flirting, and the rush of first-time sex, I started to want a real relationship. Trust, companionship, intimacy, you know—and pubic hair." He lifted the duvet and planted a kiss on Lisa's curly brown triangle. "None of them had any pubes."

She smiled feebly, her confidence evaporating.

"So that's when I cancelled my monthly hotel reservations. And then I met you."

Lisa felt scrawny, old, and even more anxious about sex. "Let's get some air. We can't spend the whole day in bed."

Dan looked up at the window and back to her. "I was thinking, if it worked with your leg, could I sleep here with you tonight?"

The question made her feel better. "I'd like that."

They spent the afternoon outside. Lisa managed her crutches well enough to walk across the cut grass and around Dan's little orchard before they had tea and grilled cheese sandwiches at the front of the house.

Later that night, when they were in bed together, she drew circles on his shoulder. "You've been so sensitive and generous, giving me that glorious massage with such a wonderful finale, I'd like to do something to please you." She slid her hand down past his stomach. He was already hard. "Anything."

He kissed the top of her head. "I love giving you pleasure, you don't have to pay me back."

"But there must be something you'd like." She pressed her body into his. "Right now."

He closed his eyes. "Okay, but you've got to promise not to laugh. I've never asked anyone to do this."

"I promise." She prayed it wouldn't be anything too kinky.

"When I was a kid, imagining what it would be like to have sex, I used to stroke the hairs on my arm the wrong way. I loved how it made me tingle. It was my secret pleasure and I thought that when I grew up, that's what sex would feel like, except all over."

Lisa's heart filled. "You want me to stroke the fuzz on your arms the wrong way?"

Dan looked embarrassed.

"That's the sweetest thing anyone's ever asked me."

The hairs on Dan's forearm were still blonde from a summer in the sun. Lisa skimmed them, softly and slowly, as he closed his eyes. She could barely feel the hairs under the pads of her fingers, but as she kept lightly stroking, she saw the muscles of his face relax. After a while, her hand travelled over the velvety fuzz higher up his arm. He exhaled slowly as her fingertips whispered through the soft, slightly springy hairs on his chest, being careful not to touch the skin. The curls on his tummy were silkier. She wanted to continue down to the smooth expanse of his erection but resisted and travelled back up his body, teasing the hairs some more, ending with his other forearm.

Dan turned onto his side, his lids heavy with sleep. "Now that's what I call *good* sex. More tomorrow?"

Thirty-eight

For two glorious days, Dan and Lisa were the only inhabitants of their own world, and arriving at the police station on Monday morning was like thudding back on earth without a parachute. There was mayhem on the steps outside as four uniformed men surrounded a woman with no teeth who seemed drunk, or drugged, and was screaming. The heavy glass doors to reception were covered in greasy palm prints and the person stooping to talk through the hole in the bulletproof glass screen was yelling. "I said before, it's not my fault. No one told me to bring it."

As Lisa and Dan sat waiting, the distant smell of disinfectant reminded her of the hospital. Was that really only three days ago?

Everything about having their fingerprints taken was disturbing. After watching so many movies where the suspect had their digits rolled on an inkpad and then onto a piece of paper, Lisa hadn't expected to be scanned. It felt invasive, like having a part of her taken that she didn't want to give away, and the station made her nervous. Working at the art school had meant coming in for an annual police record check, but she'd never been beyond reception. Here, there were too many glass panels and closed doors, locks, and protocols. It didn't seem to bother Dan. "They're just doing their job," he whispered back. "And they're used to people a lot less compliant than us."

Lisa also found it more tiring than she anticipated. Managing the station stairs and corridors with her crutches took a lot of energy, and she felt herself sweating under the thick fleece Dan had lent her. She needed to go home and get some clothes. Everything seemed to take forever, and she was relieved as the forensic expert walked them back to reception, but they met Constable MacLean on the station steps. "I was just going to phone and bring you up to date." He caught the door that was closing behind them. "Hey, do you mind coming back in and I'll tell you where we're at?"

He led them to a little interview room and they sat on wooden chairs around a steel-topped table. There were no windows, the white walls were blank, and Lisa felt trapped and worried about whether to mention Skye.

MacLean leaned back and cracked his knuckles before starting. "We've done a neighbourhood canvas, checked the pawn shops in town as well as Redstock, and found nothing. We've spoken to your neighbour, Norm O'Brien. He was at the house last Wednesday, that's five days ago, and the window wasn't broken then. He thinks he saw Ashley in a Colville taxi coming out of your driveway sometime after that."

The few drops of energy Lisa had left drained away. The more MacLean talked, the more she wanted to express her suspicions about Skye, but she kept thinking of what she'd said in her argument with Dan—that having a sketchy past didn't make a person a thief.

MacLean was still talking about Norm. "The problem is that he can't be sure when he saw Ashley. He did notice her going to the house once before, and thinks that was a couple of weeks ago, when he figured she was just collecting more of her stuff. That time she was with a young man in a brown station wagon."

Lisa spoke quietly. "That's her boyfriend's car. He's got an old Chevy that belonged to his father."

MacLean nodded. "Ashley's not answering her cell, or returning my messages, but I have managed to locate the boyfriend. I got his address from Patricia Adele."

Lisa looked puzzled.

"The owner of the pub on Charlotte."

"Of course, Patty's."

"Patricia also remembered the name of the bar in Toronto where Ashley is currently working. The manager phoned her for a reference."

Lisa's mind flipped from worrying about why Ashley hadn't returned the constable's calls, to whether her student visa would still be operational if she wasn't attending the art school, and if she should mention Skye. She had to be sure she wasn't doing it out of some sort of subconscious revenge.

"So we'll be heading to Toronto tomorrow or Wednesday to take some prints and interview Ashley."

She decided to leave Skye out of it until the police came back from Toronto. The constable promised to stay in touch and Lisa's leg ached as they drove away from the station. Dan put a comforting hand on her thigh. "At least they haven't found anything incriminating."

She looked at him gratefully, but her stomach knotted as they passed the Thrift Store, Ashley's favourite hang-out, and the new chip truck, where she had talked Lisa into having them loaded with jalapeno cheese. As she sniffed back a tear, they stopped at the lights and Lisa noticed the woman crossing pull out her phone.

"I forgot to turn on my cell." She sighed, shuffling through her bag. Two texts from Susan, the first was sent at 7 a.m.: Landed. Coming straight to see you.

The second arrived a few minutes ago: Almost in town. Are you at home? I'll drop off Grant and be right over.

Lisa turned to Dan. "Susan's nearly in Colville and wants to see me. She's on her way to my place. Can I ask her to come to yours instead?"

"Of course. *Mi casa es tu casa.*"

Lisa took a deep breath and didn't cough. A bubble of happiness was forming. This was real. They were starting to feel like something she could trust. She texted Dan's address and instructions for how to get there, and as they drove out of town, Lisa saw a sign by the side of the road. "Stop!"

Dan pulled over. "What's wrong?"

"Nothing, it's just—could you go back? I want to see that sign."

He laughed and put the van into reverse. As her eyes rested on the words, Higgins House Raising & Moving, an idea started to take shape. Lisa held up her phone and clicked.

Dan started back out onto the road. "What was that about?"

"Let me do a bit more research and then I'll tell you."

They arrived at his place moments before Susan's Jeep appeared in the driveway.

"Oh, my God." She jumped out, arms extended. "I was expecting you to look fifty shades of terrible, but you're glowing." Lisa took in her newly tanned friend and realized how much she'd missed her. Susan cautiously slipped her arms between the crutches and pressed her round, reassuring body into Lisa's, speaking more softly. "You've been through so much, I'm sorry I wasn't here."

Lisa leaned in closer. "Thank you for all the texts and phone calls. They really meant a lot."

As they made their way toward the kitchen, Dan was already making coffee. Susan looked at the expanse of windows. "This place is breathtaking."

Lisa was proud. Proud that Susan was seeing her here with Dan and proud that she seemed impressed. Dan explained that the house was solar passive, talked about its construction, asked how Susan took her coffee, kissed Lisa, and grabbed his jacket. "Fido and I are going to check out that fallen birch by the road. You know where everything is."

Susan sat down next to Lisa. "Honey, are you *really* okay? On top of everything else, to go home and find the place broken into—"

"I know, that's been devastating." Lisa decided not to say anything about Ashley. "But one good thing is that it brought me here, closer to Dan."

"I can see. I've only been away for a few weeks and you're living a whole new life."

Lisa wanted to squeal "yes, isn't it fantastic" but there was something in Susan's tone that made her hesitate. Her friend walked over to the counter, picked up a mug with a bee on the side, peered at it, and put it down. "I hate to stick a pin in that bubble you're floating on, but wasn't Dan meant to be moving to Manitoba to be with some other woman?"

"He was, but—"

"What changed his mind?"

"I did, I guess. When he heard I was in hospital he came to see me and the connection was instant." Lisa looked away.

"Maybe it's none of my business, but I love you and can't help feeling that your happiness is just a teensy bit my concern."

Lisa felt hot. She didn't want to hear any more.

"Dan just doesn't seem very, grounded. One week he's moving to Manitoba to live with a woman he loves there, the next he's in love with you, and then there's all that stuff my niece said about the women in Toronto, for all those years."

"Three years, and it was consensual. Dan didn't lie or cheat and he wasn't hurting anyone."

"He told you about it?"

Lisa nodded.

"So who were these women that he was being so upfront and honest about?"

This wasn't the conversation Lisa wanted, but she could understand Susan's worry, so she patiently explained about the internet dating, ending with the fact that when the excitement had worn off, Dan realized he needed something different, something more."

"Which he thought he'd found in Manitoba until he decided he'd found it here instead. Are you sure this is the kind of man you need?"

Lisa desperately wanted her friend's support. "Can't you just be happy for me?"

"But what about your independence? You were so adamant there was no space in your life for a partner."

"Maybe I was just choosing safety. Emotional abstinence. One thing that Dan and the car crash have made me know for sure is that I don't want the life I had. I have no idea where we're going or where we'll end up, but right here and now, he makes me happy. It's not as if I've got anything to lose."

Susan's eyes filled with worry. "Honey, that's not true. It's taken twenty years for your heart to mend. Do you really think it could stand another fracture? Anyway, he just doesn't seem like the kind of person who's ever going to fit in."

"With what?"

"Your life. Our friends. Can you really imagine him wanting to go to retirement parties? Whereas Mitch—"

"Mitch! So that's what this is about?"

"He rang my cell when I was at the airport yesterday. He's worried. He said you'd suddenly disappeared."

Lisa covered her mouth with her hand. "Oh no, I said I'd call him back and then I turned off my phone and forgot. You're right about Mitch. He is a good man and the last thing I want to do is hurt him. I'll call and apologize."

"Couldn't you just keep an open mind? Don't write him off yet. I honestly believe that in the long run—"

"The thing about Mitch is, I'd probably be a better person if I spent time with him, but he's just, he's too—"

"Open, honest, and reliable?"

"I'm not sure I want someone suitable for retirement parties." Lisa stopped. She was criticizing Susan's life, the life they had shared until now.

The rest of the visit was strained. Susan gave Lisa the purse she'd bought for her in Madrid, showed her a few photos of her trip, and then left, saying she should go home and help Grant with the unpacking. Lisa was still sitting at the kitchen table when Dan came back from the woods.

"Everything okay? I thought you'd be all charged up after your big reunion."

"Not really. I guess we were both tired."

She looked into his eyes. Suddenly their relationship felt fragile, like a thing that needed protecting. "I think I'd like a hug."

He rested the palm of his hand against her cheek. "Why don't we have a horizontal hug?"

Lisa longed to be close, to feel his tenderness and strength and keep exploring. Their bodies were learning a new language. When he slipped into bed beside her, she brushed the hairs on his chest the way she had the night before. "Now you lie still and let me do some more touching."

"If you insist," he answered with a big smile, settling down and raising one arm so his hand was under his head.

She watched the muscles move beneath his skin. It was a new experience, learning a body without the distraction of hands or lips touching her own. She tasted each finger in turn, traced the blue veins on his forearm, drew patterns across his shoulder, and then used her tongue to circle each nipple. Dan lay absolutely still, his breathing growing deeper as she worked her way down his body. His tummy was smooth and taut, his hip bones solid, and after some careful repositioning of her big boot, Lisa moved down to his thighs. She started by stroking the hairs, then massaged and squeezed his muscles.

"I don't think I can take much more." He pulled her up the bed and she lay on her side as they kissed, his penis pressing into her thigh. She took it in her hand and he slid his down to guide her, and soon his hips started to move. It took a while to find the right rhythm, but when she did, he closed his eyes, his breath hot on her face. His hips pulsed and he clutched her tight, burying his head in her hair as he was coming.

It was dusk when they woke up and went back into the kitchen. Lisa sat at the table chopping salad while Dan whisked an omelette. When they'd eaten, they moved to the chairs by the woodstove and watched the blinking flames through the smoky glass window, lazy with happiness.

"Do you know something I've always wanted to do?" Dan reached out for Lisa's hand. "Visit the Kirstenbosch Botanical Gardens. They're in South Africa. Want to go together?"

She looked at his face, glimmering in the firelight, and remembered, years ago, reading an article about the opening of the Mandela Museum. "And I'd like to go to the Nelson Mandela Museum. I think it's in Johannesburg."

"I bet there's a good game park we could visit, too."

A nugget of peace settled. They were making plans.

Thirty-nine

The next day, Lisa swung along on her crutches to Dan's office. "Could you drop me off at Norm's on your way to see Warren? And, if it's okay with you, I'd like to pop home and get some clothes."

Dan looked up from the pile of mail he was opening. "I was going to ask if you felt up to going to your place. We should check on it."

She was wearing his sweatshirt. Lisa still only had the pinafore dress and T-shirt that Ashley had brought to the hospital. "Right now, the need for my own clothes trumps everything."

"Good. Then I'll leave you at Norm's while I take this stuff to Warren, and we'll go to your house afterwards. All these bills and bank statements are his to deal with now and it feels great."

"Really?" Lisa leaned on the doorframe. "No regrets about selling the business, or giving up the job at the university?"

"To be honest, it's a relief. I wasn't looking forward to being in an office so much of the time or dancing to someone else's schedule."

"But what about the future? Doesn't that worry you?"

"I've never had this much free time, and so far, I'm loving it. Selling to Warren has given me enough cash to relax a little, and I've just made an appointment to see Caitlin Jeffrey."

"Principal of the art school?"

Dan nodded. "One of the big draws of working at the university was the promise of developing an aquaponic garden. They said I couldn't teach, as I don't have the qualifications, but they were super interested in my ideas for on-site ecology. So I thought I'd see if the art school here was interested. They have courses on sustainable building design and botanical arts, why not something to do with garden design? And an actual garden. We could involve the students, or kids from the local school, or seniors." Dan's eager ten-year-old was back. "What do you think?"

"It's perfect. Just the right timing and I have a feeling Caitlin's going to love you." Lisa crossed her fingers. She didn't want to be the only thing keeping Dan in Colville. As they drove to her place, he chattered about irrigation systems and little-known varieties of native plants, and when they turned off the road into Lisa's laneway, Fido started bouncing around in the back of the van. As Dan slid open the door, the dog rushed to the house.

"He thinks he's going to see Ashley." Suddenly sad, Lisa lowered herself out of the passenger seat onto her crutches. She had managed to push Ashley to the back of her mind, but now the doubt, worry, and suspicion were back. She gave Dan her key to unlock the door and as she followed him in, Fido sniffed around suspiciously. The teacups were by the sink, where Constable Burrie had left them, and two chairs were still pulled out from when he had taken Dan's statement. As she walked into the stark silence, a chill ran through her.

They went into the downstairs rooms one by one: the living room was cold, there was a tap dripping in the bathroom, and the sunroom was still strewn with books and papers, drawers gaping. Realizing that Ashley could have done this was too much, made Lisa wanted to turn around and go, but she struggled up the long flight of stairs, trying not to look at the empty walls. Dan walked behind, balancing her every time she swayed or faltered, but she didn't want him near. She was close to unravelling and couldn't do that with him there.

Seeing the wreckage in her bedroom—her private place, her sanctuary—made it worse. Dan scooped clothes from the floor and put them on the armchair as Lisa went to the closet to get her overnight bag. It stared down, taunting her from the top shelf, too high to reach. She assessed if she could knock it with her crutch but didn't trust her balance. Gritting her teeth, she tried to choose some clothes, but they were all on slip-free hangers, done up with buttons and ties. She couldn't do anything without asking Dan for help, and now she was too irritable to do that. She pursed her lips and refused to call him over, carelessly tugging until she had freed a few things. Leaving a clumsy pile of underwear, shirts, sweaters, and track pants on the bed, she hobbled into the bathroom for toiletries.

Dan came in quietly behind her. "Doing okay?" He was carrying her holdall. Anything I can help with?"

"No, let's just go." She was surprised to see his face next to hers in the mirror. "You were right, this does feel like too much today. Can we come back and tidy up another time?"

Leaving Dan to lock up, Lisa wondered how she'd cope until the police got back to her with news of their interview with Ashley. Back in Dan's van, she took slow, deep breaths to calm herself before seeing Norm.

* * *

Norm was sitting on the porch waiting. Lisa had called earlier to say she'd be dropping by, and he had been into town to buy doughnut holes and grapes and laid them on an oval platter on the kitchen table, next to a rawhide bone. As he filled the kettle, Lisa reminded him she didn't take cream, which made the instant coffee more palatable. Fido was thrilled to be there, and a rare grin spread across Norm's face as he sat down and gave the dog his treat.

"I've had an idea." Lisa parked her crutches against the wall. "And spoken to a man called Ken Higgins."

Norm frowned. "His father was as crooked as they come. Charged one woman for taking out a cracked septic, and when I went to dig in the new one, it was still there. We almost had a scrap when I tried to get the money back for her. His brother ended up in jail for breaking into the boss's shop and stealing tools."

Lisa sighed. "Well, Ken sounded honest, and maybe he can save your home."

"I wouldn't trust anyone called Higgins as far as I could spit him."

"Just hear me out. Please."

Norm folded his arms.

"They can't tear down the bungalow if it's not here, and that's what Ken Higgins does, he moves houses for people."

Norm's face was creased and he needed a shave, but his eyes started to gleam. "So you're saying they could pick it up and haul it somewhere else?"

"That's the idea. The thing is, it's expensive. Really expensive."

"Did he give you a price?"

"Only a rough estimate, based on what I told him."

Norm started fidgeting with the corner of the tablecloth.

"We're looking at somewhere in the region of $25,000."

Relief flooded the old man's face. "That's okay. I can give it to you now."

"Surely you don't keep that kind of cash in the house?"

"It's not under the mattress, if that's what you're thinking, but it'd only take a couple of minutes to lay my hands on it."

Lisa would talk to him about banks later. Right now they still had a lot to work out.

"But I'm going to need a damned permit to move it, and then I'm back to Holtz and his pissing applications and he's not going to smile on anything I want to do."

"I asked Ken about permits and you do need one to move the house, he can't do it without, and a police escort."

Norm's shoulders slumped.

"And you're right, you will need a permit to build a new driveway, and foundations and utilities."

"All that's going to take time, even if the buzzards do approve, which they won't."

Lisa leaned forward. "Here's my idea. If we can get permission to move the building, Higgins says he can raise the bungalow and build a trailer under it. Then we can shift it and leave it on the trailer until the other permits are in place."

Norm's eyes fixed on Lisa.

"When I was putting your papers into piles on your kitchen table, I noticed two different surveys. It looked like you had two separate pieces of land, with a different lot number on each."

"I severed a piece years ago, to give my son for his twenty-first birthday, but then he ran off to Toronto. I put it in our joint names to stop the rascal from selling it, so it's still a separate parcel."

Lisa grinned. "Then you could, theoretically, move the bungalow onto that piece of land, and you wouldn't have two homes on one property."

Norm looked more excited than she'd seen him in the twenty years they'd been friends.

"If you agree, I'll go to the Township tomorrow and see if it's viable."

"D'you think they'll buy it?"

"I think it's worth a try. The building inspector didn't strike me as unreasonable, he just wants you to play by the rules."

"Sitting there in his friggin' suit making them up as he goes along, being a smart-ass when you don't stick to them."

Lisa looked directly into the old man's eyes. "Norm, you are going to have to cooperate for this to work. I can go and see Holtz, but you're the one that'll be dealing with him after that."

Norm pulled down the corners of his mouth but then sat up straight. "If you can get him to agree, I'll play so nice he invites me for a round of golf."

Lisa popped a doughnut hole onto her tongue and washed it down with now-cold coffee, praying Holtz would live up to her prediction.

Dan picked her up a few minutes later and they went into town for groceries. "You can stay in the van, if you're tired."

"No, I want to come." Lisa was ridiculously excited at the idea of going into a grocery store. Since her time in the hospital, she was enthusiastic about a lot of things that she used to find tedious.

They walked up and down the aisles side by side, the back wheel of the cart wobbling as Dan pushed, Lisa swinging along between her crutches. They'd never been shopping together. They agreed the best apples were Honeycrisps, that they liked their bananas just yellow with slightly green tips, and said in synchronicity, that avocados in a bag were a bad idea because they all got ripe at once. Their tastes diverged when it came to potato chips: barbeque flavor for him, lime and black pepper for her. They treated themselves to the most expensive granola for breakfast and went for exotic vegetables to roast for supper—eggplant and celery root alongside shallots, peppers, and baby purple potatoes. By the time they got to the checkout, it was sinking in: she was in a relationship and loving it. But there was a sadness too. Could she have given this to herself years ago?

An hour later, watching Dan lower the tray of vegetables into the oven, Lisa wished the meal was over. She wanted to be back in bed exploring him, learning more of who he was without words. When she'd touched a man before, it was always *trying* to please him. Now with Dan, the connection felt mutual and effortless.

Later, lying face to face, Lisa's booted leg propped on a pillow, her eyes didn't leave his as she ran her fingers very gently over his neck and shoulder. The skin was smooth, stretched over muscle and bone. She kissed the inside of his wrist and when he rolled onto his back, she felt the rhythm of his ribs and the soft firmness of his stomach, her fingers brushing the line of hairs below his navel. As she moved down to stroke his thighs, his knees rolled out and his legs opened slightly, still freckled from the summer sun. She kissed her way to the more tender skin higher up and, as his hips started to move, she had an urge to sit astride him.

"Oops." They both burst out laughing. She'd almost knocked him out trying to swing her boot over his chest. They were still laughing when she finally settled. "Now I know why I've been going to yoga for all those years."

They kissed. He stroked, licked, and sucked her breasts. She was so wet, she was tempted to try putting him inside her, but she resisted. Since her mammogram, Lisa had stopped using the pessaries and if she and Dan were going to be together, they needed to find a different way. So she sat on his lap, and as she started to move, his breathing changed. His hips rocked in time with hers, she felt rooted, and as she focused on their movement, she came. He followed and afterwards, as they lay together, she could feel the energy coursing from her, through him, and back into her.

"I love you," he said quietly.

"I know. I love you too."

Forty

"I'm afraid it's too late. The demolition trucks are booked."

Lisa had been waiting in Garnet Holtz's office for half an hour, trying to avoid the gaze of the stuffed fish that was still pinned to its plank behind his desk.

"But they won't be able to pull down the bungalow if it isn't there."

This stopped him mid-stride. His eyebrows popped up. "And where's it going to be? Norm'll be in worse trouble legally if he moves that building now. He needs a place to put it, with a permit, and he'd need permits for the septic and hydro. Not to mention a driveway and an entry permit."

"I believe that Norm's got another piece of property next to his with a different lot number. He severed it for his son to build on, but his son moved to Toronto. It's in their joint names. What if the bungalow was moved onto the adjoining property and it stayed on the float until the permits were in place?"

Holtz sat down. He picked up a file and tapped it on the desk, aligning its contents perfectly before replying with caution. "That could work."

Lisa held back her smile. She needed to be sure.

"Theoretically the Superior Court could say O'Brien has contravened their instructions by moving the building instead of demolishing it and so find him in contempt of court. He could get thirty days in jail or a fine of \$5,000 for contempt." Holtz picked up a stray highlighter, checked the cap was secure, and put it in his chrome pen pot. "But if the order was on a specific property for lot and concession, because that's been moved, legally speaking, that order has no purpose in effect."

Lisa let herself grin.

"I'd have to check with the solicitor to make sure the municipality is not in contempt of a court order."

"Of course." She put her hands in her lap, hoping that everything about her indicated compliance. "And if Norm assured you he was going to get all the permits and put in a foundation that met code?"

"If the planning department was convinced that he was working toward resolving the issue, we might be able to support him."

"So what would it take to convince you?"

"He'd have to come in here himself with all the applications and the money to pay for them. And I would insist that you continue to be involved until the final inspection and the permit is signed off."

Five minutes later, Lisa left happy. Dan was waiting in the van outside, studying his phone. "I've found this great article about companion planting." He looked up. "From that smile, I'm guessing you got a good result with Holtz?"

"Better than good. I think we may have the solution. I'll tell you about it while we drive, and could we make a quick stop at the pharmacy?"

"For sure, I'll wait outside. Can you pick up a paper while you're in there?"

The sharp smell of rubbing alcohol hit straight away. Someone had just dropped a bottle and the cashier was cleaning it up. Lisa leant on her crutches, reading the overhead signs: Shaving Needs, Foot Care, Cough & Colds. *Maybe Feminine Care?* She stopped to ask a young woman wearing a *Hello, I'm Abigail* drugstore badge. Looking more closely, Lisa recognized her as an ex-student from the art school. Bravado slipping away, she drew a deep breath. "I'm looking for lubricant. Sexual lubricant."

"Yeah, no one can ever find it cuz it's next to the baby products. Stupid place to put it, if you ask me."

Lisa followed the young woman across the store, relieved not to be recognized and sad that someone who'd spent two years getting a diploma in digital image design was working in the pharmacy. When they arrived at the appropriate shelf, Abigail turned and her cheeks pinked. "Hey, aren't you Principal West?"

"The very same, but retired now."

As her ex-student stared, Lisa's confidence ebbed. Finally, she prompted, "Lubricant?"

Abigail led the way. "We've got four kinds: silicone-based, water-based, oil-based, and hybrids." Her cheeks were fuchsia now.

Seeing her so embarrassed gave Lisa confidence. "Can you tell me a bit about them?"

Abigail talked to the shelf. "The rep was in a few weeks ago explaining. The silicone-based ones are usually thicker, and last longer, but the water-based ones wash off more easily."

"So which would you recommend?" Lisa was playing with her now.

"This one's full of plant essences and works great with a condom, but maybe you don't —Do you—"

"I think I'll take the silicone one."

Abigail handed her a brown plastic bottle that looked like hair shampoo. "I could ask Shelly, she's older—"

"No need. You've been most helpful."

Abigail managed a faint smile.

Lisa smiled back, a bit too enthusiastically, and wished she wasn't on crutches so she could get away faster. As the glass doors closed behind her, she realized she'd forgotten to buy a paper, but wasn't going back to get one.

When they arrived at Dan's place, she saw a police cruiser outside and froze. Constable Maclean asked to come in, saying he had an update on the break-and-enter. Lisa's heart pummelled as they all made their way into the kitchen and she tried to keep her voice normal as he asked questions about her broken leg.

"So." He took off his uniform cap and placed it carefully on the table in front of him, unhooked the portable radio from its holder on his belt and set it next to his cap, taking forever to unbutton his jacket and settle onto the chair. "We've made an arrest."

Lisa put her hands in the pockets of her fleece, worried she might start shaking.

"We went to Toronto to interview Ashley, who told us that she hadn't been in Colville in the past week. She said she was working at a bar downtown in Toronto every day, and that lots of people saw her there."

Lisa exhaled.

"But when we interviewed the manager of the bar, he told us that she wasn't at work on Thursday, that she had quite specifically asked for the day off. That was our real red flag, when we think she came back here to stage a break-in. Sometimes a lie is as good as a confession. Anyway, the lie gave us enough to take her to the Toronto Police Division and sort out a search warrant."

Lisa let out a whimper and turned it into a cough.

"Then we were straight back to the boyfriend's and found the cash—twenty grand—rolled up in socks in a drawer, and a receipt from a nearby photography store for the sale of cameras. That was all we needed."

"Did she confess?" It was the first time Dan had spoken.

"Didn't say a word. As far as I know, she still hasn't. We went back to Toronto Police Station to take a statement on camera and she refused to talk, but she was charged with breaking and entering and possession of stolen property exceeding $5,000. We took her boyfriend back to the station too, but upon further investigation, it appeared that he was not part of the break-and-enter and had no knowledge of the property being in his apartment."

Lisa felt nauseous. "Where is she now?"

"She's been remanded to Lindsay Detention Centre, where she'll spend the weekend until her next court appearance in Colville on Tuesday."

Lisa tried to appear calm and pay attention to what the constable was saying, but her head was spiralling. It was the image of $20,000 hidden in socks that made it real, such an Ashley thing to do.

"We're still puzzled as to why she didn't take your laptop or jewellery, things that would be easier to sell."

Because the cameras and photographic prints had belonged to her father. Was that the plan all along, to get what Ashley thought was hers? Am I such a sad lonely old woman that I've been completely taken in by a self-serving stranger? She hardly followed what Maclean said next and was still sitting at the table, too stunned to move, when Dan came back from showing him out. Her voice trembled as the truth she hadn't dared face turned to anger. "If you're about to say I told you so or anything similar--"

"Hang on a minute. I don't know why you're mad at me, I was just going to ask if you wanted a cup of tea."

"But I bet that's what you're thinking, that I was a fool to trust her in the first place." Lisa was worried she might explode. She pushed her chair away from the table, unable to be around Dan, or anyone. She needed to be alone, in her own home, and she couldn't bloody get there. "I'm going to lie down."

A few minutes later she saw Fido following Dan as he strode across the grass in front of the house. She didn't want him to be witness to her stupidity. Maybe she could call a cab? But she couldn't face being at home either, staring at the walls that Ashley had stripped. Lisa lay down and closed her eyes but didn't sleep. *I hate being dependent on Dan. I was pathetic to think this could ever work.* She remembered what Susan had said about how different they were, and how quickly Dan had shifted his plans from being with Julie in Manitoba to staying in Colville. "I was a fool to trust Ashley, and I've been a fool to fall so hard for him," Lisa muttered, and then yelled, "FUCK" as she wrenched her leg turning over.

Forty-one

A couple of hours later, Dan knocked gently and spoke from the other side of the door. Lisa pretended to be asleep. He came in quietly and sat on the bed. "Can I get you anything?"

"I just need some time," she muttered into the pillow without turning around.

"I know, and I realize you haven't had any space since the accident. I was thinking, I've got some papers to sign and people to see in the city. My plan was to take a couple of days next week, but maybe I should go now? I could stay in town, arrange some meetings for tomorrow and then come back at the end of the day."

Lisa rolled over. He looked freshly showered and shaved and was wearing clean jeans. She took his hand. "I'd like that. Even when I was in the hospital, alone in my room at night, there was always something going on, and—"

"Since you came out, we've been together twenty-four seven. I get it."

She nodded. "Thank you."

"That's decided then. I'll just throw some stuff in a bag. There's plenty of food in the fridge, wood by the stove." He leant over and kissed her forehead. "I miss you already."

Lisa forgot her doubts and drew him in for a real kiss. "I love you."

"Isn't it great?" He grinned. "That I love you too?"

In the end, Dan stayed in Toronto for two nights. Lisa revelled in the aloneness. Wrapped in a blanket, she spent a lot of time outside. She did her physio exercises, snoozed in the daytime, flicked through old newspapers, left her dishes in a pile in the sink, watched TV with Fido snuggled by her feet, and after taping a plastic bag around her lower leg, managed to get herself into the tub. That was a high spot, her first bath since the accident.

But the thing she did most was think about Ashley. Lisa back-tracked their whole summer together, searching for clues, signs of oncoming betrayal, and she couldn't find any, which made it all the more confusing and difficult to accept.

On Sunday morning she started missing Dan. She went around the house, trailing her fingers over the empty honey jars in the kitchen, picking up and opening the pine box he'd made in shop class at school, slipping her hands into his leather work gloves. She studied the pin board in his office and looked at photos spanning the years of Anna: dressed as Edward Scissorhands for Halloween, graduating, blowing out birthday cake candles, holding something that looked like a part of a car engine. Lisa had just unpinned a picture to have a closer look at Dan when he was younger, when her phone pinged his message: Be home in an hour. Can't wait. xxxx

She turned into a teenager going on her first date: re-brushed her teeth, took off Dan's sweatshirt and put on her fleece, took off her fleece and put on a sweater, and wished she'd thought more about the clothes she'd brought. She tidied up as best she could and when he finally arrived, she dropped her crutches and hugged him. "Thank you for being in my life."

"Thank you for letting me be in it." He kissed her forehead, her nose, and then her lips. "I never expected to be this happy again."

They brunched on ciabatta, buffalo mozzarella, and perfectly ripe tomatoes Dan had picked up in Little Italy. When he asked what she wanted to do with the rest of the day, Lisa said she'd like to go to her place and find some smarter clothes. "I've decided to go to court. I need to see her. Maybe it'll give me a sense of resolution."

"I get that. You know, I really am sorry it turned out this way."

She nodded. They were still sitting at the table.

"Do you feel strong enough to do some tidying when we're there?"

"Absolutely. In a funny way, I think it might help me feel better."

Dan took her hand. "Would you like me to go to court with you?"

Lisa looked into his hazel eyes. "That would be wonderful. I'm sorry I exploded at you on Friday."

"Don't worry. I could see how devastated you were, and I can understand why." He started to clear the dishes.

"There is something else I'd like to do. Could we stop at the florist and pick out something for Susan? Her house isn't far out of the way."

With a bouquet of orange chrysanthemums and yellow roses carefully tucked behind the seat, Dan's van pulled into Susan's driveway, next to a pristine Honda Crossover SUV that could only belong to Mitch. Lisa's first impulse was to suggest they drive away, but that would take more explaining than she was prepared for, and Susan would have heard them arrive. She had ultrasonic hearing when it came to other people's comings and goings, as well as their conversations.

"Hello?" Lisa pushed open the front door and smelt fresh baking.

"In here." Susan's voice came from the kitchen. "I've just made banana bread."

"Then we timed it right," Dan called out. When they got into the kitchen, he handed Susan the bouquet. "The flowers are from Lisa, but I'm still the bellboy, as long as she's on crutches."

Lisa followed him in, knowing Mitch would be there, wishing Dan didn't sound so coupley. Susan seemed touched by the flowers and gave her a big hug, before turning to introduce Mitch to Dan.

As she shared her latest photos of her daughter running the London Marathon, Lisa filled with guilt for forgetting to phone

Mitch back twice, and for turning up with Dan. When they all settled around the kitchen table, she hardly said a thing. Mitch avoided eye contact with everyone but managed to keep chatting and eventually, when the coffee was drunk and the banana bread eaten, he said he had to take his Honda to the carwash. This excuse was so feeble that Lisa grabbed her crutches and went after him.

Mitch was getting into his car.

"I'm so sorry," Lisa called out as she approached. "I don't know why I didn't phone you back, but I wish I had. You deserve better, you're so good and trusting and loving."

"You make me sound like an aging Labrador."

"It's just, I can't really explain it, but—"

"It's fine. I get it. And I'll get over it. After we'd, you know, finished seeing each other, I talked to Susan and made the mistake of feeling encouraged. Apparently you told her what a good man I was, but I should have recognized that for what it really meant. Truth is, the nice guy never gets the girl."

This felt profoundly true, yet Lisa didn't want to see Mitch drive away and out of her life. She wanted them to stay friends but knew the suggestion would sound like second prize. "Forgive me?"

"There's nothing to forgive, I just like you more than you like me. It's probably not an unusual occurrence."

She looked into Mitch's eyes, hoping hers were expressing the gratitude and affection she couldn't find words for.

He turned away. "I wish you well, and now I'd like to get going."

As they drove to Lisa's, Dan admired Susan's home, wished his banana bread was as good as hers, and didn't ask about Mitch. Lisa was thankful. She'd tell him in time, but right now she was too unsettled.

Her house looked beautiful in the warm autumn light. Maybe the break-in hadn't totally tarnished it. Maybe she could love it again. As they opened the kitchen door, her phone rang—Garnet Holtz from the Township office. Dan signalled that he was going upstairs.

"Sorry to call on a Sunday. I was just catching up on some work and opened an email from the municipal solicitor, verifying that if O'Brien moves his bungalow off the property in a legal manner that will satisfy the demolition order, it could work."

Norm was going to keep his home. Holtz kept talking—something about the legalities of going to another property, needing to know Norm was going to get another permit. Lisa was nodding into the phone with a huge beam on her face when he asked, "Are you there?"

"Oh yes, sorry."

"The most important thing to convey to O'Brien is that putting the bungalow on a float and taking it to the other property, and leaving it there, will only work if he applies for the relevant permits right away."

Lisa was still sitting at the table grinning when Dan came downstairs. "You look happy, what's going on?"

She couldn't stop smiling as she relayed Holtz's call. "If you don't mind, I'd like to phone Norm and tell him right away."

Dan nodded. "To be honest, there's not much more to do. I just put the stuff in your bedroom back into drawers and the wardrobe and it looks fine. Why don't I do the same in your office while you're on the phone, and then we can get out of here. I'm assuming Ashley's room can wait."

Lisa's stomach clenched at the thought of going through Ashley's things. Norm didn't pick up, so she left him a message, explaining what he had to do and reminding him to *please* cooperate. Then she headed toward the basement to find a jacket and skirt to wear to court. She paused at the top of the wooden stairs, they looked so steep and worn, and decided to slide the crutches ahead and go down on her bum. When she got to the bottom, the basement was like a tomb. It was too quiet. The furnace was off. Only a tiny shaft of light came through the almost-opaque window and made a dim white square on the floor.

As she was going through her rail of fall clothes, Lisa noticed an unfamiliar shape covered in a dust sheet. Lifting a corner, she saw the pile of picture frames and her insides turned to lead. Ashley must have taken each photo out of its frame and—yes—Leonard's zip-up portfolio was gone.

Once again, the deception hit Lisa like a blow. Needing to sit down, she limped over to her collage table, dropped her head into her hands, and closed her eyes. Past tears, she just had to accept the fact that she'd been a complete idiot. Then she noticed scissors and torn-out magazine pages that weren't there the last time she was: a picture of a doll with a missing arm, an ad for floor cleaner, and an abandoned barn on what looked like a prairie. And underneath them, scrawled across the front page of a newspaper in huge black writing:

HOW THE FUCK COULD YOU LEAVE ME TOO.

Lisa's heart ripped open with a rush of love. She remembered sitting in this very chair as Ashley described watching her mother die in hospital, when Ashley was only sixteen, leaving her with no one and nothing. She had worked out how to fend for herself, survive alone, and that's exactly what she'd done when she thought Lisa was dying. She had taken care of herself the only way she knew how, by making sure she wouldn't be stranded with nothing.

"She can't go to jail, it'll destroy her," Lisa said to the empty room. "I have to stop this from happening."

Forty-two

"What are you thinking?" Dan asked as they turned off the highway.

"That I need to call Constable MacLean. I've got to get him to drop the charges."

Dan started to say something and stopped.

"I'm going to phone the police station. It's probably too late, and MacLean might not be there, but at least I can find out what I have to do tomorrow to stop this going any further. The hearing's on Tuesday."

"Are you sure that's a good idea?" Dan spoke gently. "Maybe you need to think this through."

"There's nothing to think about. I know exactly what I want to do, and that's make sure Ashley doesn't go to prison."

As the leafless trees sped by, Lisa told him about the writing in the basement and how she now understood why Ashley had done what she did. Lisa could hear the judgement in Dan's silence. She didn't say any more, she wasn't going to defend herself. As soon as they got back to his place, she went into the bedroom and rang the police station.

"Constable Maclean won't be here until the morning." The woman who answered the phone had a slight Scottish twang.

"Isn't there anyone else I can talk to? What about a superintendent or the Chief of Police?"

"They're not here either. It's Sunday evening and I'm afraid this doesn't classify as an emergency. You have a good night and call in the morning."

Lisa threw her phone at the pillow. She wanted to talk to MacLean and make him understand that the person he'd arrested wasn't a criminal, but a wounded young woman who'd made a mistake. She wanted to talk to Ashley, to tell her she understood and was going to make it alright. The person Lisa didn't want to talk to was Dan, but she couldn't see any way of avoiding it. And, if this relationship was to survive, he'd have to accept that she had a will of her own.

"MacLean isn't there. I have to call again tomorrow." She lowered herself into the armchair next to his by the woodstove.

Dan was holding a half-drunk glass of wine and Lisa was glad to see another, empty glass, next to the bottle. It meant he hoped she'd be joining him. They both sat staring into the flames until he spoke. There was no anger in his voice now. "I just don't get it. She came into your life, manipulated you into thinking she was some kind of substitute daughter and all the while she was working out how to steal the most valuable things you had. That print collection was worth over a quarter of a million and I googled the value of the Leica—she probably pawned it for a pittance. Don't you want her to pay for what she's done?"

The words substitute daughter hit hard, but Lisa wanted to make Dan understand. "It's not that simple. Don't you see that Ashley loved me, that's why she panicked when she thought I was dying?"

"Lisa, she was playing you and it seems she still is. Even if what you say is true, every criminal has some kind of sad story. Actions should have consequences. How's she going to learn from her mistakes if she doesn't suffer consequences?"

"Time in prison isn't a learning experience, it's a life-altering event that brands you forever, especially for someone like Ashley."

"Especially? What is it about this girl? I don't understand why you're always making excuses for her."

"Isn't that exactly what you'd do if it was Anna?"

"Of course I would, but the point is that Ashley isn't your daughter. It's like you're desperate to—"

"To what?"

Dan shoved back his chair as he stood up. "I'm going for a walk. Should I take Fido?"

Lisa shrugged. "Do what you like."

Staring into the empty room, Lisa realized she hadn't eaten all day, but she was determined not to be in the kitchen when Dan got back, she didn't need his scepticism. "Damn," she mumbled, realizing she couldn't carry anything. In the end she put some bread, cheese, and a bottle of fizzy water in a shopping bag and managed to keep it looped over her wrist as she thumped her crutches back to the bedroom. She was going to make notes about what she wanted to tell the police. She *had* to talk to them before Ashley's hearing.

Dan must have slept in his office because Lisa lay awake most of the night and he didn't come to bed. As dawn seeped into the sky, she sat up and revised her notes, rehearsing what she planned to say to Constable MacLean. When he finally picked up his phone at precisely eight o'clock, as the woman on the switchboard had said he would when Lisa called at seven, seven thirty, and seven forty-five, she just spat out, "I don't want you to press charges."

MacLean asked her to give him a minute, and as she listened to the sound of a chair dragging and papers shuffling, she thought she would burst. It was forever before he came back on the phone. "So why have you decided we shouldn't press charges?"

And again, forgetting her carefully constructed notes, Lisa blurted everything she knew about Ashley and her past and how she hadn't stolen Lisa's laptop or jewellery or any of her other possessions, and that she'd only taken stuff that belonged to her father.

The constable didn't interrupt and when Lisa stopped, he stayed silent. Her hand was so sweaty the phone slipped onto her lap. She put it back to her ear. "I'm sorry, I dropped ... Did you say something?"

MacLean chuckled. "You need to write this into a letter addressed to the Crown Attorney and copy the Chief of Police and investigating officers—that's me, and Constable Burrie. State clearly that you do not want to see these charges proceeded with, and stress that Ashley only took stuff that had belonged to her father and she felt was hers." He paused. "You could add that you agree it should have been hers."

Lisa let out a long breath. "Oh my God, thank you."

"Take the letter to the court and say you want to leave it for the Crown attorney. Get it there first thing on Tuesday morning, before Ashley is called up. You could also find out the name of the Legal Aid person who's going to stand for her. Oh, and ask to make sure the duty counsel gets a copy too."

Now Lisa spoke fast, her voice full of gratitude. "This is so wonderful. I really didn't know how you'd react. It's so great to have your support."

"Whoa there, slow down." MacLean sounded serious. "I'm only telling you what you can do. I've got no idea what the outcome may be, and because of the tight timing, it's unlikely that you will either, until the hearing."

Forty-three

Lisa had often passed Colville County Court, perched on top of High Hill, overlooking the lake. Sometimes after yoga, she shared a bench, coffee, and croissants with Susan in the little park in front of the two-hundred-year-old building, but until today, Lisa had never had cause to go in. In fact, she had never been in a courtroom before.

Despite of the tubs of Thanksgiving chrysanthemums, and the bright red and white flag fluttering outside, the grey stone exterior was austere. Lisa didn't want to use the ramp, but she found the wide steps difficult with her crutches and couldn't pull open the big wooden door and manage them at the same time. She stumped her way over to the square push-button and hit the disability symbol. Her whole life felt disabled. It was going to be months until her leg was mended, she still took painkillers at night to sleep, her house didn't feel like home, and her truck was smashed to bits—not that she could drive. Dan had offered to bring her into town but she'd called a cab. She didn't need his judgements.

Sitting in the high-ceilinged, wood-lined court, Lisa remembered the day that Ashley had appeared at her door. They were both different then, and who knew what was going to happen for either of them now. Lisa's stomach was on the verge of upset as she imagined her precious friend being led out of the room in handcuffs.

The people next to Lisa shuffled as someone manoeuvred their way along the bench. Susan sat down and took her hand.

"How did you—"

"All rise for Judge Jackson. The court is now in session."

The judge's face was surprisingly warm and open, and in spite of the long black robe and starched white collar, she looked approachable. "Good morning." She turned to a man in a suit. "So what are we dealing with today?"

He glanced at the stack of files on the table in front of him. "Perhaps we could turn our attention to Miss Ashley Aitkin. I've received information that causes the Crown to believe this case will not likely be successful at trial. In consultation with the police, we've agreed to withdraw the charges, so the Crown is not going to be proceeding."

The Chief of Police must have agreed and Ashley was going to be released. Lisa wanted to cheer. Susan squeezed her hand.

The judge nodded. "Is Miss Aitkin in custody?"

"Yes, she is."

"Well, let's get her up."

A huge smile spread over Lisa's face as she sniffed back her tears.

Susan took a mini pack of Kleenex out of her pocket and handed one over. "I didn't understand how much she meant to you."

"As well as everything else, she's made me see how stuck I've been."

The court clerk asked for silence and turned to face a door beside the judge's platform. Ashley looked awful. Her hair was in tufts, the skin under her eyes was purple, her T-shirt grubby, and she was clutching her favourite baggy jeans to stop them falling down as she moved, sliding her feet because there were no laces in her Doc Martens. Two uniformed women with tasers walked on either side of her and motioned to a bench near the council. Ashley sat down and stared at her hands.

The judge turned to face her. "Miss Aitkin."

Ashley put her thumb to her mouth and ripped a piece of skin off the side of the nail before looking up.

The judge paused, giving her time. "So, Miss Aitkin, we have been advised that the Crown is not going to be proceeding any further."

"I don't understand." Her voice had no energy.

"All charges are being withdrawn on consent of the Crown. You are free to go."

Ashley stared at the judge, face unmoving.

"Please return down with the court officers to get your personal effects."

She swallowed before speaking. "You mean it's done?"

"That's exactly what I mean. The officers will take you back downstairs now to get your things."

For the first time, Ashley scanned the room. Her face was thinner, her top lip cracked. When she saw Lisa she paused, a tiny smile trembling.

Lisa mouthed, "Meet - you - outside."

When Susan and Lisa got to the top of the courthouse steps, it was raining. Susan told Lisa to wait while she found out where Ashley would be released and Lisa gazed at the maples that fringed the park, wondering how Ashley would be and how it would feel to see her. Susan was gone a long time, and when she reappeared, Ashley was walking a few paces behind, clutching her old leather camera bag.

Susan waved her forward. "I'll get the car and meet you back here in a minute."

As Ashley climbed the stone steps, her eyes didn't leave her boots. Lisa leant one of the crutches on the wall behind her and stretched out her arm. "Come here and give me a hug."

Ashley didn't look up. "I'm sorry."

"I mean it, I've missed you. I need a hug."

Slowly, Ashley raised her eyes. Lisa no longer saw Leonard when she looked into them, she saw a young woman she loved.

"Come on. There's lots of time for apologies and explanations later."

Ashley moved hesitantly into Lisa's arms. She felt boney and cold. Using the wall for support, Lisa took off her jacket and put it around her friend's shoulders.

"Thanks." Ashley's eyes returned to the ground, but Lisa saw a tiny movement at the corner of her lips that could be the start of a smile.

"I love you. I don't care what you've done, I'm just happy that you're safe."

Ashley slipped her cold hand into Lisa's. They walked down the ramp together and as they settled into Susan's car, windscreen wipers sloshing rhythmically, she turned to Lisa. "Your place?"

"That would be splendid." Lisa touched Susan's sleeve. "And thank you so much for being here. How did you know?"

"Dan rang me this morning and said you could do with some support. I'm so sorry—"

"So am I."

Water splashed up from the tires as they drove past Patty's, Lakeside Locks, and the thrift store. As Susan was indicating to take the road out of town, a small voice came from the back seat. "Can we go to Timmies?"

"Oh my God, yes." Susan changed course. "You must be starving. Why don't we go somewhere nicer and get you some real food?"

Silence.

Lisa turned. "Choc dip doughnut with a caramel hot chocolate?"

Ashley nodded.

"Timmies it is." Susan changed lanes to head for the edge of town.

The car smelt of coffee and sugar, and the rain had almost stopped as they turned off the highway. Approaching Norm's, Lisa saw some kind of big machinery. "Good grief, it's happening." Glancing behind her, she lowered her voice. "Ashley's asleep. Can we stop, just for a couple of minutes?"

"Sure." Susan turned into Norm's driveway. "Is this something else I've missed?"

"Let's talk when we get out of the car," Lisa whispered, as they parked amid the mass of trucks and noise. A team of men in hard hats seemed to be knocking holes in the side of the bungalow's basement, there was a crane unloading huge beams onto what looked like big rollers, and in the middle of it all was Norm, happier than Lisa had ever seen him. "I'm just heading into town to get coffee for the crew." His eyes were sparkling. "Want me to get one for yous?"

"We've just been, thanks. How's it going?"

"Should be off the foundations tomorrow. Then we've just got to wait for the police escort. Holtz is bringing the paperwork any minute. Maybe I'll give him a call and see if he wants a coffee."

Lisa smiled. "I need to get home, but I'll find a way to be here tomorrow."

Instead of ruining his life, this whole event seemed to be giving Norm a new lease. He climbed into his truck and waved at the foreman as he drove away. Ashley was still asleep in the back of Susan's Jeep when they arrived at Lisa's and she woke her gently. Susan left the car running. "I'll head off. You two have a lot to talk about."

Minutes later they were in the kitchen. Lisa opened the fridge. "We haven't got much in the way of fresh food. I've been staying at Dan's since I left the hospital, but there's long-life milk, bread in the freezer, and baked beans in the cupboard. How about beans on toast and a cup of tea?"

"Maybe. I've kinda lost my appetite. All I really want is a shower and then to burn these fucking clothes and never see them again."

"Of course." Lisa leaned her crutch against the sink. "I'll put the kettle on."

Sitting down, she felt her exhaustion. It had been a huge day and it was only lunchtime. She and Dan had hardly spoken since their explosion. Lisa wanted to ring and tell him the verdict, to share her relief, but wasn't sure how the news would be received. She checked her phone—nothing.

In all her years with Leonard, they had seldom fought. With Dan it felt different, sturdier, like they were working out who they were, together and separately. She'd give it a bit longer and then call.

Ashley reappeared in a sweatshirt and pyjama bottoms. "I don't know what the fuck I'm wearing. All my stuff's in Toronto. Shit—" Her face crumpled. "I've got to call Chase. I feel so bad about how I treated him." She looked at Lisa. "But that's nothing compared to what I did to you."

Forty-four

Ashley was gasping for air, trying to cry and breathe at the same time, with tears pouring down on either side of her nose. Lisa spooned sugar into a mug of tea, stirred, and passed it over. Then sat silently. Maybe she should have resented Ashley for what she'd done, but Lisa couldn't. She understood, and part of her was relieved to be rid of reminders of Leonard hanging on every wall. She wanted to move her chair around to Ashley's side of the table, to sit close and hold her, but knew that her friend needed space. So Lisa waited, trying to keep her own emotions in check, but the more she saw of Ashley's upset, the closer she came to her own tears. She thought of herself at the same age, how she'd clung to Leonard for security, and how Ashley had come to Canada hoping he might be the key to her happiness. Instead, they'd found each other.

Eventually Ashley looked up, but when her eyes met Lisa's she heaved even heavier sobs. Lisa knew that these tears came from somewhere old, from forever ago. They needed time and attention, and she wanted to give it, in a way no one had ever given it to her. So she kept sitting and silently sending all the love she knew how, wishing she could let herself cry from so deep a place, and after a while she did. She cried her own quiet tears for all the years of loneliness, the family she missed, and the children she never had, until Ashley dragged a sleeve across her wet face and lifted her eyes, snot still running onto her upper lip. "Hang on, why are you crying?"

Lisa wiped the back of her own hand across her face. "Because I love you, and I'm so glad you didn't go to prison, and because I want you to have a wonderful big life—the life I never dared to give myself."

Ashley came round the table and wrapped her arms around Lisa. "When you had that thing in the hospital, the embolism, I freaked out. Seeing you in there was more than I could handle, and then when you couldn't breathe, and I heard the nurse say it was critical ..." She sat down, sucking back more tears. "I'd seen them rushing into Mum's room with all the same monitors and stuff and, I just couldn't—"

Lisa waited.

"Then I came back here and the place was empty, just like—it fucked with my head."

"I know. I found what you wrote in the basement."

Ashley looked puzzled.

"In the collage corner."

"Oh yeah, I forgot I was down there. So I rang Chase and the more he said nice things, the more I lost it. In the end, he just drove up here and took me back to Toronto with him. He said we could phone the hospital every day from there, to keep tabs on how you were doing." Ashley started to gnaw at the skin on the side of her finger. "And then they said you were in ICU and it might be a good idea for me to come and see you, like it might be the last time, but they never actually said that. I was gutted. Chase drove me back to Colville but when we got here, I couldn't go into the hospital, I just couldn't. And that's when—"

"You took the prints?"

Another round of sobbing. Now Lisa felt calm, able to support Ashley, but also keen to hear what happened.

"I just grabbed the cameras to start with. I hid them in my bags of clothes. Chase was clueless, and that's when I started thinking about the prints. Somehow, cuz I knew they belonged to Leonard, I'd never steal from you, even if you were—"

"I know." Lisa took Ashley's hand between hers. "That's what I told the police, that the stolen goods belonged to your father, that you had an entitlement."

Ashley pulled her hand away. "But I *did* steal from you. I sold your stuff and you'll never have it back."

The truth of this landed in Lisa's stomach, making her wonder if she'd forgiven Ashley too fast. "Where did you sell it?"

"In the city."

She nodded.

"It wasn't easy. Well, the cameras were okay, I took them to a camera shop, but the prints were a nightmare. I went to a dealer and he only wanted some of them and then he asked for provenance and receipts verifying ownership." Ashley stopped to catch her breath. "He said that anything over $1,000 had to be authenticated, and by then I'd taken all the photos out of the frames and I was scared to come back, so I dragged the portfolio down to a pawn shop south of Shuter and finally this guy set me up with a dodgy dealer."

These details were too real. "How much did you get for them?

"In the end $65,000. It's more money than I've ever seen, let alone stuffed into a pair of socks. Well, I only put some of it into the socks, the rest's behind the baseboard in Chase's kitchen."

The thought of all that money crammed into Ashley's socks made Lisa laugh, and she knew Leonard would have laughed too. "You know the picture of John Lennon and Yoko Ono is worth $20,000. The whole collection's insured for $260,000."

Ashley put her hand up to her mouth, but the sobs couldn't be kept in. Her voice was muffled. "I'm so sorry. I've still got the money—well the feds have got some of it now. Will they give it back?"

"Look at me." Lisa was careful not to sound scolding. "I want you to look at me."

Ashley opened her eyes.

"I don't care about the prints or the cameras. In a way, I'm pleased they're gone. I wish it had happened under different circumstances, and that we'd got what they're worth, but I understand why you did it and I respect the fact that you only sold stuff that belonged to your father."

There was a quieter quality to the sobbing now. Lisa leaned in and put her arms around Ashley, relishing their closeness, still loving having someone in her life that mattered. When the phone rang, she hoped it might be Dan, but didn't pick up. Instead, she went to the cupboard. "How about I make us that food now?"

Ashley nodded and looked at the empty hook where the picture of an old couple by a beach had hung. "I didn't sell that one, it's still at Chase's. I'll bring it back, I promise, and the rest of the cash that the feds didn't find."

Lisa wondered whether to let Ashley keep the picture, but she did want something as a reminder of Leonard's collection.

"I need to go to Toronto, if Chase'll see me. He didn't know anything about what I was doing, and the police were digging all around his place, accusing him as well." Ashley wiped her nose on her sleeve. "If he's up for it, I'm gonna get the six o'clock bus."

"And then what?"

"I'll go home." Ashley looked down. "Well, back to London."

Lisa's heart plummeted. "You know you don't have to leave. What about art school, your photography course?"

"I couldn't show my face, even if they'd have me. This was meant to be my fresh start."

Hoping Ashley wouldn't see her upset, Lisa turned to open the can of beans. "Where'll you go?"

"Not sure, I haven't worked that out. I can crash at a place in Camden, with the guy who's got my stuff."

"You know you'll always have a home here."

Ashley ran over and hugged Lisa from behind. "We're def gonna stay in touch, texting and–" She sniffed. "Maybe you'll come to London?"

Lisa turned and they stood with their arms around each other for a long time. "Maybe I will. We're family now."

Ashley sniffed. "On no, not more bloody crying."

Lisa's phone rang again.

"You get that. I've gotta call Chase."

Ashley was halfway up the stairs by the time Lisa picked up her phone. She saw Dan's name and longed to feel him holding her. "Hi," she answered weakly. "She's with me now. They dropped the charges."

"I'm pleased."

"Really? After everything you said last night?"

"I guess being in love magnifies the bad stuff as well as the good. I think, on some level, I felt jealous or threatened or something, but I never wanted her to end up in jail."

"I'm sorry too, I was completely overwrought. I'm just waiting to hear if Ashley's going into Toronto. She's got a lot to clear up with her boyfriend there, as well as say goodbye."

"She's leaving?"

"Going back to England."

"Oh my, I know how much you'll miss her." Dan hesitated. "Should I come over and bring Fido? And if she's going into the city, I could give her a ride to the bus depot. Apart from anything, I'd like to meet this notorious young woman before she leaves the country."

As Lisa imagined Dan's warm smile, she wasn't sorry Ashley would be in Toronto. She wanted to think about the future, not the past.

* * *

"So you're Mr. Tricky," Ashley grinned as Dan came into the kitchen. Fido bounced in and leapt on her and within seconds they were a tangle of arms and paws on the floor. When Ashley surfaced, she was beaming. "He missed me."

"He's not the only one." Dan looked at Lisa.

Ashley wiped her eyes. "Don't do this to me, not right now."

They had a quick chat, mostly about Fido, and Norm's bungalow moving, and then all piled in Dan's van. Ashley dozed with Fido's head in her lap for most of the journey, then she had to rush to get the bus.

"She's a one-off. I can see why you like her so much." They watched the slender silhouette stride into the Greyhound terminal. When she was out of sight, Dan turned to Lisa. "Back to my place? It's closer than yours."

"Yes please, I'm worn out with waiting and worrying."

"Too tired to fool around after dinner?"

Lisa laughed. "That sounds so teenage."

"I know. Isn't it great to feel fifteen?"

She nodded. "And get to work it all out, the way I never could then."

Forty-five

Dan undressed and sat on the bed next to Lisa. "You do look bushed."

"It's been tense."

His finger glided over her lips, down her neck, and across her naked shoulder.

She kept completely still. "I love the way you touch me."

"Back rub?"

Lisa rolled over and stretched her arms on either side of the pillow. Dan switched off the light, gently pulled down the duvet, and kneeled astride her. His hands were warm and strong, and after a while, Lisa felt the muscles in her back soften. Her breathing deepened and followed the path of his fingers as they traced her spine, trailing right down until they teased the tops of her thighs. Her voice was thick. "If I turn over, maybe you could release some of the tension on my front?"

"I was about to suggest the same thing."

As his hand slid over her breast, Lisa pulled Dan down for a kiss—a long slow kiss that excited him as much as it did her. His erection pressed into her belly. They licked and kissed, stroked and tantalised, until Lisa was near bursting. "I need you in me."

"You don't have to do that for me. We could—"

"The doctor said that some women can manage when they're *really* excited." She kissed him again. "And I definitely qualify. Maybe being so turned on and a bit of extra viscosity—" They both laughed as she squeezed some lube into his hand. As soon as he touched her, she came—an easy orgasm filled with joy, but as Lisa guided him to her, she could feel his apprehension. "I promise I'll tell you if it hurts."

She exhaled, feeling a sharp pang as he entered, and focused on relaxing.

He stopped. "I'm nervous."

With her hands on his hips, she pulled him into her very slowly and inhaled deeply, taking the breath right down. Sensing herself expand, she lifted her hips to meet his and they moved together in gentle rhythm, breathing in sync. She felt him in waves, and as he grew in confidence, her back arched and she lost herself, consumed by his body, their breath, her own opening, and she came again. He came soon after, his energy travelling through her. Afterwards, they lay in stillness, dissolved into the darkness, and slept.

* * *

"Wish me luck." Dan slid his tablet into an efficient-looking leather case. "And remember I'm going straight on to Warren's after my interview at the art school, to help him work out that patio design. I don't know how long it'll take."

Lisa was still in bed. She couldn't stop thinking about their lovemaking and how good it had felt to have Dan inside her without pain. She knew it wouldn't always be possible, but she also knew he'd be happy with their sex life, however it unfolded.

"Want me to ring Serge and get him to pick you up for your hospital appointment?"

"I'll do it. You go and enjoy telling Caitlin about aquaponic gardening. She's going to be crazy about your ideas."

Lisa dozed and when she woke up, a deer was nibbling just metres from the window. It looked both gentle and strong, responsive to every sound, ready to move instantly, yet still grounded. She wanted to live like that. Today she felt she could. She decided to cook, to make something delicious for Dan. He'd done everything domestic since she'd arrived, and now it was her turn to contribute, starting with Thai squash soup. She'd have to google the recipe and the number of Serge's cab company in Brockton.

Slipping on Dan's big hoodie, Lisa found her phone, but she'd forgotten to charge it. The battery was only 8%, so she made her way into his office to use the landline. Dan must have been in such a rush that he'd left his laptop open. She perched on the stool and as she moved the mouse, Lisa noticed her own name in the first line of an email from Anna. What on earth did Dan's daughter have to say about her? She hovered the cursor over the subject line, trying to resist, then clicked.

Hey Dad

I can't wait to see you. Not long now. We'll pick you up at the airport. I was going to talk about this when you got here, but I've decided to write so you can think about it before you come. Please don't hate me but I'm scared you're making a huge mistake with Lisa. Nothing about her sounds right. She's way too old and I can't see what you've got in common. What are you going to do, burn all the money from selling the business going on cruises? You've always been a sucker for a bird with a broken wing. Are you sure she isn't just a rescue mission? You and Julie were so great together, and I know she'd have you back in a heartbeat, and the guy who's been doing your job at the university isn't working out. We need you! I went to see the scary dragon who did your initial interview and she said she'd hold the job till you get here on the 9th. So the life you want is still waiting. I miss you soooooooooo much. You always say I know you better than you know yourself so maybe now's the time to listen, before you blow everything that's still waiting for you here. xoxo

Lisa read the email again, her body clenching tighter with every word, her head throbbing as she looked at the attached photos: Dan and Julie sitting outside a tent, their faces alive with laughter. Dan, Julie, Anna and a young man who must be her boyfriend, drinking beer on a patio in the sun. And the most amazing view of a river, lined with trees, beneath a huge blue sky. Why hadn't Dan told her he was going to Manitoba in two weeks?

Forty-six

Still sitting in front of Dan's laptop, Lisa looked down at the back of her hand, splashed with age spots, and remembered running into him with Julie in the summer—how vibrant she had been and how happy they were together. Lisa glanced back at Anna's email, it was the word rescue that hurt the worst. She didn't want to be someone who needed rescuing. She didn't want to be someone who needed. Or depended on people who lied to her. Or disappeared. She wasn't going to let that happen again.

Opening a new tab, she searched for the number of the cab company in Brockton, her confidence tanking. *Why would he want someone old and atrophied when he could have a younger unretired university professor, and a new job, in a new place full of exciting people? Maybe seeing me in the hospital coincided with him having last-minute nerves and I was just a convenient excuse? Or I was a rescue mission, and it was pity, and he got carried away?*

Lisa used what was left of the battery in her phone. "Do you have a car that's free now and will take a dog? I need to go to Colville—well, about two kilometres outside town—to drop off the dog and my bags, and then carry on to the hospital. I have to be there by eleven."

As Lisa stood waiting by Dan's front door, a beaten-up Sunfire turned into the driveway. *Not now. Please, not now.*

Skye got out of the car, and as she marched up to the house, Fido growled.

"Warren said you might be here." The young woman's face was set hard.

"This really isn't a good time."

Skye eyed the bulging bag of clothes at Lisa's feet. "I can see that, but what I want won't wait. I need $900."

Lisa had no energy for this, she already felt like pulp. "Skye, this has to stop. I'm not going to give you money, now—or ever."

Skye took her phone out of her jacket pocket. "Sure about that? It would only take one call to dirty that spotless reputation of yours."

Lisa saw a Dodge Caravan turn into the driveway—her cab. She mustn't be late for the hospital appointment. "Listen Skye, I don't have a reputation. I don't even work at the art school anymore."

A mean smile curved the corners of the young woman's lips. "But you are on the board. How d'you think they'd feel about their newest member fiddling the books and failing to report a student's fraud?"

Lisa stiffened as the cab pulled up.

Skye squeezed the side of her phone and it lit up. "I've already put in Bob's number. Just one call."

"Bob?"

"Robert Boswell, Chairman of the board?"

Lisa looked past Skye and called to the cab driver. "I'll be with you in a minute." As she turned back, she imagined Robert listening to Skye's story and arranging an emergency board meeting. She could see the raised eyebrows and looks of disapproval, hear the whispers around the table.

Skye took a step forward and lowered her voice. "Just think about it, getting fired from the board, everyone knowing."

Lisa did. She thought past the scandal and imagined not being there for all those important discussions and decisions and, unexpectedly, she felt lighter. As the excitement tingled in her chest, she breathed into it, sensed it grow, and smiled. The art school would be fine without her, and more to the point, she'd be fine without it. Leaning a crutch against the door, Lisa took Skye's phone. "Here, let me do that for you." She pressed *call* and Robert's number went straight to voicemail. "Hi, Lisa here. I'm ringing to say that I'm resigning from the board and I'd love to tell you why over coffee next week. Give me a call and we can arrange a time."

Skye gaped.

Lisa waved at the cab driver. "Please could you help me with my bags?"

***

As she sat in the back of the Dodge Caravan, Lisa rubbed Fido's head and wondered if this was her destiny—to be alone. She stared out of the window, and as the houses and trees whizzed by, she remembered sitting in Leonard's near-empty penthouse on her forty-first birthday. London drizzle coated the windows, distorting the spectacular view. She had bought herself a single-sized bottle of champagne to celebrate closing the sale. Leonard's shares in the ad agency had already been sold to his partners, and they had been kind enough to take on selling his Porsche and her hardly-driven MGA.

The weeks since the funeral had been horrendous and Lisa was desperate for all the practical stuff to be over, but as the grey outside faded to black, she didn't feel closure, she felt resolution. "That's it. I'm done." She lifted her glass to her reflection in the huge windows. "Whatever happens, I am never, ever, feeling like this again."

It had taken twenty years to break her promise. Was she sorry? That promise had protected her. After Leonard's death, it had given her a way to move forward and helped her to survive, to move to Canada and feel safe. "But I'm finished with surviving," she said quietly. "It's time to start living."

The driver carried Lisa's things as she followed on her crutches, then unlocked the door. Fido rushed in and she felt bad leaving him as soon as they'd arrived. "I won't be long."

At the hospital, she gave the driver a hefty tip, before taking the ramp up to the glass doors. Breathing in the comforting smell of coffee and sugar, she remembered her triumph at making it to the little Tim Hortons in the foyer to meet Frank. He had helped her more than he could know. She made her way toward the elevator, past the gift shop, and stopped. Long legs, broad leather-clad shoulders, and neatly cropped grey hair. His voice made her warm, even though he was talking to the teller. "You're welcome. Let's hope they sell."

Lisa remembered how sweet and vulnerable Mitch had been, and how needed he'd made her feel. He turned around and his whole face smiled. "Wow, look at you."

She took a step toward him.

"I've just given the gift shop all my wooden birds. I usually let the Scouts sell them at their Christmas Bazaar, but I decided to support the hospital this year."

"Generous to your core." Lisa felt the value of the words. "It's wonderful to see you, but I'm meant to be at the orthopaedic clinic in two minutes."

"How are you getting home? I could wait and give you a ride, unless, of course ..." Mitch looked down at the floor.

"No. I mean yes. But I may be a while. I'm having an x-ray and, hopefully, getting a boot that's able to take more weight."

"No problem. I could do with a coffee." Mitch nodded toward a table on the other side of the reception area. "I'll be sitting right over there."

And Lisa knew he would be. As she headed for orthopedics, she passed patients in hospital gowns, sitting in wheelchairs and hobbling on crutches, and felt like she was witnessing a distant dream. So much had changed since the accident. She had changed so much since then. Or had she?

"Good work," the surgeon pronounced. "Now you can gradually increase the weight on your boot to 50%."

Lisa felt like she'd won first prize for a school project.

"And when you've done that, you can start moving around with one crutch."

Thrilled at the prospect of being more mobile, Lisa made her way back to reception. She didn't want a coffee and Mitch was on his second, but she was glad to sit and wait while he finished it. He asked how her appointment had gone and looked genuinely pleased to hear about her progress. Just being with him grounded her. And he seemed different, brighter, more confident.

He stood up. "You stay here. I'll get the car and ping you when I'm outside."

"My phone's dead. I left it at home to charge, but I'll give you a few minutes and then wait by the door."

Lisa thought about how good it was to see Mitch, but the heaviness from leaving Dan was still there in her chest.

She settled into Mitch's passenger seat. The traffic was backed up on the road outside the hospital and he turned, speaking almost shyly. "Could we grab some lunch? We never really had a chance to ... to talk about what happened between us, and I want to tell you what an impact you've had. Your accident was my turning point, made me reevaluate my priorities."

As Mitch took the car out of *park,* they inched forward and Lisa felt tears prickle. Only a few hours ago she'd been bereft about Dan. "Could we take a rain check? It's been a big day already and I'm not sure I can say anything sensible."

"Sure, but we'd better make it soon." The traffic speeded up and Mitch turned onto the road leading out of town. "I fly to Guatemala on Friday. My bike's being shipped there as we speak, and then I'm riding down to Patagonia. Won't be back until at least late spring, maybe some time in the summer."

Lisa's heart lifted at the thought of Mitch on his open road.

"Danielle, my youngest, is going to stay in the house while I'm away and I'll be moving into her apartment when I get back. It's too small for her, now she's got the baby, and I don't need so much space."

Lisa was going to miss him.

"I'll send you a selfie from the southernmost tip of South America."

"Amazing," she said quietly. "I'll give you a ring tomorrow, make a date for lunch." As they pulled up outside her house, she leant forward and kissed him on the cheek.

* * *

Closing the kitchen door behind her, Lisa's old life reappeared. Only now it didn't feel safe, it felt sad. Fido leapt up, his tail thumping, his joy reassuring.

"Hello sweetie. I guess it's just the two of us again."

As she plugged in her phone by the fridge, she saw the fading flyers that had been her retirement project: Hugs for Healthcare, Garden Club, Colville Singers, Highland Hikers. That seemed a lifetime ago. She rang Norm.

"Not long now." His voice was full of anticipation.

Of course, the bungalow is moving this afternoon. "I won't keep you. I just wondered if you'd like to stay here when the weather gets cold, until your place is hooked up."

"Would I ever. I wasn't looking forward to a winter without water or power. But it's a long time since I bunked with anyone."

"Don't worry, I'm not going to be here. I was hoping you could look after Fido."

"Everything okay?"

"Absolutely."

Forty-seven

Lisa called Susan to tell her about Anna's email, that Dan was going to Manitoba. "You were right," she ended. "I wasn't suitable for a man like Dan. It never would have worked."

"Don't you dare talk like that," Susan erupted into the phone. "None of this is your fault. Once a player always a player, and we all know that a weasel like him won't change his spots." Her voice softened. "But I am sorry. This is the last thing you need, especially after all the drama with Ashley."

"Thank you. I just hope I'm doing the right thing by taking myself out of the equation."

"Well honey, I'm about to tell you something that's going to make you feel a whole lot better."

Lisa wasn't sure she wanted to hear.

"I spoke to Shauna last night, you know, the niece that works in the hotel where Dan stays in Toronto? She's coming for Christmas. Anyhoo, she told me that he was there, in the hotel, over the weekend."

"I know." Lisa exhaled her relief. She didn't need any more convincing that she'd made an idiot of herself. "I stayed at Dan's while he was away. He went into the city on Friday afternoon and got back on Sunday morning."

"But did you know he had one of the *women* with him? He checked in and she arrived an hour later and went straight up to his room. Shauna recognized her, said she'd seen her there before."

Lisa was stunned. Had she really fallen for another Leonard? Trusted another man who was terminally unfaithful?

"You still there, hon? I'm only telling you this to make it easier to let go."

"I know," Lisa mumbled miserably. She fumbled her way through a bit more conversation and then ended the call, telling

Susan she was tired and would speak to her soon. Moving slowly, she lit the woodstove in the living room and lay down on the couch, battered and betrayed, but strangely okay. *This is an ending, but it's not the end,* she told herself, and within seconds she was asleep.

"Lisa?" Dan was standing in the middle of the room.

Shit. I didn't lock the door.

"I don't get it. Why are you back here, at your place? And you took all your stuff. What's going on?"

Clever responses like "you tell me," "ask Anna," or "let's phone hotel reception and find out," flitted through Lisa's brain. Instead, she pulled herself upright. "It's over. I don't want to do this anymore. I think you should go to Manitoba and I know you spent Friday night with a woman in Toronto."

Dan looked baffled. "This is ridiculous. Who do you think I am?"

Maybe the real question is who do I think I am?

"Why would you say any of those things?"

"I read Anna's email. I know I shouldn't have, but I'm glad I did. When were you going to tell me that you had a flight booked on the 9th?"

"Huh? Okay." Dan dropped his jacket onto a chair. "I guess you didn't read my reply. If you're going to snoop through my mail, you should at least do it properly." He took a step forward. "When I decided not to go back, I deferred my flight and had to give the airline a date, so I randomly chose the 9th. That's when Anna thought I was coming, but I'd already decided to defer again." He paused. "Don't you trust me at all?"

"That's rich, coming from the man who's exhausted by meaningless sex. Or wasn't Friday night meaningless?"

Lisa could see the anger in Dan's eyes, but he kept his voice calm. "What do you think you know?"

"How about you just tell me what happened."

"For Christ's sake. Why can't you trust me?"

"I thought I did. You always seem to come up with some kind of convincing explanation, but Susan—"

"Ha! Susan. You believe everything that comes out of *her* mouth."

"So what *were* you doing with a woman on Friday night?"

Dan was near shouting now. "I met up with her and we went for dinner. That's all. Yes, we had a thing a while back, she's the one I told you is married."

"You also told me that you'd had a few extra-marital nights since the wedding."

"But this wasn't one of them. She emailed and asked if I'd be coming into the city soon and I told her I was attached. That's why we just met up for a meal."

"In your hotel room?"

"No, in Chinatown."

"But you were seen, she was seen, going up to your room."

"Jesus, are you having me followed? She wanted to change out of her work clothes, that's all. She's a nurse in a rehab centre near the hotel. Here." Dan took out his phone and started scrolling. "I'll show you the reply where I told her we could only meet up as friends. I went back to my room alone."

"Another plausible explanation—" Lisa suddenly heard herself and wanted to crawl under the couch.

Dan shoved his phone back into his pocket. "You know what, I can't do this anymore." He picked up his jacket. "I need to be with someone who trusts me, not thinks the worst every time I leave the house."

Groping for her crutches and struggling to get up, Lisa desperately wanted to take back her words, but Dan marched out of the room. She heard the kitchen door slam and then his van crunch down the driveway.

Fido nudged her hand with his nose, but she stayed motionless, staring at the spot on the rug where Dan's feet had been. Lisa knew he loved her, even though she couldn't always have crazy conventional sex. "He's not the problem. It's not about me trusting him, it's about me trusting myself." Fido replied with a wag. "I'll give him time to get home and then call."

She went around the house, putting things away as best she could, peered into Ashley's room, and decided to text: How's it going with Chase?

She replied straight away: Took a lot of explaining and tears, but we're good now. VERY good. Best sex ever. [thumbs up]

Still planning on leaving the country?

[sad face] Yep. But he says he'll visit.

Any idea when you'll be back here?

Couple of days? Then I'll sort out my room and book a flight. I'm going to miss you soooooooooo much. Promise we'll stay in touch.

Lisa stared at the screen, her eyes welling. In the end she just sent three pumping red hearts.

Moments later the phone rang, it was Norm. "Happening soon, police escort 'n all. I'll come and get ya."

But I need to talk to Dan. I'll have to do it later, when I get home.

Norm picked her up and at four o'clock she was in the cool sunshine, watching his bungalow towed on a trailer. It looked like royalty, perched on a platform that moved slowly down the drive and out into the road, where two cruisers were waiting. Their lights flashed as the tiny motorcade turned into the lane and, almost immediately, into the new driveway that had been built a hundred metres away. Followed by the building inspector, a handful of contractors, Fido, Norm, and Lisa, keeping up well with her crutches.

When they were in the neighbouring field, Lisa leaned one crutch against a tree and stood, with her weight on the other, watching the men manoeuvre the trailer back and forth. It was noisy and muddy but somehow perfect, and she was totally engrossed as she felt a hand slip into hers. She looked up, into hazel eyes.

"I'm sorry," he said.

"So am I."

"Can we keep trying?"

Lisa tilted her head toward his. "That's what I want more than anything."

Dan tipped his so their temples were touching. The trailer made a loud jolting noise and he turned to look. "This really is something."

"Isn't it?"

"And you made it happen."

"With a little help from a lot of other people."

It took a while to get the trailer in place, but when it was, the men unhitched it and everyone clapped.

"Such a good thing to see." Lisa sighed as she climbed into the Down to Earth van.

"And talking about good things, Caitlin Jeffrey offered me a retainer to develop the aquaponic module for the art school, and she wants me to start work on the actual garden in the spring."

Lisa's heart settled. They spent a gentle evening together in front of the woodstove and then, both exhausted, went up to bed early.

Dan folded his jeans onto the armchair by the window. "Feels different from the last time I slept over."

"Which, bizarrely, was the first time." She pulled aside the duvet and propped her leg before resting back. He snuggled in beside her.

"I've offered Norm this place for the winter, until the new foundations are built for his bungalow."

Dan broke into a huge smile. "I've been thinking about where we should live and how." He turned to her. "And I think we should get married."

She stroked the side of his face. "You know, I'm finally learning how to love, and finding it more exciting than frightening."

"Me too."

"I can't wait for big adventures and cozy times at home. We're going to laugh and fight and have great make-up sex and I want it all—but right now, marriage isn't what I need."

He held her gaze.

"As soon as my leg is healed, I'm planning to go to England. I have a sister and a father there and I want to get to know them. And I trust they'll want to know me."

"So you're turning me down?"

Lisa ignored the flutter of panic in her chest. "Not you, only the ring."

Dan paused, looking at her intensely before they kissed again. A long kiss that she felt down to her toes.

"Well then," he said. "I guess you'll find me right here when you get back."

Lisa nuzzled closer and hoped she would.

ACKNOWLEDGEMENTS

They say it takes a village—mine took a metropolis. My biggest thanks go to the person who is consistently supportive, patient, encouraging, listened to, and helped with every word—Lino Hilsdon. My writers' group has also been there for every word, sometimes several times over: Natalie Lougher, Peter Spasov and Keith Smith. I am super grateful for the help and advice from my early editors: the inspiring and diligent Heather Tekavec, insightful Judith Mason, and super-supportive Kelly O'Neill. Thanks to Jericho Writers, who taught, encouraged, and provided practical help and advice. And huge thanks to my early readers: Jenny Stevenson, Michele Karsh-Ackerman, Jill & Chris Howard, Carol Forbes, Ellee Sturgeon, June Powdrill, Joanna Nash, Rebecca Bradford, Jules Burns, and Cath Adele.

More thanks to Kaitlin Murphy for her fab web-making skills and social media advice, Jane Collins for her editorial guidance and proof reading, AOS editor Julia Bifulco for her suggestions, and Chanelle Poupart for their cover design.

I couldn't do anything without the many friends who support, share and believe, especially Judith Mason, Wendy Bristow, Michele Karsh-Ackerman, Karen Shenfeld, Mary Cranston, Andy Cowles, Sue Odell, Jules Burns, and Lucy Hughesdon. Big thanks to Maryse Baya, who helped me talk like Ashley, police people Staff Sergeant Dan Maclean and Ken Jackman, legal eagles Janet Mason and Ken Greer, medical advisors Brigid Johnston, Enzo Scarsella and Jocelyn Brown, building inspector Tim Powell, environmental biologist Alain Parada, house mover Vince Johnston, and beekeeper Glen McMullen. And to all the women who have so generously shared their experiences of sex and relationships in older years.

Ramune Luminaire was born in Montreal, moved to England when she was ten, and returned to Canada thirty-four years later. She has degrees in Sociology, Sculpture with Ceramics, and a Post Graduate Creative Writing Diploma. She has worked as a magazine editor, TV scriptwriter specializing in "talking head" documentaries, visual artist, educator, and abundance coach. Ramune now writes and makes visual art in her studio near Peterborough, Ontario.

If you enjoyed this novel, sign up for Ramune's newsletter at **ramuneluminaire.com** (and get a free short story). That way you can follow her writing journey through the back woods of a fictitious town called Staghorn—the setting for her next book—and get to know the four brave women who are trying to make a life there together. You can also find out more about Ramune, how she became a writer, and read her regular book reviews.